Return of the Eagles

Mark L. Richards

ISBN: 153985258X
ISBN 13: 9781539852582
Library of Congress Control Number: 2016918356
CreateSpace Independent Publishing Platform
North Charleston, South Carolina

For my wonderful wife, Margaret, and two daughters, Mary and Melinda. Also for the future generation, my five grandchildren: Ian, James, Owen, Kara, and Mera. May a strong wind always fill your sails on the journey ahead.

Preface

In the early fall of AD 9, the Roman Empire suffered a catastrophic defeat at the hands of a coalition of Germanic tribes. Their charismatic leader was a military genius named Arminius. The battle occurred deep in the heart of northern Germania far from the safety of the Roman fortresses on the western bank of the Rhine. The conflict, known as the Battle of the Teutoburg Forest, resulted in the annihilation of three elite Roman legions, over fifteen thousand troops, under the command of Publius Quinctilius Varus. The three legions were attacked by a numerically superior force in a primeval forest and, over the course of three days, whittled down and then massacred. As a result, all territory that Rome had painstakingly expanded her influence to east of the Rhine over the past twenty years was lost.

Rome, as a rule, did not take kindly to defeat. It was said that Rome only lost battles, never wars. More often than not, her response was to throw more legions at the problem. This was no exception. Rome amassed a mighty army of eight legions plus auxiliaries, an invasion force of perhaps sixty to seventy thousand men to reclaim her territory, kill the German leaders, and seek retribution for the terrible defeat in the Teutoburg Forest. Above all, Rome sought to recapture the three sacred, legionary eagle standards, the *aquilae,* lost by the Varus army. The eagles were held in extreme reverence by the men of the legion and even venerated at a shrine when in an encampment. To have the eagle standard captured was a matter of lost honor and deep shame.

Return of the Eagles is a fictional account of the Roman Army in its quest to redeem lost honor and to return the German lands under the heel of Rome. This book is the sequel to the author's previous work, *Legions of the Forest*, a fictional account of the Battle of the Teutoburg Forest. The story follows the exploits of Tribune Valerius Maximus and Centurion Marcellus Veronus, fictional protagonists and survivors of the Teutoburg disaster in *Legions of the Forest*. Like my previous work, aside from Valerius Maximus and Marcellus Veronus, many of the characters noted in *Return of the Eagles* were historical figures in Roman antiquity.

Prologue

Rome
Palace of Augustus Caesar, Palatine Hill
Autumn AD 9

It was a council of war. This was no mundane conversation concerning the everyday affairs of the empire: the status of the grain supply, the selection of individuals to foreign posts, or the improvement of road systems and aqueducts. The three most powerful men in Rome were sequestered in a small study in the imperial palace on the Palatine Hill. Based upon the grim expressions on their faces, the discussions were not going well. They stood crowded around an ornate wooden table surrounded by several plain wooden chairs. The seats had been vacated some time ago as the tension in the room escalated. Upon the table lay a map of Germania, their central topic of debate. That territory was so close to being annexed as a Roman province and client state until the events that had transpired approximately one month ago. Three Roman legions, the Seventeenth, Eighteenth, and Nineteenth, almost fifteen thousand men, and their commander, Publius Quinctilius Varus, were vanquished in the Teutoburg Forest deep in the heart of Germania.

It was a crushing defeat that resonated traumatically with the emperor, Caesar Augustus. The elderly ruler, now in his seventies, was shaken to the core. His gaunt countenance was etched with weariness from the strain of governing the Roman Empire for almost forty years.

Accompanying the emperor was Tiberius Caesar, stepson of Augustus, heir apparent and an accomplished military general in his own right. It was claimed that Tiberius had never lost a battle. Although he was an astute and capable commander, his troops had little love for him. He insisted on iron discipline and was by nature a taciturn individual. Now in his fifty-first year, his expression was dour, the lines in his face clearly visible. Also present was Germanicus Caesar, not yet out of his twenties, the youngest of the three generations in attendance and the nephew of Tiberius. He was the antithesis of Tiberius, a rising star in the political arena, charming, and the Roman populace loved him and his fashionable wife, Agrippina, granddaughter of Augustus.

All servants and slaves had been banished from the area. The future military strategy of Rome was under deliberation, perhaps more aptly described at this point as an outright spat.

The emperor directed his terse remarks at Tiberius, his demeanor clearly agitated. "Let me understand this. You want to assemble a force of eight legions plus auxiliaries and cross the Rhine to invade Germania. What would that be, fifty thousand men?"

Tiberius, not to be deterred, commented dryly, "More like sixty to seventy thousand."

Augustus erupted. "You want to risk almost a third of Rome's military strength after we have just witnessed the elimination of three of our finest legions, nearly fifteen thousand trained legionnaires. This is madness," he spluttered, his ire rising.

Tiberius continued, "It is in Rome's best interest to recapture the territory lost to us."

The emperor replied, his tone sarcastic, "You are so certain of this?" He bunched his fists as his rage boiled again. *"Damn those Germans. I want my legions back."*

Augustus's elderly wife, Livia, entered the room. She was a daunting persona in her own right, assisting Augustus in his rule of the vast domain. "What is all this shouting about? I can hear you all the way down the corridor."

"Your son dares to lecture me on military strategy," the emperor barked. "I am the *imperator*, and I make the decisions about how the business of Rome is conducted. He may be my heir, but he is not in power yet."

Livia raised her chin and gave her husband a scornful gaze. "Tiberius and Germanicus are your military advisors. You should listen to them."

Augustus gave an exasperated sigh. "Not you too."

Livia sniffed and turned to exit. "And please keep your voices down. The whole palace can hear your outbursts."

Tiberius quickly interjected before things got out of control. He raised his arms slightly as a placating gesture. "Sire, of course you are in charge. No one would ever dispute that. Can we just go through this one more time? Please, just listen to what we propose."

The emperor, his voice weary, relented. "All right. Go ahead."

"Our plan is as follows. We would draw legions from various parts of the empire, the Second from Hispania, the Eighth from Pannonia, the Ninth and Twentieth from Illyricum, and the Sixteenth and the Twenty-First from Raetia. As you are aware, we have already moved the First and the Fifth from Moguntiacum in the south of Germania to the north. All of these legions would mass at Vetera on the Rhine. This would be the jumping-off point for the invasion."

For effect, he stabbed the map with his finger, pointing to an area at the lower reaches of the Rhine. "There."

Augustus reflected briefly. "In addition to exposing our forces to great danger in this invasion plan of yours, do you not think that this will weaken our military presence in those areas where we have withdrawn the legions?"

"Yes, sire, but only in the short term. I would deem it to be a slight risk. This campaign against the Germans will not be protracted. If we cannot accomplish our objectives of killing their leader, Arminius, and destroying his tribe, the Cherusci, then we will withdraw to the safety of the Rhine. Of course another alternative to pulling legions from the provinces is to reconstitute the three lost legions of the Teutoburg, the Seventeenth, Eighteenth, and Nineteenth. Then we will not need to draw eight from the other provinces, only five."

The emperor erupted again. "*Never!* Those legions are the embodiment of me, the imperator. I did not lose the eagle standards; they did. It is their shame, not mine. Those legions will never be reinstated as long as I live, and I emphasize the word *never*. Please continue with your plan and objectives."

Tiberius, somewhat taken aback by the outburst, calmly and purposely made his case. "Our strategic goal is to regain the lost territory and annex the province of Germania. To do this we must kill Arminius and destroy his Cherusci tribe. Secondarily, our invasion will demonstrate to the other provinces that we have not lost our will to fight and gone soft. Our forces will exact terrible retribution on the Germans. Those client states that contemplate rebelling against Rome will think twice about it. Oh, and while we are at it, we will recover the captured eagle standards."

Augustus's face remained impassive. "What about command and control? Also supply?"

Tiberius nodded toward Germanicus. "My nephew will have overall command. He is a capable general, although young. I will personally designate the other Roman commanders to assist him. He will have the best senior officers the legions have to offer accompanying him. I will have General Tubero as his second-in-command, and General Stertinius—"

The emperor interrupted. "Not now, not now. I do not need to know the details."

"Of course, sir."

"Now, what about supply?"

Tiberius spoke. "Stores and equipment will be transported through our naval vessels up the North Sea and then the Rhine."

Augustus was not yet convinced. "I still do not like this. Germania is lost. We have extended ourselves too far, and those people are unruly barbarians. The Rhine should be a sufficient barrier to discourage them from future raids."

Germanicus, who had politely deferred to his uncle in leading the discussion, spoke. "The Germans have raided across the Rhine for many years in the past. Why would they stop now?"

The emperor was silent for several moments, and then murmured quietly, "They probably would not." He sat and quietly stared out the small window down toward the busy forum area. Tiberius gave Germanicus a warning look with a slight shake of his head, signaling him not to interrupt Augustus's contemplation.

At last Augustus spoke. "All right, all right, I will accede to your wishes, but you had better not lose any more of my legions in those infernal Germanic forests. If you do, I will take it out of your hide. I can always change my will you know."

"Yes, sire. Germanicus and I will take full responsibility. We will exercise caution when venturing into the enemy territory. Planning will begin right away." The two subordinates exchanged knowing grins. They had prevailed.

The fate of the empire had been cast. Many lives would be torn asunder. The brutal military campaign against the Germans was about to begin. Would the Romans recover their honor? Would Germania become a province of the Roman Empire? Would they return the three eagle standards lost in the Teutoburg disaster? This is that story.

I

Aventine Hill, Rome
Autumn AD 9

"You know, Tribune, I could get used to this living in Rome. I mean, the chariot races this morning were everything I imagined they'd be, and visiting the bath with a massage as well made my day. By the way, Tribune, how much did you win at the races today?" Offering a wry grin, Centurion Marcellus fingered the heavy bag of coins attached to his waist.

Tribune Valerius Maximus countered the gibe. "Very funny, Marcellus. Rub salt in an open wound. So you got lucky this time."

"No luck whatsoever, Tribune. Did I not tell you to bet on the greens today? I know my horseflesh. I have been to chariot races before, just not as grand as this one in Rome. Why do you think I wanted to go early and study the horses in their warm-ups? Just because I'm from one of the northern provinces doesn't mean that I'm not a good judge of stallions. You think I'm some sorry-ass country bumpkin."

"I didn't say that."

"No, but you were thinking that."

Valerius grinned knowingly. "Perhaps a little."

There was a break in the back and forth banter between the two. It was not an uncomfortable silence as between strangers. The men knew each other well and had formed an uncommon bond of friendship molded in the crucible of the chilling hours and days in the Teutoburg Forest in Germania. While Valerius was technically, as a tribune, the centurion's commanding officer, this proved not to be an impediment to their friendship, although Marcellus continued to address Valerius formally as tribune or sir, much to Valerius's annoyance. The two survivors of the Teutoburg disaster sat facing each other in the atrium of Valerius's parents' house. The late afternoon sunshine provided summerlike warmth on this autumn day. Nearby, a stone fountain gurgled and splashed its contents in a smooth marble basin.

Marcellus sipped from his wine cup, and then continued in a more staid tone, "How long has it been now, what, three weeks, since you broke the news to the emperor and five weeks since we escaped from the Teutoburg Forest? I almost feel human again. Most cuts and abrasions have now disappeared."

Valerius paused in reflection. Yes, it had been three weeks since he had barged into the imperial palace well after dark and beyond the hours when business was normally conducted to break the news to Augustus Caesar that his three legions of the Northern Rhine no longer existed. The legions had been wiped out almost to a man in the Teutoburg Forest. The magnitude of the military disaster was enormous—three legions, over fifteen thousand elite soldiers of the Roman imperial army—had been destroyed. This was in excess of ten percent of the twenty-eight standing legions that served to protect and defend Rome's interests. In the last several hundred years, Rome had suffered such an ignominious defeat but a few times. The grand design to absorb the German lands and her people into an imperial province was dashed, at least for now.

Valerius recalled with great clarity that fateful night on the Palatine Hill when he had delivered the news. He had interrupted a social gathering of the imperial family. After riding for almost two weeks practically nonstop from the legionary fortress at Vetera on the Rhine, his uniform was in tatters, and he was filthy and smelled like a goat. In the end, his gaunt frame and ragged appearance may have saved him. Perhaps the words "may have" ought to be emphasized, for he was not out of the woods yet. His future was, at best, precarious.

There had been great anger directed at him, especially by Augustus Caesar and his adopted son, Tiberius, the next in line for the imperial throne. One did not want to be on the wrong side of these two men. Augustus had wailed for Quinctilius Varus, the commander of the ill-fated army, to give him back his legions. Remarkably Valerius had gained an unexpected ally in the emperor's dining room that fateful evening. The nephew of Tiberius, Germanicus, who was closer to Valerius in age, appeared favorably disposed to him. The young prince and rising political figure in the Roman world had taken Valerius aside and told him he had admired his pluck for presenting himself in his grimy condition to the emperor, even hinting that there might be a place on his staff for him.

The old adage of "kill the messenger" weighed heavily on Valerius's thoughts. For the first few days after he had arrived home, he was fearful that he would be arrested and then executed for delivering the awful news about the destruction of the legions, but that was three weeks ago and nothing had happened. Should he consider himself safe? Surely imperial justice would have been served by now if it was to occur. Over the course of the twenty-some days since they had arrived in Rome, Marcellus and Valerius had lived a life of leisure, indulging in the comforts and pleasures that Rome offered. Their battered bodies were almost healed. Almost!

By a strange quirk of fate, Valerius and Marcellus had defied the odds and managed to survive the horrors of the Teutoburg disaster. Both had been assigned administrative posts primarily responsible for the payroll records, outcasts in the legion's hierarchy. By a combination of military prowess, tenacity, and luck, the two officers plus a few others lived to fight another day. The other fifteen thousand men of the army of the Northern Rhine had been butchered by the Germans and were now moldering corpses on the forest floor.

The pair had been awash in blood and gore as the two armies clashed amid a fierce rainstorm in the primeval forest. Even the victorious Germans had suffered horrendous losses of men. Chased by the Germans for almost a week, the two officers along with a few others barely made it to the safety of the Rhine fortress.

The two men were in stark contrast with each other. Marcellus was the grizzled centurion, a veteran of many battles. Now in his late forties, he was heavily muscled and well accustomed to the physical demands of the legions. Although handsome, his countenance reflected the many years spent outdoors in the heat and cold, mostly in Germania. Valerius, on the other hand, was slim in stature and much younger, a relative newcomer to the legions. His face featured prominent cheekbones framed by short brown hair and blue eyes. Germania had been his first assignment.

Marcellus, despite his many years of service and having fought countless battles in Rome's name, had never been to the imperial city. He was a guest at Valerius's parents' house. Valerius had been curious how his mother and father would receive Marcellus. Valerius's patrician parents, Sentius and Vispania, could be a bit snooty on occasion, but Marcellus, a commoner who had worked his way up to the rank of centurion, had quickly won them over with his self-effacing stories of his times in the legions. He had regaled them at length with tales of adventure and humor that were the edited versions, for the centurion's wit could be extremely coarse on occasion.

Valerius glanced across at Marcellus. How fortunate he was to have linked up with him. Otherwise, he would have been a rotting corpse with the other fifteen thousand soldiers of the three legions. The two men resumed their mocking repartee.

"Marcellus, the chariot races will be held again tomorrow morning. Why don't we give it another go? You can enlighten me on who to bet on so I can recoup some of my losses."

"Not a problem, Tribune. You just listen to me and—"

In breezed the love of Valerius's life, Calpurnia, her long raven hair trailing behind her, accompanied by Horace, the elderly servant who manned the door. The room immediately brightened with her presence. She was the tribune's unsanctioned betrothed, as his parents did not approve of the union, a problem Valerius wanted to remedy one way or another. She smiled brightly at the two men.

Valerius spoke. "Calpurnia, I was not expecting you, and I did not hear the door."

Horace, a wide grin creasing his face, spoke. "I saw her coming, Master Valerius, and escorted her in from the street."

"Calpurnia, you should not be walking the streets alone," said Valerius.

"Oh nonsense," she replied. "I have been walking the avenues of Rome unaccompanied for years."

"I am glad you came. Please join Marcellus and me in a cup of wine."

"Gladly. By the way, how did you both do at the races today?"

"Don't ask. It's a sore subject."

Marcellus laughed and held up his purse of coins, jiggling its contents so that the coins clinked together.

"Where's your purse?" she asked. Valerius frowned in response.

Marcellus jumped right in. "The tribune chose not to follow my advice, and it cost him dearly."

Calpurnia looked at her beau. "Why didn't you listen to Marcellus? After all, he probably has much more experience on these matters than you." Her voice rang with laughter.

"See, Tribune? She knows."

"Enough of this. Marcellus and I have already discussed my shortcomings with respect to the horses."

The front door of the house reverberated as someone hammered the large brass knocker. Horace hurried toward the front door. There was a brief silence, followed by the sound of rushing footsteps.

Horace returned, a harried look on his face. He spoke with a trembling voice. "Master Valerius, there are armed Praetorian guards demanding to speak with you."

Valerius arose calmly. "Stay here. Let me see what they want."

Valerius, his heart pounding, strode down the hall and then opened the massive door. He stared at the group of guards. He quickly identified the officer in charge and addressed him, "I am Tribune Valerius Maximus. How may I be of assistance?"

The Praetorian officer did not introduce himself, but sneered. "Your presence is requested at the imperial palace immediately."

Valerius didn't say a word, but stared hard at the figure. He was a large man with a swarthy complexion and a jagged scar running down the left side of his face. Valerius knew the intention of the Praetorian was to intimidate him. Perhaps their idea of fun was to see how much they could frighten someone from the aristocratic class. There was no sense in asking why his presence was requested. He was sure they would not tell him anything. He decided to counter their rudeness and arrogance with his own.

"Wait here while I change into my uniform." He slammed the large wooden door in their faces.

Valerius walked back to the atrium. Marcellus looked at him anxiously. Valerius's parents, hearing the commotion, hurried into the atrium, their faces fearful.

"It seems my presence is requested at the imperial palace. I am going to change into my uniform."

"I am going with you, Tribune."

"I am not sure that is a wise choice, Marcellus. Your association with me could be extremely hazardous to your health, if you get my drift."

"Perhaps so, Tribune, but I believe it is my duty to go. Besides," he smirked, "I have never been to a palace before."

"Are you sure you want to do this?"

"I am certain."

Valerius had no idea what fate awaited him in the imperial palace, but he was relieved Marcellus was coming with him. Three weeks seemed like a long time. If they were going to punish him, surely they would have done it by now. While the wheels of the government moved slowly, he knew from his knowledge gained as a result of living his lifetime in Rome that justice was often delivered swiftly. He quickly changed into his uniform and was waiting in the atrium when Marcellus emerged from his quarters on the right. Valerius noted the centurion had his dagger and gladius strapped to his side.

"Marcellus, you are never going to get near the imperial palace like that."

"Why not?"

"You will not be admitted with your weapons."

Marcellus offered a sheepish smile. "Oh, I never thought of that. As I said, I have never been to a palace before."

Valerius turned toward his parents. The pair stood together, unsettled by the turn of events. His father, Sentius, had a grim expression. His mother looked equally aghast. Calpurnia rushed over and gave him a tearful hug.

"Mother, Father, please do not concern yourselves with this matter. I can handle myself with the imperial household. I will be back here later today. If this was something more serious, I believe it would have occurred long before today."

He hoped his tone had enough conviction behind it and did not sound diffident. With a wave, he bid his parents and Calpurnia farewell.

The two exited the house and were immediately surrounded by the Praetorians. The officer in charge looked at Marcellus.

"Who is he?"

Valerius replied in a laconic tone, "He is my centurion, and he is accompanying me."

"My orders are to escort only you. He will have to stay."

Valerius remained steadfast. "I said he is accompanying me. The centurion's knowledge is critical to answering inquiries regarding certain events. What part of this do you not understand?"

The officer and Valerius glared at each other. The other members of the guard stared straight ahead, feigning disinterest in the clash, but listening to every word spoken between the two officers. Finally, the Praetorian relented.

"Fine, if that is what you want. It is your funeral."

They were marched through the streets in the center of a hollow square formation of the Praetorians like common criminals. After a short journey through the busy avenues of Rome, they arrived at the imperial citadel on the Palatine Hill. They entered a colonnaded garden with flowers and lush trees and from there proceeded into the heart of the citadel. Marcellus, a newcomer to Rome, gaped at the splendor of the palace, particularly the marble statues and lavish courtyards. They made several turns before entering a long narrow corridor paved in glistening marble. At this point, the phalanx of guards separated with the exception of the leader. From there, a door was opened leading to a small room. There were no chairs.

"Wait here," said the Praetorian officer. They were left alone.

Valerius and Marcellus stood in silence. Finally, Marcellus could contain himself no longer. "Did you see all of those fountains and statues? By Jupiter's gray beard, I have never seen such opulence. At least we are not in a dungeon."

Valerius pointed with his arm. "The Marmertine prison is that way. Most of those who go in never come out. The field of Mars, where they perform military executions, is in that direction." Before he could continue, the door opened.

In strode Germanicus Caesar, tall and aristocratic in bearing, trailed by a retinue of officers. "Good to see you again, Tribune Valerius. You look a bit more presentable today than the last time I saw you." He smiled smugly.

He gestured toward Marcellus. "And you are? Wait, don't tell me. You must be Centurion Marcellus Veronus."

"Correct, sir; at your service."

Germanicus continued, "You might ask how do I know the centurion's name? Very simple." He waved several pages of documents that he was holding. "This is the transcript of the military tribunal conducted by General Saturnius at the Vetera fortress on the Rhine concerning your escape and flight from the Teutoburg battle back to the safety of Roman-occupied territory. He is highly complimentary of you, Tribune, and you also, Centurion."

Valerius stared forward in disbelief. "He is?"

"Yes, he was impressed with your military demeanor and the fact that you survived the massacre, and then made your way to Vetera through many miles of hostile territory. I must say, I agree with him."

"Thank you, sir, but my centurion, Marcellus, is the one who guided us and was the person who made it all possible. He knew the landscape and a lot about fighting the Germans."

Germanicus beamed at the two. "Now listen up. You might inquire as to why I asked you here. I need good officers like the two of you. We are planning a massive campaign against the Germans in retribution for their treacherous ambush of our legions. The size of our force will be at least eight legions plus the auxiliaries. It will take months to get the legions up to full strength before we begin the invasion. Are both of you willing to be part of my staff and exact some revenge on those nasty German barbarians?"

Valerius and Marcellus looked at each other in acquiescence, and then responded together, "That's affirmative, sir."

"Excellent. Take some personal leave. This is going to be a lengthy planning process, so you might as well take some time to recover from your ordeal. You will be contacted when you are needed. I am glad you have decided to join me. You are dismissed."

Valerius and Marcellus performed a smart about-face and marched down the corridor side by side escorted by the palace guard. The centurion glanced over at the tribune and spoke softly out of the corner of his mouth so as not to be overheard.

"You stood up to that Praetorian prick of an officer like you knew everything would go smoothly. You did not flinch one bit. How did you discern that when the Praetorians showed up at your home, their purpose was not to transport you to the dungeon or some other such nefarious place?"

Valerius proffered a shamefaced grin. "I did not know."

Marcellus snorted. "As I said before, Tribune, you have the makings of a good officer."

II

Several days later Valerius sat alone in his room contemplating his future. His military role seemed assured for the next several years after his meeting with Germanicus Caesar earlier this week. Thus far he had only completed about six months of his obligatory three-year stint as a tribune in the Roman Army, for he was only commissioned as a tribune this past spring. His assignment to Germanicus's staff for the planned invasion of the German homeland was good duty considering what might have happened to him. While his military future seemed assured, it was his personal prospect that was a bit stickier. Six months ago when he had departed his home in Rome for his posting in Germania, he had been at odds with his parents, especially his father.

For people of the equestrian class such as Valerius, it was customary for the parents to arrange a marriage so that it would enhance their son's career and social status. Valerius's father, Sentius, had strong ambitions for his son. He wanted him to be a senator, and marriage to the appropriate family was a stepping-stone to a political career. Valerius was indifferent to his father's urgings and was enamored with a commoner, Calpurnia. She was whom he wanted to marry. His mother had softened her stance and shown sympathy for her son's plight. Just before he had departed six months ago to Germania, she had confided to him that she actually liked Calpurnia and would be supportive of the marriage. While he was elated by this revelation, it was only half the battle. He had to convince his father.

During his flight from the Teutoburg, Valerius had vowed that if he survived that debacle, he would marry Calpurnia no matter what. Since his return, he had been with Calpurnia almost every day, even boldly inviting her into his home. He was challenging his parents to say something about her, savoring a confrontation, but they had remained silent. On the contrary, his parents had been cordial to Calpurnia, seeming to enjoy her company. Valerius was bewildered. He did not know where they stood on the matter. It was time he had "the chat" with his mother and father and got things out in the open. Germanicus had granted him personal leave while the senior staff began planning the invasion. If he was to be married, now was the time. He would speak with his parents tomorrow. No, on second thought, he would speak with them today. This could not be postponed any longer. He would do it now.

He found Marcellus regaling his parents with one of his tales. Valerius stood unobtrusively outside the doorway so he could listen, yet not interrupt the centurion.

With his hands gesturing animatedly, the centurion spun his story. "Now we were down to only four men. All of the other legionnaires of my small unit were slain. The Syrian bandits were closing in on us. There must have been thirty of them. The ground was littered with a large number of their comrades' corpses. My small unit had given a good account of ourselves." Taking a sip from his wine goblet, he paused a brief moment for effect.

"I looked about for an escape route, but there was none. My ears perked up. In the distance I heard the horns of the legions. I had some hope after all. The horns blared again, yet they seemed distant. I knew reinforcements were coming; if I could just hold on a bit longer...But the three remaining men of my unit were cut down. I was alone facing these bloody bandits. They all charged at me. I cut two down with one sword stroke, but there were just too many."

Valerius's parents listened in rapt attention. Marcellus was silent. Valerius's father, Sentius, spoke. "Then what happened?"

Marcellus burst out laughing. "Well, I got killed." He cackled raucously at his own humor.

Sentius grinned, and Vispania laughed. "Oh, Marcellus. You had us going there. You must have hundreds of these stories."

Valerius entered the room. "He told that one to me when I first met him back in Germania, and yes, he does have hundreds of these stories. I hope he has not recited any of his famed poetry. It's quite bawdy."

Sentius chuckled. "He has not, but I would like to hear it sometime."

Marcellus would not recount his poetry with Vispania present. Judiciously, he replied, "Maybe later."

Valerius directed a knowing gaze at Marcellus. "Centurion, would you mind if I speak to my parents in private?"

"Of course, Tribune." The centurion quietly exited.

The speech Valerius had rehearsed and the logic of why he was going to marry Calpurnia went out of his mind in an instant. He did not know where to begin. He continued to stare at his parents, unable to speak. The ensuing silence was uncomfortable.

His mother rescued him. "Valerius, you wish to discuss something with us?"

He blurted, "Mother, Father, I am going to marry Calpurnia in the near future. You should know that I made a vow when I was escaping from the Teutoburg disaster that if I ever survived, I would marry Calpurnia when I returned to Rome despite your objections."

Before he could continue, his mother interrupted. "Valerius, while you were away, your father and I discussed this matter at length. We both concurred that it would be best for you if you married Calpurnia. You have our blessing."

He stood there dumbfounded, his mouth agape. Finally he spoke. "I have your blessing?"

His father spoke. "Yes, Valerius, we want you to be happy above all else. Your mother and I agreed it would be foolish to force you to marry someone of our choice when you are in love with another."

Though his father had spoken the words to allow him to marry Calpurnia, they lacked conviction. Valerius knew it was his mother's doing. This was further corroborated by his mother's expansive smile and his father's tight-lipped expression.

Valerius hurried over and hugged both of them. "We will need to schedule this soon. I have leave time to sort out my personal affairs before I am shipped to Germania. I must go and tell Calpurnia. There is much to be done."

A few nights later, Valerius sat at dinner with Calpurnia, Vispania, Sentius, and Marcellus. Several braziers had been hung from the ceiling to ward off the autumn chill. The tables were festooned with the remnants of the small feast. The informal dinner had featured aimless chatter about the wedding, but now it was time to get down to business. Vispania sat poised with her wax tablet to make the guest list for the wedding celebration. She looked toward her son. "Valerius, I need to know the names of your friends so I can include them on the list."

Valerius shrugged his shoulders. "Mother, most of my friends are fellow tribunes. They have been posted to the four corners of the empire and are not in Rome."

She frowned. "But surely you must have some friends that are not tribunes."

"I do, Mother. I will give it some thought and give you the names tomorrow."

Vispania directed her gaze toward Marcellus. "You have been unusually quiet tonight. Do you have any suggestions for the wedding celebration?"

"I do not, and for good reason. I have never attended a formal wedding before." He grinned awkwardly at everyone.

Vispania, taken aback by his comment, spoke. "How can that be?"

Valerius cringed at his mother's question. She had no idea about Marcellus's life in the legions. For sure it did not include dinner parties and formal affairs of any kind. While his mother's question was well intentioned, she had unwittingly exposed the huge social gulf that separated the patricians of Roman society from the commoners.

"My friends were all in the legions. Strictly speaking, except for the officers with the rank of tribune and above, we were not permitted to marry. Now sometimes the rules were bent just a bit, and a few of my fellow centurions paired up with female acquaintances, but the celebration of the event was hardly a formal affair. Most often everyone drank themselves silly. It was just one giant party."

Vispania spoke. "How thoughtless of me, Marcellus. I did not mean to embarrass you."

"It would take a lot more than that to discomfit me, and I do look forward to a formal wedding. I am certain it will be quite a bit different from the celebrations I have graced with my presence. By the end of the day, most of the participants ended up in a state of undress if you know what I mean."

Calpurnia's voice tinkled with laughter. "I am sure you will find a formal Roman wedding stuffy compared to the events you have attended. Maybe you could share some of your stories with us."

Valerius quickly jumped into the conversation. "I am sure he would love to, but perhaps we should save that for another time."

Calpurnia pouted and feigned anger. "Oh Valerius, the women never get to hear any of the juicy tales you men are so fond of."

Valerius smiled back. "I am sure Marcellus would be delighted to entertain you with some of his anecdotes, but not at the moment." He gave the centurion a warning glance not to pursue the subject any further.

Vispania, eager to change the subject, continued on about the wedding plans. "Now the food caterers are all arranged, so we can put that aside. Sentius, how are you coming along with the wine selection?"

He proffered a wide grin. "That is a topic on which I am well qualified. It is a tough job, but somebody had to do it."

Everyone chuckled. It was no secret that Sentius loved his wine and occasionally over-imbibed. "To answer your question, I have personally sampled various vintages that I would believe to be fitting for my only son's wedding. It was a difficult decision, but I have selected some excellent wines that I believe all will enjoy."

Vispania replied sarcastically, "I know how hard it must have been for you to find the right choices."

Calpurnia turned toward her future mother-in-law. "I must admit I am feeling nervous about the wedding and meeting all those new people."

Vispania spoke. "Nonsense, my dear. There is no need to be anxious. Just remember that in the end, this is all a celebration. After all, what could wrong?"

Calpurnia directed her gaze at Vispania. "Would you help my mother and I select a gown to wear? I would appreciate your insight."

Vispania beamed at her soon to be daughter-in-law. "Of course, dear. I know just the shop to visit. It is on the Esquiline, a small shop but of exceptional quality. They have an outstanding selection."

Valerius looked at his bride-to-be and smiled. She was the sly one. She had tactfully let her mother-in-law assist her in the choice of gowns, no doubt solidifying their relationship. Furthermore, her mirth was an infectious laughter that made everyone around her smile. He knew his mother had warmed to the girl, and his father, who was a bit more aloof, appeared to be taking a liking to her also. This was going far better than he'd ever expected. He was a lucky man.

Several weeks later amid the feverish preparations in the house of Maximus for the upcoming wedding, Valerius was again summoned to the imperial palace, this time by way of a messenger, not a Praetorian escort. He was politely informed by the courier that Germanicus Caesar wanted to discuss several matters with him. Valerius changed into his best uniform replete with shining armor and sculpted cuirass and then made haste toward the Palatine Hill.

Valerius was ushered into a sparsely furnished room. There were several chairs and a large table with numerous piles of documents upon it. Germanicus was seated at the table viewing a scroll. Standing next to him was a civilian who Valerius assumed was the general's personal secretary. At his approach, Germanicus looked up.

"Maximus, good to see you again. Have a seat. I have several matters to discuss with you." He cleared some documents off to the side and waited for Valerius to be seated before continuing. "Now then, our expedition against these Germans is under discussion at the highest levels. Augustus is not keen to any large movement of troops crossing the Rhine. On the other hand, my uncle Tiberius and I want a full-scale invasion. We believe at least eight legions will be needed to conquer the

German homeland. My uncle and I prevailed. This is a highly sensitive matter, and I ask that you not repeat anything discussed here today."

Valerius nodded. "Of course, sir."

Germanicus continued, "Tiberius and I convinced Augustus that a punitive incursion is the best course of action. By the time we are finished with them, the Germans will think twice about ever attacking Roman forces again. By the way, when you enter and exit the palace, please try to avoid being seen by the emperor. You are not viewed favorably by him, and he is still upset by the loss of the three legions. I thought he had calmed down, but he was set off again yesterday."

"How so, sir?"

"A courier arrived from Germania with a package that contained Varus's severed head. Apparently Arminius sent Varus's head to King Marobodus of the Macromanni tribe as a means of procuring the king's future support. Marobodus wanted nothing to do with it. His tribe has an uneasy truce with Rome and has no wish to inflame her ire. He sent Varus's head to the emperor. The severed head rekindled the emperor's anger about the whole disaster. So you are persona non grata. Understood?"

"Yes, sir."

"Good. Back to the plan. My uncle is handpicking the legates to command the legionary force. Several of them are in Rome, and I was thinking of hosting a meeting so we can get to know one another. It will be held...Cornelius, when is that get-together with the legates?"

The clerk shuffled through some papers, and then consulted a wax tablet. "It is tentatively scheduled for next Saturday, sir. The invitations have not gone out as of yet."

"How about it, Maximus? Are you ready to meet the legions' finest?"

With a sinking feeling, Valerius suddenly realized that next Saturday was his wedding day. Now what? He uttered, "Sorry, sir, I cannot attend."

"What? Now explain to me why you cannot attend. Please consider my invitation an order."

"Sir, the last time we met, you stated I had leave time to take care of any personal business, and that is what I'm doing. I'm getting married that day."

Germanicus grinned. "Oh, I see. I guess that is as good an excuse as any. Cornelius, why is it we don't have Maximus's wedding on my schedule? After all, it is customary for subordinates to invite their commanding officer to their wedding."

"Sir, I don't recall receiving an invitation."

Valerius offered Germanicus a sardonic smile. "It must have gotten lost in the mail."

Germanicus replied, "I see. He proffered a knowing smirk. "The planning session with the generals can be rescheduled, for I really want you there."

"Sir, you are most welcome to attend my wedding."

"I will discuss the wedding matter with my wife, Agrippina. Perhaps there is an outside chance we can make an appearance."

"It would be an honor if you could join us, sir."

"And so, Tribune, who is the lucky woman?"

"Her name is Calpurnia. She is a commoner, sir, and not of the nobility. I am truly in love with her, and I desire nothing else but to be married to her. I am sorry, sir, but I doubt you will know anyone at the wedding except for Centurion Marcellus and me. There will be no senators attending."

Germanicus chuckled. "And what makes you think I want to converse with any of those windbags? Listen, Maximus, you've got the correct idea in marrying for love. Me, I'm lucky. I've got the best of both aspects of marriage. As you know, my wife, Agrippina, is Augustus's granddaughter. Ours was an arranged marriage, but as it turned out, we are madly in love with each other. I can't imagine coming home to a wife that one detests. That would make life miserable. So if I might say so, you are making the correct choice."

"If you must know, sir, my marriage was a matter of contention with my parents, but they came around to my point of view."

"I trust then that everyone is on good terms?"

"Yes, thank the gods."

"Now then, Maximus, I have one more thing." He turned to his secretary. "Cornelius, you may leave us; I have something to discuss with the tribune in private."

Cornelius departed, shutting the door softly behind him. They were now alone. Germanicus continued, "When you gave your account of the Teutoburg disaster several weeks ago before the imperial audience, I sensed that you posited the sanitized version of events. Would you please tell me what really happened and what went so terribly wrong for our legions."

Valerius frowned. "Sir, what you really mean is you want to know about Varus."

Germanicus nodded. "Yes, precisely. Why don't we go over here to this small table? I have some nice wine ready for us. I have sampled the contents. It has a marvelous essence." The two men sat, and Germanicus poured the wine. Valerius tasted the wine. Germanicus was correct. It was of a mellow flavor and of excellent vintage.

Valerius sipped his wine again and paused in thought, contemplating how he would explain the disaster that had befallen Rome. "Sir, permission to speak freely?"

Germanicus stared back. "Absolutely, Tribune. Whatever you convey to me stays within these four walls. I need to know everything. It's not every day that three of Rome's finest legions are destroyed." He nodded reassuringly at Valerius.

Valerius began. "First, you need to know that General Varus and I were not on good terms."

Germanicus interrupted. "How did you manage that in just the short time—what, five months—that you were with the legions?"

"It's a long story, but basically I was set up by a fellow tribune, a broad-striper, Castor Nominatus. He was seeking revenge upon me because I beat the crap out of him during our training days on the Field of Mars. He was an odious turd. Pardon my vulgarity, sir, but he is, or should I say was, a despicable worm. Castor's family is very powerful and good friends with the Varus family. His father is a senator."

Germanicus spoke. "I do not believe I know the family, but I'm sure my uncle is acquainted with them. Please continue."

"So upon his arrival, Castor persuaded the general I was an unworthy officer and should not be assigned appropriate duties befitting a tribune. I was exiled to the payroll records. That is where I met Centurion

Marcellus. He was also an outcast for his past transgressions. General Varus often exhibited this type of petty behavior. He surrounded himself with sycophants who thought like him. Unfortunately, most of his confidants were political appointees and had little military experience."

Germanicus stared at Valerius. "Interesting observation. Are you sure you are not letting your personal feelings about Varus get in the way here?"

Valerius spoke. "I have a lot more to convey. I will let you make that judgment when I'm finished. Let me talk about the German leader, Arminius. As you are aware, he is a German national schooled and trained by Rome. He served with the legions in Pannonia, and I heard he was knighted and given equestrian status by your uncle, Tiberius. He became one of Varus's top advisors. The general relied upon him heavily. In defense of Varus, Arminius was effective in dealing with issues concerning the German people. As I recall, he single-handedly resolved a nasty tax conflict with some of the tribal leaders and brought back the head of a German chief who led a minor rebellion. Varus trusted him implicitly and included him as part of his inner circle. Ultimately, he assigned Arminius and his forces the responsibility of the rear and flank security of the three legions on the fateful march into the Teutoburg."

Valerius paused in his delivery so that his words and his message would be fully understood.

Germanicus frowned. "Varus assigned Arminius, a German national, the security of the entire army on the march? That is certainly not standard operating procedure. In my mind it is flawed judgment. So I assume you have met this Arminius?"

"Yes, sir. He is a powerful-looking individual and not to be underestimated. He is a man of guile and intelligence, not some barbarian from the German wilderness."

Germanicus asked eagerly, "So go on."

"Varus called a meeting of all officers, perhaps better described as a council of war, about a week before the march back to the Rhine to our winter quarters. He explained his alternative plan, with some robustness I might add, about changing the route of march through the Teutoburg Forest before returning to the Rhine fortress. It was his desire to make war upon the rebellious Chatti tribe. They had revolted and killed some of his tax collectors. This was a personal affront to him and a slap in the face to Rome. He insisted on teaching them a lesson and making an example of them so the other German tribes could see the consequences of opposing Rome. He made boastful statements about crucifying the entire population of the Chatti.

"General Licinus, legate of the Seventeenth Legion, attempted to warn him of the perils and the logistical nightmares of marching the entire army into hostile territory over very rugged terrain. Licinus's message was quite tactful and in no way critical of Varus's plan. Varus erupted. He chastised Licinus in front of the entire officer corps, stating that he was the commanding general and this was his plan and that he expected it to be executed. He dismissed Licinus from the room. It was humiliating."

Germanicus spoke. "I knew General Licinus. He was a no-nonsense soldier, a man of iron. My uncle Tiberius was also appreciative of him and held him in high esteem." He paused briefly, and then continued, "So now the legions march out?"

"Yes, but there is one more twist to this sad tale. I was told by credible sources that one of the loyal German nationals, Arminius's own father-in-law, I think his name was Segestes, attempted to warn Varus of Arminius's treachery. Varus ignored the warning. So we marched out of our encampment on the Weser heading north instead of south as we normally would have. The first few days were actually relatively easy, but then the army pivoted and moved west. The terrain changed from a well-defined military road to a mud trail through ravines and bogs. The trees of the forest were towering, blocking out almost all light. Then the first storm struck us. It was a gale with pounding rain and battering winds. The German forces attacked out of the forest. Casualties were heavy, and the marching column was stuck. Fortunately, General Licinus rescued the army. He commanded the lead legion, the Seventeenth. He advanced his forces, breaking through the German blockade position at the front of the column, and established a protective laager in a meadow for the entire army."

Valerius paused again to let his words sink in. Germanicus spoke.

"So Licinus saved Varus's butt, at least temporarily. Talk about poetic justice. By Mars's ass, we should have had that man in charge of the army. If so, the three legions of the Northern Rhine would be intact."

"Sir, you will not get an argument from me on that matter. That night in the laager, there was a meeting of the officers to determine our next course of action. I believe the casualty figures were in the range of twenty percent to twenty-five percent. Varus was paralyzed with indecision and could not believe what had happened to his army. He was coaxed by the other legates to abandon the baggage trains and break out of the laager early in the morning with the hope that perhaps the Germans had spent themselves.

"Sir, you should know that the legions gave a good account of themselves that first day. Although we were ambushed and outnumbered in bad terrain, there was little panic. We slew a lot of Germans. Unfortunately, they were far from finished with their assault upon our forces. On the second fateful day, they attacked us again, deeper in the forest. The barbarians concentrated their forces on the command element and broke through the protective corridor. Varus was badly wounded, and many of his staff were killed.

"Licinus assumed command as Varus was incapacitated. We incurred more casualties over the course of the day. The Germans fiercely hurled themselves at our lines. At this point we were down to about fifty to sixty percent strength. We again made a fortified overnight camp. Another officers' council was convened. Licinus's plan was to break out before sunrise the following day and get out of that bloody forest. We almost made it to the plain, but the Germans were waiting for us. They funneled us into a narrow pass bordered with hilly terrain on one side and marsh on the other. That was where the remainder of the legions were destroyed. Varus fell on his sword to avoid capture. Those of us who escaped did so in a second horrific storm of blinding rain and buffeting winds."

Germanicus stroked his chin in thought. "So perhaps a more prudent leader might have avoided this catastrophe?"

"Yes, sir. Varus was definitely culpable for this disaster, but I will say this again, Arminius is not your typical barbarian leader. He knows as much about the tactics of the legions as most senior officers. He is not to be underestimated."

"Your warning is heeded, Tribune. We will need to be especially careful." He paused for a moment. "Enough about this unfortunate Varus business. Now listen up, Maximus, I do have an assignment for you, if you choose to accept it. If these Germans are as duplicitous as you say they are, I need a trusted officer who understands their language and their culture. Therefore I want you to learn the Germanic language and their customs over the winter and spring months. You will not be an interpreter, but rather someone who can tell me if the interpreters are speaking the truth. What do you say?"

"Certainly, sir. I would be willing to do that." He chuckled. "If I can learn Greek, I can learn any language."

Germanicus gave him a knowing smile. "Good! I believe that concludes our discussion for the day. If by some slim chance my wife and I are available, we will try to attend your wedding. Best of luck on your upcoming nuptials. You are dismissed."

Valerius was escorted by two Praetorians down a long corridor toward the palace exit. His mind was buzzing over his latest conversation. Germanicus had stated that there was only a slight chance that he and his wife might attend his wedding. Wouldn't that be something? Perhaps the most popular political figure in Rome appearing at his nuptials. Valerius decided not to mention this to his wife or parents, since it was unlikely the couple would attend. It would just add to the stress and pandemonium that accompanied most wedding plans. As Valerius walked with the Praetorian guards, his preoccupied mind failed to notice the large retinue of soldiers surrounding a toga-clad individual approaching him from the opposite direction. The two groups passed one another.

"Wait. You there, halt."

Valerius noticed that his escort had stopped, so he did likewise. A figure clad in a tan-colored toga shuffled toward him from the group of guards. Valerius looked up and realized the emperor, Augustus Caesar, was approaching him. Oh shit, oh shit. Now what? Germanicus had warned him to avoid the emperor's presence. But what could he do?

"I know your face. You were the one who informed me of the Teutoburg disaster."

Valerius was petrified. He did what was expected of him. He stood straight and answered, "Yes, sir. It was me. Tribune Valerius Maximus at your service."

"Well, I see you are better attired this time."

"Yes, sir.

"What are you doing here?"

Sir, I was conferring with General Germanicus about the German tactics and their leader Arminius."

Augustus grimaced, and his face turned red. "I have lost three of my finest legions thanks to Varus and the treachery of those Germans." His voice was raised, almost shouting. Valerius remained silent, not knowing what to say. His fingernails bit into the palms of his hands as he waited for the coming explosion. It was not a good thing to have pissed off the most powerful figure in the Roman Empire.

Germanicus suddenly appeared on the scene. "Grandfather, I was looking for you. I was just meeting with Tribune Maximus, and he was briefing me on the German tactics. It appears we have our work cut out for us. Would you like me to brief you now?"

Augustus appeared to lose some of his fire. He hung his head in sadness. "Yes, that would be fine."

Germanicus gave Valerius a knowing look to convey to him to get out of there now and motioned for his Praetorian escort to get moving.

Valerius and Calpurnia stood arm in arm among the invited guests attending. The wedding ceremony went smoothly without incident. The ladies were resplendent in their flowing *stolas* and bedecked in glittering jewelry. The men wore their finest togas—all that is, except for Marcellus. Valerius and his father had dragged the centurion to a suitable tailor so he could be outfitted with the appropriate attire for the wedding. The centurion had never worn a toga before. It had been quite a scene, with Marcellus vehemently rejecting the formal clothing. He had complained that the garment would fall off his shoulder, thus exposing "his fat arse" to the entire wedding assembly. Valerius and his father had both shrugged their shoulders in resignation and agreed to let the centurion wear his uniform.

As handsome as Valerius was in his cream-colored toga, he was easily outshone by Calpurnia in her pale green stola. For the moment, the couple was free of any guests. Holding hands, they gazed at the assembled throng in Valerius's parents' home. Festive garlands and beautiful flowers adorned the atrium. Subdued chatter filled the air as huge platters of food and containers of wine were brought forth by the staff to serve the guests. Soft music from lutes filled the air.

Calpurnia gazed longingly up at her husband. "You were correct, darling. The ceremony was much easier than I anticipated. I was silly to be so anxious about such a matter." She squeezed his hand in affirmation of her relief.

As with most Roman weddings, it was a simple affair. Her mother had dressed her this morning as custom demanded. In addition to her green stola, she was adorned in a long silk veil pressed down upon her head by a garland of flowers. The brief ceremony featured an exchange of vows. Valerius had asked her if she would be the *mater familias*. In return, Calpurnia had asked him if he would be the *pater familias*. Once the vows were exchanged, everyone present shouted their congratulations. This was followed by the placing of some cake on the altar of Jupiter and Juno.

"I am relieved it is over, and now I just want to enjoy myself." She was about to continue when a sudden collective gasp went up from the crowd, followed by a hush. She looked about, noting a handsome couple entering, flanked by four armed escorts.

"Valerius, who are that man and woman with the burly guards?"

The tribune was stunned and remained silent. All the while, Calpurnia looked at him inquiringly. Finally he spoke. "Uh, Calpurnia, those are not just guards; they are Praetorians. That is Germanicus Caesar, and the woman with him I assume to be his wife, the Lady Agrippina."

Calpurnia paled and looked at him with her mouth agape. "You did not tell me they were invited. It's only the emperor's granddaughter and her husband, who is perhaps the most popular political figure in Rome.

What is he, second in line as Augustus's successor, and you didn't tell me? How could you do this?"

Valerius returned her look sheepishly. "The matter of our wedding came up at our meeting last week. Germanicus told me there was only an outside chance he and his wife could attend. I didn't want to make you even more apprehensive. Come on, let's go over and greet them."

Calpurnia balked, remaining in place. "But what will I say to them? I have never talked to the imperial family before."

Valerius turned toward her. "Just be yourself and follow my lead. Ready?"

Valerius grabbed her hand and half dragged his reluctant bride toward the imperial couple and the four burly guards.

Valerius hailed Germanicus. "Sir, I am so glad you could come." He turned toward the woman, a lady of striking beauty. She was attired in a beautiful peach-colored stola that fit her perfectly. Around her neck she wore a shimmering necklace, inset with a tasteful number of glittering jewels. Her hair was styled perfectly, with cascading ringlets down to her shoulders. "You must be the Lady Agrippina. Welcome to our wedding. I am Tribune Valerius Maximus, and this is, as of a few moments ago, my wife, Calpurnia."

Agrippina took Calpurnia's hand as if she had known her for years. "It is so nice to meet both of you. Germanicus has told me so much about your husband. I insisted we cancel our previous plans and attend the wedding. Sorry we missed the ceremony, but we had earlier official functions to attend."

Germanicus spoke. "It was an easy choice. It would have been your wedding or another boring banquet at a senator's house."

Masking her trepidation, Calpurnia jumped right into the conversation. "Thank you so much for coming. You honor us. It is a pleasure to meet both of you. My lady, you look gorgeous in that color gown."

"Please call me Agrippina, and none of this my lady stuff. Why don't the two of us excuse ourselves from the men and have a nice chat? You can tell me all about your plans and where you will be living." With that, Agrippina linked her arm with Calpurnia's and guided her away.

The two men gazed at the retreating figures. Valerius beamed. His wife had handled the entire situation smoothly and without a hitch. Calpurnia might be a commoner, but she exuded class.

"Good choice, Tribune. Looks like you have a charming and beautiful wife."

"Thank you. She is a little miffed at me because I did not inform her you were coming."

Germanicus spluttered with laughter. "Not a good way to start a marriage, Tribune, and you thought fighting the Germans was difficult? Welcome to the world of being a husband. I would gladly give you some pointers, but I believe I am not the most qualified to speak on the subject. Look, since the ladies are out of hearing range, let me discuss a little business with you. I know this is your wedding day and all that, but this will only take a moment. A tutor for your German lessons has been selected, and you should be hearing from him shortly. I met him briefly. He is a German national who speaks both languages. Wothar is his name. He was a Praetorian guard, but as you may be aware, all of the German nationals who were part of the guard were dismissed as a result of the Teutoburg disaster. His Latin is rather strongly accented, but you will be able to understand him. Please keep me apprised of your progress. I know I am asking a lot from you, but having a Roman officer who speaks the German tongue will be invaluable to me. Now that we have that out of the way, let us get some wine, and you can introduce me to your parents."

III

Valerius bolted upright from his marriage bed, gasping in a cold sweat. Beside him, Calpurnia lay in blissful sleep, a rounded hip exposed from the tangle of bedcovers. He regarded her naked form, admiring her sleek lines. Valerius rose and padded across the room to the curtained window. Peering into the inky darkness outside, he observed the silent streets below. Looking back to see if Calpurnia was still asleep, he used the drape to dry the sweat from his body.

The dream was the same one he had had last night, the night before last, and the night before that. He saw swarming Germans overwhelm the Roman lines. The eagle standards of the Seventeenth and Nineteenth Legions toppled over into the hands of the enemy, and then he was running for his life through the forest. He and the band of Roman survivors were dashing through the heavy rain and howling wind. Suddenly, they were surrounded by snarling, spear-wielding Germans. He killed several with his sword. Next to him Marcellus was similarly engaged. More Germans appeared out of the heavy woodlands, cutting off all hope of escape. Their spears were thrust at him. He beat aside with his sword their jabs, but there were too many to ward off. He felt the shafts plunge into his torso, and that is when he awoke.

He had come close to suffering that fate on several occasions. He thought back to his meeting at the palace with Germanicus: he had agreed to go back to Germania and assist in the destruction of the Teutonic warrior tribes. What in Hades was he thinking? Just the thought of entering the German woodlands gave him the chills. But no, this was something he had to do, regardless of his foreboding. He would not let haunted dreams and his personal misgivings prevent him from achieving retribution. Besides, and most importantly, Germanicus's request that he join him for the invasion of Germania was in reality a thinly veiled order. He had no choice. One did not reject an offer from one of Rome's most powerful figures. Like it or not, he was returning to the German woodlands.

Damn that Arminius and his German brethren who had orchestrated the deadly ambush. Rome had recognized him as a friend and bestowed the rank of equestrian upon him, and look how he had repaid them. He remembered meeting Arminius. He was a daunting physical specimen, with blazing blue eyes. Germanicus had said that the Roman forces would consist of eight legions plus auxiliaries. By all the gods, it would be an army with which to be reckoned. He estimated maybe sixty thousand men, perhaps more. That would be a lot of soldiers. In his mind they would need every one of them.

He again peered down at the empty streets. A soaring dark shape to his left diverted his gaze upward. What was that, an owl? These birds were considered bad omens. Of course, he didn't believe any of that crap, just as he didn't buy into the priests looking at the entrails of goats and chickens to see the future. Still, the presence of the ill-omened bird sent chills down his spine. Was he tempting fate once too often by returning to the German woodlands? A gust of wind rattled against the windowpane, deepening his dread. His dark thoughts were interrupted as Calpurnia called out to him, "What are you looking at, dear? Come back to bed and keep me warm."

He stared out into the black night for a moment longer, and then hurried back to his bed, the image of the owl forgotten for now. If he only knew what the Goddess Fortuna had in store for him, perhaps he would have preferred to have perished in the Teutoburg.

His day began early the next morning. He was mulling over his breakfast, listening to Calpurnia prattle on about her upcoming social engagement. She had been invited to the imperial palace by the Lady Agrippina so that they might continue their budding friendship. Calpurnia asked him what she should wear, but Valerius knew she didn't give a fig about his opinion. She was just talking to dispel her nervousness. He was about to change the subject when one of his servants announced that he had a visitor, a German dressed in Roman garb.

"Well, my dear, it appears as though my new assignment is about to begin. Remember I told you that Germanicus had tasked me with learning the German language? My sense is that this is my tutor."

"You are going to have your German language lessons in our house, not at the palace?"

Valerius laughed. "Yes, Calpurnia. Better here than at the palace. There are certain powerful individuals who reside there that would not be pleased to see me. So here is where we will conduct our business. Now if you will excuse me, I'm off to meet my new taskmaster."

Valerius approached the vestibule. Waiting to meet him was a tall individual with broad shoulders. Like most Germans he had a beard. It was short and golden in color. His hair was long, framing a handsome face. He was attired in cloth trousers and a cloak to ward off the chill. He was heavyset, no doubt a powerful individual. He gazed at Valerius and spoke in a heavily accented Latin.

"My name is Wothar. I have been dispatched by Germanicus Caesar to teach you the German language."

Valerius studied the man briefly. Wothar returned his gaze, not a hard stare, but one that reflected a kind of respect. After a brief pause, Valerius spoke. "Tell me about your background, Wothar. What tribe are you from, how did you end up in Rome, where do you want to be?"

"I am from the Batavi tribe. My fellow warriors and I were part of the Roman auxiliary cavalry with the army of the Rhine. I served five years with that unit. It was good duty, and it beat farming for a living. I heard the Romans were recruiting Germans for the Praetorian Guard in Rome, so I volunteered along with some of my comrades. I enjoyed my time as part of the imperial guards. The pay was good, and I appreciated the comforts of the city. But as you know, all of the German Praetorians were dismissed by the emperor after the Teutoburg disaster. We are all looking for work. One of Germanicus's aides sought me out for this assignment. I hope I can help you. I want to stay in Rome. I kind of like it here."

"Very well, Wothar. Let's establish some rules right now. I want to learn the German language. I will write down the German words in Latin so I can study the language. Also, I want to be educated in more than the language. I want to learn how to think, eat, sleep, shit, act, and fight like a German. I have been to Germania, so I know a little of their ways. You will teach me everything you know about the Germans and their customs. If I find you are not truthful or not giving me your full knowledge, I will discharge you immediately. Understood?"

Wothar nodded. "Fine with me, Tribune. When do you want to get started?"

"We will start today."

It was past lunch, and Valerius concentrated on the words and phrases of the German language. The instruction had been going on for hours with little progress. Attempting to enunciate a particularly lengthy German word, Valerius garbled it, as he did most others.

"Enough. I believe I have reached a stopping point. Let's move on to something else. Wothar, I want you to begin telling me about the German tribes and their customs."

"What do you wish to know, Tribune? As I said, I am of the Batavi, but all of the tribes are different."

Valerius frowned. "I understand that, but they have some things that are shared, and then you can tell me how they are different. Come now, I have met some of the chieftains of the various tribes. They appeared to have more in common than not."

"What you say is true, Tribune. We have much in common, but we are all different. Let's start with the various tribes. None of them have any permanent towns or cities. We Germans tend to move around and not stay in one place. That has always been the way. They all herd animals, a few cattle and especially horses. There is some farming."

Valerius nodded. "Go on."

"Because they move from place to place, there are frequent disputes about land ownership. This is one reason why there is no unification. In terms of deities, almost all worship the gods of the woodlands. It is common practice to sacrifice captured enemies to the gods to keep their goodwill."

"All right, I will do my best not to get captured."

Wothar chuckled.

Valerius asked. "What about the gods? I know something of them, and I have met one of those German priestesses."

Wothar grinned. "It is best not to interfere or in any manner affront those priestesses. It will not end well for you. Although there are many gods, the main one is Wodan. He is equivalent to the Roman god Jupiter. The other powerful gods are Donar, god of thunder, and Ziu, the war god."

Valerius interjected, "Tell me about their family structure and the leadership of the tribes and clans."

"Men have only one wife. The husband, wife, and children live in the same dwellings. Some of the larger clans have a royalty structure with respect to the leadership of the clan. These nobles oversee the day-to-day affairs of the typical village. Leaders are also selected based upon their prowess as warriors. So in times of war, this becomes even more important. Usually each village has a champion who represents them in combat. For example, sometimes disputes between tribes are settled by the two village champions. It is a fight to the death. A captured enemy is sometimes offered the opportunity to fight the village champion in order to avoid execution."

Wothar went on in great detail about the religious festivals, of which there were many, the defensive characteristics of the German hill forts, and what the people ate and drank. Eventually he paused, looking at Valerius expectantly, hoping this might be the end, for he had been talking for a long time.

Valerius stroked his chin in thought. "I think that is enough for today. I will study the German words and phrases you taught me today. We will do this again tomorrow. Also I would ask that you procure the German fighting weapons, you know, the spear and shield, so

I can begin my learning of how the Germans fight. You are dismissed for today."

Wothar nodded in acquiescence and departed.

The following day Wothar arrived towing a bulging cloth satchel. He grinned at Valerius. "I have the weapons you desire. We can begin training whenever you are ready." He untied the ends of the satchel and proudly displayed their contents. He retrieved two rectangular shields, made of wood and covered with leather.

Valerius hefted the shield. It was much smaller than the Roman legionary version. The Roman shield was designed to protect most of the body from arrows and other missiles, and acted as a ramming object. Oftentimes the Roman lines would overrun the foe by sheer brute force, using the shield as a battering ram. The German shield was much lighter; its primary purpose was to deflect sword and spear thrusts when engaged in individual combat. It was meant to be mobile, versus the Roman stationary version.

Valerius swung the shield from side to side and up and down, surprised at the light weight of it.

"What else do you have there?" he asked Wothar.

The German produced wooden shafts about six feet long, with padded tips instead of the double-edged iron point that was typically affixed to the shaft. Wothar grinned and twirled the spear in his hand, then swung it back and forth.

"This is the primary weapon of the German people," said Wothar.

"Let me have one of those," said Valerius.

The tribune held the shield in his left hand, the spear in the other. He felt awkward. He had trained and drilled many hours with the Roman sword and heavy shield. The new combination of weapons was foreign to him. Where the Roman weapon was short, the German spear was long, and the German shield was small versus the Roman version, which was large. Perplexed, he waved with the shield and gave a half-hearted thrust with the spear.

"You must do better than that, Tribune. It's like this."

Wothar stepped swiftly to his left, guarding his side with the shield. He thrust hard with the spear at an imaginary foe, and then returned to the ready position, his feet balanced and shield ready to deflect any counterstrike.

Valerius took note of how agile Wothar was and the certain crispness of the spear thrust. "I believe this is going to be as difficult as the German pronunciations; I have no idea how to fight with these. Show me."

The German began a series of movements with the shield and spear. He started slowly, then picked up the pace. Soon his actions became a blur as he darted in and out, back and forth. His spear twirled and delivered not only thrusts, but slashes as well. In one move, he reversed the spear and used the butt end to deliver a blow that would have knocked an opponent senseless. Wothar halted his display, smiling in a boastful manner.

"Like that, Tribune."

"My turn. Like this?" Valerius assumed the ready positions as he had seen Wothar do.

"No, no, Tribune. You are standing too upright, and your shield is not square to your body. You need to grip the spear farther down the shaft for better control." He moved Valerius's hand toward the tip. "Now try it."

Valerius realized he could handle the spear more nimbly, but it had the disadvantage of shortening the length of the weapon. And so it began. The use of the spear and light shield were perplexing to him, but the footwork he had learned fighting with Roman weapons was comparable. One always maintained good balance so as not to be bowled over. To be on the ground was a death sentence for any warrior. The feet were spaced wide apart, and one never crossed one leg over the other while moving about.

After several hours with Wothar demonstrating the defensive use of the shield and how to thrust with the lance, Valerius was eager to do some one-on-one with the German. He knew his skill level was not even close to Wothar's, but he needed to understand what this combat was like.

The two men faced off against each other. Valerius was mindful to keep the shield square to his body and at midtorso level. He was in a half crouch, waiting for Wothar to make his move. A lightning-like thrust by Wothar followed by a heavy shield blow pushed him backward. This was followed by another spear thrust that unbalanced him. Wothar, attacking from Valerius's left, charged into the tribune, knocking him to the ground. The blunted tip was poised at his throat.

"You retreated straight backward, Tribune. You need to shift to the right or left and attack your opponent's exposed flank. Again?"

Humiliated at his quick defeat, Valerius nodded. They began again, with similar results. He rubbed the spot on his torso where Wothar had jabbed him, none too gently. Valerius flushed with anger, but then caught himself. He had asked for these lessons. He was supposed to be learning the German tongue, not thrusting about with spears.

Wothar silently regarded the Roman. Valerius looked at him. "Begin," he said.

The two circled. Wothar delivered a series of feints with the spear before charging at Valerius. The tribune deftly jumped to the side and counter jabbed. It did not connect, but it was the first time he had delivered an offensive blow. Bolstered by his minor triumph, Valerius seized the initiative and thrust again at Wothar. His blow was blocked. In an instant, his opponent was past his guard, and he was jabbed with the blunt spear. Defeated again, but it did not end there. The pair continued for another grinding hour of endless repetition.

"I think I have had enough of this for today. Let's get back to the German language." Rubbing his sore torso, Valerius professed, "Learning the words is easier and not as painful. We will do this again tomorrow."

The next day the two men continued in the basics of the German language. Wothar spoke the words for various articles of clothing, foods, and weapons. Valerius recited the words back. The language structure was simple, with a limited vocabulary, but the guttural pronunciations were difficult. Valerius would write the words on a wax tablet using the Latin letters so he could study the pronunciation later. There was nothing even close to the Germanic sounds in the Latin—or for that matter Greek—language. He would need to concentrate his efforts on the enunciation of the strange words.

Later in the afternoon, the two men began their combat once again using the German weapons. Valerius was faring poorly. Valerius thrust with the spear and advanced. Wothar retreated. It was at that moment that Marcellus entered the premises. Valerius signaled for the sparring to cease.

"By Venus's pert ass, going native on us, Tribune? I thought you were supposed to be learning the language, not training to be a gladiator."

Valerius offered a wry smile and wiped the sweat from his brow. "I am expanding my horizons to encompass other Germanic customs and behaviors. Please keep this between the two of us."

"Most certainly, Tribune. I must admit you look fairly nimble with that spear and shield."

"I have a long way to progress before I may be considered skilled at this. Wothar has been beating my ass with regularity, but I am learning. Want to observe some more?"

Valerius gestured to Wothar to begin. The two clashed. Each thrust was parried, then counterthrust. The Roman put on his best display yet, lasting some length of time against his opponent. In the end, Valerius lost. He looked toward Marcellus. "Believe it or not, I'm getting better at this," he said.

The centurion snorted. "If you say so, Tribune. As for myself, I will stick to the Roman gladius with plenty of Roman armor to protect me."

That evening, Valerius hurried along the darkening streets toward the imperial palace. Tonight he was dining with Germanicus and several of his generals. This was the meeting that had been rescheduled as a result of his wedding. There would be some of the top-ranking generals in the Roman Army attending tonight. He would most likely be by far the lowest-ranking officer in the room. He decided he would maintain a polite façade and a low profile.

Upon arrival, Valerius was surprised to see Germanicus and his senior staff already there. They must have started early. A goblet of wine was thrust into Valerius's hands by a servant. He took a deep swallow, enjoying the mellow flavor. *They sure know how to select their wine in the imperial palace,* he thought. Shortly thereafter Germanicus gestured for everyone to take their places. He pointed out the far couch on the left side for Valerius. He was farthest away from his superior, which he expected as the lowest-ranking officer.

Germanicus remained standing and spoke. "Let me introduce to you a new member of my staff. This is Tribune Valerius Maximus, who, along with a few others, was fortunate enough to have survived the Teutoburg disaster. He was the one that brought the unfortunate news of the defeat to the emperor. General Saturnius at Vetera on the Rhine gives him high praise, and so do I. He is a warrior and a survivor.

"Tribune, these are some of my senior staff. To my immediate right is General Seius Tubero, my deputy commander and most experienced legate. To my left is General Licinius Stertinius, who will be my cavalry commander. Over here are Generals Publius Vitellius of the First Legion and Cassius Apronius of the Twentieth. The commanders of the two army corps for Germania Inferior and Germania Superior are not here and are on station on the Rhine."

Valerius nodded and smiled at the small group of officers. In return they gave him curious glances. He returned his gaze to Germanicus, who remained standing.

"Gentlemen, let me conclude the business portion of our get-together with a few remarks concerning the upcoming campaign against the Germans. As you can imagine, this will be a massive undertaking. We will be creating a new army with the purpose of subduing the rebellious Germans and killing or capturing their leaders. Our forces will be comprised of eight full legions plus auxiliary forces. The crusade against the German homeland will not occur until sometime in early summer. The exact date has not been finalized at this time, but preparations have already begun. I have authorized our naval forces to begin shipping supplies and materials up the North Sea and then the Rhine. You are all aware of course that this is a bit risky given the conditions at sea in the winter and spring months, but it is a peril that must be faced. We must begin the accumulation of stockpiles now. With the exception of Tribune Maximus—who has other assigned duties here in

Rome—we will be departing next month to assume command of our forces. The movement of the various legions to our headquarters at Vetera on the Rhine will begin shortly. It is my intention to have the army battle-ready and fully provisioned by early summer. We will end our campaign by early autumn. That concludes my remarks."

The various commanders all stood as one, including Valerius, and raised their glasses. General Stertinius spoke. "Sir, to a successful campaign."

Germanicus beamed at the men. "Thank you. You are the finest military leaders that Rome has to offer, handpicked by my uncle Tiberius. Now, let us enjoy our dinner."

The meal was delicious, with various courses provided by the imperial kitchens. Valerius was especially fond of the pork dish with a glazed honey sauce. He decided to limit his wine intake to a few goblets. It was best to have all of one's wits about with this assemblage. The exchange was light at first, but then morphed into deeper subject matter. He attempted to follow it, but much of what was spoken was above him. The people and places they discussed were foreign to him. As more wine was consumed, the conversation became more boisterous. He continued to place himself on the periphery of the dialogue, only speaking when spoken to. He was startled when he heard his name being called by Germanicus.

"Tribune Valerius, the legates present here tonight have been briefed on the Teutoburg disaster, but I would like to have you give your account of what transpired."

Valerius had no idea he would be called upon to provide an overview of the Roman defeat. He should have anticipated this, but he had been so focused on his wedding that the thought entirely escaped his mind. Well, too late now. It was time to act. He paused, and extemporaneously cobbled together some talking points. He began, "Of course, sir. Many of you probably place the blame on General Varus and his staff, and in truth, there were some critical errors in decision-making. I will not stand here and defend the general, but the real problem was Arminius. For those of you not familiar with the man, he is a German national educated and trained by Rome and one who served with distinction in the legions. He is a crafty individual who understands our tactics and knows both the strengths and weaknesses of the Roman Army. He developed a tactical plan that was brilliant and executed with precision.

"I would articulate his tactical successes as follows. First, he achieved total surprise. How he kept the plot secret with so many involved is difficult to fathom. There was one warning by another loyal German, but at the time Varus did not deem it to be a credible source. Second, the ambush was sprung at a time and place so that the legions could not retreat to their previous base and the army was too far from any reinforcements. Third, he attacked with an overwhelming force on terrain of his choosing and not suited to the legions. The army was at a distinct disadvantage in the woodlands. Our battle tactics of shock and maneuver were useless."

He paused in his delivery in case there were any questions. He was met by blank stares, their expressions neutral. He continued, "The tribes were united by Arminius, and although the Germans incurred heavy losses of men, they continued attacking until the legions were whittled down to a force that could be overrun. Our forces fought bravely and with discipline. I will not bore you with the grisly details, but over three days, the Germans eventually destroyed the army and its three legions. I will try to answer any questions you might have."

There was a brief silence.

Seius Tubero, the deputy commander, spoke. "So, Tribune, how long did you say you have been with the legions, and what exactly were your duties as an officer of the Rhine legions?"

Valerius attempted to mask his frown. He had noted the penetrating stare from this officer during his brief presentation. The figure had a haughty countenance and cruel dark eyes that seemed to be perpetually angry. From the gist of his questions, obviously Valerius's remarks had not been well received.

Valerius stared straight ahead, not at all ashamed of his service or his responsibilities. "Sir, I joined the legions in the spring. General Varus appointed me to oversee the payroll and to secure the pay records of the legions."

"I see, yet with your limited time and experience in the service to the legions, you have the temerity to lecture the generals assembled in this room on tactics? You would have us believe that this Arminius, this Latinized savage, is someone to be feared."

Valerius's face flushed. His anger bloomed. Yes, he had limited experience in the legions, but he had observed firsthand what transpired in the Teutoburg. He replied in a laconic tone, respect be damned.

"Yes, General Tubero, I have minimal knowledge of tactics. All of you in this room have much greater experience than me on these matters, and I would not presume to lecture you or any of the others present here tonight on battlefield strategies. But I am a survivor and an eyewitness to this debacle, while fifteen thousand of my fellow legionnaires are rotting corpses in the German woodlands. I have met Arminius—have you, General? No, of course not. So unless you want one of those German spears stuck up your noble Roman arse, I would suggest you heed my warning concerning this—what did you call him—a Latinized savage?"

Before the room could erupt, Germanicus smoothly interceded. "I would ask that all of you have some respect for Arminius. He has proven to be a formidable opponent to Rome's interests. We will need to make plans on how to best defeat this Germanic leader. Why don't we all call it a night, if that's agreeable to everyone?

"Tribune Valerius, would you please stay? I have some matters to discuss with you."

The others slowly exited; Tubero proffered Valerius a withering stare. Several of the other generals smirked, knowing Valerius was in for a first-class ass-chewing from his commanding officer. When all had departed, Germanicus spoke. "You certainly don't mince words, do you? I believe you were a little terse with General Tubero. What did you say—something to the effect of a German spear shoved up his noble Roman arse?"

Valerius was ashamed of his outburst. "I apologize for my behavior tonight, sir, but I have no desire to witness the eradication of any more of our legions. They must understand the grave danger that Arminius poses to Rome."

Germanicus responded, "There are more subtle ways to reply to my generals. I understand your passion concerning the potential threat to the legions by these rebellious Germans, but you need to appreciate this from the perspective of Tubero and the others. They are not used to taking advice from tribunes, no matter how well intentioned the remarks. Understood?"

"Yes, of course, sir. The fault was mine. I should have been more judicious in my choice of words. Again, my apologies."

Germanicus grinned back at him. "Apology accepted. Besides, Tubero's remarks were offensive, and perhaps he did deserve some of your ire. Now, as I noted at dinner, we will be departing for the Rhine by the end of next month. That includes Centurion Marcellus. He will be tasked with training my Praetorian cohort of personal bodyguards to fight the Germans. However, you will be staying here for a while. I want you to continue with your language lessons."

"But, sir, I could bring my German tutor with me."

"No, there would be too many distractions. Besides, I don't want others to know that you comprehend the language, and as you know, nothing is secret in an army camp. It is important to me that you learn the Germanic tongue. I will need your input. I don't know if I can trust these German interpreters or not. Consider it a wedding present from me that you will spend some time with your new bride. My decision is final, so I don't want to hear any arguments from you."

"I understand, sir. I will look forward to our meeting on the Rhine."

"Good. You are dismissed."

The next day Valerius sat with Calpurnia at their morning meal. He hardly ate anything and stared off in the distance. Calpurnia frowned. "I was asleep when you arrived home last night. Judging from your silence, I take it that the dinner with the generals was not a smashing success."

Valerius laughed. "That would be an apt description."

"What happened?" she inquired.

"Attending the banquet were some of Rome's most senior legates. I attempted to maintain a low profile among those senior staff. You know, only speak when spoken to. The level of conversation was way over my head in terms of who one knew and what campaigns one had been on. Out of nowhere, Germanicus asked me to provide some insight into the Teutoburg disaster for the benefit of his assembled legates. Apparently they were not pleased that a low-ranking tribune—that would be me—could provide any profound insight into the battle, even though I was actually there."

"So what happened? What did you say?"

"I took offense at their demeaning remarks. I believe I told Germanicus's deputy commander, General Tubero, that if he chose not to listen to me, then he was at risk of having a German spear shoved up his noble Roman arse."

Calpurnia gasped in laughter. "You didn't?"

"I did. You should have seen Tubero's face. It looked like he swallowed a turd. I later apologized to Germanicus after his generals had departed, but they need to realize the extreme danger they will face when the army clashes with Arminius. The man is not to be underrated. Somehow I must convey to them the peril of crossing the Rhine in pursuit of the Germans."

"So what is your status? What happens next?"

"There is some good news. It seems the entire staff is packing up to move to the Rhine, including Marcellus. I will remain here and continue my language lessons. Germanicus will summon me when he is ready. It will be some time before the legions are ready to advance into German territory. He said that my retention here in Rome was his wedding gift to you and me."

Calpurnia grinned. "Good. I shall have you all to myself except for that German guy."

"Wothar."

"Who?"

"His name is Wothar."

"Oh, yes, that's him. Now tell me how your language lessons are progressing—is it difficult?"

In response, Valerius spoke a series of German words.

Calpurnia looked back at him quizzically. "What does that mean?"

Valerius proffered a lewd grin. "Roughly translated, it means I want to ravish you upon the breakfast table."

Calpurnia arched her eyebrows. "I'm not sure how you are going to be of service to Germanicus if you only learn phrases like that. Also, the answer is no—the servants are all around us—but if want to follow me into our bedchamber, so be it."

IV

Somewhere in the German Woodlands

Arminius sat at the crude wooden table along with the chieftains of a number of tribes. Outside the mud and timber walls of the crude dwelling, snowflakes danced in the wind. A small fire bloomed in the hearth, providing a modicum of warmth on this brutal day. In attendance were members of the Chatti, Bructeri, Marsi, Angrivari, Dolgubni, and Arminius's own tribe, the Cherusci. Seated next to him was his uncle, Inguiomerus, his father's brother. Arminius did his best to exhibit a calm demeanor, but inwardly he cringed at some of his uncle's suggestions. Far from being a voice of reason given his age and status, his uncle championed aggressive action against the Romans to the point of recklessness. One would think that someone of his age and experience would exercise restraint when dealing with the Romans. Outside of the Teutoburg victory, the Germans had not fared especially well against the might of the legions. More to the point, the Germans had lost badly when they opposed the legions on open ground.

His uncle spoke. "Arminius, tell us why we cannot attack the Roman forts along the Rhine. We have humbled the Roman legions with the massive defeat inflicted upon them, but as long as their strongholds stand on the banks of the Rhine, we will never be safe as a people. They can strike us at any time from across the Rhine. The river provides no barrier against the Romans. They can build their bridges in a short time and cross with impunity into our lands." There was a muttered chorus of approval from the assembled throng.

Arminius sighed in annoyance. He had explained the reasons why they could not attack the Rhine forts to them once before. They had not listened. He patiently began again. "I agree that these forts pose a threat to us. The Romans can launch an offensive across the Rhine into our territory. As you, I would like to eradicate these citadels, but it would be disastrous for us to attempt this. Let me explain why. In order to undertake a siege of the Rhine forts, we would need many boats, which I would remind you we do not have. The Romans control the few pontoon bridges that span the river, and these could be destroyed by them quickly.

"Assuming we could cross the Rhine, we would need to establish a supply line to feed our warriors. Why, you might ask. Because it would be a lengthy siege, and we would need to stockpile provisions and weapons. Of most importance, we have no siege equipment like the Romans possess. If we are to take these fortresses, we need the Roman ballista. Furthermore, our warriors would be extremely vulnerable to a counterattack from Roman forces. The legions are capable of quickly mobilizing forces and moving them rapidly from one province to another with their elaborate road systems. Then we might become the besieged instead of them."

He continued, "Listen to me. We have suffered some heavy losses as a result of our victory in the forest over the Romans. I fear we would lose many more men in an attack of the Roman forts and probably not have a successful outcome. I would ask that you put aside these thoughts of invading across the Rhine for now. What we should be concerned about is what the Romans might do in response to their defeat. Winter is upon us. My sense is that the Romans will do nothing until the spring. Our spies tell us that the Romans have reinforced their garrisons along the river. I am not sure what they plan when the weather warms, but we must be vigilant for a Roman offensive.

"Frankly, I don't believe they will do anything. While the Romans don't take kindly to defeat and their typical response is to deploy additional legions, this is different. They have lost a great deal. Three of their finest legions are gone, and all of the territory they believed to be secure is now back in our hands. The cost of retaking this land would be enormous in terms of resources, and to what end? What would they gain? The Romans will never conquer the German spirit. Even if by chance they recaptured our lands, we would counter with another Teutoburg. In my opinion, Rome will recognize they have lost the German lands east of the Rhine. Then again, if we attacked their citadels on the Rhine, this would be viewed as a threat to their Gallic provinces, and they would have no choice but to respond in full force. So why provoke them?" Finishing his remarks, he gave his uncle a pejorative glance.

Inguiomerus did not care for his nephew's retort. "We could scale their walls without the siege engines. You give them too much respect."

"Uncle, have you ever seen the devastating effects of Roman artillery? I have. Those bolts from their scorpion bolt throwers can go through two people. Believe me, it is not a pretty sight. The Roman fortresses are bristling with artillery pieces. They would cut down thousands of us before we reached the walls. Then we would have to navigate the ditches while the Roman defenders released their stones, arrows, and spears. I am telling you all once again, storming the Roman strongholds is a bad idea."

Gilix, the chief of the Chatti tribe and faithful ally of Arminius, spoke. "How are we to know if the Romans cross the Rhine and attack our lands?"

Arminius paused in thought. "We will need to post observers along the river to spot any deployment of their units."

"How many legions might the Romans mobilize to attack us?" asked a Marsi chieftain.

"Unknown, but my guess is that if they do come after us, it will be more than three legions, the number that we destroyed in the forest."

Gilix of the Chatti responded. "So what you are telling us is to go back to our tribal areas until the spring and, in the event of a Roman invasion, be prepared to battle the Romans again."

"Yes, and if they do cross the Rhine, we will lure them to forested terrain, where once again we can defeat these invaders. I don't care who their new commander is; I will deal with him like I did with Varus. When we take their eagle standards again, they will never cross the Rhine in the future."

There was a murmur of agreement among the chieftains. Inguiomerus, angry at his nephew's rebuke of his suggested course of action, hastily gathered his things and stalked away.

V

Many weeks later, Valerius sat at dinner with Calpurnia. A baked fish was featured, along with some dried figs, bread, and various cheeses. Outside the wind whistled down the narrow streets of the city. Winter was upon them. It was dark, and it was cold. The small dining area was heated by several charcoal braziers to ward off the chill. Valerius leaned back on the couch. He winced slightly from the effects of Wothar's spear thrusts. Another blast of cold rattled the windows. Valerius stared glumly at the darkness, picking at his food, but not really eating.

"Why the long face, dear?"

"Oh, sorry. I think I much prefer the warm weather to the cold and gloom. And another thing, everyone is gone to the Rhine but me. I feel like someone who is left behind."

Calpurnia smiled at him. "I have some news that might cheer you up."

"What is that?"

She beamed back at him and was silent for a moment. "You, Tribune Valerius, are going to be a father."

He stood up and pulled Calpurnia to her feet, then hugged her. "That is wonderful news."

She grinned and asked, "What would you like, a boy or a girl?

"It does not matter to me. I am so excited. When can we tell our parents?"

"Anytime you wish."

"When are you expected?"

"I'm not really sure, but most likely sometime this summer."

Wothar panted with exertion. He watched as the tribune warily circled and then reversed course to the right, always on guard for any sudden thrust. Wothar's expression was one of uncertainty. The confident manner that he exuded over the last four months was gone, replaced by one of doubt, for as much as he hated to admit it, his pupil had surpassed him. He had several bruises on his torso to remind him of how much progress the tribune had made. The Roman officer had integrated his uncanny speed and grace into the German style of fighting. His small shield and spear now moved in coordination with each other so that his movements flowed, his thrusts a blur.

Wothar, his shield angled in a defensive posture, pondered his next move. Perhaps the right words would distract Valerius. He knew he could not provoke him with insults. The tribune had a cold and calculating mind that would not permit his anger to bloom. No, that would not do, but perhaps the right amount of praise would be sufficient to create that momentary slip in concentration. "You fight well for a Roman." Wothar detected a faint change in his posture. He acted.

Wothar closed on his opponent and then dropped to the ground, rolled, and smashed the length of his spear into Valerius's lower legs. With a cry, he tumbled to the ground. Wothar, now on his feet, finished him with a thrust of the blunt end of the spear.

"That wasn't fair."

Wothar laughed. "Of course it was."

Realizing he had been bested, Valerius grinned. "I suppose you wouldn't mind showing me that maneuver. I have never seen that before."

Wothar spoke. "And for good reason. It was taught to me by one of the older warriors, who swore me to secrecy about it. It is not a maneuver to be used unless one is in a desperate situation, meaning you know you are about to die unless you do something miraculous. Only then should you employ it. It requires to be practiced many times. If you don't do it correctly, you are a dead man. One must bring the man down with a proper blow to the legs; if not, well, that is it for you."

"Would you teach me that? I promise not to tell anyone and will employ it only if I'm in a last-chance situation."

Wothar frowned. "I will, Tribune. But you need to understand that sometimes even if you execute this ploy perfectly, your opponent will counter the move or not go down as expected. It is a gamble that should only be used under the direst of circumstances."

"Understood. Now show me how you tricked me just as I was about to defeat you."

Wothar moved into a ready position, gesturing for Valerius to do the same.

"It's like this, Tribune. First, you must be close to your opponent. If you are some distance away, this will require you to roll on the ground toward your enemy. That is a slow and cumbersome process. He will be able to move faster than you. Bad idea. Wait until your enemy strikes out at you and gets close, then act. Drop to the ground and use your spear to trip him or injure his legs so that he is no longer standing."

Valerius practiced several repetitions of the ground-roll movement, all of them clumsy and resulting in failure. The two men sparred late into the afternoon, much longer than usual. Valerius finally got it right, or maybe Wothar was tired and let him execute the tricky maneuver. By the time they were finished, both were perspiring heavily despite the coolness in the air. Valerius grabbed two towels and handed one to Wothar. He nodded to one of the household staff to bring some wine. Both men retired to a bench.

"Wothar, I want to thank you for the language lessons and introducing me to the German style of fighting. Thanks to you, I know what to expect when I am facing these barbarians. No offense, I hope."

"Tribune, this is why you hired me. No thanks are necessary. As to the barbarian reference, no offense taken. Those rebellious German tribes are barbarians and a savage adversary."

The chilled wine arrived. Both men drank greedily. Valerius paused in thought. He had come to trust Wothar. He was not really friends with the man, but he liked and respected him. He would be a definite asset to Valerius in Germania. "Let me offer you a proposition. My sense is that I will be called to the Rhine in the spring. I would like you to come with me. I'm sure I could arrange to have you added to the staff at a Praetorian's stipend. You could serve as my aide. I know you said that you like it here in Rome, but I am offering you employment. There is an element of danger, no denying that, but such is a soldier's life. You could return to Rome when the army is finished with its business across the Rhine. It is supposed to be a campaign of short duration. What do you say?"

Wothar was silent. He stared at the tiled floor. Finally, he looked up. "Thank you for the offer, Tribune. When I first came to you, I had resigned myself to put up with the arrogance of some rich tribune, but that was not the case. Please, no offense with the tribune reference."

Valerius smiled back. "None taken. To characterize many tribunes as rich and arrogant is an accurate description. Please continue."

Wothar nodded. "You have treated me well and are an eager learner of the German ways. I never would have revealed that ground maneuver to anyone else."

"I am flattered. Does that mean you will come with me?"

Wothar put up his hand. "Please, Tribune, not so fast. I vowed that I would never cross the Rhine and return to the woods and fields of Germania. My family was slaughtered there by members of the Cherusci tribe. My parents and young bride were murdered in a raid many years ago. I have nothing back there but bad memories. While I thirst for revenge against the Cherusci for the killing of my people, I have found a new home here in Rome. I will need to think on your proposal. I will let you know."

Valerius clapped his German tutor on the back. "Please take my offer seriously. I want you to join me in Germania. Would you give me an answer by next week?"

The German nodded. "I will."

VI

Roman Fortress of Vetera on the Rhine
Spring

Stroking his chin in thought, Marcellus examined the papyrus document on the wooden field-table. Ignoring the soft pattering rain on his tent, he studied the six names of the centurion commanders of the Praetorian Guard and their experience levels. Each officer commanded a century of eighty men. The six centuries made up the Praetorian cohort of 480 men. Their mission was to provide security for the overall commander of the army of the Rhine, Germanicus Caesar, and to act as a reserve in any forthcoming battle with the Germans.

"Hmmm," he muttered. Marcellus was pleased. They were all good men, capable centurions deserving of their leadership position. All had combat experience and were career soldiers. He grinned in anticipation of his upcoming meeting with the centurions. He was delighted with his new duty. He could not believe he was back in the rank and file of the legions, and not some staff do-nothing as he had been relegated to in Varus's command. That had been intolerable.

He was assigned as the training centurion for the Praetorian cohort. He knew there would be some resentment from the centurion commanders. He would feel the same way under similar circumstances. He, an outsider about whom they knew nothing, was placed in charge of their training. If he attempted that "I know better than you" routine, his efforts would fail. Marcellus understood a thing or two about leadership and human nature. He would take a soft approach and win them over. That would start tonight. He had several containers of half-decent wine to help lubricate his efforts.

A short while later, the six centurions of the Praetorian Guard appeared at his spacious tent. It would be cozy with all of the six centurions, but not too uncomfortable. Marcellus greeted them warmly, although he could tell by their glum expressions that they were not especially happy to be here. The centurions included Crispus of the first century and overall commander of the cohort, Clodius of the second, Brutus of the third, Quintus of the fourth, Albinus of the fifth, and Decimus of the sixth. Marcellus produced the wine and the drinking cups. Their expressions appeared to ameliorate a bit. After introductions, several cups of wine, and somewhat strained conversation, Marcellus decided to begin.

"I have reviewed your records. You are all outstanding centurions. Obviously, the legate has selected well with respect to his centurion leaders. Furthermore, my inquiries about the fighting capabilities of the Praetorian cohort reflected high praise. Why then, you might ask, have I been selected to train you? You are all dedicated officers who know how to drill your troops. You can probably do it better than me, but there is one thing I know, and that is how these Germans fight. I have served in Germania almost my entire career and was one of the few survivors of the Teutoburg disaster. I never want to see something like that again. Gentlemen, the Roman legions are the finest fighting force in the Roman world. There is no doubt of that. But if we get caught in undesirable terrain of the enemy's choosing, our superior armor, weapons, and training will not save us."

Marcellus was pleased that the centurions appeared to be listening to what he was saying.

Quintus of the fourth century spoke. "So what do you propose, Centurion Marcellus?"

"Please call me Marcellus. I would suggest this. We begin by reviewing the standard battle drill that you have repeated over and over again with your troops, and then modify it to potential German threats. For example, after discharging your javelins, what is standard doctrine?"

Crispus spoke. "The lines are to advance rapidly upon the enemy with sword and shield."

Marcellus responded, "But you cannot charge the enemy when you are surrounded by forest. The shield wall and formation would be broken apart by the terrain. We will need an alternative course of action."

There was silence among the group. Not a good sign.

Marcellus continued, "Listen, just give me a chance to demonstrate to you some of these tactical maneuvers. I know you are a little skeptical, but I don't believe I'm asking a lot given what's at stake. Your lives may depend on how quick your troops can react to the German tactics. What do you say?"

The centurions nodded in unison.

Marcellus smiled. "Good. We will begin tomorrow with the first century."

It was the next morning, and Marcellus was anxious to start. He waved his arm toward the adjacent parade ground. "Centurion Crispus, put them through their paces. Let me see what the first century can do."

There were several reasons he had selected the first century to begin his lessons in tactics. The first was always the best of any cohort. They usually established the initiative in any tactical response. Also, Crispus was the overall commander of the cohort. If he could convince him of the benefits of the training, then the other centurion commanders would follow his lead.

Marcellus watched them maneuver in the open space of the parade ground, the formation of ten men abreast and the ranks eight deep. He scanned the soldiers visible to him on the outside ranks. They looked good. Their uniforms and armor were up to standard. So far, fairly impressive. Upon command, the formation smoothly shifted to four lines, with the centurion out in front.

"Open ranks. Make ready. Pilum release."

The four lines of legionnaires effortlessly opened ranks so that each man had space to throw his pilum. Suddenly, a shower of javelins from the eighty men plummeted into the target zone.

"Close ranks. Shield wall. Draw swords."

Immediately the formation compacted. The large rectangular shields were almost touching one another, and a bristling line of swords jutted ominously from the front row.

"Advance."

The century moved forward in crisp formation.

"Wedge formation."

The ranks smoothly transitioned into an arrowhead shape three ranks deep, with the centurion and the optio at the head of the point. The wedge moved forward before the next command was issued by the centurion.

"Testuto."

The second and third interior ranks raised their shields overhead, thus covering the entire century against overhead projectiles, while the outer ranks utilized their shields to protect the sides, thus creating a carapace of shields. The large and heavy shields would withstand the sharpest spear or arrow attempting to penetrate.

"Halt."

Marcellus walked over to the century. "Centurion Crispus, why don't we reconvene in the shade of those trees over there?" The group of legionnaires walked over. "Centurion, with your permission, I would like your men to sit and relax. They are free to remove their helmets."

Crispus smiled at Marcellus. "Certainly." He then turned to the men and bellowed, "You heard the man. Sit down, relax, and remove your helmets." The men were sweating heavily from the maneuvers in their heavy suits of iron.

Marcellus strode to the front. "Legionnaires of the first century, not a bad performance. In fact, it was damn impressive. I wish my old century could maneuver like that. Your movements were precise, and the change in formations was flawless. I don't intend to teach you any more standard battle drill. You have certainly mastered that." He paused to get his thoughts in order and to prepare the men for the next phase of his plan.

"I want you to meet someone." He signaled with his arm. A figure that had remained hidden in the bushes came forward.

"This is Draxir. He is of the Triveri, a German tribe friendly to Rome. Please note his appearance and weapons."

The figure was attired in cloth trousers and a long-sleeved tunic. A cloak was worn around his neck, pinned at the shoulder with a broach. He carried a long wooden spear with a leaf-shaped iron point and a small rectangular wooden shield. Fastened to his waist was an iron knife.

Marcellus began his tutorial. "Please note the absence of any armor. Also, there is no helmet. His primary weapon is the *framea*. It is a thrusting weapon with a wickedly sharp iron point. It comes in many sizes and is used in close quarters, and it can also be thrown with great accuracy. Some of the Germans are armed with swords and axes, but most use the spear."

Marcellus slowly paced back and forth. "Not very impressive when compared to the Roman legionnaire, is he? If that is the case, how did an enemy like this destroy three of our finest legions?"

There was silence among the eighty men as they stared at the German warrior. Marcellus continued to pace back and forth. "Men equipped just like Draxir massacred three of our legions. How? I will tell you how. First, hordes of these men tracked the legions through the forest without being spotted. Can you imagine legionnaires outfitted in our heavy armor and shields doing the same thing? No, of course not. So our German adversary has the advantage of mobility, especially in heavy terrain. The Teutoburg battle was fought over several days in horrific weather with deluges of rain. Do you think the rain is going to bother Draxir? Perhaps some, but not nearly as much as our iron-suited legionnaire. Let me continue. When the Germans fought us over three days, they were hidden in the trees much of the time, and then they sallied forth against the legions' shield walls. Now, I saw you employ your wedge formations and throw your pila, but that will do you little good in heavy woodlands. Your javelins are going to hit trees and not much else, plus it will be impossible to maintain a cohesive formation when advancing through heavy foliage. Do you want to go dashing into the forest, not knowing what awaits you? No, I think not."

Marcellus stopped speaking. He eyed the group of soldiers, noting their somber expressions. *Good,* he thought. *I have their attention. They need to understand the tactics these Germans employ.*

"We are going to have a little demonstration of these German maneuvers. The first century will be the unfortunate prey. The enemy will be represented by some of our auxiliary units of Germans friendly to us. These include members of the Triveri, Uri, and Batavi tribes. Please do not become overzealous and stab them. They are our friends and allies. For training purposes they will be hurling blunted javelins without iron points at you."

"Draxir, you are dismissed and may join your comrades." With that Draxir hurried down a road leading away from the fortress walls. "Centurion Crispus, I would like you to march your unit down that road over there." He pointed with his wooden staff for effect.

"It is a Roman road lined on both sides by heavy forest. It will serve as a good example of the possible terrain our forces may encounter. Form up in a standard six-man marching column."

The century moved out with Centurion Crispus in the lead accompanied by Marcellus. They marched down the road. Soon dense foliage obscured sight lines on both flanks. It was perfect for what Centurion Marcellus wanted to demonstrate. "Centurion Crispus, I hope you don't mind if I temporarily usurp your command. I will turn it back over to you shortly."

"Not a problem, Marcellus. I am curious what you have planned for us."

"You shall see shortly. We are almost at the ambush point."

The century marched onward. The verdant forest was encroaching on the road, so that low-hanging tree branches were impeding movement. Very little light filtered through the forest canopy, and the air was dank and fetid. Pesky insects swarmed about legionnaires. Marcellus was in the lead at the front of the century and walking backward so that he could address the legionnaires. "I want you to have your shields up to deflect any of the wooden spears. Make ready and listen to my commands."

The century advanced farther down the road. Suddenly there were screams from the forest on both sides of the trail. The century was showered with a deluge of wooden lances. Most struck harmlessly against the big Roman shields that covered most of the legionnaire's body. A few got through, as indicated by the moans of pain.

"Halt. Drop pila. Shield wall. Draw swords."

After some initial confusion, the century formed its shield wall, three ranks deep facing each side of the trail. More javelins descended on the century. The century presented a deadly wall of steel. The men regarded the forest but could see little movement, only occasional glimpses of men throwing their spears at them. After a brief pause, the Germans charged out of the timber, howling at the Roman lines. They charged to within several feet of the formation and then halted.

Marcellus looked toward his German auxiliaries. "You may withdraw." The Germans quickly blended back into the heavy timber. Marcellus looked at the men. "This exercise is not finished. We are going to advance down the road almost using a sidestep motion. Be sure to have your shield square to the threat from the trees. *"Advance."*

The men were not accustomed to this kind of movement and shuffled awkwardly down the road. It was almost comical as the men tripped over one another. There were no more massed German charges, but there were more spears hurled from the timber bordering the road. This continued for perhaps two hundred yards.

"Halt. Let us move over here to this small clearing for a critique."

Marcellus gestured with his arms, gathering the troops around him. He looked about. There appeared to be no serious injuries. A few men were rubbing their bodies where the wooden spears had struck them. "I hope I gave you some appreciation for what it is like to fight in terrain that is not of our choosing. I wanted you to experience how difficult it is to maneuver on a road with bunches of spears flung at you. It is not the best of situations. Many of you are probably wondering why we do not just avoid that kind of terrain. Unfortunately, if we are going to invade Germania, this is the type of topography we will be challenged to overcome at some point during the campaign." Marcellus pointed in the direction of the Rhine. "Gentlemen, once we cross that river, there are few Roman roads, and we will be forced to navigate through the woods and swamps. The enemy knows that kind of land is not to our advantage, and he will seek to strike us there."

Marcellus turned toward Centurion Crispus. "With your permission, I would like the other five centuries of the cohort to go through a similar drill, if that's all right with you?"

"You have me convinced, Marcellus. We should schedule them as soon as possible. Can we start today?"

"Affirmative, Crispus. Let's get moving on this right now."

VII

The Western Bank of the Rhine
Early Summer

Valerius sat with the other officers of Germanicus's command. He attempted, with some difficulty, to concentrate on what was being said. Outside, the rain drummed heavily on the tile roof of the headquarters. The weather had not changed much since the last time he was here a year ago. His mind continued wandering from the briefing. One of the senior tribunes, acting as the supply officer, droned on about how many wagonloads of grain were required daily. Germanicus believed that it would be a good experience for Valerius to attend these briefings so that he better understood the workings of the legions. In his opinion, it was a waste of time. To make things interesting, he silently translated the words of the tribune into German. He smiled smugly. He was getting good at this. Wothar's language lessons had borne fruit. The endless repetition of words and hard study on the part of Valerius had made him fluent in the language of the Germans.

He had arrived at the Vetera fortress on the Rhine two days ago. He was amazed at the bustle of activity and the military sprawl of the camp. Last fall, he and Marcellus, plus a few other survivors, had reached the safety of Vetera after being pursued by a posse of angry Germans following the Teutoburg defeat. Back then, Vetera was a fortress built to house two legions. It was only occupied by one when he staggered in there last fall. It now contained the forces of eight legions plus auxiliary troops, completely overwhelming the capacity of the encampment. Because of the shortage of available quarters, junior officers such as Valerius were relegated to a tent in temporary camps constructed adjacent to the main fortress. Great swaths of land had been cleared by the legions' engineers contiguous to the fortress. A great sea of tents extended almost to the horizon.

He thought back to the sorrowful farewell with Calpurnia. He had wanted nothing more than to remain there with her, but duty beckoned. Besides, his commander, Germanicus, had been away from his wife, Agrippina, for the birth of two of their children. If his general could endure this hardship, then so could he. When Valerius departed, Calpurnia was showing her pregnancy, her belly plumping. His parents and his in-laws were present at his departing. They all vowed to look after Calpurnia in his absence. Valerius was somewhat relieved by their assurances, but he could not dispel his anxiety of leaving her in this state. Wothar, who had decided to join him on his journey northward to the lands of the Germans, had stood silently by. Calpurnia, her face streaked with tears, spoke softly to him. "Please return to me and our child. Be careful in Germania and travel cautiously."

"I will, Calpurnia. I promise to return safely and as soon as possible." With a last hug, Valerius had said good-bye to his love, wondering if they would ever see each other again.

Valerius's musings returned to the briefing. The droning tribune was not finished. "And so the legions will have up to four thousand horses and thirty-five hundred pack animals, which will need to be fed. While the animals are expected to graze, nevertheless the need for huge quantities of barley oats and hay will be required on a daily basis. The annual consumption for an *ala* of horses is close to twelve thousand pounds of hay and two thousand pounds of barley."

Who cares? By the gods this was worse than his assignment of payroll records under Varus. *Well, maybe not,* he thought, *but close to it.* Valerius shifted his butt on the hard wooden bench. *How much longer can this continue?* He had promised Marcellus and Wothar to join them for the evening meal. His stomach grumbled, telling him it was getting late in the afternoon. The officious supply officer prattled on...

Marcellus, Valerius, and Wothar sat at a small wooden table on a low bluff overlooking the Rhine. It was quiet here. The surrounding vicinity was packed full of soldiers as more units swelled the ranks of the burgeoning army. The three had sought an unobtrusive place to relax away from the clamor of the encampment. Many of the legionnaires frequented the civilian settlement directly down the main road and within sight of the fortress ramparts. It was jammed with makeshift brothels and low-quality taverns stocked with wine that had all the qualities of horse piss. The brawls that occurred in the civilian settlement were frequent and often violent to the point of death. So the three men sat on the outskirts of the encampment, enjoying a jug of wine that Valerius had procured.

Valerius had had little time to converse with Marcellus since his arrival. The tribune attended one meeting after another devoted to the planning of the upcoming excursion into the land of the Germans. Now was his opportunity to catch up on what was happening.

"Marcellus, how has your instruction been received by the Praetorian cohort?"

The centurion proffered a grin. "Overall, it has been a great success. I must say that training the troops is a much better assignment than payroll records. The centurions and their units have taken an interest in my drills, which feature moving along forested roads with some of our friendly German auxiliaries attacking out of the woods acting as the enemy. They have come to understand how difficult it is to fight Germans on their terrain. What's more, as a result of my training, they have adapted to those conditions so that they present a stout defense to the German ambush tactics that you and I are so familiar with. It doesn't hurt that the Praetorian cohort is one tough outfit that knows their stuff. They are superbly trained, which makes my job much easier."

Valerius spoke. "I have never seen you this enthusiastic about your assignment. So you have finished the training?"

Marcellus took a sip of his wine. "I am, but I have not. Apparently word has spread about my instruction on German tactics. Germanicus stopped by to witness one of our drills with the Praetorian cohort and the German auxiliaries. He was so impressed that he ordered me to expand the training to the other cohorts of the legions. Each day I have a new unit to indoctrinate in the German style of fighting. There is no way I will have them all trained, but I am making progress."

Valerius looked toward Wothar. "Do you think you could help Marcellus? I'm sure he could use some assistance. For the moment I am bogged down in one administrative meeting after another, and I have nothing meaningful for you to do with the exception of our sparring with the German weapons."

"Gladly, Tribune. That is if you don't mind me not being available to you?"

"Not at all. You will serve me best by assisting Marcellus. I will let you know if I need you."

"I could certainly use the help, Wothar," quipped Marcellus.

"Good," said Valerius. "Now that this matter is settled, let's enjoy our wine."

The three men gazed out upon the river. The evening air was still warm, and the river current gurgled and flowed. The boat traffic had ceased for the day, and the trees lining the bank cast shadows as dusk approached. Insects chirped and droned in the evening air.

Valerius broke the tranquil silence. "It's hard to believe that on the opposite bank is a foreboding land. The last time I was there, the Germans chased my ass almost to the riverbank."

Marcellus chuckled in remembrance.

"It was an experience I won't forget. How we made our way across those hostile lands and survived was miraculous. I wonder if someone is watching us now. What say you, Wothar?"

The German paused in thought. "Aye, they are observing this fortress and the activity of the legions. My guess is that the German tribes have disbanded for the present, but when the army crosses the Rhine, they will mobilize. This battle is not over."

Valerius spoke. "Those are sobering words. I guess I expected as much."

Wothar continued, "I know the tribes that are in Arminius's alliance. The larger ones include the Chatti, Marsi, Bructeri, Usipetes, and Angrivari. They are no doubt proud of their victory in the Teutoburg and will never be friends of Rome. Their warriors will be eager to take up the spear again. The only choice the legions have is to destroy those tribes that are allied against Rome."

Valerius frowned. "I agree. There can be no reconciliation. They believe they have the upper hand and will never submit to Rome unless it is at the point of a sword. From what I saw in the Teutoburg, there are a lot of angry Germans out there on the opposite side of the Rhine."

Marcellus joined in the conversation. "Everything that we had accomplished over the last twenty years in pacifying the German population went up in smoke in the Teutoburg. If you ask me, this is a hopeless quest, but who am I, a lowly centurion, to question the wisdom of our imperial leaders? You are spot on, Tribune. There are a lot of angry Germans out there, and they know how to fight us and on what terms. Now pass me that wine jar. My cup is empty."

Several days later, Marcellus appeared at the entrance of Valerius's quarters. It was almost dusk. "Come on, Tribune, we are going to a drinking establishment outside the encampment."

"I thought you mentioned a few nights ago that these places were dens of iniquity and to be avoided at all costs."

"I did, Tribune, but I know of a place called the Braying Mule that is worthy of our attendance. It is reserved for officers only, so Wothar will not be able to accompany us."

"No matter. He is out carousing with his Batavi brethren tonight. I am sure he will have a late night. What was that place called? The Braying Mule? Sounds charming. I'm not sure about this. Besides, I'm tired."

"Tribune, you are taxing my patience. It will do you good to get out. You cannot stay in your quarters mooning over Calpurnia. She isn't here. I know you miss her, but you need to live. Stop being so reticent. Get yourself together, and let's get out of here. The tavern awaits us."

Valerius let out a sigh. Reluctantly, he strapped on his sculpted breastplate. He slowly tied his marching boots on and stood. "Lead the way."

The two men sauntered out of the encampment and past the wharf. Valerius noted many ships berthed at the docks. As a result of the military buildup, the quayside had been transformed to a large river port capable of handling large ships laden with men and material. The two officers continued their trek into the booming civilian settlement outside the fort, where everything and anything was for sale. Women appeared out of the dark recesses exposing a long leg or plump breast, waving seductively with their hand. They neared a tavern filled with raucous shouts and laughter. Valerius gave the place an anxious glance. "That's not it, I hope."

Marcellus grimaced. "Of course not. Do you think I would frequent a place like that?"

Valerius shrugged. "How much farther?"

Marcellus said, "Not much. In fact it should be just around the bend of this road."

They approached a wooden building with a solid door and several glass windows. Hanging from a chain was an iron effigy of a mule. A large torch mounted above the door illuminated the entrance.

Valerius beheld the place. He had to admit it looked much better than the other establishments they had passed on the way here. Maybe this would exceed his low expectations.

"Tribune, here we are, the Braying Mule. A tavern of good wine and refined conversation."

Valerius snorted. "You first."

The two men opened the heavy wooden door and entered. Murmurs of quiet conversation echoed in the single large room. There were perhaps thirty tables, mostly occupied. A small bar area on the right side of the entrance was a site of frenzied activity as the staff rushed about to fill the wine orders. Oil lamps hung from the rafters, illuminating all but the darkest recesses. Marcellus gestured to a small empty table with four chairs. The two sat down. A young woman with a rather large cleavage materialized in front of them.

"Marcellus, how nice to see you again. I have missed you oh so much."

The centurion spoke. "Brida, two wines of your best vintage." The barmaid turned to get their drinks.

"Wait," said Valerius. "Brida, is it?" She nodded. "Where is the wine from?"

The young woman shrugged her shoulders. "I don't know. You can ask the owner if you want. He brings it in by ship. I don't get too many complaints."

Valerius smirked. "No, I'm sure you don't."

Marcellus gave him a look of disapproval, letting him know he did not appreciate the tribune's humor.

Valerius turned back to Brida. "All right, you may bring the wine."

She brushed Marcellus with a shapely hip as she walked past the table. Valerius turned to the centurion, mimicking the serving girl. "Marcellus, how nice to see you again. I have missed you oh so much."

The centurion shrugged his shoulders, offering a sheepish grin. "So I have been here a few times before. Is that a crime? Would you deny this old centurion the pleasure of female companionship?"

"The waitress appears smitten with you."

"The young lady and I are well acquainted if you know what I mean."

"Marcellus, you old dog."

The centurion, anxious to change the subject, spoke while gesturing with his hands. "So what do you think of this place? Did I steer you wrong?"

Valerius replied, "It will do. I must admit it is better than I anticipated. Oh, before I forget, I received a letter from Lucius and Julia. It is posted from a little town called Belilarcum in Gaul. It arrived shortly before I departed from Rome. Would you like me to read it to you?"

"By all means. Read on. I am anxious to hear what they have to say."

Valerius produced a piece of parchment from his tunic. He unrolled the document and cleared his throat. "Greetings, Tribune Valerius

Maximus. I trust you arrived safely home to Rome and that life is bestowing many blessings upon you and also to Centurion Marcellus."

Valerius paused and looked up at the centurion. Marcellus beamed, pleased to know he was mentioned in the letter.

Valerius continued, "Lucius and I owe our lives to you, and we will be forever grateful. Please know that you will always have a special place in our hearts for leading us out of the German lands to safety. We survived because of you. Now for the big news. Last month I delivered twin boys. We named the boys Petrocolus, after my father, and Cassius after our friend. They are a joy to behold. We are living with Lucius's family for the present but soon hope to have a house of our own. Again, we owe all of this to Marcellus and you. Also, I am holding you to your promise to host us in Rome one day. I know Lucius would love to visit the city and see both of you again, as would I. I'm not sure when that might ever happen, but we would love to call on you. I have noted our address below if you would be so kind as to let us know how you are doing. I pray to Minerva every day to keep you and Marcellus safe. We may be far apart in distance, but you are in our thoughts and prayers. Sincerely, Lucius and Julia."

Valerius folded the parchment and put it back in his tunic. Both men wore somber expressions.

Marcellus spoke first. "You know, Tribune, that warms the cockles of my heart to hear those words. They are safe and now with a family of their own. No matter what happens, you and I are responsible for creating some good in this world. Ours is a domain of death and destruction, but look what we managed to salvage."

Brida arrived with the wine and set the two goblets on the table. Marcellus offered a toast. "To Julia and Lucius, and Petrocolus and Cassius." Both men took a healthy swallow. Marcellus raised his glass again. "To defeating the Germans and a safe return to Rome." The two sipped the contents. Valerius was about to comment that the wine was actually not bad when a voice from the far side of the room bellowed above the clamor and din of the tavern.

"By Jupiter's balls, is this a ghost I see? Is that you, Tribune Valerius Maximus?"

Marcellus looked at Valerius quizzically. The tribune knew that voice. There could only be one person who had that lung power laced with profanity. Out of the shadows emerged an older man in the uniform of the Roman Imperial Navy. The jaunty-looking figure sauntered up beside Valerius's table, his face weathered and worn. Valerius's face split with a wide grin.

"Why, Captain Sabinus, what an unexpected pleasure."

"Unexpected pleasure, my ass. You're alive. I had given you up for worm food, but here you are."

Valerius offered a wry smile. "Let me introduce you to Centurion Marcellus. Centurion, this is Captain Sabinus. I sailed on his good warship on my way to my posting to Varus's army on the Weser. He taught me a few things about navigation on the way. The captain runs a tight ship and harangues his crew at every opportunity, but they love him. Many of them told me that there was no finer leader than the captain when in battle."

Sabinus returned the grin. "Thank you for those words, Tribune. By Hades I'm glad to see you are alive. Now if I recall, Tribune, the last time I saw you, there was a promise to buy me some wine the next time we met."

"I have not forgotten that promise." He stood, caught Brida's eye, and gestured to her to bring a full jug of the wine. After a few moments, she appeared at the table with a large clay container.

Valerius poured into Sabinus's goblet. They all drank deeply.

The captain spoke. "My thanks for the wine." He raised his goblet high. "To your continued good fortune."

Marcellus and Valerius in turn raised their goblets. "To good fortune."

Sabinus spoke, his tone more serious. "So, how did you make it out of the Teutoburg?"

Valerius looked at Marcellus, then spoke in a subdued tone. "The centurion and I managed to evade the Germans and escape to the Rhine. We were extremely lucky."

The captain inquired, "Was it as bad as they say it was?"

"Far worse. We witnessed the destruction of three legions and the loss of the eagle standards. On the last day of the battle, we were engulfed by a horrific storm, which provided a means to our escape. We fought our way out of several confrontations and evaded the Germans for almost fifty miles of wilderness. Marcellus knew something of the terrain and led a few of us to safety. I must say, Captain, your lessons on celestial navigation came in handy."

Sabinus grinned widely. "Did they now? I'm thankful for that."

"I owe you my gratitude. By the way, Captain, what are you doing here?"

Sabinus scowled. "The imperial navy has rid the seas of pirates, and there are no more sea powers like Carthage to oppose us, so my warship is once again..."

Valerius joined the captain in the next few words, "a fucking transport."

Marcellus laughed lightly. "It seems to be a touchy subject."

Sabinus spoke. "You have no idea, Centurion. Now, Tribune, as I recall, there was an incident in a port that we stopped by to get new provisions, and you professed to know nothing about it. Care to expand us on that, because my old sea nose tells me something different."

Valerius replied, "Somehow I knew you would bring that up."

Marcellus, his curiosity aroused, stared at Valerius. "I never heard about this. Do tell."

Sabinus smirked. "I can't wait to hear this."

Valerius sighed. "All right. I will confess. It went like this. After weeks at sea, make that very boring weeks at sea, we stopped at a port in Gaul for fresh water and new provisions. The good captain warned me about leaving the ship. He told me the town was a sewer filled with villainous characters of dubious parentage. I didn't care. I needed to feel solid ground under my feet and get some decent food. I am not one to complain, but the food aboard a Roman warship makes a legionnaire's rations appear like a gourmet feast. Marcellus, have you ever seen an overweight sailor?"

Marcellus frowned in thought. "Now that you mention it, no."

Sabinus interrupted. "Enough. No need to disparage the naval rations. Get on with your story."

Valerius continued, "Despite the captain's warning, I departed the ship. I looked around and found overnight accommodations, and then ventured into the heart of the town for a decent meal. I must say the captain was correct. The place was a sewer."

Sabinus nodded. "Of course, I told you that. So you are looking for an evening meal. What happened next?"

Valerius paused in remembrance. He then took a small sip of wine. "Believe or not, I actually enjoyed some half-decent food and wine. As I recall, I had bread and cheese plus two goblets of wine. I was on my third cup when I saw these two iniquitous-looking characters appraising me. I didn't like their looks if you know what I mean. Heeding the captain's warning, I didn't finish that last goblet of wine. I paid the bill and started back toward my room. When I exited the dining establishment, there was not a soul in sight, and it was pitch-black, with a bilious fog rolling in from the sea. I made my way in the direction of my room, when I thought I heard someone following me. I looked back, but all I could see was wafting mist. I continued on and heard the sounds of someone behind me again. I'm now cursing myself for not following the captain's warning."

Valerius paused to drink some of his wine. Marcellus and Sabinus sat there riveted, waiting for the tribune to continue.

"I hurried through the fog, scared and in a panic mode. I heard the sounds again, like someone running from behind me. I drew my sword and turned, slashing in one continuous motion. My blade struck home. I heard a loud shriek, and then I saw two men racing away, one supporting the other. At my feet was a wicked-looking dagger dropped by my would-be assailant. I sprinted to my room without any further mishap. I bellowed for the landlord to get me some wine, not realizing that my face and clothing were covered with a fine spray of blood. I didn't sleep at all that night."

Sabinus chuckled. "Tell Marcellus what happened next."

Valerius continued, "I returned to the ship early the next morning. The captain had told me the night before that the ship would sail just after dawn. We're about to leave the port when the town constable shows up with his two brutes. They have cudgels with them and demand to board the ship and question any of the crew who were ashore last night. It seems one of the town's fine citizens had perished as a result of a slash to the head and neck from a sword. The captain informed the constable that if they attempted to set one foot on his ship, he would cut them up in little pieces and feed them to the sharks or something to that effect. He told the constable in no uncertain terms that while he may represent the law in the town, this ship was part of the Roman Imperial Navy, and he was the master of that vessel. Did I put that right, Captain Sabinus?"

Sabinus smiled. "I believe that was the gist of the conversation."

"Thank the gods that they were not allowed access to the ship. The proprietor of the inn where I stayed saw me covered in a mist of blood."

Sabinus laughed. "Nice beginning as a tribune in the Roman Army."

Valerius frowned in remembrance. "Actually, it got worse. Upon arrival at the base on the Weser, I clashed with General Varus as a result of Tribune Castor's perfidious scheme."

Sabinus appeared puzzled, and then his countenance brightened. "Ah yes, Tribune Castor, he was that fat-ass excuse for an officer on our ship."

Valerius replied, "One and the same."

Marcellus spoke. "Enough of this past history crap. You survived your encounter with the murderous thieves in the disreputable port, the ill will of Varus, and the Germans. Not bad for a new tribune." They all raised their goblets as a toast to Valerius.

The captain drank deeply. He wiped his mouth with his sleeve. "So here you are against the Germans once again. If I recall, I made you an offer to join the imperial navy. Looks to me like you should have accepted my proposition."

Valerius frowned. "You are probably correct on that account, but what is done is done. When I'm finished here in Germania, I'm through with the legions. I have a beautiful wife back in Rome who is expecting a child."

Sabinus half raised his goblet. "Congratulations, Tribune."

Valerius nodded in response and then arose. "Now, gentlemen, if you will excuse me for a moment, I need to relieve myself." Valerius stood and exited at the back door of the tavern.

Sabinus gazed at the retreating figure of Valerius, waiting until he was out of earshot. "So, what do you think of our tribune?"

Marcellus contemplated the question for a moment, and he put on a serious face. "When he first arrived, he was as green an officer as you will ever find. On top of that, he managed to get on Varus's shit list thanks to Tribune Castor. Things were not going well for the young man, but he fought through that adversity. When we were this close to Hades," Marcellus showed a small gap between his thumb and forefinger, "he rose to the occasion. I have never served with a finer officer. He is a real warrior and continues to impress people. When we finally managed to reach the safety of the Rhine after fleeing the Teutoburg, he managed to convince the commanding general of the fortress that he and our small band of survivors were the best soldiers in the Roman Army. If not for him, the whole lot of us might have been executed as deserters."

Sabinus smiled. "I knew that boy had the makings of a good officer. As you said, he was a bit raw."

Marcellus continued, "It gets better."

"How so?"

"The commander of the Rhine fortress, General Saturnius, ordered the tribune to deliver the news of the defeat to Augustus Caesar. We rode for nearly two weeks, almost nonstop. We arrived in Rome late at night. He interpreted his instructions from General Saturnius verbatim, deciding to go to the palace that night. I was there when he was given his orders. The general told him to proceed to Rome with all possible speed and personally inform the emperor of the defeat. So that's what he did. His uniform was in tatters, and he smelled like a goat. He barged into an imperial family banquet and delivered the news."

Sabinus laughed. "He really got into the palace to see the emperor covered in filth? I would love to have witnessed that."

"Most people would have been executed for what he did. Instead, he comes out of this smelling like a rose. He impressed Germanicus

Caesar so much with his gumption that he was appointed to the general's staff, and here we are."

Marcellus was about to continue when three hulking centurions, obviously intoxicated, materialized out of the gloom to stand in front of their table. The one in the middle pointed at Sabinus. "What's he doing here?"

Marcellus glared at the three. "What do you mean what's he doing here?"

The middle one, apparently the leader, spoke again. "He's in the navy."

"How astute of you. Any more shrewd observations?"

The leader's face reddened in fury at his belittling remarks. "We don't like navy folks in here."

"Tough shit, he's a friend of mine. Now leave."

The three inebriated centurions were looking to pick a fight, and nothing was going to stop them. Marcellus intuitively knew what was about to happen. He gave Sabinus a knowing glance, and then he erupted out of his seat. He punched the leader squarely in the mouth, and then stomped on the foot of another. Sabinus was ready. He head-butted the other centurion, and then things spiraled out of control.

Valerius came in the back door and was startled to see his two friends engaged in a brawl with three massive centurions. He needed to even the odds. Without hesitation he charged into the fray. The tribune hurled his body into the burly centurion closest to him. He bounced off the solid figure as if he were made of stone. The centurion turned toward him. Valerius charged again, the top of his head aimed at the man's face. He never made it. He was repulsed by a forearm seemingly made of solid oak. Valerius sprawled on the floor. He quickly jumped to his feet, his fists cocked. His adversary threw a punch that he partially blocked. The unblocked part hit him above the eye. His vision swam from the force of the blow. He scurried out of range, noting the contemptuous grin on the centurion's face. Valerius darted back in, delivering a punch to his opponent's nose. The man cursed as blood spurted from his injured appendage. His sights squarely on the tribune, the hulking figure advanced menacingly.

Valerius was filled with dread. Now what? He was no match for this behemoth. Before the man could close with him, Marcellus grabbed his arm, and he was dragged out the back door. The three officers hurried down the alley, each looking back to see if there was any pursuit. There was not. They laughed in unison, and then went in search of another drinking establishment. The night was still young.

VIII

All of the senior officers gathered in the *principia,* the colonnaded headquarters of the Roman legions. This was no ordinary meeting. Supply officers would not be droning on about the number of amphorae or wagonloads of grain needed to feed the legions. This was a council of war. Germanicus, adorned in his finest armor, stood at the head of the long table. On either side of him were the two corps commanders of the Germania Inferior and Germania Superior. Commanding the four legions based out of Moguntiacum of Germania Superior was Gaius Silus. Opposite him and responsible for the four legions of Germania Inferior out of Ara Ubiorum was Aulus Severus. At the moment, the three were engaged in a hushed conversation aside from the other gathered officers. The lower-ranked officers present knew intuitively not to interrupt Germanicus and his two corps commanders.

Valerius stood apart from the milling group waiting for the proceedings to begin. He was anxious to hear what Germanicus had planned. He looked up and caught Tubero glaring at him. Obviously the verbal confrontation back in Rome was not forgotten. There was no love lost there, that was for sure. Not wanting to risk a confrontation, he discretely directed his attention across the room.

Apart from Tubero, he received curious glances from some of the other officers. His presence was conspicuous from the discolored swelling above his right eye courtesy of the centurion's punch during the brawl in the tavern. Valerius had attempted unsuccessfully to conceal the results of the blow to his face. He had applied a cool soaked cloth to the swelling but to no avail. Marcellus had laughed at his efforts, stating that through numerous personal experiences, he knew only time would heal the discoloration.

The three senior officers disengaged and faced the others. Germanicus spoke. "Gentlemen, please take your seats." He waited for the officers to sit, and then continued, "We have much to discuss here tonight. It is my intention to convey to you the strategy we will employ to defeat these Germans and take revenge for our defeat in the Teutoburg Forest. Before we get to that, let me address the subject of the minor mutinies that have occurred within several of our legions. The unrest was a direct result of the extension of enlistment terms from twenty to twenty-five years. This edict was decreed by Augustus as a result of the German crisis. While I have some sympathy with the men in the ranks concerning this pronouncement, seditious behavior will not be tolerated. The ringleaders of these mutinies have been identified and dispatched. I don't want to risk any further rebellions within the legions. Therefore we will engage the Germans shortly. Once we are out on campaign, this should distract any thoughts of insubordination. Believe me, they will be too busy and too exhausted to think about anything but the enemy before them.

"Our ultimate goal is to destroy the German tribes as a fighting force and kill or capture their leader, Arminius. He is the individual responsible for the terrible loss of our three legions last fall. How are we to do this? I will tell you how. We will cross the Rhine on several fronts and engage those tribes allied with Arminius. We will raze the settlements of these tribes and destroy their forces. In the end, the legions will isolate the Cherusci tribe, that of Arminius, and crush them."

Tubero spoke. "When are we to begin this quest? I can't wait to wreak havoc on these Germans."

Germanicus grinned. "Soon, General Tubero, although an exact date has not yet been set. The first phase of our strategy will be to engage the Marsi tribe. They are the enemy closest to the Rhine. We will advance on a broad front of about thirty miles between where the Lippe and Ruhr Rivers join the Rhine. I intend to send the entire eight legions across the Rhine and devastate their territory. Once we have dealt with the Marsi, our forces will advance to the next occupied land, that of the Bructeri, and after them the Chatti. I fully expect that Arminius will mass his forces once again and then challenge us to battle. This is what we want. We need to decisively defeat the German coalition and capture or kill Arminius.

"Will we be bringing the *ballistae*?" inquired one of the senior tribunes.

"That's affirmative. The artillery may be needed to subdue those settlements that have fortified positions. Are there any more questions?"

There was silence among the small group of officers.

"Good. I will reconvene this group once I have decided on the date and time of our invasion. In the interim I would suggest you all prepare your legions for the campaign. Rome will get its revenge and then some."

The officers began to file out of the building. Valerius headed toward the exit. He halted when he heard his name called.

"Tribune Valerius, would you please stay. I have an assignment for you." Valerius looked back and saw Germanicus motioning toward him. The tribune cringed. He had deliberately placed himself in the back of the room to escape notice of his ruined eye. With trepidation, he slowly made his way toward Germanicus. The general frowned, noticing the discolored bruise featured on the tribune's face. He waited until the room was empty, and then spoke. "I am going to put your Germanic language skills to the test."

"How so, sir?"

"Tomorrow one of my Germanic allies from the Trevari tribe will speak to me through an interpreter about the readiness of the Marsi tribe."

Valerius grinned. "Germanic ally? You mean spy."

"Call it what you'd like. The man claims to have firsthand knowledge of the locations and readiness of the Marsi. I need you there to listen to what he says and then let me know if you believe his information is credible. Are you up for it?"

"I am, sir. I believe I'm proficient enough in the language to understand what the Trevari scout has to say and judge if the interpreter has relayed his words accurately."

"Excellent. I will summon you here tomorrow morning. Hopefully the Trevari scout will have good news for us. Our invasion plans are dependent on what he has to say to us."

Germanicus turned to leave, and then stopped. "Oh, and Tribune, I expect my officers to be a little more circumspect in their behavior. Understood?"

Valerius felt his face flush. "Yes, sir."

He arrived at headquarters the next morning. He was ushered into the conference area and observed the commander in deep conversation with Tubero plus the two army corps commanders, Gaius Silus and Aulus Severus. Germanicus nodded to Valerius and pointed to a chair next to the table. The four generals exchanged additional remarks, and then broke apart.

Germanicus addressed Valerius. "Our Trevari scout and our interpreter will be ushered in momentarily. I need you to study their words so that we have a good understanding of what is communicated to us."

Valerius replied, "Just so I understand, am I to infer that the Trevari scout does not speak any Latin?"

Germanicus spoke. "That is affirmative."

"And what tribe is the interpreter from?"

"I believe he is of the Ari clan."

There was a flurry of activity at the entrance. One of Germanicus's staff ushered in the two German nationals. The pair were dressed in traditional German garb—woolen leggings and woolen shirts. The two men remained standing as they faced the seated officers. No introductions were made. This was not a social visit, but more like an interrogation.

"Please report what you discovered about the Marsi," said Germanicus.

The interpreter relayed the command to the Trevari. He began a long rambling monologue punctuated by several arm gestures. Valerius listened. At first he had some trouble comprehending the dialect, but the longer the Trevari spoke, the better he grasped the words. The conversation flowed back and forth between the two men for a time, and then the scout finished.

The translator turned to the officers and spoke in guttural Latin. "He says he has been across the Rhine in the land of the Marsi. He posed as a seller of horses. He even made some money doing it. He says the Marsi are watching the river to see if the Romans will cross it, but he believes they are of the opinion that the Romans will not invade their lands and that we are still licking our wounds from the terrible defeat. He also says that the warriors have not mobilized, and they are in their villages. The settlements are dispersed throughout the land of the Marsi, and there is no major concentration of forces. There are no signs of any of the other tribes in the area. It is assumed they have returned to their own lands."

The Trevari warrior began speaking again in an animated tone. He gestured with his arm, then laughed.

The interpreter addressed Germanicus. "He says that in six days, the Marsi will be celebrating the festival of Tamfana. That is all they have been talking about. Everyone gets drunk and copulates. That would be a good time to attack."

Germanicus exchanged glances with the other commanders and then turned to the interpreter. "Ask him if he has anything else to add."

The interpreter barked a question at the German scout. He shrugged his shoulders in response. Germanicus nodded to an aide, who then tossed a small sack of coins to the Trevari scout. The two German nationals exited.

Germanicus turned to Valerius. "Did you follow that? Please give me your thoughts on that exchange."

Valerius paused and then spoke. "Sirs, at first I had some difficulty with the dialect of the Trevari, but I quickly got into the flow of his diction. He appeared sincere in his report of the activity of the Marsi, although I can't vouch absolutely for the veracity of his remarks. With respect to the interpreter, I found his translation to match what I would have stated."

Gaius Silus, one of the corps commanders, spoke. "What about this festival of Tamfana—do you know anything about it?"

Valerius hesitated and then responded. "I have heard about it in my study of the German language and culture. It is a major celebration." He turned toward Germanicus. "Sir, I would like to confirm with Wothar, my German aide and tutor, the exact date of the Tamfana. I will locate him and get back to you directly."

"Please do, Tribune. Get back to me quickly. Our planning of this invasion may depend upon your response. I have another appointment, but I will leave word with my staff to interrupt me when you show up."

As luck would have it, Valerius could not find Wothar anywhere. He looked in all the obvious places, but could not find him. He knew Germanicus was expecting him, so his search was intense. Some distance from his quarters, he found Marcellus giving some of his instructions on defeating the Germans to several centuries of legionnaires. The legionnaires in the audience guffawed at one of his remarks, no doubt a vulgar one. Valerius moved closer and gave a quick gesture with his hand to catch the eye of Marcellus.

The centurion halted his discourse. "Excuse me for a moment," he said to his audience. He walked over to Valerius. "What's with that frantic look in your eye?"

"I apologize for the interruption, but I need to find Wothar. Germanicus is waiting for us back at headquarters to discuss a matter of the utmost importance, and I cannot find him."

"Well, then you have arrived at the right place. He is down the road a bit, acting his part as a German aggressor for my troops." Marcellus pointed with his staff for emphasis.

Already hurrying down the trail, Valerius replied with a muffled, "Thanks." Valerius found the German with a bevy of other friendly tribesmen. They were all gathered in a group laughing over some matter or other. Valerius, fuming at the length of time it took him to find Wothar, burst into the area, gesturing in agitation to Wothar. The others looked on curiously as Valerius emphatically waved for Wothar to join him. Both men hastened back down the trail.

"I have been searching all over for you. Your presence is required at headquarters over the timing of the invasion."

Wothar shrugged his shoulders. "Tribune, you told me to assist Marcellus, and that is exactly what I have been doing."

"I know. I know, but I told Germanicus I would be back shortly, and I have been wandering here, there, and everywhere searching for you."

"So what's so urgent?"

"We need to know about the celebration of Tamfana, and if it would be a desirable time for us to attack the Marsi. I remembered a bit of what you told me, but not enough to conclude with any certainty of the dates and the nature of the celebration. Now come on, we need to move; you can enlighten me on the way." The pair broke into a trot toward Germanicus's headquarters.

A short while later, Valerius entered the headquarters building with Wothar in tow. He knew Germanicus would be involved in other discussions, but he was sure he would be admitted to his presence right away. The two entered the vestibule. An aide looked up and immediately shepherded them in to see Germanicus.

Valerius and Wothar entered a secluded chamber and found the general huddled around a small table with an elderly man. The figure sported a long white beard, and he was attired in a cream-colored flowing robe of a fine weave. Embroidered on the garment were various astrological signs. The tabletop had an assortment of documents on what looked like a chart of the heavens.

Germanicus looked up as the two men entered. "So, you have arrived and have good news for me?" Without waiting for a reply, he continued, "Let me introduce to you Thrasyllus. He is my Uncle Tiberius's personal astrologer. He has been sent here by Tiberius to help me decide on the propitious moment for us to invade the German lands. Would you like to listen to what he has to say?"

Germanicus looked at the Greek astrologer. "Please continue your reading. I am anxious to hear your divination."

Thrasyllus looked up briefly at the two newcomers before returning his gaze to the heavenly charts. He began speaking in a soft melodic tone. "The planets are in a favorable alignment. I see the sun in Libra and the moon in Pisces. Mars is in Scorpio, and Jupiter in Virgo. I see Saturn in Cancer. Leo is rising, and Taurus is at midheaven. Capricorn is setting. I believe this bodes well for your plan to attack the Germans. There may be some danger. You must take care because of Mars in Scorpio, but this is more than outweighed by the rising of Leo and Venus in Libra."

Germanicus clapped his hands. "So, what do you think of that?" he exclaimed. "It appears the omens are favorable to us. The stars and the planets are configured to our good fortune. You also have news for me, Tribune?"

Valerius was taken aback by the astrological reading. He paused, somewhat baffled. Aware that Germanicus was waiting, he spoke. "Yes, sir. I brought Wothar with me so you could hear directly from him." Valerius motioned Wothar forward.

Wothar spoke in his best Latin. "It is true, sir. The festival of Tamfana will begin next week. It is a time of heavy drinking. All of the tribes celebrate in a similar fashion. I would expect whole villages to be in a stupor."

"Thank you, Wothar." Germanicus turned toward Valerius. "Tribune, based on our horoscope and the timing of this Tamfana, I believe we have established a schedule for our invasion of the Marsi lands. Dismissed."

Valerius headed toward his quarters and arrived just as the centurion was approaching his tent. Clearly agitated, he motioned for Marcellus to enter. The two men sat down. "Marcellus, we need to talk. I have studied Roman history, and this is one of the largest armies ever assembled. Correct?"

The centurion nodded. "Aye, it is the largest force that I have ever been a part of."

"I just returned from meeting with Germanicus. He was in his headquarters getting a reading of the astrological signs, so he could establish the time for the invasion. A seventy-thousand-strong army is hinging its plans on the words of some old fool dressed in a fancy robe. By Pluto's purple arse, what is this world coming to?"

Marcellus sighed. "Calm down, Tribune."

"Oh come on, Marcellus. What a crock of crap. Did you know that Tiberius Caesar sent this astrologer all the way from Rome to cast the horoscope? His name is Thrasyllus. Some Greek twit. Ever hear of him?"

Marcellus shook his head. "No."

Valerius continued, "Our glorious leaders of the empire put their faith in one of these charlatans."

"Tribune, you sound like the same green officer who showed up at the Weser camp under Varus. First, you should understand that some people believe strongly in the heavenly alignment, even those supposedly shrewd elite who govern us. Second and most important, you, Tribune Valerius, have absolutely no say in the matter, and it is best to keep silent."

"I did not mean to be petulant."

"Well, you were. I believe you are getting too disconcerted about this. Let's go back to the Braying Mule and get some wine."

"And see Brida also?"

Marcellus smiled. "Of course."

Valerius and Marcellus stood with the Praetorian Guard on the immense parade ground. They were in the front center of the massed army, a perfect place to view the proceedings. The entire army of some seventy thousand strong had marched past the reviewing stand filled with the flint-eyed senior officers of the army of the Rhine. To the blare of the horns, each legion, adorned in their polished armor and colorful shields, paraded past the reviewing stand. The drums rolled and cymbals clashed as the ranks, formed row upon row, each straight as an arrow, marched by. Each legion proudly displayed their gleaming eagle mounted on a wooden pole, followed by the cohorts with their vexilla. As the last of the legions trooped past, the cavalry entered with their fluttering pennants. It was an impressive display of military might. These were battle-hardened soldiers, not raw recruits, ready for the invasion of Germania.

It was time for the ritual ceremony. As was customary, a bull would be sacrificed to Jupiter and Mars and the bloody entrails read by a haruspex. With great fanfare, the clash of symbols, and the blare of trumpets, a pure black bull was led by a tethered rope on to the raised dais for all to see. The chief pontiff, clad in white robes, swiftly slit the throat of the animal with a crescent bladed knife. While the bull remained standing, his blood was collected in a large silver bowl. Eventually, the animal toppled over and ceased breathing. The beast's belly was then split open by two of the priest's assistants, who pulled the entrails from the steaming abdominal cavity.

The bloody organs were placed on a large wooden table to be read by the haruspex for a favorable augur. After lengthy study, the priest nodded to Germanicus, signaling that all was well. The general walked to the central stage and raised both arms skyward, indicating a favorable outcome. Seventy thousand voices cheered the results.

When the voices had quieted, Valerius leaned toward Marcellus so no one could hear him. "Pardon me, Centurion, but I believe Varus performed a similar ritual and the augurs were also favorable, and look what happened to him."

Marcellus smirked. "Tribune, cynicism does not become you. Have you no respect for the gods?"

"Apparently not after what I witnessed the last time. How could the gods be so wrong?"

Their conversation was interrupted by the events on the stage. Germanicus gripped a spear and dipped the tip into the silver chalice that had collected the bull's blood. He held the spear aloft for all to see, and then hurled the spear off the dais. War had officially been declared on the Germans. The legions broke into a huge cheer. The army was ready to invade German soil.

The invasion of the German lands began. Hoping to remain undetected and achieve surprise, the army traversed the river at night. Valerius, Wothar, and Marcellus marched with the Praetorian Guard across the pontoon bridge over the Rhine and into the land of the Marsi. With the weight of so many men upon it, the bridge slightly bucked and swayed.

Four legions were fording the Rhine at Vetera, and the other four legions crossed the river approximately thirty miles south at Ascxiburgium, where the Ruhr entered the Rhine. From the crossing points, each of the legions would fan out and, acting independently of one another, seek out the Marsi settlements and destroy them. Although one of the military maxims was never to divide one's forces, this strategy did not appear to be risky, as the Marsi forces were dispersed throughout their various villages—at least that was what the Roman scouts had reported back to the staff at headquarters. Based on the intelligence the Romans had received, it was not anticipated that any of the legionary forces acting on their own would be greatly outnumbered by the Marsi. The element of surprise would be in favor of the Romans. They would advance on a broad front, rolling up any Marsi forces as they swept over the land. The terms of engagement were simple and straightforward: Any male who was old enough to be a warrior was to be slain. The women and children would be captured and sold into slavery. Any who resisted the soldiers would be killed. All settlements were to be razed.

Valerius reached out several times to get his balance on the swaying bridge. His thoughts turned to Rome and his wife, Calpurnia. She should be fully displaying her pregnancy by this stage. He yearned to be back with her and away from his present circumstances. He broke off his musings. He was off the bridge and on the other side of the Rhine—enemy territory. It was not that long ago that he was fleeing for his life from the Teutoburg with the Germans in hot pursuit. He turned toward Marcellus. "I don't believe we are returning to these hostile lands again. It is an eerie feeling."

"I'm not thrilled with the prospect of coming back either, but we are here and will do our duty. We must keep our wits about us. Hopefully we can catch these buggers by surprise, ravage their lands, and then return safely to the other side."

Valerius was silent. The three men marched on amid the clamor of armored men on the march. The rattle of metal and heavy footsteps resonated in the night air. He could not shake this unnerving sensation. He did not know what waited for him on the east side of the Rhine, but he feared that it would not be good. He had miraculously escaped the last time he was here. Was he tempting fate? Would the Goddess Fortuna smile on him again?

He turned toward Marcellus. "I have these nagging concerns about why we are marching into the lands of the Germans once again. I have no answers. Wothar, what say you? Maybe you can shed some light on the matter."

"Me, I don't like it at all, but I do take some comfort that I have eight legions at my back. It is an impressive force."

Valerius nodded. "Aye, Wothar, you are quite right. Eight legions is a formidable army. I must stop dithering like an old lady. Let's see how the Germans stand up to Germanicus and his army."

Valerius marched on into the night. He attempted to take comfort in Wothar's words, but he could not. There was something sinister about this foreboding land on the opposite side of the Rhine. He thought back to the sighting of the owl outside his home in Rome and involuntarily shivered. The favorable omen of the bull's entrails offered little comfort. It was time to be a warrior once again.

Brinwulf of the Marsi tribe rubbed his bleary eyes, trying to understand what had awakened him from his stupor. He spied his prized drinking horn in the dirt next to him. He shook his head, intensifying his wicked headache. Although still in a fog, he realized he smelled smoke and heard screams. What in Donar's bloody name were those shrieks about? He groggily stood to his feet. His staggered toward his spear and shield, which were stashed in the corner of his hut where he always kept them. He noted his wife and two young sons were still sleeping.

He heard more cries. The shrill yells evoked death and terror. What was happening outside the walls of his hut? Brinwulf moved toward the entrance. He was startled as two Roman soldiers with drawn swords burst into his dwelling. With a rapid thrust, one of the legionnaires buried his sword almost to the hilt in the German's midsection. Brinwulf felt a tremendous punch in his stomach and then incredible pain. He staggered a few steps. His spear and shield dropped from nerveless fingers. The other legionnaire swung his gladius, cutting the German's throat. Luckily for him, he died before he could witness the ruthless dispatching of his wife and children by the two Romans. The legionnaires departed the dwelling, leaving it awash in blood. The pair had blatantly ignored their orders to capture the women and children, but who was to say they were not attacked by the members of the warrior's family.

The mission of the Roman Army was to close with and to destroy the enemy, and that was exactly what they did to the unfortunate Marsi. The German tribe was ill-prepared to face the onslaught that overwhelmed them, not that it would have made any difference no matter what their state of readiness. The legions were a killing whirlwind that left a path of total destruction. The Roman cavalry and heavy infantry swept through the Marsi settlements leaving nothing but scorched earth.

Valerius, Marcellus, and Wothar tagged along with the Praetorian cohort that guarded Germanicus and other high-ranking staff officers. They approached a settlement that had already been razed. Dead bodies, mostly males but some women also, were strewn randomly throughout the village. Animal carcasses littered the landscape. Some of the huts were already burning. Off to the right, the slave pens had been constructed for the surviving women and children. Valerius trod in a huge puddle of congealed blood. It made a squishing sound as his foot landed in the middle of the offending liquid. Disgusted, he wiped his foot on some nearby grass. Looking up, off in the distance, he could see pillars of smoke rising into the afternoon sky from other torched settlements.

Valerius frowned. "This is truly a disgusting display of butchery and human misery. It appears that Rome is getting her revenge."

Marcellus replied, "Not a pretty sight, is it, Tribune? I have seen this pillage-and-burn action twice before, and I hope it ends soon. My sense is that the farther we drive east of the Rhine, the fewer Marsi we will encounter. No doubt they will have been alerted to our presence and will have fled into safer territory."

Wothar spoke. "The Marsi should have known that there would be a terrible retribution. They were totally unprepared for the assault that has swept their lands, which are closest to the Rhine. There is no buffer zone between the Roman forces and their territory. Where are their German allies now?"

"Where indeed?" said Valerius. "I can't believe that the Germans had no plan to reinforce their fellow warriors. These people had no chance against the fury of Rome."

Marcellus quipped, "I'm not surprised. Remember that these tribes are not overly fond of one another, so mutual assistance was never in their plan. Furthermore, we have been moving against the Marsi over flat ground with little in the way of forests to hinder our movements. I would not expect Arminius and his allies to offer battle on open ground. It is not what they do well."

The three men continued walking in silence amid the carnage wrought by the legions. Valerius wondered if the next steps in the planned invasion, whatever they were, would go as smoothly. The army would advance even farther east, away from the safety of the Rhine. Again he had a queasy feeling that their continued advance might not bode well for him or the legions.

IX

It was officers' call, and the mood was ebullient. The army had exceeded all expectations. The stunning success of the army over the last three days had put a bounce in everyone's step. The first phase on the road to redemption for the legions of Rome had been accomplished. Valerius milled around with the senior officers, waiting for the arrival of Germanicus. General Tubero walked up to him, sniggering.

"Your mighty Germans were not so impressive. I have seen Egyptian women offer more resistance. And to think we lost three legions to those poor excuses for warriors. I believe this will be an easy campaign and we will have this land as a Roman province in no time."

Valerius, minding what Germanicus had told him about offending senior officers and being more tactful in his responses, nodded meekly. He knew Tubero was attempting to provoke him. "I hope you are correct, General. I am also pleased by our success." He then turned away and departed, pretending to catch the eye of a fellow officer across the room.

"Don't turn your back on me, Tribune. Who do you think you are? Just because our commanding general views you favorably does not give you the right to ignore military courtesy. I have had it with your insolence."

Others in the room were drawn to the confrontation. Tubero had deliberately raised his voice in a laconic tone, no doubt seeking an audience in which to embarrass Valerius. The tribune could feel his face reddening. He desperately sought a response that would rescue him from this confrontation. If he countered with a gibe, his disrespect would be reported back to Germanicus, and there would be a number of witnesses to corroborate the incident. He chose the tactful response.

"My apologies, General Tubero. I thought our conversation was ended."

Tubero scowled in anger. He was about to respond when the officers were called to attention as Germanicus entered. The confrontation was for the moment diffused. The general vigorously hopped to the dais, then turned and smiled at everyone.

"Please take your seats, gentlemen." He waited as a large map of Germania was placed upon the dais in front of the assembled officers. He began "The army has been extremely successful over the last three days. We have exacted a terrible revenge upon the Marsi tribe for their participation in the annihilation of Varus's three legions. Their lands have been devastated, the warriors slain, and the people enslaved. Our advance scouts in Stertinius's cavalry report that they're fleeing the region in droves. The legions have looted the land and will receive additional booty as a result of the sale of the slaves and livestock. This will take their minds away from any future thoughts of mutiny."

He paused, briefly surveying the room. Then he continued, "This is just the first stage of the plan to bring these barbarians under the heel of Rome. I informed you previously our ultimate goal is to kill or capture Arminius and in the process destroy his confederation of tribes. To do this we will annihilate those forces that are allied with him, resulting in the isolation of Arminius and his Cherusci tribe. The Marsi are no longer an effective fighting force. The next tribe to receive our attention will be the Bructeri."

He walked over to the large map set upon the tripod. An aide handed him an ivory-handled pointer.

"It is my intention to continue the campaign from here and move in a northeast direction toward the land of the Bructeri and then the Chatti." He traced the direction with the pointer. "We will move from here to here."

One of the two corps commanders, Gaius Silus, legate of the army of the upper Rhine, rose from his seat. “Sir, this will take us back in the direction of the Teutoburg Forest. Is that desirable?”

Germanicus responded, “I know where we are headed, and it is a valid question, General. My answer is that this is not a desirable course of action, but we will go wherever is necessary to defeat these Germans. I understand what happened to Varus and the tactical disadvantage to our legions of entering one of these German forests, but there will not be a repeat performance of Varus with this army of eight legions. The emperor gave specific instructions to Tiberius and me. He made it clear that we are not to put the legions at jeopardy in our campaign. I will keep his words in mind, but you all know the adage: with risk comes greater reward. Perhaps more succinctly, glory favors the bold. We are a much stronger force than Varus had and will be on the lookout for any type of ambush. Our scouts are trustworthy and not part of Arminius’s confederation.”

Valerius asked himself if he had heard correctly. Surely Germanicus would not lead them back to the Teutoburg. *Had he not listened to my account of the Varus defeat?* The Germans could amass overwhelming numbers—yes, even against eight legions—and strike the army from their hidden positions in the woodlands. He suddenly realized Germanicus was calling his name.

“Tribune Maximus, where are you?” Germanicus craned his neck looking about the crowded enclosure. Spying him, he spoke. “Oh, there you are. You all know Tribune Valerius Maximus by now. He was a survivor of the Teutoburg. What say you?”

Valerius stood and cleared his throat. This was not the time or place to argue with the general’s plan.

“Sirs, as you have just witnessed, the German tribes are no match for the Roman legions on open ground. We win every time. The Marsi were dispatched rather easily. We were the superior force by far. The Germans fare much better when they can operate in forested terrain, where the legions cannot maneuver and use their massed formations to overrun the enemy. This was the case in the Teutoburg. Now I wouldn’t especially like to return to the Teutoburg.” There was some muffled laughter in the room. "But as our commander has stated, we have eight full-strength legions, not three understrength legions as with Varus, and we are keenly aware of the Germans' predilection for ambush. There will be no surprises this time."

Valerius sat, leaving his statements open-ended. Germanicus eyed him briefly, and then continued. "There you have it, gentlemen. We have eight legions plus a large number of auxiliary troops, and we will not be unsuspecting as was the army of Varus. We will go wherever is necessary to defeat these German barbarians. Unless there are any more questions, you are dismissed."

Valerius found Marcellus in his quarters, enjoying some fresh figs. He looked up from his repast, eyeing the harried-looking tribune. "What is it this time? You look like the entire army is marching into the Teutoburg."

"Exactly, Marcellus. Our esteemed general is taking the army northeast to engage the Bructeri and then the Chatti. The Teutoburg is directly in our path. I'm not sure I can handle that scene again. You know, torrential rains and thousands upon thousands of furious Germans with those spears and axes."

"What did Germanicus say?"

"He said that the overall strategy was to isolate the tribe of Arminius, the Cherusci, by eliminating his allies. To accomplish this the army must move over the lands of the Bructeri and the Chatti, even if that means going back into the Teutoburg again. He asked for my opinion in front of the entire senior officer corps. Me, a lowly tribune who had the good fortune of escaping the Teutoburg thanks to a certain savvy centurion that I know. It's as if Germanicus was testing me and my loyalty to him."

"What was your retort? I hope you did not disparage the general's grand plan in front of all those senior officers."

"No, of course not; I was diplomatic. I decided to joke about it. I noted that I had no desire to return to the Teutoburg. I noted that eight legions was a formidable force. I also said that our army would be extremely vigilant for any sign of an ambush, unlike Varus and his unsuspecting legions."

Valerius paused, contemplating his next remarks. "I have been catapulted into a role of a senior officer despite my lowly rank, and elevated to a high status. Germanicus asks my opinion on all things German. I am obviously flattered, but Marcellus, in the grand scheme of things, I do not know that much. I am a survivor of the Teutoburg, and I have had lessons in the German language and customs for about six months. That does not qualify me as an expert on military tactics and interpreting intelligence information on our German foe. You should see some of the resentful looks I get from some of these senior officers."

Before Valerius could continue, Marcellus held his hand up.

"Tribune, you must understand some things. First, at the moment, all Germans are considered to be disingenuous given their perfidiousness in the Teutoburg. They are not to be trusted. Case in point, the emperor removed all of his German Praetorian guards the day after you delivered the bad news at the palace last autumn. Germanicus is placing his trust in you because he has no other options. He will not rely on any of the German nationals that are supposedly friendly to Rome. Do you think for one moment his selection of you to learn the German language was on a whim?"

In reply, Valerius shrugged his shoulders.

"Well, it was not. He needs someone to verify any evidence coming to him and with good reason. He is protecting his noble Roman arse. As to the tactics, my sense is that he is a bold commander who is not afraid to take aggressive action even though these strategies might be considered risky. This daring is tempered by the rules of engagement dictated to him by Tiberius and Augustus. He must not lose any more legions. So given all of that, were your remarks well received?"

"I believe so. Germanicus smiled at me as I departed, so I guess I passed his loyalty test, but I still do not like it. This is another disaster waiting to happen. If he leads the army into those infernal woodlands and bogs, bad things can ensue. You know what he also said?"

Marcellus gave him a quizzical look.

Valerius responded, "He said that glory favors the bold. I say glory favors the bold, my ass."

Marcellus spluttered. "I know it is not a laughing matter, but you need to put these thoughts aside for now. Come on, we need to get to the archery range and practice with our bows. I don't believe we have had any drill lately. What do you say?"

"Let's go. I need to get away from this stuff for a while."

Marcellus and Valerius were practicing with their huge compound war bows. They had moved the archery targets almost twice the distance away as they were for the standard bows. In a designed exercise, the two men unleashed a volley of five arrows apiece at the outlying targets. Even from this distance, the results looked impressive. Both were concentrating on their archery so much that they were startled as a voice spoke from behind them.

"By the gods, you two never cease to amaze me. What in Hades are those weapons you have?"

Marcellus and Valerius turned to see Germanicus and his retinue of senior officers mounted on their steeds.

Valerius smiled at the group. He held up his giant bow. "This is an ancient Egyptian war bow. Marcellus has one also and taught me to shoot it. Thanks to these beauties, we survived the Teutoburg. Want to try it?"

Germanicus chuckled. "No, I don't think so. I remember something in General Saturnius's report about these bows. Now that I see them, I can understand what awesome weapons they are. What is the range of that thing?"

Valerius grinned back. "Not exactly sure, but it goes a long way. Do you want to see another demonstration?"

"I think I would."

Valerius turned toward Marcellus. "On my mark, we shoot a volley of seven at the targets. Are you ready?" Marcellus nodded.

The two men smoothly drew their bows back and unleashed a shower of arrows at the targets. There was no hesitation or fumbling. Their movements were calculated, but quick. In a short time span, all fourteen arrows were on target. The distant straw bundles were bristling with arrows.

"I don't believe I have ever witnessed anything like that before. Where did you get those weapons, and can we get some of them for the army?"

Marcellus spoke. "Thank you for the compliment, sir. Unfortunately, they do not make these bows anymore. It is a lost art. I procured two of them when I was stationed in the East many years ago."

"Too bad. We could use those in coordination with the bolt throwers. That combination would be a most impressive array of long-range weaponry. I would like to observe the effect of those bows during combat. Perhaps soon, when we meet Arminius and his forces face-to-face."

Germanicus nodded to his retinue, and they continued on their way.

Valerius gasped for air under the hot summer sun, and then swatted at the swarm of insects buzzing around his face. The heavy body armor and iron helmet encased his body. While he was grateful for the protection it afforded him, it was extremely uncomfortable to wear in the summer heat. He looked to his right and was reassured by the presence of Marcellus and Wothar. They looked just as miserable, their faces streaming with perspiration. Valerius gazed straight ahead. He could see the Bructeri massing for an attack on open ground. Obviously the word had spread concerning the legions' advance and subsequent devastation of the Marsi lands. The Bructeri had managed to gather a portion of their forces here to defend their homeland.

Valerius, along with Wothar and Marcellus, trotted into position with the Praetorian cohort. The three men were situated in the rear of the cohort's lines. Although Valerius was entitled to be on a horse because of his rank, he rejected that privilege. He was not that accomplished as an equestrian, and he would rather fight with his friends at his side. The cohort took the center position in the battle formation. For today Germanicus's Praetorian cohort was attached to the Twentieth Legion. The commander had taken a fancy to the Twentieth and committed his soldiers and staff to this unit. The seven other legions of the Rhine army were off and about acting independently of one another and were seeking the Bructeri in their settlements.

Shielding his eyes with his hand, Valerius squinted against the glare of the sun to observe the movement of the Bructeri. By his estimate they were about six hundred paces away from the Roman lines. It appeared they were forming into individual units, something he had not seen Germans do before. They were acting more like Romans than a bunch of berserk barbarians. He tried to guess their number, but it was difficult from this far away. More than likely they outnumbered the force of five thousand men of the Twentieth, but not by much. He gazed to his left and right. There were the ten cohorts of the Twentieth, five on each sides of him, all at full strength and eager for battle.

The Praetorian cohort were massed in front of the command staff, protecting Germanicus and his retinue, including General Apronius, legate of the Twentieth. The signal horns of the legions blared, indicating preparation for battle. Centurion Crispus, senior centurion of the Praetorian cohort, initiated movement. *"Open ranks."*

The five other centurions of the cohort followed his lead and bawled their orders, as the six centuries of the cohort opened ranks in preparation for discharging their javelins. The five hundred men of the cohort were ready.

Valerius returned his scrutiny to the Bructeri. They appeared to be moving slowly forward. What was their strategy? Surely they were not going to oppose the legion head-on. That would be a huge tactical mistake. The Germans were lightly armed, with no body armor and only a small oval wooden shield for protection. They would be charging into a wall of iron-suited legionnaires. Either their leader had taken leave of his senses, or they were desperate to stop the Roman invasion of their homeland. This was not the Teutoburg and the Bructeri would have no forest to hide and protect them.

The Germans approached closer to the Romans lines. The gap between the two forces narrowed. Suddenly, the enemy charged forward, screaming their shrill war cries. The legion stood steadfast and silent, with the exception of the centurions, calling out to their centuries to remain calm. Valerius gripped his long sword tightly. His weapon was not the standard short stabbing sword issued to the legionnaires. It was a longer, suppler weapon that could be used to thrust or slash. It had saved his life on a number of occasions in the Teutoburg disaster. Thanks to Mars, he was not in the front ranks. That was where the fighting and dying occurred. He stood at the rear of the formation, which was three lines deep. The legionnaires were spaced apart, ready to hurl their javelins. Once that was done, they would tighten the formation so that they formed a shield wall. It was all going to happen soon. The Bructeri were closing fast.

The Germans were about a hundred strides away. Valerius could make out the individual features of the snarling mass that was rapidly approaching. It was time. The first commands were shouted by the centurions. The Germans advanced nearer, the din mounting. Their eyes widening, the men in the cohort tightened their grips on their pila in anticipation of the command to throw. The gap narrowed even more, and the ground shook from the German charge.

"*Make ready.*" The soldiers cocked their arms, prepared to throw upon command. The barbarians were about thirty yards away. "*Release pila.*"

A swarm of javelins filled the air, smashing into the German front lines. The forward momentum of the charge stopped as those in the forefront fell to the deadly javelins. With no protective armor, the spears wreaked havoc and death among the Bructeri. Amid the groans of the dying, the Germans resumed their advance. The second rank and then the third flung volleys of javelins at the advancing Germans, with similar deadly results.

Centurions bawled the next commands. "*Shields up. Draw swords.*"

The German ranks collided and like a giant sea wave smashed into the Roman shield wall. The Roman lines buckled in a few places from the savage charge, but held. The Roman short swords jabbed at the German warriors through the small gaps in the shield wall, slaying the Bructeri at will.

The familiar din of battle engulfed Valerius. The mortal cries of agony mingled with the screams of triumph in a thunderous vortex. The familiar sounds of steel on steel, punctuated by the sickening thud of blade on flesh, filled the air. Two German wedges rushed forward and struck the lines of the Praetorian cohort, breaching the center of the Roman formation directly where Valerius, Marcellus, and Wothar stood. A group of four penetrated deep enough in the ranks so that they met face-to-face with Valerius, Marcellus, and Wothar. The three men rushed forward and attacked the Germans with their swords.

Marcellus dispatched his man with ease. Wothar swung his sword at the neck of the German to his front. His razor-sharp blade connected, sending a pulsatile fountain of blood into the air and into the face of Valerius. Temporarily blinded, Valerius backed up, holding his blade to his front. His adversary gave a shout of triumph. Valerius wiped his eyes with his left arm just in time, and then parried the thrust of the German's spear. His sword parry was so strong that it cut the German spear in half. The man cried in dismay at the stick remaining in his hand, which moments before had been his weapon. Valerius thrust his sword through the German, killing him instantly. Marcellus and Wothar dispatched the remaining German, sealing the small breach.

Valerius stood ready, but there were no more enemy in the vicinity. He turned to his left as he heard his name called. Germanicus sat astride his horse.

"Good sword work. Now I see how you survived the Teutoburg."

Valerius nodded at his commander and then turned back to the front. The piles of German dead were growing in front of the Roman shield wall. The ranks of the Roman legionnaires pushed deliberately forward. Upon a whistle signal from Centurion Crispus, the cohort smoothly changed ranks so that the second rank was now in the forefront, and the first rank was now the reserve. The fresh legionnaires now occupying the front tore into the tired Bructeri warriors, further decimating the barbarian lines. The Bructeri slowly began to retreat by ones and twos. This quickly turned into a frenzied attempt to escape, but it was too late. The Romans charged after them, slaying them with abandon. It was another victorious day for the legions.

Elsewhere, about ten miles southwest of the Twentieth Legion, Legionnaire Severus of the First Germanica Legion leaned wearily on his shield; its colorful emblem, a prancing lion with a sword in its paw, decorated the business side of it. A small trickle of blood streaked down the left side of his face from his eyebrow to chin, courtesy of a German shield. That had been a close one. The heavy ridge of his helmet above his forehead had absorbed most of the blow that otherwise would have rendered him senseless. Instead, he lived to fight another day. He knew his craft well. While he was perhaps not officer material, his sword could always be depended upon. His ten years in the legions had hardened and seasoned him so that others of less experience looked up to Severus when the going got tough, and today was a tough day. His chain-mail armor and the shiny lion emblem were splattered with blood from the carnage that his legion had wreaked upon the Bructeri over the course of the morning hours. This was the third village they had attacked, and yet the day was only half over. He savored the thought of taking a deep draught from his goatskin water container, but he knew he had drained that long ago. He absently picked up a pebble from the ground, wiped off the dirt, and popped it into his mouth. He sucked on the stone to assuage his thirst, but it offered little in the way of relief.

He numbly looked about at the fellow legionnaires of his century; there were not as many as there were this morning. Their faces were smeared with blood, soot, and sweat. Several coughed and spat the offending contents on the earth. The weary soldiers stood in a huddled mass, perhaps sixty in number, waiting to hear their orders from their centurion. They were in the middle of a large Bructeri settlement. Greasy plumes of black smoke emanated from the village. It had been a tough go for the men of the second century. Unlike the Marsi, the Bructeri knew the Romans were coming and had reinforced their stronghold. In the end they were no match for the Roman forces, but their resistance was fierce. The stockade-like walls had been recently breached and the defenders slain, but this was not the end. There was more work to do, and it would be bloody. The surviving Germans had retreated into the various longhouses that populated the settlement, and then barricaded the doors.

Their officer, Centurion Antonius, commander of the second century of the fourth cohort, strode up to his men. "I want you to stop resting on those shields now. Strap them on and make ready. Start looking like legionnaires. I know you're tired, but you have been through worse than this before. We are going to assault that building there." He pointed with his gladius to a longhouse a short distance away. "We will use a log as a battering ram against the barricade. You six men," he pointed to the men on his right, "go get the log from where we breached the main gate. And make it fast." The six men hurried off.

Centurion Antonius turned back to his men. "Here is what we are going to do. We will hammer that barricade and force an opening into the building. Once inside, kill everything in sight. No prisoners. That includes the women. Just because they do not have a prick between their legs doesn't mean they can't kill you." He turned to walk away, then stopped. "Oh, and try not to do anything stupid like get yourself killed."

Legionnaire Severus glared at his officer with murderous eyes and seethed. *Just what we need,* he thought, *centurion humor after this morning's butchery.* It had been a hard day for the second century. Two of his friends, Cato and Decentius, would no longer be on the legion's roles. Both had succumbed to the deadly German throwing spears while storming the walls. Severus was exhausted and ill-tempered. Further stoking his anger, the soldiers had been ordered not to loot. They were told there was no time. Their orders were to kill and then advance to the next Bructeri stronghold.

The six men returned carrying the heavy piece of timber. They struggled in the afternoon heat to maneuver the heavy object. The century quickly massed in front of the entrance to the longhouse. Centurion Antonius screamed, *"Now."*

With a roar, the second century charged the doorway. With a resounding crash, the heavy log easily splintered the barricade. They were inside. Severus, who was slightly behind the front of the pack of legionnaires, trampled over several dying Germans once inside the enclosure, and then past a dying legionnaire, bleeding out from a gaping wound in his throat. He paid them no mind. He fanned out to his left, searching the dim interior for the foe. A German darted in front of him and thrust at him with his spear. Severus quickly raised his shield. The spear point raked harmlessly along the surface. Severus slammed his heavy shield into the man, then stabbed swiftly with his sword upward into the man's chest, twisting the blade to ensure a lethal stroke, killing him. He charged onward down the length of the longhouse. He was now alone, ahead of everyone else. With a screech a woman leaped at him with a knife held high above her head. The legionnaire slashed her neck with his gladius. He was rewarded with a spray of blood that covered the existing grime and detritus on his body.

He advanced toward the far wall. He could see a small alcove that somehow seemed out of place with the surroundings of the longhouse. He needed to investigate that further. There could be more Germans hiding in there ready to spring out and kill. Severus approached the enclosure cautiously. Nearing the opening, he pondered his options. He could quickly peer around the corner, or he could charge directly into the room. If he selected the first option, he might be rewarded with a sharp spear in the eye. That would not do. If he chose the second possibility, he might be overwhelmed by a superior number of Germans. *Fuck it,* he thought. He leaped inside with a shout, his sword held in front of him. It took him several moments to get accustomed to the gloom. There were no Germans there, but what he saw made his jaw drop.

Valerius sat with the other officers in their commander's tent. He sipped his wine and leaned back in his chair. It had been a relatively uneventful day for him. There had been some fighting, but nothing like the Teutoburg. It was early on this summer evening that retained pleasant warmth even as the sun moved to the west. Germanicus, surrounded by his senior officers, was in a jovial mood, and why not? His eight legions, operating independently of one another, had sliced through the land of the Bructeri, killing their warriors and leveling their crops. Dispatches had been arriving throughout the day reporting favorable results. True, the legions had lost some men and material, but that was to be expected. For the most part, the legions had operated with impunity. Germanicus's strategy was working. He had destroyed the Marsi and now the Bructeri.

General Lucius Stertinius, commander of the Roman cavalry, stood up. He was a highly regarded officer, and his cavalry units had been hugely successful on this day. Stertinius spoke. "Sir, I would like to propose a toast to the army of the Rhine, the greatest Roman army ever assembled. We will have our revenge, and Rome will regain the lands she lost as a result of the Varus disaster."

The officers all rose and cheered the words of Stertinius. Germanicus smiled and nodded his thanks. There was a temporary silence as the officers politely sipped their wine. The quiet was broken by raucous cheering and men shouting outside the tent. The officers all looked at one another quizzically. Germanicus stood. "I wonder what in Hades that is all about."

Ignoring military protocol, one of Germanicus's junior aides barged into the tent, interrupting the discussion. "Sirs, you have to come out and see this." The officers rose abruptly and hurried out of the tent. Approaching the group of senior officers was a mass of legionnaires cheering and shouting. Leading the pack was Legionnaire Severus of the First Germanica. He carried a wooden pole, on top of which was affixed the Roman eagle standard of the Nineteenth Legion, one that was lost in the Teutoburg Forest.

X

Valerius hurried down the main thoroughfare of the temporary Roman camp toward the command tent. He had been in the process of writing Calpurnia a letter when he was interrupted by a messenger requesting his presence before Germanicus Caesar. He had no knowledge as to why he was summoned—only that he was expected to be there immediately. His mind raced with thoughts of possible transgressions he might have committed, but he could think of none. He smiled smugly. Yes, he had been a model tribune as of late, and as much as he would like to vent his views concerning the future campaign in the direction of the Teutoburg Forest, he had dutifully held his tongue. He had avoided a verbal confrontation with Tubero, so there was no trouble from that quarter.

When he reached the entrance, the guards ushered him into the tent. He was greeted by an unpleasant sight. A German warrior was curled up in a fetal position, wrapped up in heavy iron chains, his face bruised and bleeding from a beating. Valerius stared at the pathetic figure on the ground, wondering who he was. Around the prisoner stood Germanicus, General Publius Vitellius of the First Germanica, a German interpreter, and several Roman soldiers.

Germanicus spoke. "Welcome, Tribune. You know General Publius Vitellius. It was his legion that captured the eagle from the Bructeri."

He looked at the curled figure on the ground. "This is Ergrom, a chieftain of the Bructeri." Germanicus snorted. "Well, he was a chieftain. His clan no longer exists as a result of our incursion. We have been questioning him concerning the whereabouts of the other eagles. He said that only two of the eagle standards were captured in the Teutoburg. He also says he heard that Arminius was furious that only two of the standards were accounted for and that Arminius believed that one of the tribal chieftains took one of the eagles for himself. He informed us that Arminius gave the two captured eagles, one each, to the Bructeri and the Chatti, as a reward for their efforts. I want you to listen to what this German states and tell me if you think he is telling the truth."

Valerius nodded in reply. "Certainly, sir. Let me hear what he has to say."

Germanicus motioned to two legionnaires standing in the background. They hoisted the German prisoner to his feet. The German interpreter barked a series of questions at Ergrom concerning the eagle standards. The prisoner looked down and did not answer. It was as if he did not hear the questions. Germanicus nodded to one of the legionnaires. He rushed over and smashed his fist into the man's face. He stuck a wooden staff under the man's chin, forcibly raising his head up.

"Tell him to answer the questions."

The German interpreter again shouted a series of queries. Ergrom gazed at Valerius, his bloody face beaten to a pulp. He offered a look of hate, yet weary resignation. His harsh Germanic words were slurred as a result of his swollen lips. "As I said repeatedly, there were only two eagle standards that were captured. I have heard no rumors as to who might possess the third. Arminius awarded the two captured eagles to the Bructeri and the Chatti for their assistance in defeating the Romans."

Ergrom was then silent, continuing to glare at Valerius.

Germanicus looked at him quizzically.

Valerius glanced at the prisoner, then spoke. "May we confer in private, sir?"

"Certainly."

Valerius and the two generals walked toward a cordoned-off section where Germanicus kept his field desk. The tribune spoke. "Sir, as to whether or not all three eagles were captured by Arminius, I have no idea. It could be that one of the chieftains secretly kept one as a prize. I guess there is also the possibility that one of the eagles was hidden by the legion's standard-bearer, but that appears unlikely given the tactical situation in the Teutoburg. We were in close contact with the Germans. They surely would have noticed any effort to conceal the standard, which they so highly prized. Perhaps the more pertinent question is why the Bructeri chieftain would lie. To what purpose? More beatings? I would have to go with my instinct that the man is telling the truth and that only two eagles were handed over to Arminius. As to his statement that the Chatti have the second eagle, I would again ask, why would he attempt to deceive us? They are not his tribe."

Germanicus stood in silent thought, and then looked up at Valerius. "Based upon what you witnessed in the Teutoburg, you don't believe the third eagle might have avoided capture?"

"Wishful thinking, sir. I guess it's conceivable, but not probable. The Germans had us surrounded and were in close proximity. They would have observed any attempt to hide the eagle."

"All right, I am inclined to believe what the prisoner said. We will try to confirm his story from other captives. I know you are opposed to going through the German forest to invade the land of the Chatti. If I were you, I would probably feel the same. I'm also wary of the prospect of entering one of their dreaded woodlands, but we have no choice. Caution be damned. The Chatti have one of the emperor's eagles, and I'm going to get it back. Furthermore, the Chatti are on the targeted list of tribes for us to wage war upon. We will just need to be vigilant."

Valerius attempted to keep the resignation from his voice. "Yes, sir. Vigilant is the word."

Germanicus replied, "Good. Since we will soon be invading the land of the Chatti, I have one more request of both you and Centurion Marcellus. It is my intention to find the Teutoburg battlefield and bury the dead. I also want to build a cenotaph in their honor to those who perished. Do you think you could help the army find its way there? I intend to travel lightly. I will send the ballista and all but the essential wagons back across the Rhine before we depart. I do not want the column bogged down."

Valerius was silent for a few moments, and then spoke. "Sir, you must appreciate that the Varus army didn't know exactly where they were at the time of the final battle. It was only a guess. If I remember correctly, the generals believed we were near the edge of that cursed forest and close to the plain. How close, I am not sure. Their strategy was to break out of the woodlands and establish a tactical formation more suited to the legions on open ground. Centurion Marcellus and I will study any maps you have of the area, but you must understand there were no terrain features upon which we could determine our location. It was all one bloody forest, with nothing but towering trees and bogs."

"Understood, Tribune. If you can get us in proximity of the battlefield, the cavalry scouts will do the rest. Thank you for your help on this. You are dismissed."

Several days later early in the morning, the eight legions exited a wide plain and entered a series of woodlands. The scouts were out in force reconnoitering, looking for Germans. It was slow going as the army column slugged its way along the dirt track. This had to be the edge of the Teutoburg. From the border of the Chatti tribal lands, they were now moving into the heart of the Teutoburg. Fortunately, there were no signs of any sizable enemy forces. The senior staff was hopeful that the coalition of German tribes had not yet had the time to unite.

"By Jupiter's rotten teeth, I have no idea if we are on the correct path."

Valerius stared at the map, ignoring Marcellus's diatribe. He was surprised the centurion had not spewed forth more invective given their circumstances. Insects buzzed around their heads, looking for an inviting spot to bite. Marcellus suddenly swatted his neck, then looked at the offending contents smeared upon his hand. "Got you, you bloody bugger."

The pair was with the advance guard of the army, leading the search for Varus's lost legions. If Valerius's reckoning was correct, they were on a trail heading in the opposite direction of where the ill-fated Varus army advanced. If, and it was by no means certain he was correct in his assumptions, the army continued down this dirt trail, they should eventually intersect with the location of the final battle.

Valerius stared at the map one more time, and then waved his arm forward. The mounted centurion of the forward element of the legions acknowledged his signal with a nod of his head and urged his horse forward. Valerius and Marcellus mounted their newly issued steeds and rode after the cavalry scouts. The tribune gazed at the surrounding forest, its foreboding presence sending chills down his spine. They continued down the crude trail, deeper into the gloom of the woodlands. Sensing a presence above them, the tribune craned his neck skyward. A ghostly shape swooped past them and soared deep into the dense stand of trees. He had only caught a glimpse of the raptor, but he knew it was an owl. Valerius shuddered. Again this ill-omened bird appeared before him, first in Rome and now here. He chided himself for being a superstitious fool, but he had a sense of dread. Something bad was going to happen. It was an eerie feeling, one he could not dispel. Marcellus looked at him quizzically. The tribune shrugged his shoulders. He needed to overcome his fears and soldier on. Germanicus was depending upon him.

The legions continued blundering through the oppressive forest. Valerius hoped like Hades he was correct in his supposition that the battlefield was on this particular trail. Otherwise, he was leading the entire eight legions to who knows where. Marcellus was not much help. He just stared at the map, scratched his head, and swore. But Valerius had an advantage in his understanding of their location. He had attended the final officers' briefing in the Teutoburg, while Marcellus had not.

The tribune remembered vividly the map on display that night at the briefing and the discourse concerning General Licinus's strategy. The council was held after the second disastrous day of the German attack. The legions were in desperate straits. It was the collective belief of Varus's generals that they were within a day's march of exiting the forest and entering open ground. Of course, they could have been mistaken of their actual location, for they did not know for sure. The ill-fated strategy had been for the surviving members of the legion to exit the encampment before dawn and move with all possible speed through the forest to the plain beyond. They never made it that far. If Valerius's belief was correct that this was the road that the legions had hoped to travel on to escape the Teutoburg, then the battlefield should be close, somewhere up ahead.

Marcellus and Valerius cantered on into the early afternoon. Through occasional breaks in the massive treetops, they saw the bright sun shining in a blue sky. Neither spoke. Occasional riders galloped past them, alerting the main body of the cavalry of the terrain ahead. They plodded onward. Marcellus retrieved some hard biscuits from his saddlebag and proceeded to munch noisily. Valerius leaned over his saddle and spoke to the centurion. "By the gods, every German in the forest knows where we are now after hearing you eat those bricks you call food."

Marcellus smiled mockingly. "Care for some, Tribune?" He was about to continue when a mounted centurion thundered up the trail. He halted in front of them, his face ashen.

"We have found the battlefield."

Relieved, Valerius stared back at the cavalry centurion.

"Good work, Centurion. We will need to inform General Germanicus immediately and have him come forward."

"Yes, sir. Tribune, the battleground sight is ghastly. I can't express in words the horror of it."

Valerius held up his hand. "Stop it right there. I can imagine what it must be like. As I said, we need to bring the general forward immediately. Understood?"

"Yes, sir." With that the centurion kicked his horse into a gallop back toward the headquarters element. Valerius turned to Marcellus. "We shall remain here for Germanicus to arrive."

They did not have to wait long. The general, along with his retinue of senior officers and personal guards, rode into view.

"This way, sirs," said the mounted centurion.

The group of generals, surrounded by a retinue of guards, followed the centurion a short distance. He led them off the trail and through the timber toward a small knoll overlooking the land below. The group emerged on to the hillock. The wind blew, gently swelling the trees in their general vicinity. A stronger gust whistled through the forest, creating a keening sound. The men looked at the macabre scene before them. Not a word was spoken. As far as the eye could see, there was a lengthy trail of bleached bones stretching in both directions along the dirt trail, bordered on one side by forested high ground, and on the other, a bog. In some places there were piles of desiccated bones, as if the men had died one on top of the other. In places, vines grew through the empty rib cages of the fallen. On trees, skulls had been nailed to the trunks. Scattered among the bones were shattered javelins, battered shields, and remnants of clothing.

Valerius took a deep breath and let it out slowly. He glanced at Marcellus, who shook his head in disgust. Valerius returned his gaze to the scene below. This was worse than he imagined. The number of skeletal remains up and down the trail appeared endless. He looked toward Germanicus. The general sat upon his horse staring with a tight-lipped expression, not quite believing what lay before him. He then slowly dismounted and walked toward the downslope of the small hill. The other officers remained mounted.

Valerius alighted from his steed and made his way to Germanicus's side. The general, his face pale, turned toward Valerius, then back to the bleached bones. He spoke in a subdued tone. "We will collect all these bones and bury them in deep pits. But before we do that, I want every legionnaire, from the lowest-ranking legionnaire to the highest legate, to witness what we see here. I have heard rumors that some believe we are being too harsh on the German population and that our methods are too brutal. After they see this, there is not one legionnaire that will not be thirsting for revenge."

Germanicus paused and then turned back toward his officers. "Tribune Aldorus, where are you?"

One of his junior aides dismounted and eagerly rushed forward. "Here, sir."

"Listen carefully. I want you to ride with haste back to the main body. Get hold of the senior centurions of each of the legions and have them organize the troops so that they all witness this battlefield. They will also designate work parties from each legion to dig the burial pits. Understood?"

"Yes, sir."

"Good. You have your orders. Now get going."

It was late afternoon several days later. Valerius sat on his cot, exhausted from the day's activities. The legions had been on the move all day, probing deeper into Chatti territory. Germanicus had not tarried at the site of the Teutoburg battle. The bones of the dead were hastily buried in pits. Piles of stones were erected to mark the spots. The legions had then hastily departed the area. The troops, as well as the officers, disliked the place and considered it a bad omen to remain. Germanicus understood their fear, for he also had anxieties about the site of the massive defeat. He needed no urging to leave.

Fortunately for the legions, the two-day march northward was marked by a swift exit from the heavily forested terrain and a return to open ground without interference from the German forces, but word of their arrival had spread. They marched through wide pastures absent of any grazing beasts, and the Chatti settlements they encountered were abandoned. All the legions found were empty dwellings devoid of any food or possessions. In some cases, the hearth fires were still smoldering. The eight legions swept through the terrain and encamped for the night on favorable ground, a wide meadow, but once again to their front was a heavily forested area of unknown dimensions. They would be entering another ominous forest. Tomorrow would be a trying day.

Valerius was relieved when the army had exited the Teutoburg. In fact, he was elated. He had chided himself at his premonitions and ominous thoughts. He silently scoffed at his fear and the recent sighting of the owl. In the end, it was all for naught. It was superstition, nothing more. He needed to focus his attention on the rest of the campaign over the course of the summer season. True, they would be entering another series of woodlands, but it was not the dreaded Teutoburg.

His musings were interrupted when a messenger from headquarters appeared at the entrance of Valerius's tent. "Sir, I'm to inform you that you have a dispatch from Rome. You may pick it up at the Praetorium."

"Thank you. I will retrieve it shortly." Valerius wearily buckled his armor back on. It was a short journey to the headquarters area, but the standing rule for both common legionnaires and officers alike was to be attired at all times in full armor, including helmets, when outside. Valerius frowned. It was unusual that a dispatch should be delivered to him while on a major campaign. Only the senior officers received mail, and it was usually messages delivered directly from the imperial palace in Rome. Personal mail was waiting for the legions back in Vetera on the western side of the Rhine.

Valerius entered the headquarters tent. The place was bustling with activity. He inquired of an officious-looking clerk about his dispatch and was directed to one of the staff officers. Valerius approached a young tribune seated at a field table.

"My name is Valerius Maximus. I was informed you have a letter waiting for me."

"Of course, it is right here. Please sign here stating that you have received the document." He produced a rolled piece of parchment sealed with wax and handed it to him. Valerius thanked him and turned to leave. At that moment, Germanicus and an entourage of officers strolled through the area. The general moved past him and gave him a peculiar look. Valerius was not sure what that meant. He shrugged his shoulders and departed. Generals were strange men sometimes. He could not figure them out.

Valerius returned to his tent and sat on his cot. He removed his helmet and broke the seal on the scroll. He could tell immediately that the message was from his father. He recognized the familiar scrawl and smiled in anticipation of the contents. He began reading, and his world ended.

Wothar ran toward Marcellus's tent. He entered, interrupting the centurion eating some biscuits. Wothar spoke, his breath coming in gasps. "You must come right away. Something terrible has happened. A great wailing is coming from the tribune's quarters."

The two men rushed toward Valerius's billet. Marcellus parted the tent flap, and both Wothar and he entered. The tribune was sitting on his cot holding his head in his hands, not speaking. He did not acknowledge their presence, but stared at the ground instead.

"What's wrong, Tribune?" Marcellus asked.

Valerius gestured to the rolled parchment on the ground beside him.

Marcellus picked up the document and squinted in the gloom of the tent. He began reading, and then stopped, slowly lowering his arm holding the parchment.

"I don't know what to say, sir. I can't imagine how painful this must be for you."

Valerius looked up for the first time, his eyes swollen and red. "Why did this have to happen? My wife and child died in childbirth, and here I am, stuck in this German wilderness. Some husband I am." He paused. Marcellus was about to speak when the tribune started again. "Marcellus, this is why I survived the Teutoburg? The gods spared me so I could bear this pain? I would be better off being one of the heaps of bones that we threw into the pits."

Marcellus spoke. "Tribune, Wothar and I are sorry for your loss. Your wife was a breath of sunshine in this latrine we call a world."

Valerius, his face ashen, looked up at Marcellus. "Not much I can do about that here in Germania. Why am I here? Why did I come back to this forsaken land? I should have been home with my family—then none of this would have happened."

Marcellus replied, "Tribune, you were doing your duty in the service of Rome."

"So duty trumps family life?"

Marcellus knew better than to argue with the tribune. "You will have to make that judgment, not me."

Wothar approached Valerius. "Sir, I lost my family years ago when the Cherusci slaughtered them. I felt as you do now. You must get over this tragedy. I know how hard it is, but I did it; so can you."

Valerius stared back, saying nothing.

They turned toward the tent entrance as General Germanicus entered, taking in the doleful expressions. He nodded to Wothar and Marcellus. "If you don't mind, I would like to speak to the tribune in private."

"Of course, sir," answered Marcellus. The two men departed, closing the tent flap behind them, and then moved a discrete distance away.

Germanicus sat next to Valerius. "I am so sorry about your wife and child. Agrippina sent me a dispatch, which I opened just prior to you receiving the terrible news. She is dreadfully upset. She really adored Calpurnia." Germanicus paused. "Listen to me, Tribune. I would like to see you take some leave to get over this, but I cannot. There is no time. The legions are about to enter one of these German forests again, and I need your expertise. Besides, there is no way I could send you back through hostile territory to the safety of the Rhine by yourself. You are here for the duration, like it or not."

Valerius spoke woodenly. "I understand."

Germanicus, his voice hardening, continued, "Furthermore, you will conduct yourself as an officer in the Roman imperial legions. I don't want to see you doing a suicidal charge into the German lines. I have seen that sort of behavior before, and it will not do. I will not have it. You are here to serve me and Rome, and that's what I expect of you."

Valerius turned toward the general and stared into his eyes. "Don't worry about me, sir. I will do my duty."

Germanicus clapped Valerius on the shoulder. "Good. I really do need your help." He rose and departed, giving one more glimpse at Valerius. He did not believe a word the tribune had said. He emerged from the tent and spotted Marcellus and Wothar discretely off to the side, out of hearing range.

"I have spoken to the tribune. I told him there was no time to take any leave and mourn. I need his services now. I also told him it would be unacceptable behavior for him to perform any suicidal charge at the Germans. I am worried about his state of mind. I will need you two to keep an eye on him for me and try to raise his spirits. Understood?"

Marcellus spoke. "I am also concerned about his state of mind. We will watch over him, sir."

"See that you do. Now I must be on my way. Take care, Centurion."

Perhaps ten miles away from the Roman encampment, deep within the German woodlands, another meeting was taking place, one not friendly to Rome. A gathering of Germanic chieftains was about to begin. No one had spoken, yet there was an undertone of anger in the air. It was almost palpable. There was a menacing look in the men's eyes. Assembled were representatives of the Marsi, Bructeri, Chatti, Cherusci, Usipetes, Arpus, and Angrivari. Other lesser tribes were also in attendance.

Arminius gestured with his arms and spoke in a perfunctory tone, as if nothing was amiss. "Please have a seat. We have much to discuss." He paused in his remarks, waiting for everyone to get settled. He began his rehearsed speech. "Not far from here is the Roman encampment. The legions are intent upon razing the land of the Chatti. In order to do this, the Romans need to advance through the woodlands that we now occupy. They must come through us. There are no other alternatives unless they retreat, which they will not do. I have another Varus here. They will march through the forest, and there we will defeat them." He was about to continue when Frenmar, chieftain of the Bructeri, interrupted him.

"How do we know they will enter the forest? Maybe they will stop and turn back toward the Rhine or attempt to find a way around the woodlands?"

Arminius spoke. "They will go through the forest. Their leaders are arrogant and believe they are better prepared than Varus. You all saw—"

Again he was interrupted, this time by one of the surviving chieftains of the Marsi. "Where was everyone when the Romans invaded my lands? My people suffered terrible losses, and our crops and villages are destroyed."

Now it was Arminius who interrupted, his voice angry. "Yes, and you were supposed to keep an eye on the Romans and to inform everyone if you observed them crossing the Rhine. It was a complete surprise to everyone here that the Romans invaded. Perhaps if your warriors had been more vigilant, your people would not have been slaughtered."

Hunulf, chieftain of one of the clans of the Dolgubni, a small tribe, spoke. "Arminius, you stated last fall we would achieve a great victory, which we did. You also said we would rid ourselves of the Romans on this side of the Rhine, but here they are back again. I lost many good men in our victory in the Teutoburg, and now we must fight them once again." There were murmurs of agreement among the chieftains.

Arminius put his hands up for silence. He waited until all was still. "If you remember, I spoke of this possibility when we met last over the winter. I didn't anticipate this, but I'm not surprised. The Romans don't take defeat lightly. They are a proud bunch and have come back after us. I was hoping their leaders in Rome would come to the understanding that it is not worth the cost to make these lands a province of Rome, but they foolishly believe that they can still accomplish this. We will defeat them again. The Romans cannot conquer us in our own forests."

A chieftain from the Chatti spoke. "Our scouts tell us that they have a mighty force; I believe eight eagles."

"And yet we have more men than they do," Arminius retorted. "Listen to me, mighty chieftains. I'm also disappointed that the Romans have come back. I thought they would be sensible and leave the German people alone, but they have not. So what are we going to do, sit here and whine like a bunch of old women? We can't stand by and let them ravage our lands. We must take action, and the Romans have given us the perfect opportunity. Just like the Teutoburg, they will be on a heavily wooded trail. We will attack and destroy them. We will have eight more eagles to add to our treasures."

There was a rumbling of assent from the German leaders. Arminius's uncle, Inguiomerus, stood and spoke. "I know some of you are unhappy at the developments that have occurred, but Arminius is right. We need to do something about it, not remain idle while the Romans plunder our land and kill our people. What do you propose, Arminius?"

The Germanic leader paused, briefly surveying the faces of the assembled leaders, and then spoke. "They have a sizable force, and our numbers are not as overwhelming as the Teutoburg, so this is what I suggest. We launch an attack and concentrate our forces on the baggage train in the middle of the column, and at the same time we attack the rear. We don't have to swallow this army whole, so let's do it piecemeal. I suggest a small force to harass the front of the column and impede forward movement. I would espouse the same tactics as before. We rush out of the forest, inflict casualties, then retreat. Our aim is to raid the baggage train and then isolate the last legion in the column. When the day is over, I hope they have one less eagle and their supply wagons are destroyed. The Roman Army cannot mount a lengthy campaign if their supply lines are disrupted. That plus the destruction of one of their legions should convince them to return back to the Rhine. If not, we will continue to attack the next day and the day after, until we will have their eagles."

The chieftain of the Angrivari, Odovacar, arose. "I agree with Arminius. This is a sound plan. We must put aside our dissension and defeat these invaders. No one could have foreseen the Roman foray into our lands, so let's pull together on this, and rout these conquerors once and for all."

"Thank you for your support, Odovacar. I beseech all of you to put our differences aside for now. We must start planning the attack on the Roman column. Before we begin the detailed preparations, we must have our ritual sacrifice to Wodan. Are we in agreement?"

There was a resounding shout from the chieftains.

Aulus Capronius had been a proud optio for the first cohort of the Nineteenth Legion, one of Varus's ill-fated units. Unlike his legionnaire brothers, he did not perish in the Teutoburg Forest. He had been captured, along with a few others, and made a slave to the Cherusci tribe. As far as he was concerned, his fate had been worse than death. For the past ten months, he had been subjected to constant humiliation. The women had spat at him, and the men had pissed upon him. He had been beaten, starved, and nearly worked to death. He was but a gaunt effigy compared to his former self.

The optio shifted his position on the ground. The heavy chains binding him clinked, alerting his guard. The German warrior looked at him briefly, then resumed sharpening his knife. Aulus Capronius remembered that horrible day in the forest when he had been captured. He was fighting desperately with his comrades to hold off the besieging Germans. There were thousands that had encircled the small number of survivors of his unit. The Germans had given a mighty shout and charged the remaining group of men amid a blinding rain. The butt end of a spear shaft had knocked him senseless. The next thing he knew, he awoke in a wooden cage. He wished he had died then.

The Roman soldier was appalled at what he had become. He was dressed in assorted rags and no shoes. His marching sandals had long since rotted away. He was covered in grime, with an unkempt hair and beard. There had been other Roman slaves of the Cherusci. He had been forced to watch one by one the torture and execution of each of his fellow legionnaires. The Germans loved to sacrifice their prisoners to their infernal woodland gods. It was carried out with pomp in front of the entire tribe. Sometimes the ending was quick. The woman priestess would saw open the belly of the prisoner and hold the entrails up for all to see. Those were the fortunate ones. Other times, the man was subjected to horrible acts of torture. The eyes were plucked out and the tongue cut off, and then the person was emasculated. The Germans seemed to relish the agonizing screams of the dying. Slowly burning a victim to death in a wicker cage was a popular alternative.

Aulus sought to calm himself. He knew his end was near. He was informed that he had been brought along with the warriors so that he could be sacrificed to Wodan. He looked at his warrior guard with pure hate. What he wouldn't give to feel the pleasure of his gladius sliding into the belly of one of his captors. He was determined not to cry out and give them the satisfaction of witnessing the pain of his death. He focused his mind with steely resolve. Yes, he must do this final thing before his life ended. He would show them how a Roman legionnaire died.

He did not have to wait long. Two German warriors approached and dragged him to his feet. One of them smashed his fist into the prisoner's mouth, knocking out several teeth. Through bloody lips, the optio grinned at his tormentor. The man hit him again. Aulus laughed, further infuriating the German. The two men roughly dragged him into a circle of German chieftains. His chains were removed, and he was securely tied to a stone altar. His rotting garments were ripped from his body. Two priestesses loomed over him. They began chanting in their guttural language. He thought back, away from the terror of the present, to his old legion and the friends he had known. He involuntarily gasped when the priestess plunged the knife into his belly. The pain made him bite his lip and draw blood, but he did not cry out. From far away he heard the chieftains shout in triumph. There was a bright flash, then darkness as he died upon the stone altar.

XI

Valerius had little time to mourn for Calpurnia. The massive army was on the move and into its second day in the forest. They were following an old Roman road constructed many years ago. It was certainly better than the dirt trail that Varus's army had marched upon in the Teutoburg, but the road had its problems. The avenue was wide enough to accompany the standard marching column of eight men abreast, but the bridges and planking across swampy areas had deteriorated to such an extent that they had to be replaced with new timber, making for slow progress.

Valerius stood watching the latest construction of the causeway. The men making the repairs sweat and swore as they laid down fresh-cut timber to replace the old, rotten wood. Occasionally he diverted his gaze to the surrounding forest and the towering trees of oak and beech. Here and there patches of sunlight filtered through the dense foliage. He fidgeted with his sword, sliding it halfway out of the scabbard and then back in again. Marcellus stared at the tribune's gesticulations, hoping he would get the message that he was damn annoying. After Valerius completed several more cycles, he caught the centurion's glance.

"What?"

"I'm not exactly at ease under the present circumstances. Yes, I am as nervous as you, maybe more so, but do you have to keep playing with your sword?"

"Sorry about that. It's just apprehension."

"I know."

They both stood there in silence observing the latest repair work. Despite the efforts of the engineers to overhaul a small span over a deep gully, the wooden planks had splintered under the weight of a grain wagon, sending the cart, along with the driver and the oxen, plummeting into the gulch below. It was not a pretty sight. The injured oxen, bellowing in pain from their shattered legs, were quickly silenced with a cut to the throat. The teamster of the wagon had attempted to leap free of the plunging cart, but he had not jumped far enough. His crushed body lay in the shallow ravine. The army would be delayed even more as the bridge was mended once again.

After a short while, Valerius began the fidgeting with his sword again. He caught himself doing it and stopped. He turned to Marcellus, who gave him a disparaging glance, and then they both started laughing. At that moment a rider approached and halted in front of them. "General Germanicus immediately requests the presence of Tribune Valerius Maximus and Centurion Marcellus at the headquarters element."

Valerius responded, "We will be there shortly." The two men wended their way down the trail toward the command element. It was only one hundred strides away. Valerius could see the commander's pennant just up ahead. The summons had sounded urgent. They went into a trot. The two officers found Germanicus conferring with several generals, one of which was Seius Tubero. Germanicus broke away from his conversation when he saw Marcellus and Valerius approaching.

"There you are! I need your guidance given our current circumstances. I know you don't like our present tactical position, and frankly I don't either, but we have no alternative if we are to invade the land of the Chatti. This is what I have ordered to protect the army and expedite our progress through these woodlands. I have sent an ala of cavalry ahead to reconnoiter and determine how much farther this forest extends. I ordered the cavalry to scout our flanks to warn us of any Germans lurking in the area. Also, the forward legions are deployed to serve as road builders so that we can get through here as quickly as possible. I had no idea our progress would be this slow and the column so elongated. We are reduced to a crawl. Any other ideas? Your thoughts would be welcome. I value your advice."

The centurion and Valerius exchanged glances. Valerius paused to measure his words. "Sir, it appears that you are taking all the appropriate measures to avoid an ambush and to further our progress through these woodlands. As I see it, there are a number of issues. First, the army can only move as fast as its slowest vehicle. We are therefore inhibited by the wagons. We are forced to bridge some of these watercourses solely because of the wagons. If there were no supply carriages, these culverts could be traversed by the army without the repair work. Sir, I know you have reduced the number of carts in the baggage train to the bare minimum, but my sense is that if the Germans will attack our legions in this forest and prohibit us from advancing forward, our first priority should be to rid ourselves of the wagons."

Marcellus jumped into the conversation. "Sir, I agree with the tribune. Back in the Teutoburg, Varus's army was able to advance much quicker once the wagons were aborted. This terrain is just too inhospitable for the baggage train."

Germanicus frowned. "I would not like to abandon the carts with all of our supplies, but I see your point. What else?"

Valerius spoke. "It's the Germans, sir. This is their element. I would like to believe that Arminius and his allies remain scattered across Germania and have not reunited, but if they have coalesced again, which as you are aware, our latest intelligence believes they have, then they will certainly attack us here. You may have your cavalry scouts alert us to their presence, but once they attack us on this forested trail, the advantage is theirs."

"How will they come at us, Tribune?"

"My sense is that they will concentrate their forces and attack one section of the column. The Germans will attempt to breach the integrity of the column, isolate that piece, and then destroy it. They will strike out of the forest, then withdraw, then strike again. We cannot maneuver and advance our forces because of the forested terrain. As I have mentioned before, Arminius knows the strengths and weaknesses of the legions. He may even attack the headquarters element, seeking to destroy the command and control structure."

Germanicus nodded sagely, pondering the tribune's words. He offered a wry smile. "Let us hope not."

General Seius Tubero had been listening to every word. Ignoring Valerius and Marcellus, his snub intentional, he addressed Germanicus. "Sir, these barbarians are no match for our legions. We have routed them at every turn. I agree that we must be cautious, but we will be out of this forest soon enough, and then we can continue killing Germans and destroying their lands."

Valerius decided to be polite and chose his words carefully. "General Tubero, sir, I know we have had our differences in the past, and I regret some of the words I spoke in Rome, but please consider that Varus's army comprised arguably three of the best legions in the Roman Army, yet they were massacred almost to a man. I'm just suggesting to you that this is a perilous situation, and we need to be prepared in the event the Germans attack."

Germanicus intervened. "My thanks for your advice, Marcellus and Valerius. We must be vigilant. Come, Tubero, let's confer with some of the staff about our next steps."

The two generals strode off together. Valerius turned toward Marcellus when they were out of hearing range. "I thought I was quite tactful in my choice of words with General Tubero, don't you think?"

Marcellus smirked. "He still hates your guts. Stay away from that one."

Over the course of the next several hours, little progress was made. The army advanced but a short distance because of the required road repairs. There was a commotion at the headquarters area as legionnaires gathered and shouted. Marcellus and Valerius hurried toward the command area to see what was going on. General Stertinius, commander of the cavalry, sat upon his lathered horse. His expression was grim, his appearance haggard. Behind him was a decurion, leading a string of six horses. The horses had tied and braced in their saddles six legionnaires—minus their heads.

Stertinius dismounted and then faced Germanicus. "Sir, these were my advance scouts. They were directed to explore the end of these woodlands and report back to me. The Germans are sending us a message. They are letting us know that they are in this forest, and they are going to attack."

Germanicus grimaced. "Do we know how far these woodlands extend? Was their mission in vain?"

Stertinius replied, "There were no survivors from this group, but I sent a second detachment, and a few made it back. They reported to me that the forest extends perhaps another ten miles, maybe a bit more. My men also stated that there are a lot of Germans out there." He gestured with his arm for effect.

Germanicus frowned. "This is not totally unexpected, Stertinius. You are a very capable commander. I know it is dangerous and you may lose more of your men, but I need your cavalry to continue to scout the territory ahead and to our flanks. It is imperative we know where the enemy is and, if possible, his intentions."

Stertinius replied, "Yes, sir. As we speak I have patrols out to our front and our flanks."

"Thank you, Stertinius. I knew I could count on you. You are dismissed."

That evening Valerius, Marcellus, and Wothar sat in front of a small fire enjoying the heat. While the day had been pleasantly warm, the night brought a chill. The encampment for the eight legions was huge. The earthen walls had been built to the legions' specifications and then some. The ramparts were over nine feet tall, plus a deep ditch surrounding the entire fort. On top of the walls, palisade stakes had been embedded, further discouraging any possible attack. The mood of the three men was a shade above glum.

Valerius spoke. "Wothar, what do you think? What will the Germans do?"

Wothar replied, "There is no doubt in my mind they will attack tomorrow. The when and the where I don't know. They hope to trap the legions in this forest and prevent them from reaching the open ground.

My guess is that they would have attacked today, but their forces must just now be marshaling together."

Valerius turned toward Marcellus. "Your thoughts?"

"I agree with Wothar. They will come at us out of the forest and attack us tomorrow."

Valerius countered, "But eight legions is a formidable force. Can they really overcome this massive army?"

Marcellus replied, "They will try—and they don't have to kill every one of us. All they really need to do is force Germanicus to retreat. A stalemate favors them. A Roman withdrawal back across the Rhine is all they really need to achieve. Don't forget, the mission of this army is to isolate the Cherusci tribe and kill or capture Arminius. Only then can Rome absorb the German lands into a Roman province. Unless we can decisively defeat the Cherusci, our mission has failed."

Valerius, his voice morose, responded, "By Mars's arse, all we need now is a horrific gale to repeat the Varus battle."

Marcellus responded, "Do not even go there. It would be a nightmare. I cannot fathom going through that again."

Valerius rose abruptly. "I need to be by myself for a while if you don't mind."

Wothar protested, "Stay with us, Tribune. We will keep you—"

Marcellus interrupted. "It's all right, Wothar. The tribune needs some time alone. See you in the morning, Tribune."

Valerius waved his arm in acknowledgment and ventured into the darkness.

When the tribune was out of earshot, Marcellus continued, "He needs time to mourn and to figure out his place in this world. His future has been ripped to shreds. We will need to observe him carefully. With fighting the Germans imminent, we can't have him distracted, or his future will surely end here."

Wothar responded, "When I faced similar circumstances, I didn't care if I lived or died. I hope he recovers from this, and quickly."

Marcellus nodded. "It is a bad thing he is going through. We will provide him support in the days ahead."

It was midday. Legionnaire Flavius Gallus of the First Germanica Legion leaned wearily upon his long axe handle. His unit was in the vanguard of the legions. He was covered in mud and grime from the never-ending day of road repair through the German forest. He spat dirt out that somehow had found its way into his mouth. His arms and shoulders ached from the constant chopping of trees, but no amount of rest was going to make the pain go away. Because of the imminent threat of a possible German attack, he was attired in his full armor plus helmet. These heavy accoutrements made his task twice as strenuous. Their progress had been achingly slow. By his estimation, the legions had advanced but three miles today.

He numbly stared at the wooden bridge that spanned the small stream. It had been torn up recently by the Germans. Scattered timbers and stones from the abutment lay scattered about. He silently cursed the Germans for their destruction. His centurion plus several road-building engineers attached to the legions viewed the debris and consulted as to what the next steps should be. His fellow legionnaires and he designated for road repair were not alone. They were protected by a cordon of several centuries of alert soldiers, with swords drawn and at the ready in case of an attack. Word had passed down that the Germans were nearby and that they might sally forth at any time. Flavius Gallus felt somewhat secure, but he would gladly trade duty with any of his armed protectors rather than chopping wood and clearing the causeway. He wiped away the grime from his face and began hacking with his axe once more.

The forest erupted as screaming Germans charged from the trees. Flavius quickly dropped his axe and drew his sword. Compared to the heavy axe, his sword seemed incredibly light. He could hear the centurions screaming to form their shield wall. Flavius picked up his shield, which was kept nearby, and rushed over to the nearest group of legionnaires. The German charge was initially repulsed. He saw more Germans edging closer. Many threw their deadly spears. He heard the distinctive thump of javelins striking the Roman shields. There were cries of pain echoing from the ranks. More Germans dashed out of the forest and crashed into the shield wall. Their disciplined and repetitive training served the Romans well. The attack was stopped with no penetration of the lines, but one thing was certain: there would be no more progress of the legions through the forest today.

The Twenty-First Legion was tasked with the security of the middle of the Roman column, where the baggage train was positioned. Every Roman soldier from the highest general to the lowest legionnaire of the Twenty-First knew there were Germans shadowing their movement in the forest. They had not seen the enemy, but knew they were out there. Yet it came as a shock when the Germans charged out of the woods directly at the baggage train. One moment all was still, and the next, it was total chaos. The Roman shield wall formed quickly, but the massive force of Germans managed to penetrate the lines and reach the supply carts. Gaps were created by the wedge-shaped charges out of the forest by the Germans. They swarmed over the carts, killing the drivers and overturning the vehicles on their sides. The precious grain cargoes were spilled on the earth. The oxen drawing the carts panicked, sending the vehicles careening off the causeway and overturning in the mud. Several of the vehicles were torched by the marauding Germans. The Roman cavalry rallied to defend the baggage carts. The Germans countered using long twelve-foot spears to kill the horses and send the riders sprawling in the mud. It was a confusing melee of horse, oxen, and men bent on slaughtering one another.

Marcellus, Valerius, and Wothar stood with the Praetorian cohort. They were deployed so that they encircled the command staff in a protective ring. From his vantage point about several hundred paces away from the baggage train, Valerius could see that things were going badly. Breaches had occurred in several locations. The wedge-shaped German charges had exploited the initial openings, resulting in total chaos. He was not especially surprised. It was a vulnerable spot and not easily defended. Valerius silently cursed Arminius and his horde. The damage was nowhere close to what had happened in the Teutoburg, but the Germans had once again hit the most vulnerable spot of the army column.

Marcellus huddled with Centurion Crispus, the senior officer of the Praetorian cohort. He glanced back toward the supply wagons and then back to Crispus. "I overheard Germanicus discussing how to seal the breach in our lines. My sense is that our general is going to send reinforcements to the wagons, and this will include your cohort. Remember what I said about keeping your lines and shield wall intact. Are you ready?"

Crispus shouted back above the din. "We have practiced for many hours the tactical formations you showed us. As soon as we receive the word, my men will charge the Germans and kick their collective arses out of here. We will leave our javelins grounded here. This is strictly sword work."

Marcellus spoke reassuringly. "Good. The tribune and I will be there with you."

Germanicus waved his sword from his mounted position and pointed toward the Germans. The Praetorian cohort broke into a trot. When they were within fifty yards, Crispus issued the command: "*Charge*."

The wedge-shaped lines of the six centuries of the Praetorian cohort surged against the surprised Germans. The swords glinted in the sun as they plunged into the lightly armored foe. Additional reinforcements soon arrived from the other cohorts. The supporting centuries charged into the flank of the attacking Germans with a resounding crash, sealing the breach. Slowly the Germans gave way, and then vanished into the forest. All was quiet with the exception of the moans of the wounded.

Elsewhere, the Twentieth Legion, Valeria Victrix, Germanicus's favorite and everyone knew it, was designated to defend the rear of the column. It was one of the most vulnerable locations. The Twentieth had interlocking protection to its front with the Eighth Legion, but behind them, there was nothing. The commander of the Twentieth, General Apronius, understood his precarious position, but was unafraid. In fact, he embraced his assignment, and he made sure that all of his officers adopted the same can-do philosophy.

Apronius sensed the attack before it actually occurred. He had read the accounts of the Teutoburg disaster and grasped the German tactics. There was no doubt in his mind that they would employ the same strategy. One moment he was looking at the foreboding forest, and the next instant, it was a boiling mass of crazed Germans seeking to breach his lines and destroy his legion.

His legion was prepared. From the ten cohorts to the sixty centuries down to the individual legionnaire, his unit moved as one. The Roman defensive shield wall was in place almost immediately. The Germans stormed out of the woodlands and were stopped in their tracks at the impenetrable Roman lines. The enemy died by the hundreds as the razor-sharp swords of the legionnaires darted out between the large rectangular shields seeking flesh. If a Roman legionnaire fell in the front ranks, he was immediately replaced with another.

More Germans charged out of the forest, but the Roman lines held. It was the Germans who were punished. Where the German spears found gaps between the shields, frequently their spears broke upon contact with the Roman armor.

Arminius had positioned himself so that he could observe the assault against the Roman rear of the column. He stood a short distance away, viewing the carnage. His warriors hurled themselves at the Roman shield wall but to no avail. Piles of dead formed in front of the Roman lines. He cursed in dismay at the ineffectual charges. He realized that there would be no victory against this steadfast legion on this day, and most certainly, there would not be another eagle standard to add to his collection. He turned toward his trumpeter and signaled for him to sound the recall. Furious at his lack of success, he stormed back to the gathering place deep within the forest.

Marcellus, Wothar, and Valerius advanced toward the command center. They were allowed to enter the ring of Germanicus's personal bodyguards. Valerius saw the general in deep conversation with his staff. The senior officers were huddled together, trying to make some sense of their situation, and then they broke up. A bevy of messengers waited for their instructions. Germanicus addressed them. "Go forth to your designated legions and tell the legates we are going to establish an overnight laager here. It is late in the day, and we have some open ground. I want the First Legion at the vanguard and the Twentieth Legion at the rear to move their men to this location. Construction will begin immediately."

Valerius observed Germanicus. While he appeared sure of himself and his command voice was steady, there was a glint of fear in his eyes. There was no doubt Germanicus was a bit shaken by the sudden turn of events. In Valerius's opinion, his commander was fortunate that things had not gone worse. Thus far the damage to the marching column was minimal with the exception of the baggage train.

Arminius stood before his assembled chieftains in the fading twilight. Their mood was somber. With the exception of their success against the baggage carriages, they had not breached the Roman column; they also had not captured any of the prized eagle standards. Arminius was about to address his lieutenants. Though he was dissatisfied at the results of today's foray, he was not discouraged. He began, "I know many of you are frustrated with the outcome of the battle waged against the Romans. They are a much more formidable force than Varus, but we all knew that. We did achieve a kind of victory today. Many of their supply carts were overturned and their contents spilled upon the ground. The Roman Army cannot advance without a constant flow of rations and fodder for their horses and draft animals. They will not be able to continue their invasion into the German lands without their precious supplies. Our forces were not able to isolate the rear legion from the Roman column and destroy it. My suggestion is to attack again tomorrow using the same strategy."

His remarks were met with sullen glances. This was not a good sign. A chieftain of the Usipetes arose and spoke. "Not far from here, the forest begins to thin out and then ends completely. While we have the advantage now, we won't for much longer. I say we attack them in their laager at dawn. We can breach their walls and cross their ditches; I know we can."

Arminius's uncle, Inguiomerus, rose and spoke in a boisterous tone. "I agree. We have the Romans fixed in this one location. Once we enter the earthen fort, they will be in a panic. I say we attack at dawn." There was a chorus of approval.

Arminius held up his hands for silence. He did not like this alternative. Damn his uncle for advocating this strategy. It was foolhardy to attack a Roman stronghold. Their casualties would be huge, but on the other hand, some of the tribes might become discouraged and leave if he pushed for his plan. "Most of you know I don't espouse aggressive tactics against the Roman fortified camp. Their forces are more susceptible on the forested trail. Attacking the Roman column on the trail served us well last year. Why should we change that? In my years of fighting for the Romans, I never saw a defensive position taken by Rome's enemies, but I am willing to have a vote on this. All those in favor of attacking the encampment at dawn, raise your hands."

Some slowly raised their arms. Inguiomerus elevated his arm high in the air so all could see. As he had a large contingent of loyal followers, they quickly raised their arms. Others, unsure of the best strategy, looked about and joined their brethren. Most of the men had their arms upraised. It was done; they would attack the Roman laager tomorrow morning at dawn.

Inside the Roman encampment, Centurion Brutus Flavius of the Sixteenth Gallica Legion stared at the ten men lined up in front of him. They stood erect in the light of a single flickering torch, ready for their assignment. Upon closer scrutiny, the men wore no armor and had their hands and faces blackened with a mixture of charcoal and water. All were armed with a sword and dagger. They were all volunteers for this risky but necessary assignment. Their mission was to exit the encampment under cover of darkness and scout the perimeter of the Roman laager. They were to report how close the enemy was to the walls, and if possible, bring back a prisoner or two for interrogation.

The men shuffled their feet, anxious to get under way. Centurion Brutus Flavius performed an inspection of each man to ensure there was no dangling equipment that would make noise and that any exposed skin was properly blackened. The centurion spoke in a calm tone. "All right, you know the drill. No noise and no talking. If you got to piss, better do it now."

The centurion led the men in single file toward the main gate of the encampment. They slowly exited the encampment and blended into the darkness. The sentries manning the wall looked on from their perches above, thanking Jupiter, Mars, and any other gods they prayed to that they were not part of that assignment.

The squad of Romans ventured approximately two hundred strides from the walls. They glided through the darkness and encroaching brush without making a sound. Best of all, they were unobserved. The centurion halted the men. This was where things would get hairy. One group of four legionnaires would proceed to their right, and the other group of five would go to the left. The centurion and one man would stay put, waiting for the two squads to report back.

The centurion and his men huddled together in the darkness. He spoke to his men in barely a whisper. "All right, one more time. I do not need to tell you there are a lot of Germans out here. If you are detected by the enemy, run for your lives to the gate. Do not engage the enemy, do not yell out a warning to me—just run. Your first priority is to gather any intelligence concerning the location of their forces. If you can snag a prisoner, that would be a real coup. Now move."

The two teams departed to his left and right, leaving him alone with a single legionnaire. Centurion Flavius stood immobile, his gut churning. This was the hardest part—waiting. At any moment he expected to hear a cry of alarm from the Germans, but all was silent. The centurion stared at the sky, pleased that the moon was now obscured by a cloud. More time passed as the centurion waited for his men to appear. The sole legionnaire accompanying the centurion fidgeted. He was quickly reprimanded. "Marius, stay still and make no sounds. Understood?" The man nodded in the darkness. No sooner had he done so when the bushes to their right rustled, and four legionnaires appeared, dragging a German, his mouth gagged and his hands tied.

The centurion spoke in a hushed tone. "Good work. Take him inside the walls for questioning. I will wait to hear from the other group."

The men nodded in acquiescence and began moving toward the camp, relieved to enter the protection of the Roman fortification.

"Marius, where do you think you are going? Stay here with me." The legionnaire reluctantly returned to the centurion's side to wait for the second group. The night was quiet as the two Romans stood alone. More time passed. The centurion weighed the dilemma before him. They should have been back by now, yet he had heard no sound of alarm. So what was happening? Were there Germans all around them? Insects twittered in the darkness, and a solitary night bird made strange calls. Time continued to drag on. The stillness of the night was shattered by shouts of discovery.

Now it was every man for himself. Each legionnaire was to take the most direct route to the safety of the Roman wall. The centurion and his bodyguard charged out of the foliage and into the clearing in front of the walls. He was startled to see the second group emerge from the forest off to his left dragging a captive. The men ran toward the gate and burst inside the fortress. It had been a successful yet harrowing evening.

The command tent was filled with the senior officers. Oil lamps of various sizes strategically placed within the space provided sufficient illumination. General Stertinius, commander of the cavalry, addressed the legates and tribunes. He used a large sheepskin map displayed upon a tripod. "The army made some progress this morning before we were halted by the afternoon attack. My scouts have reported that we are no more than seven miles from the edge of this forest. The dense woods begin to thin out perhaps three miles from here. The road follows a course in a northeasterly direction. It is not a long march, but my sense is that it will be a tough stretch to navigate with all the bloody Germans out there."

He looked toward Germanicus for direction. "Anything else I should add, sir?"

Germanicus strode to the front of the officers. "Thank you, General. That will be sufficient." He paused, and then began articulating his strategy. "Gentlemen, we are for the moment trapped in these woods by a substantial force of Germans. I am sure you understand we are in a poor tactical position. Their attack on our column today was repulsed with relatively few casualties. They attempted to breach the column where the baggage train was located, and achieved some measure of success, and endeavored to separate the Twentieth at the rear of the column but failed. They were sent back to their forest with their tails between their legs. General Apronius, your legion's gallant conduct was exemplary. In fact, you all performed admirably today. My thanks to everyone."

He looked about, straining his eyes in the shadows of the assembled officers. "Tribune Valerius Maximus, where are you?"

Valerius waved his arm from the rear.

"Tribune, please continue to remind all of us about the dangers these Germans pose to the legion once we are in their woodlands. Now that I have a taste of their capabilities in this forested terrain, I am unlikely to put the army in this position again. The legions are too vulnerable here. We need to get out. So this is what we are going to do. First, all of the wagons are going to be abandoned. They do nothing but slow us down. Perhaps the Germans did us a favor in destroying many of the carts. To the extent possible, we will redistribute the grain and fodder to the men and to the mules. Everyone will be carrying extra rations to see us through this.

"I want the First Legion and General Stertinius and his cavalry to act as the spearhead to break us out of this mess. We will move as a compact force with all possible speed shortly after dawn tomorrow. The army will continue the same order of march. Are there any questions?"

Before anyone could respond, an aide entered and rushed up to Germanicus, whispering in his ear. The general's face lit up with excitement. "Gentlemen, there has been a new development. Please continue your discussions without me. I will return. Tribune Maximus, please come with me."

The aide led Germanicus and Valerius to an open area where a large fire burned. Two German nationals were bound to wooden posts driven into the ground. The two prisoners had been beaten about the face, their lips and noses a bloody mess. A centurion paced back and forth. Several tough-looking legionnaires and an interpreter were also present.

The centurion approached Germanicus. "Sir, Centurion Brutus Flavius at your service. As you are aware, we sent small scouting parties outside the walls of the encampment to see what the Germans were up to. Sir, these two were captured by our scouts in different places, but all relatively close to the walls of our laager. They were questioned separately, but both have the same story. They say their forces will attack the encampment at dawn."

Germanicus turned to Valerius. "All right, Tribune. Time to earn your pay. Let's start with the one over here to the right."

The prisoner, a ferocious-appearing individual with a face in a perpetual snarl, looked at the Romans with contempt. The centurion nodded to the German interpreter. An exchange of terse words occurred between the two men. They were shouting at each other. Valerius locked eyes with the prisoner during the entire exchange. His responses were boastful. He said that they would attack and kill the Romans at dawn. They would cross the ditches with prepared bundles of the sticks to fill in the space and then ascend the dirt wall of the castrum.

Germanicus and Valerius conferred in private apart from the others. Germanicus looked at Valerius. "What do you think?"

"It is my sense that the captive is telling the truth. There was a certain arrogance in his tone. Why would he lie? What would be the purpose of this ruse? I suggest we question the other."

The second prisoner was interrogated. His story was the same, not as immodest as the first man, but their statements were all consistent. Valerius again conferred with Germanicus. "Sir, I strongly believe what these men have told us. The centurion noted that they were captured in separate locations. If this is some form of subterfuge, it is quite elaborate."

"Come on, Tribune, we need to get back to the senior officers. I don't look at this as a threat, but more of an opportunity. I have a new plan."

The two men entered the command center. The room was called to attention. Germanicus strode directly in front of his generals. "Gentlemen, we have some rather astounding news. It seems the

Germans are going to attack the laager at dawn. This is what I would like to do."

Marcellus, Wothar, and Valerius stood in the darkness. The three men wore their cloaks to ward off the chill. They had little sleep that night. Dawn would come soon, and then the general's plan would be unleashed. It was a bold gamble and more than a bit risky—in fact, it was extremely risky—but Germanicus would not hear of any dissension. The castrum was shaped like a rectangle. The tactical plan was to allow the Germans to scale the western wall, one of the smaller sides of the oblong shape of the encampment, and then funnel them to the center of the compound. Hopefully the attackers would include Arminius and his senior deputies. Once the Germans gained access, the breach on the wall would be sealed by a reinforced legion. The cavalry plus a full legion, the Twentieth, would then sally forth and slay the entrapped Germans. But that was not the end of the plan. Once the German forces inside were slaughtered, the legions would rush out of the gates and attack the enemy assaulting the fortress.

Hunulf, chieftain of a clan of the Dolgubni tribe, huddled in the darkness in the forest close to the western wall of the Roman encampment. His lands were north of the Cherusci and had witnessed little in the way of Roman intrusion. Of greater concern to him were the raiding parties of Cherusci that had over the years killed his warriors and abducted the women. He preferred not to think about this now, for he had volunteered his warriors in the battle against Rome. He understood that if the other tribes, including the Cherusci, fell under Rome's boot, then the demise of his tribe would quickly follow. Despite his intense loathing of the Cherusci, he had joined the rebellion that began last fall and ended with the Roman defeat in the forest. Although he had lost many men, they had collected ample booty, and better yet, there had been no further incursions into his lands by the Cherusci.

This area of the western wall had been assigned to Hunulf along with several other tribes. Even in the darkness, he could distinguish the silhouette of the Roman ramparts. He had never assaulted a walled fortress like this one. He was uneasy about the task ahead for his warriors. His forces would be in the second wave of attackers and were to charge the earthen wall, while others would move to the base of the ramparts and fling their bundles of sticks into the deep ditches at the base of the ramparts. Once the trenches had been filled, the men would cross over the obstacle and climb the walls. It appeared to be a reasonable course of action, and none had disagreed with the concept. Given the lack of opposition to this approach, he assumed it was something others had done before. He and his men made ready. It was close to dawn.

The first light appeared as the sky brightened from a gray hue to a pallid yellow. The assault began. The Germans streamed out of the forest, many carrying large bales of sticks to fill in the outer ditch. The legionnaires manning the walls were expecting them. The auxiliary archers and legionnaires armed with bundles of throwing spears were waiting. First the archers unleashed their deadly volleys. The Germans faltered, but continued their advance forward. When they came within twenty yards of the earthen embankment, the soldiers discharged their javelins, punishing the attacking Germans. Men flew backward from the devastating volleys. Despite the deadly rain of arrows and spears, the Germans ignored their losses and rushed forward, flinging their bundles into the outer ditch. Volleys of arrows and spears descended upon the Germans. On three of the walls, the Romans were repulsing the Germans. The Germans continued to heave bundles of sticks into the ditches so that they could cross the obstacle, but the legionnaires countered with a weapon of their own. Flaming pots of oil were heaved from the walls, setting the bales of wood on fire, roasting those Germans unlucky enough to be in the process of crossing the ditch. The western wall had no fires.

As planned, the legionnaires and auxiliary forces on the western wall began to thin in an orderly fashion. It was a gradual process, a ruse that was difficult to discern. Legionnaire Gaius Paulinius of the Second Legion, third cohort, stood on the western rampart throwing his javelins at the invaders. Like the others manning their posts on this rampart, he had volunteered for this perilous duty. It was a delicate maneuver that required perfect timing. If they departed the wall too soon, the Germans would storm over the wall unimpeded and penetrate too far into the interior of the camp. If they exited too late, those on the wall would be slaughtered by the Germans. They had had little time to rehearse the movement during the night.

Gaius's centurion was responsible for directing the men in their orderly withdrawal from the wall. Many of his comrades had already melted away from the besieged spot. Gaius heaved his last javelin at the Germans scaling the ramparts. His aim was true as his lance skewered a large bearded figure almost at the top of the parapet. He looked to his centurion for the signal to retreat. It would never come. His centurion lay dead on the bastion. Gaius turned to flee, but he did not make it far. Two Germans leaped on him and stabbed him repeatedly with their iron knives. The others like him who were supposed to be the last to go suffered a similar fate.

The flaw in the defenses of the western wall did not go unnoticed. Warriors were directed at the western embankment. The first Germans triumphantly scaled the walls against the token force left to defend it. Hunulf and his men followed the others over the ramparts. He had lost a few men in the assault, but overall, he was surprised at how easily they had reached their objective. Now the fun part began. They would slaughter the panicked Romans like cattle. With a roar, Hunulf led his men.

A flood of Germans descended into the center of the encampment, including Arminius and his cadre of chiefs. The Romans sprang their trap. Thousands of Romans from the reserve force sallied forth, retaking control of the western wall. The soldiers heaved the fire pots into the ditch and flung volleys of spears at the besieging Germans, sealing off the breach. No more Germans could enter or exit the western wall.

In the middle of the camp, the Roman forces surrounded the thousands of Germans who had entered the camp. With a mighty roar, arrows and javelins filled the air from all sides, trapping the unfortunate foe that had entered the compound.

Hunulf, chieftain of his Dolgubni clan, was a veteran of many battles and had seen much combat. He and his group of warriors were one of the last to scale the ramparts. While he had never assaulted a fortification like this before, it appeared too easy. His instincts told him that there was something amiss. He was about to direct his men into the compound when he witnessed a massive force of Romans sallying forth to take control of the rampart. He looked at the carnage below and then back at the Roman reinforcements. It was a trap. Jumping to the front of his warriors, he halted the advance of his men. "*Get out. Get out now.*" He pointed with his spear to the forest beyond the fortification, and then ran to a small gap that had not yet been closed by the Roman legionnaires.

Marcellus and Valerius calmly fired their arrows into the tightly packed mass of Germans. They could not miss. Above the din Marcellus shouted to Valerius, "Be sure not to overshoot, or you will hit the friendly forces on the ramparts." Valerius nodded and then calmly released another arrow. He withdrew the next arrow from his quiver. Looking at the mass of German warriors, he felt the presence of Arminius. He visualized him, with his long flowing hair and blazing blue eyes. It was an eerie sensation, one he had not experienced before. Killing the hated German would resolve Rome's current difficulties with this unruly territory. He said a silent prayer to Mars to guide his shaft. He slowly drew the bowstring back to its full stretch. *Find Arminius,* he thought, and then he released the arrow. The missile flew from his bow in a flash. It narrowly missed several Germans and continued its deadly flight.

Arminius advanced farther into the Roman compound. He was surrounded by a posse of handpicked bodyguards. He stopped abruptly to ensure his retinue was keeping pace with him. His decision saved his life. A streaking arrow impaled one of his closest friends, striking him in the midsection and knocking him to the ground. Arminius paled at his near fate. He knelt down to aid his friend, Fredegar, but his life force was gone.

The bewildered Germans mingled about in confusion, as inside the Roman laager, death rained down upon the invaders. It became a killing zone for those unfortunate Germans that had breached the western wall. The *buccina* blared three times, the signal for the cavalry to enter the fray. They thundered into the mass of Germans. The enemy was ill prepared for the onslaught of the mounted Romans. Many were slain by the long swords of the riders. Others were trampled to death as the wave of horses swept through the mass of Germans. From the other sides, the legionnaires formed a shield wall and marched toward the center, trapping the unfortunate foe. The swords flashed, killing the German infantry at will.

Arminius and his uncle, Inguiomerus, looked about in alarm. Arminius cursed out loud, realizing they had been deceived by the Romans. Sensing his own peril, he directed his handful of bodyguards toward the wall. They needed to escape now before it was too late. He yelled for his men to retreat back over the rampart, as the cavalry thundered into them. His uncle, only a few paces away, received a spear thrust to the hip from a charging rider. He collapsed to the ground, badly wounded. Arminius looked down upon Inguiomerus, whose leg was bleeding badly. He was tempted to leave him there as punishment for orchestrating this fiasco, but instead, he ordered two of his bodyguards to pick up his uncle and continue the retreat.

Arminius and his retinue dashed forward, battling the Romans, who were now in control again of the western wall. Fortunately for Arminius, there was a slight gap in the northwest corner of the wall that had not been completely retaken by the Romans. He and his men ran toward the opening before it closed. The German leader leaped off the rampart, followed by his surviving officers. A few other Germans made it back over the wall, across the smoldering fires in the ditch, and into the forest. The remainder were slaughtered in the compound.

The buccina blared once again. First the cavalry charged out of the camp gate, followed by the infantry cohorts. The compact centuries poured out of the camp. The legates and centurions directed them toward the Germans outside the ramparts. The foe attempted to form a shield wall in a number of places, but the momentum was with the legions. They broke through the German lines. The battle became a rout.

Marcellus, Wothar, and Valerius charged out of the encampment with the Praetorian cohort. Centurion Crispus, the overall cohort centurion, calmly directed the unit to the left after exiting the gate.

Several centuries of the Twentieth Legion were meeting stiff resistance. Crispus pointed his gladius at the German lines.

"Advance." The lines of the Praetorian cohort smashed into the foe. The German lines crumbled immediately. The Roman shields pushed forward, and the swords stabbed. Valerius watched it all in grim fascination. The tribune stood, sword at the ready, along with his two friends, but they had no one to engage. The Germans fled into their forest, leaving piles of dead behind.

XII

Several days later Valerius, Wothar, and Marcellus sat on camp stools eating their rations and resting their weary bones. They had exited the forest with relative ease after the German retreat from the laager, and set up a massive camp on a broad plain. It had been an exhausting last few days. They had been informed that the army would stop and rest for a few days before continuing its campaign.

Valerius spoke. "I believe we are extremely fortunate to have escaped that forest relatively unscathed. Not only that, but the strategy of Germanicus to allow the Germans to enter the encampment over the western wall for the purpose of entrapping them was, in my opinion, reckless, but the general would hear no remonstrations from his subordinate commanders. He believed this was his opportunity to snare Arminius."

Marcellus joined in. "I concur. The idea of letting the Germans into the fortress was risky. It was a close thing back there in the woodlands. I hope our esteemed commander has learned his lesson. Let us hope that we do not venture into any more forests."

"If the Germans had waited to attack us on that seven-mile stretch from the forest to the plain, we would have suffered significant casualties," replied Valerius. "I think Germanicus has a newfound respect for fighting the Germans in these woodlands and will be reluctant to do so again. Fortunately for us, we got out of this mostly intact." He was about to continue when a courier, breathless from his dash from the Praetorium, parted the tent flaps.

"Sirs, which one of you is Tribune Valerius?"

Wothar smirked. "Now I am a sir."

Valerius replied. "That would be me."

"Sir, your presence is requested immediately at the command tent on an urgent matter. I was told to escort you."

The tribune frowned and rose. "Now what?"

Marcellus chuckled. "Have fun, Tribune. We will be waiting for you."

He followed the messenger at a trot toward the command area and was ushered into the inner sanctum of the general. Seated with him was Cassius Apronius, legate of the Twentieth Legion. Standing before the dais were two German nationals. Valerius recognized one of them as an interpreter, though he could not remember his name. The other was a stranger.

"Thank you for coming so quickly, Tribune. An urgent matter has come to our attention, and your assistance is required," said Germanicus.

"Yes, sir. How may I be of service?"

"This man," he pointed to the German to the right of the interpreter, "is Agde. He has come forth with some rather startling news. Agde, correct?"

The German interpreter nodded. "Yes, his name is Agde. He speaks only German."

Germanicus continued, "He is a Cherusci and an ally of Segestes. You have heard of that name, I presume?"

"Yes, sir. He was the one who was rumored to have warned Varus about the treachery of Arminius."

"And, Tribune, have you ever met this Segestes character before?"

"No, sir, I have not."

"You know he is Arminius's unwelcome father-in-law?"

"So I have heard."

"We are going to listen to Agde's story, which I have now heard several times. It pertains to Segestes. I want you to listen to what this German has to say. I need a thorough understanding of what our Cherusci friend is telling us." Germanicus nodded to the interpreter, who in turn barked a command at the Cheruscan. The man spoke in guttural German.

"I am a friend of Segestes. As you know, he has always been an ally and a friend of Rome. He is being held in a Chatti hill fort some thirty miles north from here and fears for his life. The only thing that has saved him from death is the fact that he is the father of Thusnelda, Arminius's wife. He is pleading for the forces of Rome to rescue him." The man paused briefly.

Valerius stared at the German. "Is there anything else?"

The figure was startled to hear a Roman officer speak his language. "Oh yes, there is a great deal more," he replied.

"Then please continue."

"Also at the Chatti hill fort is Thusnelda and her infant son, Arminius's child. Perhaps of greater interest to you is the eagle standard of the Seventeenth Legion."

Valerius was stunned. He spoke in Latin. "By Jupiter's holy ass, what an opportunity for us. Three prizes at one place."

Germanicus chuckled. "Thank you for your colorful metaphor, Tribune. What do you think of Agde's story?"

"Given what is at stake, we should assume it to be true and explore the possibility of taking this fort."

"Thank you, Tribune, but do you not think that is my decision?"

"Of course, sir. No offense intended. It is just that the prizes are of such magnitude that it would be a real coup to pull this off."

"And you believe the German's story is credible?"

"Sir, I cannot vouch for the veracity of Agde, but his words are astonishing."

"Good. That is the way I see it. I know there is risk, but given what is at stake, we need to strike this hill fort. I have General Apronius here of the Twentieth. His troops are some of the best trained and reliable."

He waved the two Germans out and called after them, "Stay in the vicinity. I will need to talk to you both later, and do not repeat this conversation to anyone."

"Understood, sir," replied the interpreter.

Germanicus paused in thought and then continued, "General Apronius and I have discussed our options earlier this evening. If we mount a full-scale assault, the Germans will be alerted, knowing we are coming, and get out of there along with our eagle standard, Thusnelda, and Segestes. So what I propose is a snatch-and-grab incursion. We will be in and out quickly with a small mobile force. This is a mission of stealth. There will be no armor, only swords and daggers. If our infiltration is discovered, I would expect heavy losses. My intention is to send but a single century."

"I would like to go, sir, and I am volunteering Centurion Marcellus as well."

Germanicus smiled. "I thought you might like to join Apronius and his crew. Besides, we need an interpreter who can be trusted." He turned toward the commander of the Twentieth. "Apronius, do you have any objections to including the tribune on this mission?"

He chuckled. "I like what I have seen of this young officer. In fact, I would insist he come along. I would like to have this Centurion Marcellus also. I witnessed that little exhibition of those two with their bows a little over a week ago. Their weapons will be useful."

Valerius spoke. "Sir, do we know the strength of the Chatti in this hill fort?"

Apronius responded, "Yes, we do. Agde told us earlier that the hill fort holds about a thousand. How many are warriors, I do not know. We will be heavily outnumbered, but the mission is to get in and out without them knowing about it. If we become engaged with the Germans, I fear a poor outcome for our mission."

Germanicus spoke. "Under no circumstances are you to discuss this mission with anyone. We have thousands of auxiliary forces, many of them German. I do not want the word to leak out that we will be sending a force after one of the Chatti hill forts. That would be a disaster. While as a whole I trust the loyalty of these troops, it only takes one disgruntled individual to ruin the secrecy of our plan."

"Understood, sir."

The next day, Valerius and Marcellus went to meet with General Apronius and his men. The general had selected a location away from the camp to avoid prying eyes. The two men, with their strung war bows over their shoulders, approached the assembled group, a century of approximately eighty men.

Apronius spoke. "Gentlemen, please welcome Tribune Valerius Maximus and Centurion Marcellus Veronus to our assembly. Please give them the utmost respect. They are survivors of the Teutoburg and know their craft well. Tribune and Centurion, meet the first century of the first cohort of the Twentieth Legion. They are the best, my finest unit. The commander of the century is Centurion Gaius Centronius."

The centurion of the century nodded in acknowledgment. Valerius surveyed the men present. They stood in loose formation, their centurion at the front. These were hard, stark, muscular men. They looked tough and dangerous. These were not raw recruits, but experienced legionnaires; killing was their trade. The return stares from the men of the century were not friendly, more like curious with a touch of resentment. After all, the two were outsiders.

Centurion Centronius, a burly figure, who appeared to have been chiseled out of granite, stepped forward. "What is it with the bows?"

In response, Marcellus rapidly withdrew an arrow from his quiver and released the arrow toward a distant tree. It struck with a distant thud.

There was a collective gasp from the century. Nervous laughter emanated from the group. Centronius spoke. "I am glad you are on our side."

Apronius stood in front of the men. "This is going to be a stealth mission. Strictly snatch and grab. We have little time to rehearse, so we will train hard in the short amount of time available to us. After that we will improvise. The mission is to infiltrate a Chatti hill fort some thirty miles north from here. It is estimated, according to our sources, that about one thousand Chatti occupy the site. Once there we will attempt to rescue a German national and a friend of Rome, Segestes, his daughter, Thusnelda, who is the wife of Arminius, and her young son. Oh, and it is rumored that the eagle standard of the Seventeenth is there also."

Apronius paused in his remarks. There was absolute silence from the men.

Finally one brave soul from the rear ranks quipped, "Is that all, sir?"

The ranks howled with laughter. Centurion Centronius turned about from his position in front of the formation, his face flushed with anger, but then he spluttered with mirth.

When the jollity had ceased, Apronius continued, "Good. I like men with a sense of humor, because we are going to need it. I will not lie to you. This is one dangerous mission and no Saturnalia party. Many of you may not make it back. In fact, we all might be slaughtered, but the prizes at stake are worth the risk. Now the first thing we are going to do is strip off all armor and helmets. Everything goes. Do it now."

Centronius turned to the men. "You heard the general. Get it off now."

The legionnaires silently removed their armor and helmets, leaving them in orderly piles. Even the general removed his heavy breastplate and accoutrements.

"Centurion Centronius, if you please, march the century around me with no cadence or bawdy marching songs."

Centronius began, "*Form up. Century, forward march.*" They were off. The century marched about halfway around the clearing before the general spoke. "Centurion, please stop them."

"*Halt.*"

Apronius approached the unit. "That was totally unsatisfactory. Your marching was superb, but the clatter and the noise will not do. We must ensure absolute silence. Centurion, I have brought tallow and various sizes of leather straps to lubricate and secure the swords and scabbards. I have also fetched the tools provided to remove the hobnails from the bottom of your marching boots. Stealth is the order of the day. Please use this time to get your men to have their equipment noiseless."

The general turned toward Valerius and Marcellus. "Please do the same with your equipment."

A while later Apronius stood before the men and laid out his plan in no-nonsense terms. "My design will be simple. It is as follows. Three teams of ten men each will scale the walls under cover of darkness and penetrate the hill fort by stealth. One squad will target the location of Segestes; another seizes Arminius's wife, Thusnelda, and her newborn son; and the third unit will target the lost eagle standard of the Seventeenth Legion. Each of the ten-man sections will operate independently once inside the hill fort. The other fifty men will be the security force and remain outside the walls of the fortress. The role of the security group is to act as a delaying force in the event we are pursued by the Germans. As each team seizes their objective, they will advance immediately to the wall, scale it, and then move to the safety of the security force. The team will then head back to our base here and not wait for the others. There are too many moving pieces to coordinate everyone leaving together. We will begin our preparations now."

Apronius approached Valerius and Marcellus. "I want you to accompany the squad that is designated to recapture the eagle. I place major emphasis on the word 'accompany,' because you will not be leading the unit and will act strictly as observers. It is probably the most risky endeavor of our three objectives that we will undertake, for surely the eagle standard will be heavily guarded. Now the optio of the first century, Decimus, will be in charge. He knows the men well and has led them before. I think it would be asking a lot of you to be in charge when you have little knowledge of their capabilities."

Valerius nodded. "Understood, General."

"Good. I want you to escort this section for three reasons. First, it would only be fitting that you two survivors recapture this eagle. I am sure it is a matter of personal pride to both of you. Second, I want you to assist the optio, Decimus, in whatever capacity you are able. That includes using the power of those awesome bows of yours. They can be a difference maker. I have explained the situation to both Centurion Centronius and Decimus. Both appeared favorably inclined to have you along, so you will get no opposition from them. Third, Tribune, your language skills may be needed, depending on how the situation develops once we are inside the compound. I am counting on both of you to make this a successful mission."

The preparation and rehearsal phase began, using a miniature mock-up of the village fort made with mud and twigs. Each of the dwellings was identified by the Cherusci loyalist. The three teams that were to enter the fort studied the mock-up village so that they could plan how to reach their objectives. The security force drilled repetitiously using various formations for a fighting withdrawal. Their main purpose was to delay the enemy in the event they were pursued. Their lives would be forfeit so that the mission could be accomplished.

Two hard days later, the eighty-plus men designated for the Chatti raid sat silently in a densely wooded cove approximately one mile from the Chatti hill fort. They had marched in a column of twos over the past day and night to reach their objective. The men were sprawled about munching on dried meat and figs while slaking their thirst with water from their goatskin containers. It was morning, and they had all day to rest before beginning their mission later that night. Absent was the usual clink of equipment and idle chatter. Silence was the rule. The legionnaires carried their swords and daggers, plus each man was given one javelin, not the standard issue of two. Once dusk approached, the men would blacken their hands and faces with a charcoal-and-water mixture. The tunics they wore had been dyed black before their departure.

Marcellus and Valerius sat with their backs against a tree, the bark cutting into their skin through the thin tunics. It had been a grueling day and night getting to this location. The gods must have looked favorably upon the small unit, for no one had become lost during the journey, and more importantly, they had gone undetected by their German foes. It had been a harrowing ordeal, especially the night march. The visibility had been reduced to almost nothing in the dense woods that they had journeyed through. The small force had stopped several times when clusters of legionnaires had been separated from the main group, but by some miracle, each time they had been reunited.

Valerius thought back to the rehearsal. He and Marcellus would be with the group to recapture the eagle standard. Assuming they made it back to the reserve force outside the walls, they would assist the security force in the retreat using their giant war bows, that is, if they made it back. There were many things that could go wrong with the plan, and many questions remained unanswered. How heavily guarded would each of their objectives be? Could each of the three squads identify the dwellings in the darkness where Segestes, Thusnelda, and the eagle were located? Would it be a problem scaling the walls? What would happen if they were discovered by the Chatti and the alarm was raised? Could they conduct a fighting withdrawal in the dark?

Valerius awoke with a start. Marcellus was nudging him in the leg with his foot. He leaned close to the tribune and whispered, "Do you want to sleep through this little exercise we are about to undertake?" He could see the gleam on Marcellus's teeth from his sardonic smile. The tribune sat up and rubbed the cobwebs from his head. He looked about and noted that the men were applying the charcoal mixture to their faces and hands. There was only a glimmer of daylight remaining. It was time.

When it was completely dark, the men advanced close to the hill fort, moving to a small copse of trees perhaps two hundred paces from the stockade wall. They would remain hidden, and then close to midnight, they would begin their final approach to the walls. Valerius looked at the structure silhouetted against the night sky. The Cherusci guide, Agde, had told them the walls were about ten feet high. He had also mentioned that at the base of the walls, there was a ditch, which was not well maintained and could be crossed easily. Valerius strained his eyes, but he could not detect the presence of any sentries. Surely there must be someone on watch. He felt a tap on his knee. A legionnaire spoke to him. "General Apronius wants to see you.

Careful not to make any noise, Valerius followed the legionnaire to the right side of the copse of trees. Apronius whispered his instructions. "This is the hardest part. We are going to sit here and wait until it is the middle of the night and everyone is asleep. Hopefully that will include the sentries. I do not believe they are fearful of being attacked. All three of the squads will climb over the wall in the same place. Once inside, we will fan out to our designated targets. Got it?"

"Understood. It appears as if there is no celebrating tonight. There is no sound whatsoever coming from the fort."

"Good. I like quiet, especially tonight. Listen, I know it is late in the game, so to speak, but there has also been a slight change in plan. Agde and I talked about the three teams seeking their objectives independently. Agde thought it would be best, and I agreed with him, that he would guide each of the teams to the dwellings where their objectives are located. The last thing we need is for any of the three sections to go fumbling around in the dark and enter the wrong hut, which is a likely scenario given the labyrinth of outbuildings. I know we had a scale model and he identified the respective dwellings, but we would be tempting fate. Your team will be the last to be guided by Agde to your objective. If the alarm is raised before that, forget your objective and run like Hades to the wall."

Valerius heaved a sigh of relief. "To be candid, sir, I was not looking forward to seeking out the housing location of the eagle standard in the black."

Apronius nodded. "The more I thought about the execution of our original plan, the more uncomfortable I became. In the end I believe this alternative, although lengthier in time, presents less risk and a greater chance of success." Apronius moved on to the next group to inform them of the change in plans.

The three teams, thirty men in total, crept toward the palisade wall. Valerius padded silently forward, his heart pounding in his chest. He now wished he had gulped some more water to quench his achingly dry throat. The pace picked up as the group edged closer. He glanced at the night sky and was pleased to note that only a crescent moon was rising. He saw no sign of any torches or sentries. The Chatti obviously did not come close to Roman standards of vigilance with respect to night watches. There would have been sentries patrolling the walls, and at predictable intervals, torches to illuminate the ground to the front of the fortification.

They reached the ditch. It had long ago succumbed to rain and collapsed upon itself. The group moved silently over the partially filled-in trench to the base of the wall. The designated men cast their ropes with looped ends over the palisade and securely pulled the loop closed over the pointed wooden ends on the top of the wall. The one crude ladder that they had decided to bring with them was braced against the wall. Silently the men climbed the ramparts, and then they were over. So far everything was going just as they had rehearsed—no glitches. Valerius was surprised that it all went smoothly. No one fell or made a sound.

The three teams entered the compound and ventured toward the center. Here and there the remains of fires cast a dim glow from the fading embers, but other than that, the fortress was obscured in darkness. The only sound was of their feet striking the ground. Now things would begin to get interesting. Through hand gestures, the Cherusci loyalist, Agde, indicated the section delegated to capture the eagle to stay put. The two other teams went with him to the left toward the location of the dwellings for both Thusnelda and Segestes. The Cheruscan would return once he had identified the abodes of Segestes and Thusnelda.

Decimus, the optio in charge, gestured for his ten men to huddle together in a small group. Valerius and Marcellus stood off to one side, nervously anticipating the return of Agde. They waited for what seemed like a long time. Valerius glanced anxiously toward the direction where they had scaled the rampart in case they needed to bolt. He observed Decimus beginning to fidget. The other men remained silent, but one could sense the tension in the air. They continued to wait, but there was still no sign of Agde. Decimus edged close to Marcellus and Valerius and whispered, "I think we should head back to the wall."

In response, Marcellus seized the man's arm in an iron grip and spoke in a hushed tone. "Do you hear any sounds of discovery? Are there any shouts that something is amiss or screams of angry warriors? "

"No," the optio replied.

"Then I suggest we continue to stay where we are."

Even in the darkness, Valerius swore he could detect a sheen of sweat on the optio. The other legionnaires seemed to have picked up on the unease of their leader. They started milling about like a herd of sheep. The tribune fretted. Now was not the time for panic. They needed to keep their collective wits about them. Valerius took action. He waded into the small group of men, whispering for them to remain still and not to make any noise. His efforts were successful. The men settled down.

After more waiting, the form of Agde materialized out of the darkness. His expression was anxious, his eyes wide. He spoke softly to Valerius.

"Sorry for the delay. It seemed that our arrival near the two huts coincided with several Germans exiting their huts to take a piss. It was a close thing back there. We had to remain motionless for some time after the men returned to their dwellings to ensure they were asleep again."

The tribune moved close to the Cheruscan. "We need to move now. These men are about to jump out of their skins. Lead the way toward the eagle. We are behind schedule with respect to the others."

The band of men followed Agde, traveling perhaps a hundred strides to the silhouette of a square dwelling set apart from the others. He pointed with his arm. There was no light visible outside or inside the hut. Valerius silently rejoiced at the general's change in the plan. His reckoning of where the hut was situated was not the one Agde identified. They soundlessly crept toward the front of the dwelling. They stopped at the entrance. Decimus withdrew his sword. The others followed his actions, the blades hissing in unison as they exited their scabbards. The men filed into the dwelling.

Valerius cleared the doorway and stared hard into the darkness. He could not see much in the deep gloom. To his left, there were piles of armor and Roman swords, no doubt booty from the Teutoburg battle. He looked toward the back of the hut, but could make out little. Off to his right, he heard a gasp.

"Here is the bloody eagle," a voice whispered. Valerius hurried over. The individual was indeed correct. Still attached to the wooden pole was the eagle standard of the Seventeenth Legion, abandoned in a darkened corner. Decimus, now more in control of events, hissed, "Now let's get out of here."

Valerius moved toward the doorway. He took a deep breath. Was it possible that they would actually survive this raid? The men crossed the compound toward the spot where they had climbed the palisade, not running, but more like a quick walk. The fortress remained veiled in silence.

At that moment, a figure garbed in woolen trousers and a long cloak materialized out of the darkness. The man barked out a question in guttural German. "Who are you wandering around the grounds at this time of night?"

Valerius glibly replied, "We just arrived. We are part of Arminius's forces. We are tired and need a place to sleep."

This bought them some additional time. The German continued approaching. "Let me get a better look at you."

Valerius rushed forward and buried his blade into the surprised German. He let out a weak moan before collapsing dead on the ground.

The men halted. The tribune hissed, "Don't just stand there; keep moving."

The group continued forward, their pace increasing. Off in the distance toward the area where Segestes and Thusnelda had been housed, loud voices rang out in the night; the absence of the pair no doubt had been discovered. Torches appeared several hundred strides away. Like angry hornets of a disturbed nest, Germans erupted from their dwellings. The small group of Romans sprinted toward their exit point and the scaling ropes.

Valerius and Marcellus ran side by side. Angry shouts were directed at them as they sprinted toward their escape point. Valerius stopped at the base of the palisade. "Bows?"

Marcellus replied, "Let's give them some discouragement."

The others of their team frantically climbed the ropes up the timber walls, while the two officers unleashed a torrent of arrows in the direction of the rapidly approaching Germans. They did not aim their shots. Targets could not be identified in the darkness, so the arrows were directed toward a location. Valerius heard a few screams of pain. The two men unleashed one more round and then flung their bows over their backs and began scaling the walls. They were the last Romans to leave the compound. They dropped over the other side and sprinted toward the rally point not too far away. Running for his life, Valerius could see Germans with their torches boiling out of the main gate to the hill fort, heading toward them.

They approached the trail, where Apronius was standing with the reserve force of approximately fifty men. The legionnaires held their javelins at the ready. The general spoke to them. "The three sections that entered the fortress have already fled with their prizes. Do you wish to stay or join them?"

Valerius answered, "It was agreed that we would stand with you. I think our bows, along with several volleys of these javelins, might discourage any German pursuit. We will stay."

Marcellus and Valerius took their bows out and made ready. The German torches were getting close. Both men unleashed a flurry of arrows toward the torches advancing in their direction. There were more shrieks of pain and cries of confusion, but the wave of torches continued to move closer. At about fifty yards away, Apronius gave the command, "*Prepare to throw.*" He waited several moments for the Germans to get closer. "*Release.*" The front-weighted missiles wrought destruction among the advancing Germans. About half the men had a second javelin, courtesy of the three teams that had already departed. "*Prepare to throw. Release.*" The German advance collapsed from the shock of the javelins.

Apronius waved at the men with his arm. "Let's get out of here." The formation of fifty soldiers turned and sprinted down the trail.

They ran on the dirt track, their breaths coming in collective gasps. Their speed was tempered by how far they could see in the darkness. Every so often, Valerius looked to the rear of the group, but saw no pursuit. They continued to trot onward. The three sections, including their prizes of Thusnelda, Segestes, and the Seventeenth's eagle, were somewhere ahead of them. They hurried onward the remainder of the night. At daybreak, the security force stopped for a brief rest. The fifty men mingled around, exhausted from their night's work. The men gulped what little water they had remaining. With a wave of his arm, Apronius signaled the men forward. They began their rapid advance once again.

Near midmorning, they crested a small knoll. It provided a perfect spot to view the land behind them. Apronius directed the men to rest, while Valerius and Marcellus ascended to the highest point of the promontory to observe. Squinting against the morning glare, Valerius saw nothing. He turned toward Marcellus. "You see anything?"

Marcellus ignored the inquiry, continuing to stare back from whence they came. Finally he spoke. "There, Tribune."

Valerius strained his eyes but could not see anything. He stopped and followed the direction of Marcellus's arm. Still nothing. "What am I looking for?"

The centurion pointed again. "You will not see men at this distance, but if you follow my arm, you will spot a dust cloud. That is a movement of men and perhaps some horses."

Valerius looked again. Now he could see it. It was a brown smudge on the horizon. He was not sure how far away.

"Shit," he exclaimed.

Marcellus replied in a laconic tone, "Shit, indeed, and we are going to be waist deep in it."

Valerius knew it was too good to be true that they would escape unscathed. He descended from his perch in search of Apronius. He found him conferring with Centurion Centronius.

The tribune interrupted. "General Apronius, Centurion, would you please come here?" A sense of urgency was in his tone.

Valerius led the officers up to the rising outcrop of ground.

The general said, "What is it?"

Valerius spoke. "Marcellus, please show him what you just revealed to me."

The centurion extended his arm. "Sir, please follow my arm to the left side of our horizon. You will see a brown smudge of dust. That is a formation of men and horses."

The general peered. "I see it. Shit."

"Yes, sir, that is the prevailing sentiment," said Marcellus.

Apronius scowled. "How far behind are they?"

Valerius looked toward Marcellus for his response. He was the one experienced in such matters.

"Hard to tell, sir, but my sense is that we are not halfway back to the legion encampment, and their warriors are fresh, while we are spent. At some point they will catch up to us. If I may be so bold, sir, we need to find a suitable ground to give them a little welcome party. We are at a disadvantage in that we are absent our armor and shields, but I am sure the men can manage with their swords and daggers."

"I concur with your thinking, Centurion. Let's get out of here. We need to slow it down a bit and find a suitable place for a Roman ambush. I do not know how many men they have, but it cannot be too many given the size of the hill fort. Your bows will come in handy as well."

Apronius gathered the men around him. "Listen up. We are being pursued by a German force of unknown numbers with possible cavalry. It is the opinion of Centurion Marcellus that they will eventually catch us. I agree. We cannot outrun them. So here is what we are going to do. We will continue forward and find a suitable place to ambush these barbarians who chase us. It is our mission to protect the three sections that have gone ahead with our captives and our eagle, so that is what we are going to do. We need to move now."

There were no grumblings or complaints. These soldiers were crack troops who knew hardship. If anything, an iron resolve was etched upon their faces. They were ready to do battle when the time came. The security force of fifty advanced down the trail.

About four hours later, Valerius and Marcellus, hidden from view by the dense foliage, stood off to the side of the trail. Accompanying them were five legionnaires, their swords and daggers drawn. They observed the distant cluster of Germans trudging up the road toward them in the afternoon heat. The ambush would be sprung up ahead on the narrow path, bordered on both sides with a dense mixture of both bushes and trees.

The plan was simple. At the point up ahead where the trail narrowed to a width of two persons, General Apronius would launch his attack from his concealed position at the front and flanks of the German force. The men were instructed to stab or slash anything on the trail. Surprise would be in their favor, plus they were refreshed from resting in their camouflaged positions, while the Germans had been moving in the hot sun. From behind, Marcellus and Valerius would unleash their remaining supply of arrows into the German force, sowing confusion. After they had expended their arrows, the two officers plus their provisional force of five legionnaires would attack the rear of the German column. Their plan had an Arminius-like quality to it. Possibly they might be successful.

Valerius turned toward Marcellus and spoke in a hushed tone that only he could hear. "What do you think of the general's plan?"

"As good as any, I guess. I sure wish we had some of those legionnaires who are escorting our prizes back to the encampment. It does not take ten men from each section, thirty in total, to escort a German national, a woman with a baby, and one of our eagles, but that is crying over spilled wine. As for our tactical situation, this is a good ambush site. I sure wish we had our shields, but again, that was the general's decision. Actually, things have gone well up to this point. Apronius made some educated assumptions that worked rather well. Pretty impressive for a general. Let's get ready. The Germans will be upon us shortly."

The Germans filed by, now about even with Valerius's position. Another eighty paces, and the Germans would reach the ambush point where Apronius and the main force waited. Valerius estimated the German band numbered easily in excess of one hundred warriors, with a few cavalry mixed in. The riders would be the first targets for their arrows and easy pickings. Most likely, the mounted Germans would be the leaders. The rear of the German column would be about forty paces away when he unleashed his arrows, a perfect killing range.

Valerius eyed Marcellus. Both men had their arrows nocked, waiting for the screams from the Roman attack that would signal the beginning. He glanced toward his reserve force of five men. They all had snarls on their faces, ready for battle. It should not be much longer. The German force advanced down the dusty trail past the hidden place of Valerius and Marcellus and toward where the bulk of the Romans were positioned. Any moment now.

There was a cacophony of shrieks as the Romans darted from their hidden positions and began stabbing the compacted force of Germans. Valerius unleashed his arrow at his first target, a bulky German rider near the rear. His arrow went wide. Valerius cursed, but was already nocking a second arrow. His next shot hit home, sending the rider hurtling to the ground. He fired again and again in rapid succession, conscious of Marcellus doing the same thing. The riders were down. Valerius directed his attention to the men on foot. The force of Germans had compacted into a dense mass of struggling figures. Valerius and Marcellus fired another five volleys with devastating effect. The pair cast their bows aside and drew their swords and daggers. They charged up the trail, followed by the five legionnaires. Valerius and his force waded into the confused and terrified Germans, thrusting with sword and dagger. It was all chaos and screams, the area strewn with bodies.

The smaller Roman force managed to pare down the number of enemies, but they remained outnumbered. The Germans recovered from the shock of the sudden attack and fought back. The small track became a mass of struggling figures intent upon slaying one another. The carnage continued as the opposing forces hacked and stabbed.

Valerius and Marcellus continued attacking the German rear, their force of five legionnaires now down a man. The number of Germans pressuring Valerius and his men at their rear became overwhelming. It seemed that it would only be a matter of time until they were overrun. Marcellus, from his years of experiencing combat, understood intuitively what was occurring and what needed to be done. The Germans to their front wanted to flee the unexpected mayhem, but could not because of the blocking force to their rear. There was nowhere to go. Amid the carnage, Marcellus screamed, "Disengage and move to the flanks." Valerius and Marcellus, plus the other four legionnaires who remained, shifted toward the side of the trail. The strategy worked. Like a herd of cattle, the Germans fled en masse back down the path from where they had come.

With the exception of the cries of the wounded, there was an eerie silence. Valerius needed to speak to Apronius as to what to do next. He found him talking to several legionnaires. His clothing was splattered with blood, and he had a jagged cut on his left arm. There were bodies scattered everywhere. Valerius approached. "What are your orders, sir?"

"Glad to see you made it through that rather nasty confrontation. If the Germans would have had a leader, I do believe we would be having this conversation in Elysium. It was a close thing. We lost about half of our force. Couldn't be avoided. Those bows of yours helped turn the tide. My thanks. Now, I believe we should make haste and get the Hades out of here. There is no telling if there are more Germans after us. Our mission will remain the same. We are to protect the three sections ahead of us so that they may deliver the fruits of our efforts to General Germanicus."

"Yes, sir. With your permission, the centurion and I are going to retrieve any arrows that are functional. Who knows? We may need them again."

"Make it quick, Tribune. I do not want to tarry here for any longer than necessary."

The next day Valerius and the survivors of the security force arrived back without further incident at the legion encampment in midafternoon. They had marched all night and then through the morning and early afternoon, half dragging, half carrying the surviving wounded. It had been an exhausting four days over the course of the mission. The three sections, along with their prizes, had safely arrived earlier amid much accolades and fanfare. Valerius had made his perfunctory greeting to Germanicus, and then hurried to his tent and cast his clothing and weapons in a pile, collapsing into a deep sleep.

Valerius moaned as someone shook his shoulder. "Go away," he snarled. The shaking persisted. He heard someone calling his name. He buried his head under his arm. "What in Hades do you want?"

"Tribune Valerius, you are wanted at the Praetorium right away."

Valerius opened his eyes, his vision bleary. He could see the erect figure of the messenger standing before his cot.

"Sir, I have been instructed by General Germanicus that your presence is requested immediately."

"What time of day is it?"

"Sir, it is just past the evening mess hour."

Valerius did some quick calculations in his head. He had been asleep but a few hours. Waving the messenger away, he grunted, "Tell him I will be there shortly."

He wearily donned his armor and trudged to the headquarters area. He was ushered in immediately to see Germanicus. There were several others present, including a tall German woman of striking beauty with a small child. Marcellus was also there, looking equally as ragged as the tribune felt.

"Ah, Tribune Valerius, you have awoken. I hope I did not interrupt your sleep?"

Valerius was irritated and let his feelings known with his impertinent response. "You did."

Germanicus smirked. "No matter. You can sleep when you are dead."

"Thanks," he said dryly.

Germanicus ignored the response. "First, let me thank you and also Marcellus for assisting General Apronius in carrying out the mission. He spoke very highly of both of you and those fearsome bows of yours. You two continue to astound me. I want you to meet the success of your efforts. This is Thusnelda and her infant son," he said, gesturing at the tall German woman holding an infant, "and her father, Segestes."

The German national, who appeared to be in his late forties, made a slight bow. "My thanks for rescuing me."

The woman, Thusnelda, looked at Valerius icily, her bearing regal in stature. She spoke in her native German with a haughty tone. "Arminius will kill you for this, and he will do it slowly."

Valerius replied in his best German, his words clipped, "I think not."

The fact that he spoke in German stunned Thusnelda. She was temporarily at a loss for words. Finally she gasped, "You speak our language."

Valerius proffered an arrogant smile.

Germanicus continued, "Thusnelda is not pleased with her father. It seems he has opposed the marriage with Arminius from its inception, and he is responsible for her capture. This family situation is not important to me, but she claims that Arminius will continue to attack us despite his losses and that he will never relent. Her words are of interest to me. I want you to talk to her and let me know your thoughts."

Valerius gazed hard at the woman. She stared defiantly back at him.

"I met your husband when I was with General Varus's army. I must say, my first impression of him was not favorable."

"You lie, Roman. No one escaped alive from the Teutoburg Forest."

Valerius snorted. "I survived. You did not kill all of us." He decided to bait the woman to see how she would respond. "How can your husband possibly counterattack the Roman Army? Has he not learned his lesson? Besides, his forces are breaking up. The German tribes are a fractious bunch."

Thusnelda spat the words back at him. "You do not know my husband. He has the loyalty of the tribes—maybe not all of them, but enough to destroy your legions. He will never give up. You and your generals will die a horrible death."

Valerius turned toward Germanicus and several of his aides. "Sir, she says that her husband has the loyalty of the tribes and will never give up. We will all die at the hands of the Germans. Frankly, as long as we avoid the forests, I do not believe we will perish. Arminius may or may not have the continued allegiance of the confederation of tribes, but I do accept as true her statement that he will never give up. Of this I have no doubt." The tribune hoped he had not pushed his quasi-intentional gibe too far with reference to the avoidance of the forest, but as far as he was concerned, it was deserved.

Germanicus frowned in thought. "So, Tribune, in your estimation, what will Arminius do?"

"Sir, if he still has the loyalty of the various tribes and they have not scattered to the four winds, Arminius will attack again despite his recent setbacks."

XIII

Arminius stood off to the side of the gathering of the chieftains. It was midafternoon six days after the ill-fated assault of the Roman encampment in the forest. The mood was glum. Instead of defeating the Romans, they had suffered a humiliating loss. The German tribal leaders hung their heads in shame. Arminius noted that they were fewer in number than previously. It had been a costly setback, but not a decisive one. The coalition was still intact, albeit in a fragile state. He pondered his words. How was he to address this group? He rejected the "I told you so" scenario. That would do little good. More than likely it would turn more of the chieftains against him, and they would go back home. If only they had listened to him. The attack on the Roman encampment had been foolish. At least his uncle, Inguiomerus, was not here. His wounds were too grievous for him to attend. Arminius felt his anger bloom in his chest. He should have let the bastard die in the Roman compound. The man's reckless ideas made him a thorn in Arminius's side during the entire campaign.

He must choose his words carefully, but what was he to do next? The Romans had exited the forest unopposed after routing his forces. The opportunity to trap them was now gone. Thank Donar for the woodlands. The Romans had not pursued the Germans deep into the forest for fear of having the Germans counterattack. If they had been on open ground, his men would have been hunted down and slaughtered. He deliberated on the alternatives open to him. If he did nothing, the alliance of tribes would collapse, giving the Romans leave to continue to raze German territory. He must act decisively to defeat the Romans or at least battle to a stalemate.

Arminius stepped in front of the assembled leaders. The murmured conversations ceased immediately. They craned their necks forward, anxious to hear their leader's words. "We may have had a setback, but we are not defeated. Our forces incurred losses, but not to a degree that we are no longer a fighting force."

"We should have listened to you," shouted a voice from the rear of the assembly. There were mutters of agreement among the men. Arminius held up both arms for silence. "What is done is done. Let us forget about what has occurred. We can defeat the Romans, but it is going to entail sacrifice from all of you."

He paused in his delivery to search the faces of the multitude. "We will have to face the Romans on open ground, which is a dangerous thing to do. What I propose is this. Our forces challenge the Romans to battle, but we select the time and place. We must scout ahead and find a site where the terrain is to our advantage. It must be a place where our warriors occupy the high ground and have obstacles to protect our flanks. The Romans will seize this opportunity to do battle. I know how they think. They did not come all this way from across the Rhine to dally. They favor aggressive action. Furthermore, I believe the Romans are running low on supplies thanks to our attacks on their baggage train, so there is some urgency to their campaign. This is our chance to defeat them, but we must choose a place that is favorable to us. Are you with me on this?"

Many roared their approval. Some did not. After the uproar had died down, Hunulf, chieftain of a small clan of the Dolgubni tribe, arose. "Arminius, I pledge my support to you for this next battle, but after that, I'm withdrawing my warriors back to my lands to the north. I have lost many men over the past year to the Roman swords. There are many new widows in my village. We achieved great success last fall when we defeated Varus, but the Romans are back in even greater numbers. When is this going to end? Their new generals are not like Varus, and their legions appear to have adapted to our tactics. You all saw how they repelled our forces in the forest. My men have been at the forefront in all of these battles. I cannot go back and face my people with even more losses. I know that many of the tribes have also suffered, but my lands are to the north of the Roman incursion. They have not as of yet entered my territory or taxed my harvest. I don't mind aiding my fellow tribesmen, but understand I am accountable to my people. So I will pledge my warriors to you one more time."

Arminius nodded to Hunulf. "I thank you for your patience and your sacrifice. It is my hope that the Romans will retreat back to the Rhine after this next battle."

Arminius maintained a polite façade, but underneath he was seething. Why did Hunulf have to bring this to his attention with everyone present? Did he want others to follow him? Was he being petulant? Perhaps the more likely explanation was that Hunulf despised the Cherusci, and this was his means to let everyone know his contempt. Hunulf could have just as easily told him in private. Now others would be entertaining the same thought. He knew his fragile coalition of forces could unravel quickly. He breathed deeply to dispel his anger. He must find a way to deter the Roman incursion and force them back across the Rhine.

Later that day, Safrax, a Cherusci chieftain, visited Arminius's uncle, Inguiomerus. Safrax reigned over a large clan of Cherusci warriors and was a devoted follower of Inguiomerus. He shared many of the same views as Arminius's uncle. While he believed in Arminius, his allegiance was elsewhere. He stood before Inguiomerus, who was propped up on his cot and swathed in blood-soaked bandages around one of his legs. The prone figure grimaced in pain.

"What brings you to my sick bed, Safrax?"

Safrax spoke with a hint of anger. "We have a traitor among us."

Inguiomerus replied, "Who? What is his name?"

Safrax grinned inwardly. He'd gotten the response he had hoped for. "It is Hunulf, one of the Dolgubni tribe's chieftains. He stated in front of all the chieftains that he was leaving the coalition after the next battle with the Romans. He said that his clan had suffered too many losses."

Inguiomerus snorted in disgust and waved his arm in dismissal. "Is it that big of a loss? Their numbers are few and account for but a small proportion of our forces. Besides, the Dolgubni fight like women and cannot be counted upon. That is why the Cherusci are always victorious over them in battle. They are inferior."

Safrax bobbed his head in agreement. "I know, but the real problem is that Arminius needs all of us now, and it is a matter of principle. If the Dolgubni depart, who will be next? If someone abandons us, they should be punished."

Inguiomerus nodded sagely. "I see your point, but Arminius would never consent to any kind of reprisal. He has banded all of us together."

Safrax continued, "Who is to say Arminius would ever know about it? After we defeat the Romans, I would like permission to devastate Hunulf's village. I hear he has a beautiful widowed daughter in need of a husband. I would like to take her."

Inguiomerus eyed Safrax. "Now I understand the crux of the matter. So his daughter is a real beauty?"

"Yes, and I would like to take her as a prize." Safrax held his breath, waiting for a favorable response.

Inguiomerus stroked his chin in thought. "All right, but you did not hear that from me, and do not do anything until after we settle things with the Romans. You can raid Hunulf's village and justify it as a blood feud. The fewer survivors, the better. Understood?"

Safrax beamed. He could not have been more pleased with the reply. "Hunulf's village borders on Cherusci land. We do not like one another, and this will be retribution for the carnage he supposedly committed against my people. I will make it appear as if he started this feud and the Dolgubni are to blame."

Inguiomerus chuckled. "All the better. If you are so intent on raiding the Dolgubni and absconding with the maiden, may Wodan be with you."

Several days later all of the senior officers were gathered in the command tent. There was an excited hum in the air as they waited for the arrival of Germanicus. A large number of people crowded into a small space, but no one seemed to mind the stuffy atmosphere. The entire encampment was buzzing with the news that the cavalry scouts had reported this morning. The Germans were but five miles away, entrenched upon a hilltop. Despite their recent humbling defeat, it appeared the Germans were offering to do battle once more.

Valerius stood apart from the others, pondering the latest news. Turning the situation over in his mind, he continued to come back to the same question—why? What was Arminius plotting, and what was to be gained? He probably knew of the supply problems the legions faced as a result of the destruction of the baggage train. He must have a strong tactical position to court the Romans in open battle away from the towering forests and treacherous bogs. What was going on in the German camp? His musings were interrupted as the room was called to attention.

Germanicus strode up to the dais. "Take your seats, gentlemen. We have much to discuss. As you all know by now, our scouts have located the German forces. They are a short marching distance from our encampment and fixed upon a hilltop. Later today I will do a personal reconnaissance of the German position and from that develop a battle plan. They obviously want to lure our forces to their position and do battle. I would have thought the Germans would have broken off after the last ass-kicking we gave them."

There were muttered chuckles from the audience. The Roman officers' spirits were buoyed from their last engagement, in which they had turned the table on the enemy and chased the German foe into the depths of their bloody forest. A boastful pride emanated from the assembly.

Germanicus held up his hands for silence, and then continued, "I must admit, I am perplexed by their recent actions. I would have thought that they would have broken off from the legions, but here they are, back again. They must know of our logistical problems. We cannot venture much farther into German territory without a massive resupply. Our scouts report that they hold terrain that is favorable to them. I am unsure if it offers them an overwhelming advantage. I will need to see this location for myself to get a better understanding of the tactical situation. So why are they desirous of engaging our forces in open battle? What sort of ruse are they planning?"

There was silence in the room. Germanicus searched the crowd. "Tribune Valerius, where are you?"

"Here, sir."

"You know these Germans as well as anybody. What are they planning?"

Valerius paused in thought. He needed to be careful of his words. "I was wondering the same thing. Sir, this is only supposition on my part. Permission to speak freely?"

"Of course. Please do. What is Arminius thinking?"

Valerius framed his words carefully. "This is just conjecture on my part, but this is what I believe is happening. Despite their recent defeat at our hands, we believe that the Germans still outnumber our forces. They now hold the high ground, and this gives them a tactical advantage, but is that enough to challenge the legions in open battle?" He paused again for effect, letting the question linger. "From what I have heard about Arminius's position on the hilltop, I think not."

Muttered conversation filled the room. Germanicus held up his hands for silence. "So again, Tribune, why is Arminius doing this?"

"Several possibilities, sir. First, you can bet your last sesterce that Arminius will engage in some form of trickery in battle. I do not know what subterfuge he will employ, but he will do something unexpected. The greater question is why he is offering to do open battle with the legions. His deceptions may not be enough of an advantage for him to win. I speculate there are factions within his fragile coalition of forces that are demanding aggressive actions against us. They were humiliated by their recent defeat at our hands and now want victory, revenge, whatever you want to call it.

"Their actions over the last week bordered on recklessness. Case in point, sir: the morning attack of our fortified encampment a few days ago was so un-Arminius-like. I do not believe he would have pursued such a foolish course of action on his own since he had our army trapped in the forest. The various tribes of his coalition do not particularly like one another. They are a fractious lot and have no patience. The tactical doctrine favored by Arminius of attack and then withdraw is fundamentally against the German beliefs of how they conduct themselves in battle. My conclusion is that Arminius is offering to engage us in open battle to appease various cliques in his coalition of forces. He must know that this strategy is a bold gamble, but he may not have any alternative. We are not in one of their bloody woodlands this time, but if he does nothing, his forces may disperse."

Germanicus stared in silence for a few moments and then spoke. "I see. So, based upon your assessment of our enemy, Arminius has his own internal problems? His hold on his alliance is tenuous at best?"

"That is my opinion, sir."

Germanicus continued, "Tribune Flacus, what is the status of our supplies? Do we have enough rations and fodder for the horses to sustain us through this next engagement?"

Flacus replied, "As you are aware, sir, our supply situation is critical. If we are to continue the campaign another week, we would need to go on half rations. Our supply line is extended back to the Rhine. Our troops can forage off the land, but the Germans are leaving us nothing the farther we penetrate into their territory." He glanced down to consult a wax tablet containing his figures. "My latest calculation show the following quantities of stores—"

Germanicus interrupted. "Not now, Tribune. As long as we have enough to sustain us for the next few days, that is all I am interested in at the moment. Gentlemen, I will make a list of those commanders that I want to accompany me on a reconnaissance of the enemy's position. We will then formulate a battle plan for tomorrow. Given our supply situation, we must make haste. *Dismissed.*"

XIV

It was a beautiful summer day. A slight breeze swelled the treetops, providing a breath of coolness to the Roman contingent riding over the slightly undulating landscape. The terrain featured cleared fields, interspersed with clumps of towering trees of beech, oak, and spruce. They crossed an occasional meandering stream, but nothing of any size that would deter the massive army when it marched forward. Valerius's horse cantered along with the retinue of senior officers. Keeping pace with the senior staff was a full ala of cavalry of about five hundred mounted men.

Valerius gazed about at the landscape. Up ahead beyond the main body of riders, Valerius could see the advance scouts out to the front and the flanks, ensuring that there would be no ambush of the reconnaissance party. They all wore drab tunics and cloaks. None wore their armor or helmets, for they did not want the sun to reflect off any polished armor. Valerius was surprised that Germanicus had invited him to accompany the reconnaissance, but perhaps he should not have been. The general had come to ask his opinion on all things German.

He did not consider himself adroit on German affairs, but given the other commanders' lack of knowledge of the German people and their culture, he was the expert by default. He knew his elevated status in the eyes of Germanicus rankled some of the senior officers, especially

Tubero, but he didn't care. After a few more miles, the advance scouts galloped back to the reconnaissance party. A decurion separated from the other scouts and walked his horse next to Germanicus. "Sir, the German positions are not far ahead. If I may be so bold, sir, I would suggest that we remain undetected and view the topography from a healthy distance. We wouldn't want to give the filthy barbarians any ideas about attacking our senior staff."

"Quite right, Decurion. Is there a hidden place where a small number of us can observe the terrain and the enemy position?"

"Yes, sir. My suggestion would be for your entourage to move below the slight rise of ground directly to our front and follow this slight vale around to our immediate left. We will come to a copse of trees that should shield us from view."

"Very well. Please select a small contingent to escort the command staff. We will follow your riders."

"Yes, sir. Please wait a moment while I get things organized. In case of trouble, we should move back to this location with all speed."

Germanicus turned to his entourage. "Stay together and, once the decurion returns, follow him. Do not draw your swords unless we are threatened. There is no need to give away our position by having the sun glint off an iron sword. Any questions?"

There were none.

The decurion and ten other riders detached from the main body. They were all armed with lances. Their swords remained sheathed. "If you will follow me, sir, we will move to a veiled position to observe the enemy."

The group advanced ploddingly along the shallow glade toward a large copse of trees. As they approached, a rider materialized from the small wood and gestured for them to come forward. The group silently slid into the trees and wended their way forward until reaching the edge of the thicket. The decurion cleared his throat. "Sirs, no disrespect intended, but please be as brief as possible. I am sure you understand that our current position is precarious. If we were somehow discovered by the Germans, there are a lot of frenzied warriors up on that summit that would welcome the opportunity to dispose of the Roman command staff."

Germanicus nodded. "Your warning is noted. We will make this quick. By the way, Decurion, what is the name of this place?"

"Sir, the Germans call it *Idistaviso*, meaning 'forest meadow goddesses.'"

"Sounds tranquil enough. Let us see what we have here."

They were on the left flank of the German-held summit, perhaps a thousand paces away. Valerius strained to see through the encroaching branches. He smelled woodsmoke. He noted slightly rising ground to a crest. Scanning the hilltop, he observed the earth redoubts along the pinnacle, curving to the left and right of the center. He noted dense forests to the rear and off to the flanks. Valerius withdrew a wax tablet and stylus from under his cloak and started jotting his annotations. He observed the upslope, noting the absence of any obstructions. The Germans held the high ground, but the gradient could be overcome by the legions. In his mind it was not an insurmountable obstacle. He was relieved, for the terrain could have been far worse. Besides the high ground, he believed Arminius had selected the site because it offered protection with the woods on their immediate flanks, and the rear was forested as well, thus offering sanctuary in case the Germans needed to retreat. The legions would not be able to pursue the Germans very far into the dense forest.

Valerius eavesdropped on the senior officers, who were gathered about twenty paces away in a close-knit group. He could barely hear the muted conversation. The tribune smirked. What? It was not like the Germans could possibly hear them from that far away. His gloating was interrupted as Germanicus addressed him. "You have something to add, Tribune?"

His silent mirth had been exposed. He offered a tremulous smile. "No, sir, I was just noting some observations on my wax tablet."

The general gave him a withering stare. "I see."

Tubero proffered a contemptuous glance. "You think this some game we are playing out here, Tribune? Your insolent behavior is intolerable. If I had my way—"

Germanicus cut him off. "Gentlemen, we need to concentrate on the task at hand. Enough!"

Valerius put his head down as if he were studying some of his notations, ignoring the harsh glances of several of the other command staff. After a short while, Germanicus turned toward the decurion. "I think we have seen enough. Now lead us out of here and back to the main body."

The cavalry officer could not help but let out a sigh of relief. "This way, gentlemen. I suggest we move as rapidly as possible."

Later that evening, Germanicus was finishing up conferring with his generals and finalizing the battle plan for tomorrow morning. "I think that about does it, gentlemen. We all need to get some rest, so let us call it a night. General Tubero, would you mind staying for a few moments?"

After all of the men had filed out, Germanicus turned to his second-in-command. "Tubero, I value your service to me, and I depend on you for a lot of things. I would ask a favor of you."

"Certainly, sir. How may I assist you?"

"I would request that you reserve your hostility for the Germans and ease up a bit on Tribune Valerius Maximus. I depend upon him as well, and he has been invaluable to me on this campaign. He is a good officer."

Tubero replied, a hint of anger in his voice, "He is impertinent."

Germanicus sighed. "That he is, and I have talked to him about that. But he is a survivor of the Teutoburg."

Tubero responded, "So he is a fast runner."

Germanicus frowned. He had hoped this discussion would have gone better. "That is far from the truth. I read General Saturnius's report of the military tribunal concerning the survivors of the Teutoburg. The tribune and his centurion friend wreaked havoc among their German pursuers. General Apronius of the Twentieth raves about him. He said that the snatch-and-grab mission was successful in large part due to the heroics of Maximus and his centurion. Though the tribune is impertinent, he is a warrior. Furthermore, I value his opinion on all things German, given his understanding of their language and customs. His comments about marching the legions into the German forest were prescient. We should have all listened to him. He has recently lost his wife in childbirth and has had a tough time of it lately. I fear for his mental state. Come on, what do you say? Can you put your dislike of him aside? I am sure he is sorry for his previous remarks."

Tubero proffered a tight smile. "Well, I certainly would not invite him to my home to attend a dinner party, but I promise to be civil to him."

Germanicus smiled back. "Good. Now let us all get some rest. Tomorrow is going to be a trying day."

The entire encampment was up before dawn, assembling into their cohorts and centuries. Their breakfasts of heated porridge were eaten in haste. Gone was the grumbling and muttered curses that usually accompanied a march out. They knew that some would die this day. The column of soldiers exited the encampment to the brassy sounds of the cornua. The massive army was headed toward the German position just miles away.

Valerius, Marcellus, and Wothar marched alongside the Praetorian cohort. They would not be positioned in the rear to observe the ebb and flow of the battle, but rather directly in the center of the Roman lines. The cohort would function both to protect their general and as front-line troops in the assault. Valerius glanced at Marcellus and Wothar. Both maintained implacable expressions. Oddly, he felt totally calm. He could not explain why. He knew he should be anxious. There was going to be a lot of killing today, and odds were, given his position in the line, that he would be right in the middle of it. Perhaps his combat experiences over the last year and the loss of Calpurnia had hardened his soul. Did he care anymore whether he lived or died? That answer fluctuated depending upon what day it was. He tried not to dwell on the subject, but he could not purge the matter from his mind. What kind of person had he morphed into? He involuntarily grimaced at the thought of his future.

Marcellus gave him a worried glance. "Something wrong, Tribune?"

"No," he lied, "but I believe this will be a tough fight today."

Marcellus waited for him to say something else, but he did not. "All fights are tough, especially if you are selected for Elysium."

Wothar snorted at the humor. "Let us all hope it is not our turn."

Marcellus continued his probing. "You appear as if you are in a stupor, Tribune."

His reply was blurted and laconic in tone. "I have hardened myself for this engagement. Now can we change the subject?"

Marcellus was taken aback by the outburst. "Just remember, Tribune: you are to stay with us during this engagement. Understood?"

Valerius remained silent, his anger tightly held for the moment.

By midmorning the legions had arrived at the base of the gentle sloping hill that the command staff had observed yesterday. The army immediately began to deploy. The archers moved forward in the vanguard, followed by the auxiliary cohorts. They advanced in a checkered formation. Behind the auxiliary cohorts were five legions, with the Praetorian cohort and the command staff in the center. To the rear of these five legions were the three other legions, acting as a reserve and to fortify the forward legions when needed.

The positioning of the army was an impressive sight. The brightly painted shields of the legionnaires gleamed in the early morning light. Each legion had a symbol on their shields. The First showed the lion. The Second had Pegasus, the flying horse. The Fifth, Eighth, and Ninth had the bull. The Twentieth showed the lion, while the Sixteenth and Twenty-First displayed the bear. The air was filled with the rhythmic cadence as thousands of feet marched in formation. The feet and ankles of the men quickly became soaked with the residual morning dew. The sun peeked out of the puffy white clouds and shone brightly.

The overall battle plan was to have the archers engage the Germans at long range. Once they did their damage, the archers would retreat through the ranks of the auxiliary cohorts. Simultaneously, five legions would advance forward to fill the checkered formation of the auxiliaries into a solid line. Stertinius and his cavalry would sweep around both flanks and harass the Germans. When needed, the reserve force would be called up to reinforce the front. It was a bold plan that required good timing. Germanicus was confident the Roman heavy infantry would withstand any German charge from the crest. They would stymie the

German advance, and then move forward to sweep over the enemy and push them off the hill.

Valerius took a swig from his goatskin container and replaced the stopper, his gaze never leaving the advancing cohorts and archers. Beyond the Roman vanguard, he saw the enemy troops massing. There were a lot of Germans out there. He stood ready with his comrades in arms, Wothar and Marcellus. His heavy armor breastplate and helmet made the warm morning even hotter. His bow was strapped to his back, along with a full quiver of arrows. His sword for the moment remained sheathed. Like every legionnaire, he wondered how this was going to play out. He glanced briefly to his right, where Germanicus and his staff sat upon their mounts.

Centurion Crispus strode to the front of his men. "Look at me, first century. Eyes on me only. Do not be concerned with that barbarian horde to our front. They will be here soon enough. You all know the drill. You have been through this before. Stay behind your shield. Block their thrusts and then smash them with your shields. When the opening appears, jab hard with your swords. Our foe has no chance against us, so listen to my commands, and everything will be fine."

Marcellus turned toward Valerius. "I like this centurion. He understands how to lead his men. I know some of the legionnaires are feeling a bit edgy about now, and that would include me, but he recognizes their fear and dispels it with words."

He had no sooner spoken when, like a giant wave, the Germans began their assault downhill toward the Roman lines. They roared their battle cries and struck their shields with spears and swords. The Roman archers let loose with their first volley, and then quickly a second. The Germans fell as the arrows struck human flesh, but it hardly slowed them down. The wall of men continued their advance. The buccina signaled the advance of the front five legions.

The roar of the German hoard grew louder. The Roman archers began retreating through the Roman lines, some not fast enough. As the ranks of the legions advanced, they were implacable. There was not a sound. At a distance of about fifty yards, the centurions shouted their commands. As one, the legionnaires reared back, using the shield as a counterweight, and hurled their deadly javelins toward the screaming Germans. This was followed by a second volley. As the Germans lacked any protective armor, the effect of the javelins was devastating. German warriors crumpled to the ground everywhere. The intense roar lost its volume, replaced by the shrieks of the wounded and the dying.

The command was issued to draw swords. There was a gigantic hiss as the deadly blades were withdrawn from their scabbards. The Roman shield wall was in place. The German advance, which had been temporarily stymied, renewed with even greater ferocity. There was a tremendous crash as the two forces collided. Roman swords darted from the shield barrier, seeking flesh. More Germans fell at the feet of the legionnaires. The Roman lines edged forward. The centurions bellowed their commands above the din. *"Push and stab. Push and stab."*

The clamor was overwhelming between the ringing of steel on steel and the cries and shrieks of the wounded. Valerius and friends slowly marched forward from the rear of the Praetorian lines. He turned in both directions and saw the mounted cavalry charging into the German flanks. So far it appeared that everything was going according to plan. There was no doubt that they would soon break the Germans and the rout would begin. Even now he could see some of the panicky foes streaming back toward the forest. Above the uproar, he heard the shrill war horns of the Germans. What could that mean? His question was answered shortly. A second massive wave of Germans swept out of the forest at the top of the hill. They charged at the center of the Roman lines, directly where he was standing.

"Marcellus, bows?"

"There is no time, Tribune. They will be on us soon."

Valerius gripped the bone hilt of his long sword tightly and dug his feet into the earth. He stared at the advancing mass of Germans. A hundred paces away, mounted on a gray steed, was none other than the figure of Arminius. He wished he had his bow strung and an arrow nocked. He would have liked to have attempted at least one shot at his nemesis, but there was no time. At that instant, the Germans crashed headlong into the Praetorian cohort. The Roman lines were pushed back. He glanced to his right. The cohort flank was crumbling, and

Germanicus and his command staff were directly in line of the German push.

Valerius did not hesitate. "Marcellus, Wothar, follow me. We need to protect our commander."

They joined a small circle of soldiers comprised mainly of the personal bodyguards and formed a cordon around the generals. The clash evolved into a series of savage individual battles. All cohesion within the ranks disappeared as the Germans penetrated the Roman shield wall. Valerius confronted a man and thrust his blade through his torso. He ran forward and engaged two Germans at once. His blade flashed a deadly arc, wounding both. He recklessly charged into a melee of legionnaires and Germans. He killed another with a thrust to the neck. Glancing about, he saw Wothar struggling with a large German warrior. The man towered over the others on the battlefield. Using his enormous strength, the German thrust his small shield against Wothar's shield, unbalancing him. That was all of the advantage he needed. His spear thrust was quick and hard, slicing through Wothar's torso.

Valerius screamed, "Wothar, no." He rushed toward his fallen comrade, realizing it was probably too late, for the wound was mortal. Sensing a presence to his left, he brought his sword up to block the blow, but it was too late. He was driven to his knees by a sword strike to his helmet. Fortunately for him, the reinforced helm saved him from death. He attempted to get up, but another blow struck his head. His face smashed into the turf, and his world turned black.

The German success was short-lived. The Romans recovered, and the two sides were at a stalemate, with neither side gaining ground. The blaring of the Roman signal horns reverberated above the din of battle. The three Roman legions in reserve hurriedly advanced to join the maelstrom of carnage in the once peaceful meadow. The backup force of nearly fifteen thousand men tipped the scales in favor of the legions. The centuries and cohorts of the reserve reinforced the Roman lines, and then relentlessly pressed their adversaries. The German lines held their ground for a surprising amount of time, but eventually the heavy infantry of the Romans prevailed and pushed the Germans slowly back. More Germans began to stream back to the safety of the forest, and then the Roman advance turned into a rout. There was total panic among the German tribes. Commands were issued to the heavy infantry cohorts of the legions to pursue and kill any Germans they encountered.

Arminius, astride his steed, cursed at the turn of events. What was worse was the attention he had drawn upon himself. Some of the Roman auxiliary forces of German origin had identified Arminius in the swirl of battle. It seemed they were all pointing at him. Arrows and javelins whistled past his head, narrowly missing him. He was not so lucky when one of the missiles grazed his left arm, opening up a lengthy gash. Surrounded by a retinue of his followers, he galloped off to his left. Moving away from the potential threat, Arminius dismounted, wiped his hand along his left arm, and smeared the blood over his face. The German leader emerged from the swirling mass of men, his features obscured by his own blood. He looked to rally his forces, but realized it was futile. His men were in full retreat back up the hill and into the awaiting forest, where they could not be pursued by the Romans.

Hunulf of the Dolgubni looked on in disgust. They were close to killing the Roman command staff, but then the Roman reserve legions arrived. He observed others turning about and running back up the rising ground and away from the battle. They were being pushed methodically back, and no amount of renewed ferocity was going to change the outcome; the Roman lines were thick with fresh troops. Hunulf turned to one of his subordinates, his voice filled with resignation. "Take the tribune with the fancy armor and large war bow back with us. At least we will have something to show for our losses."

Two men dragged the unconscious Roman back up the hill. Igomer, the senior of the two, strained to lift the Roman up the hill. There was no doubt why he was selected for this task. He stood out from the others because of his size and brawn. He muttered a curse. Why couldn't they just kill the Roman? It would be easier than transporting this lump back to their territory. Maybe Hunulf planned some sport with the Roman. A ritual killing perhaps? He was not sure it was worth the effort, but he followed his chieftain's orders. Igomer's spirit brightened. He had survived. They were going home. He would be with his plump wife and children again. Enough of these Romans and their killing ways. He and his family would be safe in the forests of their homeland.

Marcellus stood alone. The others, including the command staff, had advanced up the hill, chasing the fleeing Germans. The centurion had lost sight of Valerius and Wothar in the churning mass of humanity that defined the battle. What he did know was that neither of the two men were part of the advancing legions. So where were they? The Germans had come close to collapsing the small cordon of soldiers that protected the command staff, but in the end, the Romans had held. It was all chaos and confusion, with screams of the wounded and dying mingled with the flashing downstroke of swords. The immediate area was now devoid of Germans.

The centurion tried to calm himself, but his apprehension grew. Where was the tribune? Where was Wothar? He stepped through congealed puddles of blood and over dead bodies. He found Wothar. His face appeared calm, as if nothing was wrong, but his torso told a different story. He was pierced at least three times with what looked like spear wounds, his legs and chest covered in blood.

He knelt down and tenderly closed the German's eyes. He stood and moved on. He called out the tribune's name. All was silent. Marcellus thought back to the recent mayhem. Yes, the tribune stood right about here, not far from Wothar. He was sure of it. But there was no body. He looked again. There was no evidence of the tribune, no weapons, armor, or anything connected to him. Cursing, he hurried toward the hospital tents. Surely they would know.

The centurion entered the medical area. It was a ghastly scene. Men lay on cots and on the ground. Some stood, supported by their comrades. The moans of the wounded were interspersed with piercing screams. Off in the corner, a pile of bodies waited to be carried outside. He approached one of the physicians, his smock smeared with blood. Marcellus grabbed his arm to make sure he had his attention. "Have you treated a tribune today?"

The man shook his head. "Not that I remember, but you should ask them as well." He gestured to several other attired individuals feverishly applying bandages to stop the bleeding. "Now get your hands off me so I can get back to work." Marcellus looked up in exasperation. The other medical staff appeared totally preoccupied and would probably not remember if they had seen a tribune in this charnel house, but Marcellus was not to be denied. He hurried on to the next figure, and then the next. He was given the same answers and the same reproachful looks.

To his far right was a physician bent over a cot, examining a particularly bloody leg wound. The centurion barged in front of the patient, blocking the physician's view of the unfortunate legionnaire. "Did you treat a tribune today?"

The man frowned and scratched his head with a bloodied fingernail. "As a matter of fact, I did."

"Can I see him?"

"I suppose so. He is not going anywhere. He succumbed to his wounds. He is either in that pile over there," he gestured with his arm, "or he is outside with the other dead."

Marcellus abruptly turned away, his mind near the panic stage. He observed the heap of deceased legionnaires. To his relief, he did not see the form of the tribune. He turned several bloody corpses over just to be sure. He wiped his hands of the gore and went back outside.

Not far away was another collection of dead legionnaires. He grimly surveyed the Roman deceased and began sorting through the pile. Nothing. The group of pale flesh revealed no Valerius. Off to his right was another bunch. He noticed a glint of shiny armor befitting an officer. He turned the limp figure over. Sightless eyes stared back at him. It was a tribune, but not Valerius.

By Mars's arse, the tribune had to be somewhere. He would find the Praetorian cohort. They were the men who had been part of the fighting near the command staff. Someone had to have seen what fate became of the tribune, but first he was going back to the battlefield while there remained some daylight for one more look-see. He hurried over to the last place he had seen Valerius and Wothar. Huffing and out of breath, he arrived at the site. It remained the same as he had left it. No one had gathered up the dead as of yet. He stepped over Wothar and moved to his left several paces. There was a dead legionnaire with a gruesome wound to his neck, his head almost severed. Marcellus looked about. Nothing there. He moved on to another dead legionnaire, covered in blood. His battered shield lay off to one side. Marcellus kicked it out of the way in frustration. The centurion gasped at the revelation. There in the dirt was Valerius's helmet. There was no doubt this was the tribune's helmet. As with most officers, it was handcrafted and adorned with the figure of Mars in battle. He picked it up, observing several large dents.

Marcellus carried the helmet with him and hurried uphill toward where he believed the Praetorian cohort was located. He found them ensconced on the summit of the hill recently vacated by the fleeing Germans. The men were slumped on the ground, weary from the battle. They had been up before dawn and engaged the Germans in hours of unending combat. He observed Crispus engaged in a discussion with the other centurions of the cohort. The centurion looked up as Marcellus approached.

"Marcellus, glad you made it through that little disagreement we had today with the Germans."

"Crispus, pleased to see you and your officers on their feet and not the ground. As always, your men fought well."

"Aye, they did. It got a little dicey there for a while." He was about to continue the banter, but he noticed Marcellus's grim expression. "Something wrong? If you do not mind me saying so, you look a might stunned."

"Yes, there is a problem, and I need your help. Tribune Valerius is missing. His German aide, Wothar, was killed, and I found this on the battlefield." He held up Valerius's helmet. "I searched all of the medical tents and could not find him. His body is not on the battlefield. I thought maybe one of your men might have seen something."

Crispus replied, "Marcellus, we owe you. Nobody will admit it, but your training helped save our necks back there in the forest a few days ago. You came to the right place. Somebody in the cohort had to have seen something."

Crispus turned to his fellow centurions, who were gathered about him and had listened to the conversation. "I need you to go to your men right now and see if anyone knows what might have happened to the tribune. Let us make this quick. Get back here in two shakes of a ram's arse and let me know. Dismissed."

He returned his gaze to Marcellus. "Don't worry, Marcellus. We will find out what happened." He smiled. "Maybe he wandered off with the general's staff. We need to be optimistic here."

Marcellus frowned. "I would like to think so, but unfortunately I have this." He held up the tribune's helmet. Two of the centurions returned, shaking their heads. Nothing. Centurion Clodius of the second century returned with a legionnaire in tow. "This is Rufus. He told me he saw something that might be of interest. Tell them what you saw."

"I only glimpsed it for a moment, and I cannot really be sure, but I thought I saw some Germans dragging a Roman with an officer's breastplate back up the hill."

Crispus exploded. "And you did not bother to report this?"

Rufus lowered his head, cowered by the centurion. "I was fighting for my life at the time, and as I said, it was only a brief glimpse. With all of the men that were killed today, I did not believe that it was important."

Marcellus spoke. "Centurion Crispus, it is not his fault. He is correct. We were all surrounded by blood and death." He nodded to the legionnaire. "Rufus, is it? Thank you for the information."

Marcellus turned to Crispus. "Thank you for all of your help. I know you are all tired and in need of some wine and a good night's rest. I think we can all guess what has happened to the tribune. I must report this to the senior staff."

Crispus nodded. "I hope you find the tribune. He was a good officer."

Marcellus turned about and ventured off in search of the generals. He did not have to go far. He met Germanicus and several officers on the way back from the battlefield. There were a bevy of officers on their horses calmly discussing the day's events.

"Ah, Centurion Marcellus, glad to see you survived the hostilities, and from your appearance, not a mark on you. Where is your tribune? I need him to assist in the interrogation of the prisoners," Germanicus said.

"Sir, I was on my way to the headquarters to report to you. It appears we have a problem."

"How so, Centurion?"

"Sir, the tribune is missing. His body is not on the battlefield or in the tents of the *medicus*. A legionnaire in the Praetorian cohort has told me that he thought he saw the Germans dragging a Roman officer from the battlefield. I did recover this." He held up Valerius's helmet.

Germanicus frowned. "Have you spoken with Wothar?"

"Sir, Wothar is dead."

Germanicus's face remained impassive. "I see. This will not do." He motioned for one of his aides to come forward. "Go to General Stertinius and have him send a cavalry patrol to reconnoiter the immediate area of the German retreat and see if he can locate the tribune."

"Yes, sir." The man quickly rode away.

The general directed his attention toward Marcellus. "We will do whatever we can to locate Valerius. If you come by any more information, let me know."

Valerius awoke to the sensation of his feet dragging and an infernal pounding in his head. It felt as if someone had driven a spike into his skull. Despite the pain, he felt relieved that he was alive and he was being pulled to safety. He wondered briefly how badly he was injured when vertigo overtook him, and he started to retch. He heard muttered German curses, and he was thrown to the earth. His feeling turned to dread. Those were not Roman voices. In whose hands was he? He opened his eyes, but all he saw were blurred images. He concentrated, focusing his vision. Yes, those were Germans who were dragging him. *Had the legions lost?* he wondered. He smelled the musky odor of the forest. There was no mistaking that scent. It was a fecund aroma smell, not altogether unpleasant, and unique to the German woodlands. The musky tang was not associated with pleasant things. He saw trees, so the Germans must be retreating. Thank the gods for that. He heard a gruff voice.

"Get him on his feet. We must be away from here, the sooner the better. The Romans will send their cavalry after us."

He was roughly hauled to his feet. "Stand up, Roman, or I will end your pitiful life here."

Valerius, supported by two men, was half dragged away. His head ached. Thinking back to the battle, his despondency deepened. The death of Wothar was all his doing. He was the one that had convinced him to come back to Germania, and look what it had gotten him. Death at the end of a spear. To Hades with his life. Valerius gritted his teeth. If this was his end, so be it.

After what seemed like a long time, they stopped in a small glade for a rest. He had no idea of how far they had journeyed or what direction they were moving. He looked about at the milling group. His captors numbered some forty men. He was able to identify their leader. He was a short, older man who commanded tremendous respect. All of the warriors, though much larger and younger, deferred to him and carried out his orders without delay. They called him Hunulf. Valerius's two captors were nasty-looking characters. They snarled at him and cuffed him about the head when he could not keep up with the pack. Their feelings about him were obvious; they wanted to kill him—the sooner the better. He conjectured that for some reason, it was the chieftain called Hunulf who wanted him alive. Why, he did not know. They had already stripped him of his sword, armor, and bow. What else did they want? Perhaps they desired him for entertainment in some slow, ritualistic killing. He shuddered involuntarily. He knew how cruel these Germans could be.

He glanced up from his sitting position, avoiding the hostile glares. These men were in a bad disposition. He expected no sympathy. His situation was hopeless. There would be no pursuit from the Romans. It was too dangerous for the legions to chase the Germans into their woodlands; the possibility of ambush was too great. Besides, he was only a lowly tribune, not worth risking Roman lives. Valerius pondered escape, but there was no way. His captors were too numerous. As if the Germans had read his thoughts, Hunulf barked a command. Valerius did not catch the entire phrase, but he soon understood its meaning. His two jailers pushed him flat on the ground and bound his wrists behind his back tightly with rope. The one grinned as he pulled the knot extratight, causing him to gasp with pain.

He was hauled to his feet. They were moving at a rapid pace once again. Valerius stumbled along, barely able to keep up. His bound arms made it difficult for him to walk with any semblance of a tempo, plus his head injury made his head swim with vertigo off and on. He tripped over an exposed root and fell on his face, opening a cut over his left eyebrow. Harsh words were directed at him. He was kicked several times in the ribs, heaved to his feet, and forced to move.

The band moved through forest and field for the remainder of the day. Valerius thought he would collapse on several occasions. Even his German captors appeared exhausted. They finally stopped for the night. Several men gathered wood and built a blazing fire. Clearly the men were unafraid of any Roman presence. These were German lands. The men broke out their provisions of dried meat and gnawed hungrily on their meager rations. Valerius was given nothing except for a gulp of water. His feet were bound, and then he was tied around the waist to a tree. He was not going anywhere. He shivered in the cold night air, wondering about Marcellus. Had he survived? He hoped so. The centurion deserved a long life and a pension given his service to Rome. He trusted Marcellus would write a letter to his parents, letting them know of his fate. By the time they received it, he would probably be dead. He never finished his thoughts. Drained from the day's events, he collapsed in sleep.

Marcellus sat in his cramped quarters, wondering of the fate of his tribune. Perhaps he lived, but what would the Germans do to him? Nothing pleasant, that was for sure. Why did this particular bunch of Germans take him as a captive rather than kill him on the battlefield? He knew that in some of Rome's past conquests, military officers had been held for ransom, but the Germans did not believe in that sort of thing. His musings were interrupted by a messenger.

"Centurion Marcellus, you are wanted at the Praetorium at once."

Marcellus nodded and then rose. He stooped over and retrieved his armor, which he had meticulously cleaned the night before, scouring off grime and splattered blood. He hurriedly donned his equipment and helmet and set off in the direction of the command tent. He knew the news would not be good, and the best he could hope for was that the tribune was still missing.

Upon reaching the Praetorium, he identified himself and was immediately ushered into the inner headquarters. Germanicus and several aides were studying a map of the territory. The general looked up.

"Ah, there you are, Centurion. Let me get right to it. General Stertinius sent out cavalry patrols at least several miles into the woodlands in the direction of the German retreat. They were forbidden to travel any farther. Nothing was found except dead or dying Germans. I could offer platitudes that the tribune remains alive and so forth, but the fact is his outlook is grim. You understand."

Marcellus responded, hoping his voice would not betray his feelings. "Sir, I do. I guess at this point the only thing to say is that he may be alive, and if so, he has a chance, albeit a slim one, to get back here."

Germanicus replied, although his voice lacked conviction, "Yes, there is always a chance."

"Sir, I know it is customary for the commanding officer to notify the next of kin about these matters. I would like to take the responsibility of writing that letter. I knew him better than anyone here, and I grew fond of his parents when I stayed at his house in Rome. I would humbly ask your permission to script that message."

"I see. Yes, I think that would be a good idea. I do not relish writing such letters, and the fact that you were so close to him and his parents makes sense. Once you are finished, give it to one of my aides, and it will delivered by military courier to Rome. You are dismissed."

The centurion did an about-face and departed.

Marcellus sat in his tent and opened the flaps for light. He sat on the camp stool and began composing.

Dear Sentius and Vispania,

I hope you are well and this letter finds you in good health. I have some bad news, and I will get to it directly. The legions recently engaged the Germans, and your son has gone missing. Cavalry patrols were sent out in all directions, but the whereabouts of your son remain unknown. He is believed to have been captured by the Germans. There was one witness who stated that he saw a Roman officer dragged away by the Germans. I know this is difficult for you to grasp. I will not give you false hope and tell you everything will be fine and Valerius will return to us one day. However, as far as we know, he is still alive, and as long as he is alive, there is always hope. I cannot put into words how upset I am at these developments, and I know this is a terrible blow to you. Please know that we will do everything in our power to recover the tribune, alive. This campaign is not over, and I will not rest until we get your son back.

Marcellus

XV

Hereca walked through the center of her village, savoring the warm breeze that swelled the surrounding treetops. Off in the distance, the cattle mooed. In the adjacent fields, she observed some of her tribal kin beginning the harvest of this year's barley crop. It would be a good one. The weather had been near perfect, sunny and warm, with just the right amount of rain. Tall and strong, she continued her trek toward the village shrine. She had come to pay homage to Wodan and pray for the safe return of her father, Hunulf, and the warriors from her village. They had been gone to fight the Romans many weeks now.

The last time the men had departed to do battle the previous fall, they had returned triumphant. The warriors had brought back much in the way of bounty—armor, weapons, and coins—but for her and many others, it had been a shallow victory. She and a large number of other women had become widows. She thought briefly of her dead husband, Valta. He had been a good man, although not a great warrior. He was a follower, not a leader. Nevertheless, he had always treated her well and had not raised a hand to her. Perhaps that was because her father would probably have killed him if he did.

Hereca had begged her father to allow her to accompany the men on this latest excursion against the Romans, not as a cook or washer of clothes but as a warrior. She wanted to go to battle against the Romans to avenge her husband. She had argued that she could throw a javelin just as far as most of the men. She was strong and lithe and capable of many of the warrior feats of those who accompanied her father. He did not give it much thought, dismissing her entreaty immediately. He stated that he had enough to worry about, and the safety of his only daughter would just add to that burden. He had told her that the Romans were a tough and brutal adversary, and he would not lose his daughter to their killing ways. She had continued to plead but to no avail. He had finally lost his patience and yelled at her mother, Clonid, to take control of the situation. Hereca had sulked for days afterward, unwilling to concede that her father was probably correct in his dismissal of her request.

Hereca approached the stone shrine in the wooded glade. No one was there. She kneeled and said a prayer to Wodan, the all-father, for Hunulf and the rest of the men accompanying him. She looked up briefly, and then bowed her head again. It was so peaceful here. A single shaft of sunlight penetrated the bordering trees, and the songs of nesting birds filled the air. She wondered when the men would be back and how many would not return. She cursed the Romans for bringing death to her people. She had never met a Roman, but she hated them for what their soldiers had done. She wished again that she had gone with her father so she could throw her javelins at the Roman soldiers.

Valerius stumbled onward now late into the afternoon. He had fallen several times today and was rewarded each time with savage kicks. He did not know how much longer he could keep up this pace. He sensed the Germans were anxious to return home and increased the speed even more. The men pointed to a small clearing up ahead. They were going to stop here for the night. Valerius understood everything they said, but his German captors did not know that. Perhaps he could gain some advantage. He doubted it, but for now, it was something to hang on to. He would continue his deception until the proper moment.

He sat on the ground with his knees up. He rested his head on his legs, hiding his face from his captors. A man came over and nudged none too gently with the butt of a spear. He gestured with a skin full of water. Valerius nodded. He squirted some water into his mouth. He gulped it greedily and resumed his previous position.

Another hulking figure approached and tapped Valerius on the head none too gently with the butt end of his spear. "We do not like you, Roman. I do not know why our chieftain brought you along. We should have finished you back there on the battlefield. In any event, it is just a temporary reprieve. Your end will not be pleasant. The people of my village will be angry from our losses and demand that you be sacrificed. What do you think of that?"

Valerius looked back at the man with a blank expression, pretending not to understand. This only served to inflame the anger of the warrior. He raised his spear menacingly. Hunulf yelled at him, "Not now, Guntar. We will deal with him when we get back." Guntar spit on Valerius and returned to his clansmen, huddled by a small fire.

They traveled several more grueling days. With his injuries and lack of food, Valerius barely managed to keep up. On those occasions when he faltered, he was kicked and beaten by his captors. His facial features were distorted and swollen from the thumpings. Several times he just wanted to give up and have the Germans kill him where he fell, but something pushed him onward. Some spark kept him going. At one point during the brutal trek after he had fallen, one of his captors stood poised over him with a spear at his neck. He looked to his leader questioningly. The chieftain spoke. "Nay, hold that thrust. We have brought him this far. Keep him alive."

They trekked until dusk, stopping when it became dark. Valerius immediately fell to the turf. He shivered in the evening air, numbly looking up to the heavens, observing the stars. He thought of Captain Sabinus. He should have taken up his offer and joined the navy. His fate would have been better than this. The good captain had tutored him aboard the ship on how to read the night sky. He found the handle of the dipper and found the star that always pointed north. Yes, they had traveled that direction. He knew that much. He was far north of where any Roman soldier had ventured, even before the Teutoburg disaster, and there was no hope of rescue. None!

He ruminated briefly about Marcellus. They had gone through much together. No other tribune or centurion had survived the Teutoburg, but they had. He reckoned he had tempted the Goddess Fortuna too many times. He did not hate the Germans. They were only defending their homeland. It was not a matter of revenge that brought him back here. It was his obligation to serve. Some might say he returned to the German woodlands for the glory of Rome, but glory be stuffed. When you are on the bloody battleground, there is no such thing as glory—only courage and survival. He looked back up at the heavens, pondering how many more nights he had remaining in his life. Probably not many, he mused.

The Dolgubni were off again early the next morning. Valerius struggled to keep up. Each time he fell behind, his captors would strike him about the head and body. Eager to finish their journey, they marched hard and did not stop even for a food or water break. Later in the afternoon, the band of warriors bypassed several settlements. Valerius's spirit was bolstered by the thought that they had to be getting close. The Germans were also weary, but their mood seemed to be lifting. He heard several laugh and make boastful comments about what they would be doing with their wives tonight. Would he be able to finish the journey? He had no sooner asked himself the question when off in the distance, a horn blared a deep, mournful sound. The men cheered. Valerius looked up ahead. This had to be their destination.

The group entered a settlement that featured a large number of mud and wooden huts with thatched roofs. They were scattered about in no particular order, and none were connected. Adjacent to the village, he observed pastures with grazing cattle and horses. Directly ahead were lush fields of crops. The people of the hamlet rushed to welcome their returning warriors. There were great cries of joy, mingled with anguished moans. Valerius sensed that there were a number of new widows. He stood in the center of the throng as returning men greeted their families.

At first he was ignored, but gradually the people of the village began to glower at him, their glances filled with hostility. Some had never seen a Roman before. He stood apart from the Germans, uncomfortable with the sudden attention directed at him. He shifted his weight on his feet and cast his eyes downward, but there was no escaping the hate-filled gazes. Now what? He cringed inwardly, waiting for the first blow to be struck.

Hunulf separated himself from the embrace of his wife, Clonid, and daughter, Hereca. He held up his arms and shouted, "We have brought back with us a Roman officer, whom we captured in battle. Behold our enemy." Many jeered, and some of the men spit on him. Valerius stood with his eyes downcast. He sensed his life hung by a thread and that any moment he would be torn asunder by the angry villagers.

Hunulf continued, "He does not look so invincible now, does he?" There was more jeering and hurled insults. Clods of dirt and stones were flung in his direction. "We shall have to arrange a fitting end for our Roman captive." The villagers cheered the chieftain's words. Hunulf turned to two of his warriors. "Tie him securely to the post in the village center. We can decide his fate later."

That evening, Valerius awoke to someone staring at him. He had passed out in the mud shortly after being secured to a solid wooden post driven deeply into the ground. His arms were bound behind his back by rawhide strips, and his feet were also tightly bound. He glanced up from his sitting position to see the face of a beautiful woman. She stared hard at him. "So this is what you filthy Romans look like. Your soldiers killed my husband last year when we defeated you in the forest. There are many widows in our village thanks to your invading army." Valerius remained silent, not letting on that he understood every word she had said. She scowled at him in silent contempt.

She continued, "My father, Hunulf, is the village chieftain. By the time we are finished with you, you will beg for death. Somehow I thought you would be more imposing, but you are not. Compared to our strong German men, you are but a weakling. Look at you—trussed up like a pig waiting for the slaughter." She laughed in derision and walked away.

It was a bad night for Valerius. He was awakened from his stupor by a deluge of rain that thoroughly soaked him in a matter of moments.

It was impossible for him to sleep. He shivered as the cold rain pelted him in a bed of mud. He attempted to think pleasant thoughts, but he was too uncomfortable. He tried to shift his body to a more relaxed position, but he could not, for he was bound too tightly. The rain continued to pour, and dawn refused to come. He quivered uncontrollably. He doubted he would last much longer given his weakened state. He did not really care anymore. He wanted it to end. He would welcome death.

"Roman, look at me." Valerius felt his face slapped, but he could not open his eyes and focus. He was slapped again. He groggily looked up and was greeted by the face of Hunulf. Two warriors stood behind him. The chieftain turned toward his two men. "I do not want our prisoner expiring from the elements before we have had our sport with him. Take him to the guest hut and give him dry clothes and food. After that, tie him up again. These Romans are not tough like the Germans. They are weak. I will look in on him later this afternoon. Now get him out of my sight."

Valerius awoke, feeling almost human again. He was curled up on a floor of matted straw. A wool blanket had been thrown over him. He heard someone come in, snort in derision, and then leave. He was not sure if it was Hunulf or not. He did not care. He just wanted to rest and let his body heal. His earlier thoughts of death had been replaced with the comfort of being dry and warm. He did not stay awake for long. He passed out once more.

After several more days, he had regained some of his strength, and even the dull ache in his head seemed to be moderating. He continued to be fed and his bonds loosened. His thoughts returned to Rome and Calpurnia. His dreams had turned to ashes so quickly. He attempted to be stoic about the whole thing, but he continued to hurt from the loss. *Life could be so cruel,* he thought. He would be joining Calpurnia soon in the netherworld, of that he had no doubt. He wondered when they would come for him. Certainly it would be soon.

He had his answer two days later. He heard many voices from outside the walls of his prison. Perhaps they were approaching to get him.

Two stout figures appeared in the entranceway and unceremoniously dragged him by the arms out into the middle of the settlement. Valerius looked about and was surprised at the large number of people, perhaps five hundred, who had gathered around. There were taunts and curses directed at him. The two men held him firmly.

Hunulf strode up to him, then turned and faced his tribe members. "Here is our prize from the fight, a Roman officer. What a pathetic excuse for a man." More taunts and hoots filled the air. Hunulf was making a show out of Valerius's demise. "What shall we do with our enemy?"

Hunulf's words incited the crowd even further. "Kill him, kill him," they shouted. The chieftain smiled broadly. "Kill him, you say? Yes, but how? Shall we let the priestesses slowly open his belly, or maybe we should burn him in a wicker cage?" The crowd shouted for justice. Some yelled loudly for the priestesses to take charge; others preferred the death by fire. Hunulf raised his arms for silence. "Perhaps we shall dismember him piece by piece. Start with his eyes, his tongue, ears, genitals, and then move on to his hands and feet." There were more cacophonous shouts. The people were now in a state of frenzy.

Valerius felt his anger bloom. He would not be sacrificed like some farm animal. He was a Roman officer and would go down fighting. He recalled what Wothar had taught him of German customs. Many times captives from other tribes were forced to fight the village champion rather than be executed. This offered the prisoner an honorable death, one fitting for a warrior. If victorious, one might be spared. He did not believe he had much of a chance against a village champion given his limited fighting skills and weakened state, but it was a chance.

Hunulf held up his hands for silence. "What shall—"

"I am a Roman officer of the imperial legions and deserve a noble death. I challenge the village champion to individual combat," shouted Valerius.

There was a stunned silence. Hunulf looked at him incredulously. He rushed over to him and glowered at him, face-to-face. "You speak our words, Roman?"

Valerius stared back at him. "We Romans are capable of many things." He snorted contemptuously at Hunulf.

The enraged chieftain withdrew his knife from its sheath and placed it at Valerius's throat.

"What makes you think you deserve the right to individual combat? That is reserved only for German warriors. I should cut your throat."

The gathering shouted in agreement. "Kill him. Kill him now," they shouted.

Valerius puffed his chest out and stared boldly at the horde. "I am a Roman officer. I deserve to die an honorable death in combat. What is the matter? Are you afraid I will defeat your champion? Where is he? Who holds this title in the village?"

Valerius had chosen his words carefully. He was challenging the reputation of the tribe's most capable fighting man. He knew the figure would come forward to fight him. Pride demanded that. The village champion would be his unlikely ally in his quest for individual combat.

His ploy succeeded. A bulky warrior strode forward. It was Guntar, the man who wanted to slay him on their journey here. "I will fight you, Roman. You will beg for death by the time I am finished with you." For effect, he waved his arms upward, inflaming the crowd. They began chanting. "Guntar, Guntar."

Hunulf raised his arms for silence. Valerius seized the opening, not waiting his turn to speak. He shouted above the crowd, pointing contemptuously at Guntar. "That is your champion, that fat bag of wind? That is the best you can do?"

Guntar snarled and rushed forward, knocking Valerius to the ground. "I will fight you, Roman dog. Your death will be slow and painful." The people yelled in triumph. They wanted to see a match and the Roman dead. Valerius suppressed a grin. He had manipulated the crowd. Now all he had to do was defeat Guntar. Not likely, but at least he had a chance.

Hunulf spoke. "You shall have your wish, Roman. Be prepared to meet your gods."

Valerius was hauled to a circular bowl, a natural arena, on a nearby hillside. Preparations were hastily made for a fighting arena. Long wooden poles were laid out in a rough square to establish boundaries for the duel. The mob of villagers stood on the slope of the hill so that all could witness the fight. The bonds that fastened Valerius's hands and feet were cut away. He rubbed them vigorously to restore circulation. He gazed up and assessed his opponent. The man was much larger than Valerius. More to the point, he was huge, towering over Valerius's slim form. The German's size and strength were his advantage. Valerius would need to use his speed and guile to defeat him. He said a small prayer to Mars for having the wisdom to continue his practice with the German spear and shield against Wothar, even when they were at the Roman camp in Germania. Guntar did not know he had been trained to fight in the German style. Good. He wanted his opponent overconfident.

Valerius was handed a small rectangular shield, similar to the one he had trained with against Wothar. Next, a long spear was thrust into his hands. He examined the shaft and the pointed iron tip to ensure it was securely fastened.

Guntar used the occasion to mock his opponent. "You use the pointed end against your adversary." The gathering erupted in laughter.

Valerius looked up and grinned back at Guntar. "Too bad it will soon be sticking up your arse." His retort was carefully crafted to goad his opponent, get him enraged, and have him forget his fighting skills. Valerius had been taught at an early age in his training as a tribune that it was cold calculation and skill that won in combat, not anger. Fury, no matter how intense, often resulted in the other side winning. His training centurion repeatedly quoted the Roman writer and philosopher Horace. *"Anger is momentary madness. Control your passion or it will control you."* Anything he could do to get under Guntar's skin would be to his advantage.

Guntar scowled in rage, his eyes blazing. The men stood at opposite sides of the square. Hunulf approached him. "You got your wish, Roman. The rules are as follows. You fight with German weapons, not your large Roman shields and stabbing swords. It is a fight to the death. You are not permitted to trespass beyond the wooden boundary poles. If you do, you will be executed on the spot. Oh, and just so you know, Guntar has never been defeated. He has slaughtered many Roman soldiers." He laughed and walked away.

Valerius stood ready. He looked across at Guntar. The man appeared angry and overconfident. Excellent. This would be beneficial to Valerius. He might prevail, although he gauged his chances as slim. If he did win, he had no idea what the Germans would do to him.

Hunulf stood in the middle of the square and raised his right arm. He slowly backed toward the edge and then abruptly lowered his arm.

Valerius thought he was ready, but he was not prepared for the speed and ferocity of Guntar's attack. The huge warrior bull rushed him, almost knocking him over. The spear jabbed at his head. Valerius managed to barely parry the thrust with his shield and darted to his left. The spearpoint narrowly missed his face but gashed his left ear, drawing a crimson steam of blood. The audience howled in satisfaction. The tribune was circling warily, looking for an opening, when Guntar charged again. Valerius shifted to his right. His foe thrust out his leg, tripping Valerius. The spear descended, aimed for Valerius's midsection. At the last moment, he flicked his shield out and deflected the thrust. He quickly regained his fighting posture before Guntar could exploit the situation. The German snarled in frustration, surprised that he had not skewered the Roman by now.

Valerius stood across the crude arena, gesturing for Guntar to come. The German howled with fury and charged. The tribune quickly shifted to his right and managed to punch his opponent in the face with the light shield as he went by him, causing a trickle of blood above his right eye. It was an insignificant wound, but the audience gasped at the turn of events. This was not supposed to happen. Guntar stalked after Valerius. The tribune nimbly avoided the massive figure and the menacing spearpoint. Ever the aggressor, the German charged again and then again.

"Stand still and fight, Roman. Stop running away, and meet your death. I will be merciful."

Valerius motioned for Guntar to come get him. Mindful of Wothar's tutelage, he kept his knees slightly flexed, his shield at chest height, and his grip down on the spear shaft for better control. He looked for a weakness in the German's defense, but as of yet, nothing had presented itself. He swallowed hard, panting slightly. Guntar jabbed hard at his legs. Valerius quickly blocked the blow with his shield and counter-thrust at the German's torso. Guntar barely blocked it in time. The man gaped at him in surprise. That had been close. Valerius backed away and gesticulated with his shield arm once again for his foe to come get him.

"Come on, champion. I thought you would have me spitted upon your spear by now. This is the best you can do?"

Guntar roared in frustration. He advanced, his aim to bowl over the annoying Roman. Valerius was ready for him. He smoothly adjusted his body to the left, avoiding the charging figure. There it was. A brief opening appeared. He seized the initiative and flicked his spear out, gouging the flesh on the German's left arm. Guntar winced at his wound, hissing in pain. Blood trickled down his arm. The cheers and shouting from the villagers went silent with the wounding of their defender. Back and forth it went. A series of charges and countercharges ensued, with neither man gaining the advantage. Both men were streaming sweat and gasping for air on the warm summer day.

The tribune felt his stamina wilting. His wounds and captivity had sapped his strength. He could not go on much longer. Valerius circled again, gesturing at Guntar, egging him on and hoping for a mistake. It was the German who did something unexpected. He kicked a clot of dirt into Valerius's face. Temporarily blinded, he retreated to the edge of the arena, with the hulking German in pursuit. The man thrust with his spear. Valerius dodged left, but felt the spearpoint gouge his ribs, drawing a gush of blood. He inhaled deeply, grunting against the pain. He dared not look down lest his attention get diverted for an instant.

He gasped in agony and held his arm briefly against his side to stem the flow. The blood dripped on to the bare earth. The villagers shouted in a frenzy. They were anxious for the kill.

The confident German approached again, a large grin creasing his face. "Your time is finished, Roman."

Valerius knew he must do something quickly. His movements were no longer crisp, and his fatigue was growing. He recalled Wothar's ploy of the ground roll and tripping the opponent. It was a drastic maneuver and one of desperation, but something he needed to do. Wothar had told him it was only to be used as a last resort. He was at that point. He was out of options.

He must get in close to his opponent. That should not be a problem given the proclivity of the German to constantly attack. He waited for the inevitable advance toward him. Sure enough, Guntar came at him. Valerius stepped forward, then ducked down and rolled into Guntar's legs, simultaneously using the spear shaft to trip his opponent. It succeeded! The German crashed heavily onto the ground, stunned by the reversal. Valerius was up in a flash. He stomped on the man's spear arm, rendering him weaponless. He hovered the lethal spear tip at Guntar's throat and yelled, "*Yield.*"

There was a collective gasp from the audience. Guntar lay on the ground and snarled at Valerius.

Hunulf slowly approached the Roman. "You have the right to kill him. It is customary to finish off the defeated."

Valerius stared hard at Hunulf. "I do not want to kill him. I do not hate him. He is a fine warrior."

"You tricked me, Roman," snarled the prone figure.

"Aye, that I did—a maneuver I learned from another German like you," said Valerius. He discarded his spear and offered a hand to the prone Guntar. The man ignored the gesture, rose, and stalked away.

Hunulf gestured to several of his men. Valerius was seized and led back to captivity in the hut, but he was still alive. He knew not what the Germans would do to him, but for now, he still breathed. An old woman accompanied by two burly guards escorted him to his dwelling. The woman, who must have some skill as a healer, applied a poultice, binding his wounded side, and departed. Valerius briefly pondered his new fate, then collapsed in sleep.

The chieftain returned the next day. Valerius sat up to meet his captor, his face contorting in pain from his wounded side. Hunulf gestured to the two guards accompanying him to unbind the captive.

"I do not know what to do with you, Roman. Many of the tribal elders want to execute you. The members of my village, including my daughter, have no love for you. So again, what am I to do with you?" He paused, glaring at the tribune. There was a silence between the two men. He continued, "Roman, you are a strange one. I have never met a Roman who could speak our language and fight with our weapons. Furthermore, I noted what you did to Guntar. You taunted him, distracting him before you defeated him with that ruse. Impressive. Where did you learn such tricks?"

"I had a good teacher." Valerius remained silent except for his brief remark.

"You had a good teacher. That is all you have to say? I think there is more to it than that. Tell me more."

"My commanding officer thought it would be wise if I learned your language. He did not trust the German interpreters. I took his instructions one step more, and learned how to fight and think like a German. I know all about your culture, your beliefs."

"I see. Who is this German?"

"He was of the Batavi. His name was Wothar."

"Was?"

"Yes, he died in the last battle. He was a good friend."

Hunulf's expression remained impassive. He was silent for a time, assessing the tribune's words. "You are a Roman officer, who speaks our words and can fight like a German. When you were captured, you were in possession of a giant war bow. A strange weapon for an officer, no?"

"A centurion friend of mine taught me to shoot that. It saved my life in the Teutoburg."

The chieftain's face conveyed shock. "You were in the Teutoburg and survived?"

"I did. I made my way to the Rhine with a few others."

Hunulf spoke slowly. "I seem to recall a story about two Romans in the Teutoburg using these terrible large war bows against us. I did not put much credence to it. That was you?"

"It was. Too bad I could not have put it to better use when we last met in battle."

Hunulf glared at Valerius. "You must have powerful gods to have survived the Teutoburg and then be dragged here only to defeat Guntar, our champion. You are an unusual one. I will think more about your fate. We will speak some more later." He turned about and departed.

Valerius stood, flexing his arms and legs. He was not bound, but there were two guards at his door. Both men viewed him warily. After all, he had defeated their champion in combat. They were no longer watching a bedraggled tribune, but rather a warrior of great skill. He looked up at them, and they turned away.

He was alive. Based upon his conversation with Hunulf, his prospects did not appear as bleak. He believed they would have killed him already if they intended to do so. He pondered what his future status might be. Would he be a slave? What would be his fate?

Hunulf returned to his dwelling, where his wife and daughter stood waiting. "What are you going to do with the Roman?" demanded his wife.

Hunulf, angered at her caustic tone, snapped back, "I am not sure. I will spare him for now."

"How can you, Father?" his infuriated daughter inquired.

"Because he defeated Guntar in single combat. We have always spared anyone who could conquer our champion—you know that."

His wife snorted. "When was the last time someone defeated our champion? It was before you were even the chieftain."

Hunulf responded, "It was, but our tradition has always been to spare the victor."

Hereca's eyes blazed in fury. "Tradition be damned. He is a Roman. He should be executed."

Hunulf countered, "He has powerful gods. He says he fought in the Teutoburg Forest and survived."

"Then he could have been the Roman who killed my husband." With that, she stormed out of the dwelling. Hunulf watched her retreating form and cursed.

"I am the chieftain, and I make the decisions," he shouted after her.

His wife looked at him in disdain, and then followed her daughter outside.

Hunulf appeared the next day. Valerius rose when the chieftain entered. "You do not know how much trouble you have caused me, Roman." He frowned in disgust. "My wife and daughter want you killed. Now I must endure their scorn. I must say I was of the same mind, that is, to kill you, but you defeated our champion in battle. Therefore I felt obligated to spare you."

Valerius spoke. "Will I be a prisoner? What is my status?"

Hunulf stroked his chin in thought. "I am not sure. This has never happened before while I have been chieftain. You will be free to walk about in our village, but if you attempt to flee, you will be killed. We will hunt you down like a wounded stag. Besides, the nearest friendly Roman is a long way from here, at least five days march. You would not get far."

"Understood. By the way, my name is Valerius."

Hunulf ignored the friendly entreaty. "And another thing, Roman: be careful what you do and say. The people do not like you and would rather see you dead." He turned brusquely and departed.

Meanwhile, many days march to the south, the army of Germanicus was clashing once again with the barbarian forces. The Germans had offered to do battle once again. This time they were entrenched upon a slight ridge and had constructed an earthen wall, replete with a barricade of woven branches and vines. Two charges by the legions had been repulsed by the Germans, leaving the field strewn with Roman bodies. The piles of Roman dead in front of the German barrier were testimony to the difficulty of overcoming the German redoubt.

Marcellus grimly surveyed the scene before him. He peered forward at the barricade once more. The ballista would clear that wall in a hurry, but the ballista had been left behind many weeks ago because of the difficulty of transporting the heavy equipment in bad terrain.

Centurion Crispus approached Marcellus. "We are next. Germanicus is throwing us at the wall. It needs to be breached. The legions have lost a lot of men."

Marcellus responded, "It is a nasty business storming these barricades. Where would you like me to be positioned?"

"You are not obligated to be part of this," Crispus replied.

"Nonsense. This is my unit, and I will do what I can to move these bloody arseholes off that wall."

Crispus smiled. "I could use the help. Why don't you position yourself in the rear to keep things moving forward? Once we penetrate the barrier, help marshal the forces to exploit the breakthrough."

"Count me in. Now tell me how you plan to scale that wall and put a hurt on these Germans."

Crispus replied, "I have talked to my centurions about this. We are going to use our own men as platforms to elevate our men up to the height of the wall. First the ranks will hurl their javelins, and then we will advance in a testudo formation so that we are completely protected. Once we get close, the front ranks will advance to the base of the barricade and kneel, with the shields covering their backs. The next ranks will advance and then vault up to the top of the wall and through the makeshift barrier."

Marcellus grinned. "I like it. That's what I would do. Let's go kill some Germans."

The Praetorian cohort, along with the other reserve forces, were moved forward from the rear position. They were ready. Centurion Crispus drew his sword, pointed it at the barricade, and bawled his order: *"Forward."*

The cohort and the other legionary forces advanced. The distance was not that far, perhaps a hundred paces. *"Open ranks."*

The centuries of the cohort spread out. Across the width of the battlefield, the other legions performed a similar act. They neared the German wall to about twenty-five paces away. *"Javelins, release."*

A shower of the heavily front-loaded spears descended upon the German position. It had little impact. The Germans ducked behind their barricade and let the missiles pass overhead or strike the wall.

"Form testudos."

The ranks of the legions stormed the wall, their shields held before them covering most of their bodies. Marcellus followed the three waves of legionnaires of the first century. They reached the German barricade, and then things became difficult. The ditch and mud wall were challenging to ascend because of the steepness and the slick surface. The recent rain and the blood of the legionnaires from the previous charges had made the soil a thick ooze, which made footing nearly impossible. The first rank squatted down with their shields overhead. The second and third ranks stepped on the shields and launched themselves at the wall.

The Romans achieved some success. They vaulted upward and crashed through the barrier using their shields. The Germans countered by rushing reinforcements to the breaches and overwhelming those initial legionnaires who had penetrated the wall. More Romans died, but they eventually breached the wall in too many places for the Germans to plug all of the gaps.

Marcellus stepped forward, treading on several bodies, and then climbed up to the barrier. With a snarl, he knocked over the woven branches and engaged a German warrior armed with a spear. Marcellus deflected the spear thrust with his shield and then stabbed quickly with his sword. The blade entered about halfway through the figure's torso. His foe toppled off the wall and remained still. More legionnaires ascended the wall and slew the German defenders. It turned into a rout. The Germans fled into the forest, leaving their dead and wounded behind.

To the rear of the bloody conflict, Germanicus sat upon his steed, surveying the brutal battle taking place before him. He was surprised the Germans had offered to do battle again. Although short on supplies, Germanicus had seized the opportunity. He needed to crush these barbarians and kill Arminius. He watched as the third wave of legionnaires crossed the ditch and charged over the earth redoubt. The general grimaced as he watched the Germans melt back into the forest, limiting any pursuit.

Tubero nudged his mount forward. "Another great victory, sir."

Germanicus remained silent.

Tubero felt the need to add to his comment. "The Germans are routed again. Are you not pleased?"

"Tubero, I find it difficult to match your enthusiasm. It is late in the season, and our supplies are dwindling. We will shortly need to retreat back to the Rhine."

Tubero responded, "Retreat, sir? I would say it is more like a strategic withdrawal in force. No one is pressuring us."

"Call it what you will. We are vacating the area. Let me ask you something, Tubero. Would you be comfortable establishing a garrison here for the winter?"

Tubero frowned. "No, sir. The place is too perilous to risk the lives of legionnaires."

Germanicus spun away from the battle and toward Tubero. "Then we have failed."

"But, sir—"

Germanicus cut off Tubero's remarks with a wave of his arm. "Have we damaged the forces of Arminius's coalition? Yes, but not enough. They are still a viable foe, and Arminius, as far as we know, is still alive. We have lost many good soldiers and a great deal of equipment, with little to show in the way of our accomplishments. This was supposed to be a short campaign to bring the lands of Germania under the heel of Rome, and we have not."

Germanicus guided his horse away from Tubero and the others, then turned his attention back to the battlefield.

Noting the absence of any guards, Valerius decided to exit his former prison and stroll about the settlement. He was tired of his confinement and needed some fresh air. Unsure of what reception he might receive, he stepped outside. There were people moving about. Those with whom he made eye contact rewarded him with unfriendly glances. A woman and two young children approached. She looked up and spotted him, then quickly scurried away, pushing her children to avoid any proximity to him. This was going well, he thought. What should he do next? Standing in the village center, he paused and looked about. No one would venture near him. Disappointed, he returned to his hut.

Life was uneventful over the next few days. In fact, it was exceedingly boring. No one communicated with him. The extent of his social interaction was someone placing food and drink in his dwelling. Each day Valerius would extend his walks closer to the edge of the village. He even ventured into the plowed fields ripe with crops and into the pastures with cattle and sheep. He did not, however, tread into the woodlands beyond. They might think he was attempting to escape.

A major breakthrough came unexpectedly. Hunulf spied him wandering. "You will dine with my wife and daughter tonight. I will be expecting you." He turned about abruptly and departed.

That evening Valerius arrived at the chieftain's dwelling. He stood at the entrance, not knowing what to do. Should he announce himself? What was the protocol? This was not something Wothar had discussed with him. Before he could act, Hunulf emerged and spoke in a gruff tone. "Are you going to stand there all night, Roman, or come in?"

Valerius entered the dwelling. It was larger than most and had separate sleeping quarters, plus an area for the food preparation. The mother and the daughter were seated at the table, staring coldly at him. Valerius smiled. He was rewarded with the same icy expression. Hunulf spoke. "This is my wife, Clonid, and my daughter, Hereca. They are not fond of Romans."

"I gathered that," he said dryly.

"What did you say your name was?"

"Valerius. My name is Valerius."

There followed an uncomfortable silence broken only by the clatter of dishes as Clonid served the meal, which consisted of barley cakes, roast venison, and ale.

Valerius decided he was the one who needed to get the conversation started. "You know, we Romans are not all that bad. Just like you, we care for our children, love our families, and cherish our friends. We have our gods, enjoy a good wine, and relish a fine meal."

Hereca responded vehemently, "And you come from far away to kill our men and force us into slavery."

Hunulf barked, "Hereca, do not be so rude to our guest."

Clonid sat there, her expression frozen, not sure what to say. Valerius was temporarily at a loss for words. He needed to defuse the situation and do it quickly before things became worse. "Perhaps what you say is true," he replied smoothly. "I believe our emperor wants to secure peace across the Rhine to ensure the safety of the Gallic provinces. This has been a source of tension for many years. The designs of the Roman imperial government are beyond my understanding. For my part, I volunteered to serve in the army for three years. It has not been a pleasant experience."

Clonid probed. "What was your plan after three years? What would you do?"

Valerius responded, "I do not know. I never got that far. I had hoped to have a family, but that has been shattered."

Clonid inquired, "Because of your capture?"

He frowned. "I was informed several weeks ago that my wife died in childbirth."

Clonid spoke. "I am sorry. I did not mean to pry."

"That is all right. You could not have known."

Hereca, who had remained silent since her short diatribe, spoke. "You wish to return to Rome?"

Valerius paused in thought. "Perhaps not. I miss my parents who live there, but other than that, I have no desire to return."

Her curiosity aroused and her anger temporarily quelled, she asked, "Where would you go?"

"I do not know."

Hunulf entered the conversation. "I heard from Arminius that Rome is a large city, with many magnificent buildings. How big is Rome?"

"It is hard for me to explain without a frame of reference. If you take this village and all of the pastures, then double it and then double it many more times, that is the size." They looked at him, puzzled, not comprehending what he had said. He looked at the wooden table and picked up a small piece of barley cake. "Look, if this barley cake was the number of people in your village, then this table would be the number of people in Rome."

Hereca gasped. "That cannot be. Surely you are attempting to make fools of us."

Valerius chortled. "No, I mean every word of it. There are many, many people in Rome. It is hard for you to understand because you live in this modest village. I do not mean to disparage how and where you live, but I speak the truth. The place where they race the horses with chariots would hold the number of people in the Dolgubni nation."

Hunulf spoke to his daughter. "Hereca, I believe the Roman, I mean, Valerius, speaks the truth. Our leader Arminius, who has been to Rome, says the same thing."

Clonid asked, "What do the women wear?"

Valerius smiled at her. "Ah, I see I have piqued your interest. Many wear clothing similar to yours, woolen garb in various colors. The richer ladies wear gowns called stolas, which are made of a very fine weave. Of course their beauty cannot compare to that of the German women."

Hereca interjected herself. "Roman, you are patronizing us."

The tribune laughed. "Forgive me. I could not resist. But if you must know, the women are beautiful everywhere. The Roman women are not as tall as the German women. Their hair coloring is different. You are more of the blond and rufous color. Many Italian women have darker hair."

The conversation ebbed and flowed into the evening. Valerius kept the exchange as light as possible. He did not want his audience to feel he was lessening them. His comments on Rome were factual yet not boastful. He had no intent to demean the place where these people lived and died. He noted that it was beginning to get dark outside. He rose and thanked Hunulf, Clonid, and Hereca for inviting him to dine.

Several days later, Hunulf approached with several of his warriors, including Guntar. The chieftain carried Valerius's large war bow and quiver of arrows. He handed it to Valerius and gestured at his men. "Some have tried to string your large bow and could not. You will teach them how to make the bow ready and to shoot the long arrows."

The tribune accepted the bow and arrows. He was not sure he wanted to have these people shooting his bow. He put those thoughts aside for the moment and grinned back at the group. "I will demonstrate how to use this bow, but must warn you that it takes a lot of practice to master. It took me many repetitions to become accomplished with this weapon." They ventured to a nearby pasture. A large cowhide was attached to two wooden poles embedded in the ground for a target. It was placed almost a hundred paces away.

Valerius remembered Marcellus's instruction from many months ago. He had never taught anyone the use of this bow before, so he would mimic what the centurion had imparted to him. He effortlessly strung the bow, which was an art form of its own. Several of the warriors gasped in surprise. There was a trick to stringing the bow involving bracing of the feet and using both arms. Valerius smiled smugly at the group. Now for the next phase. He planted his feet firmly apart for a stable platform. He drew back the bowstring in one fluid motion, using his left arm to extend and his right to pull. He maintained the sight picture, held his breath, and let the arrow fly. It hit the target dead center.

The men were astonished that he had struck the target from that far away. Guntar stepped forward, wrenching the bow from his hands. Despite his enormous strength, he could not draw it back all the way. After several moments, he let the arrow fly. The shot was hopelessly wide of the target. Snarling, he drew another arrow and let that fly. It was another disaster. Some of the others snickered at his archery prowess. Guntar threw the bow down in disgust.

"You think you are better than us, Roman? Just because you can shoot this bow? How about I fight you again? I am wise to your tricks. The outcome will be much different this time."

Valerius backed away from the German warrior. What the man said was probably true. He would be defeated if he had to face Guntar again. He needed to mollify Guntar, yet not show cowardice. If he was perceived as timid, he would not last long among these people.

"Guntar, you are the village champion. Hunulf told me you had never been defeated, and I understand why. I cannot match your skill and ferocity in fighting with the German spear and shield. I know I was fortunate to defeat you, and that was only because of a bold maneuver on my part. You are most likely correct: you would best me if we fought a second time. So the answer is no, I will not challenge you again. I know better."

Guntar grunted. "Just remember, Roman, anytime you want to fight me again, let me know." He turned and stomped away.

Several of the others attempted to shoot the bow with equally dismal results. Valerius again demonstrated the proper technique. Their accuracy did not improve. After a while, the small group became discouraged and wandered back to the village. Valerius was relieved that the men were too impatient to learn. Surprised that they had not taken his weapon with them, he retrieved the bow and quiver of arrows and brought them back to his dwelling.

The next day Hereca entered his crude dwelling to bring him his midday meal of barley cakes and ale. She placed the food and drink on a small stool. She hesitated before leaving.

Valerius realized she wanted to talk to him. "Hereca, you have a question for me?

"Roman, you will tell me more about this large city where you lived."

Valerius, knowing she was uncomfortable in his presence, smiled back. Perhaps her hatred of him and all things Roman was moderating, at least a little bit. He could use every possible ally in his current quandary. "What would you like to know?"

"It is hard for me to believe the things you say about this city and all of its people. Tell me more. Where do they get the food and the water for all of these people?"

He paused in thought. How was he going to explain this? "Let me start with the food. Rome is upriver from a large seaport. Many ships travel in the great sea and bring large quantities of grain. This is transported to the city and stored in large buildings so that there is always a supply of grain for bread. Farm produce and animals are brought to the markets by way of the vast road system."

She stared blankly back at him.

He doubted she could grasp the concept of the large grain vessels unloading their cargo for the starving mouths of Rome. He decided to move on to the water supply. "The builders of Rome have constructed large stone structures standing as tall as the trees to bring the water from the mountains surrounding Rome. The water travels in conduits on top of these structures and eventually enters the city through pipes."

"What is a pipe?" she asked.

Valerius sighed. This was getting more difficult. "It is a round tube of stone, wood, or metal." He gestured with his arms to indicate the size of the circular tubes.

She returned his gaze, not comprehending. "Surely you are making this up? This cannot be." Without waiting for him to respond, she turned and departed.

She returned several days later with his midday meal. "My father stated that what you said might be true about your water system."

Valerius replied, "Might? It is all true. Why would I lie?"

She returned his gaze coldly. "Because Romans lie. Everyone knows that. What about your gods, Roman?"

Valerius frowned. Discussing religion was not a good topic to gain consensus or stay on good terms with anyone. He thought for a moment and then replied, "The Romans have many gods." He started naming a few of them. "There is the all-powerful, Jupiter. The god of war, Mars. There are female goddesses, such as Minerva and Fortuna. Some others include Apollo, god of the sun, and Neptune, god of the sea. I am sure you have many gods, yes?"

She replied, "We do. The two most powerful are Wodan and Donar."

"Hereca, I am familiar with some of them. My German friend Wothar told me about them. I guess our gods are similar to yours. Many Romans believe that any unusual occurrence is a sign the gods are speaking to them. You know, a lightning storm, the appearance of a certain bird, a rumble of the earth. The priests perform sacrifices and read signs in the entrails of a goat, a chicken, or even a bull."

She looked puzzled. "What do they look for?"

"The priests examine the entrails to see if there are any signs of disease or malformation. If there is, that is a bad omen. I do not believe any of that stuff. Surely if the gods wanted to talk to us or warn us, they would do so."

"Roman, our priest and priestesses will sacrifice an animal to ensure a good harvest."

"I see." Valerius got a gleam in his eye. "You know, Hereca, our women will take the entrails of a goat and wrap them in their hair to ensure fertility."

She gasped. "They do?"

Valerius smirked, and then burst out laughing.

Anger blazed in Hereca's eyes. She spluttered in anger and stalked off.

"You Dolgubni have no sense of humor," he called out after her.

XVI

It was evening, and the German village was illuminated with a number of large fires. It was a festival night to celebrate the upcoming harvest. There was singing and dancing everywhere, accompanied by the sounds of flutes and drums. Valerius stood obscured in the shadows, observing the celebration. By Venus's pert ass, these Germans could drink. The fermented barley brew was consumed in copious quantities by men and women alike. He much preferred the taste of wine to the bitter German concoction, but there was no wine this far north. Romans were no slouches when it came to intoxication and he had partaken his fair share of inebriation in Rome at elaborate dinner parties, but these people took it to a whole new level. The night was still young, but some were already in the falling-down stage.

He was informed by Hunulf that the reason for the festival was to celebrate the harvest and the changing of the season. The crisp autumn weather had arrived, but there was something about this revel that had a carnal undertone, and it had nothing to do with the changing of the seasons. The unmarried young women were giving the unmarried young men bold glances, accompanied by swaying of hips and other sensuous movements, leaving little in the way of imagination about what was to take place later.

Valerius witnessed the figures dancing around the large wood fire. Out of the corner of his eye, he caught Hereca eyeing him. He had believed he was discretely out of sight given the darkness, but obviously not. Knowing she had been noticed by the tribune, she turned abruptly and retreated into the shadows. Valerius silently smirked, rejoicing in his minor triumph over the haughty German. He directed his gaze back to the dancing figures, noting several of the young women giving him sidelong glances. What was that about? With the German brew buzzing in his head, he pondered briefly about joining the festivities as a full participant. Some of these women were quite attractive, especially the one closest to him on the left. She was a full-figured maiden who kept edging closer to him. The woman then directed her gaze fully at Valerius and smoothed her long hair over her breasts in a caressing motion.

He sipped some more of the brew, wondering what the night might bring, when just as quickly, a cold wave of fear engulfed him, bringing him back to reality. What was he thinking? He was not one of these people. He was a captive, who was allowed the freedom to roam the village—nothing more. Who knows what jealousies he might provoke if he became involved with one of these women? He did not know who belonged to whom or who was promised to whom in the grand scheme of things in this village. He frowned and looked at the remaining contents of his mug. He placed his half-filled wooden drinking cup down on a tree stump and unobtrusively shuffled toward his hut. He did, however, look to see if Hereca was still about. Disappointingly, she was not.

Several days later, Valerius wandered aimlessly through the village with nothing particular in mind. He had little else to do. Approaching a field next to the village, he noted a group of young men engaged in javelin throwing at straw targets. The range was about thirty paces to the straw effigies in the shape of men. The lances were about six feet long, of hardened ash with an iron point affixed to the shaft. By comparison, the German throwing spears were not as effective as the Roman pilum. The Roman javelins had a much longer iron head that was heavily weighted toward the front of the javelin for greater penetration, but still, the German throwing spear could be deadly effective. Moving closer, he noted several young women, including Hereca, participating. He stood there, observing the throws. He was impressed with Hereca's flings. Her power and distance were almost as good as the men's. He could not imagine Roman women participating in this form of activity, especially women of his class. He smirked at the thought of it.

His grin did not go unnoticed. A voice from the group of men issued forth a challenge. "So you think you could do better, Roman?" The tone of the challenge was filled with disdain, almost mocking.

Valerius decided not to risk any confrontation. "I was just admiring your throws. They looked fairly accurate."

"Come over here and show us your abilities, Roman. Or are you afraid that your skills with the javelin cannot match even our women's?" The group of young warriors chuckled at the last remark. They all looked at him expectantly. He knew there was no way he was going to extricate himself from this situation. He would need to display his javelin-throwing skills, which, he must admit, were good. In fact, they were better than good. He excelled at the javelin. No one in his military training class could best him.

Valerius walked up to the throwing line, conscious that all eyes were upon him. The man who had shouted out the challenge to him spoke. "My name is Uthrix, Roman, and I am one of the best at throwing the javelin. Why don't you show us what you can do?"

Valerius looked at Uthrix. He had seen him before, but never conversed with him. The man was powerfully built, with long scraggly hair.

"Here." He pushed a spear sideways at Valerius, bumping him in the chest, no doubt on purpose, a calculated rudeness.

The others in the group laughed at Uthrix's theatrics. They were enjoying the confrontation.

Valerius hefted the spear to get the balance of it. It seemed so much lighter than the Roman pilum. Next he looked down the length of the shaft. It was straight and true. "Sure, I will give this a try."

Valerius beheld the straw target and again hefted the spear for balance. He knew that if he missed, it would be on the high side, given the relative lightness of the spear. He would need to compensate by aiming lower on the target. He breathed in deeply, drew the spear back, and heaved it toward the target. As soon as he released it, he realized he had not adjusted his throw enough for the weight of the spear. It was sailing high and wide from the center mass. Just before reaching the target, the javelin dipped slightly and struck the straw head of the target directly in the center, knocking it off the body—a fortuitous throw. Oohs and aahs echoed from the assembled Germans.

Valerius offered a slight smile to Uthrix and turned to go. His progress was halted as the German blocked his advance with a spear across his intended path. "You do not get off that easily, Roman. It was a lucky throw. Why don't you and I have a contest to see who the best is?"

Valerius wanted to avoid any confrontation, given his standing among the Germans. He grinned back at the German. "As you said, it was a lucky throw."

He turned once again to leave. His words had the opposite effect of his intentions. His path was blocked again by the spear, this time with much more force. The German's face reddened in fury. "I said we will have a contest. Do you understand, Roman?"

Valerius was trapped. He had to take up the challenge. He could let the German win, but that was not his nature, the consequences be damned. Besides, Hereca was here. He could not back down to the German boor. Valerius gazed straight into the eyes of his antagonist. "All right, if that is what you want, but why don't we make this a little more interesting and extend the distance to say another ten paces? This will truly test our skill levels. What do you say?"

The German was startled by the challenge and could do nothing but agree to the terms. He nodded in acknowledgment. "Whatever you say, Roman. Three throws each."

Valerius smiled smugly to himself. He had just gained an advantage with the distance. His arm was more accustomed to the heavier javelin and the effort required to throw it. "Agreed, Uthrix. You can go first."

The contestants moved back another ten paces. Uthrix stood ready, frowning at the longer distance. Clearly, this was not the range he was accustomed to throwing. He picked up a javelin from the stack before him and hefted it for balance. He stared at the target and heaved the missile. It flew from his hand and punched the target dead center. The group of Germans cheered his efforts.

Valerius stepped forward and selected a javelin. He examined it briefly. Before getting into the ready position, in his mind he slowly went through the mechanics of releasing the javelin. Staring at the target, he cocked his arm and heaved the javelin. This toss was a little low. He had overcompensated for the weight, but nevertheless, struck the target on the lower left side.

Uthrix stepped forward and grabbed another javelin. He looked downrange, then threw the spear. Again he struck the target dead center. The German audience erupted in celebration. Valerius quickly stepped forward. He had already selected his next javelin. He liked the feel of it. He gripped the smooth surface and heaved it at the target. It struck dead center. He turned toward Uthrix. "How about we increase the distance another ten paces for this last throw?" Uthrix grunted his approval.

After moving back another ten paces, the German took another javelin. With the additional distance, he did not appear as confident. He looked hesitant, as he was not sure this was a guaranteed hit at this range. He cocked his arm back and then released the javelin. It streaked downrange. There was plenty of power behind the throw. It missed a bit wide. Groans emitted from his followers.

It was Valerius's turn. He chose a javelin at random and looked downrange. Remembering what his training instructor had drilled into him with endless repetitions, he imagined the javelin flying toward the target and striking it center mass. Without hesitation, he breathed deeply, tightened his grip, and then stepped forward and threw. The missile flew toward the target. There was a splash of straw as his spear struck the target in the center of the groin, the lance protruding like a giant phallus.

The gathering chuckled at the position of the lance, further enraging Uthrix. He strode rapidly toward Valerius. He extended his arms and pushed. Unprepared for the larger man's shove, Valerius stumbled backward. Uthrix shouted at Valerius, "You think you are superior to us, Roman. Come let us fight with the spears rather than throw them at straw figures. You are a weakling and no match for me. You got lucky against Guntar, but you will not with me."

Before Valerius could respond to the threat from the German, Hereca barged in front of him. "Stop it, Uthrix. You are the one who wanted this contest, and you lost. You are a sore loser. He did not goad you. This was your own fault. Stop this nonsense about fighting. My father would strongly disapprove."

As soon as she mentioned her father, Uthrix lost some of his anger. He did not wish to face the wrath of the village chieftain. He glared at Valerius once more and then stalked off. Valerius stared after him briefly. Shaken by the sudden rage directed at him, he glanced at Hereca and the others before wandering back toward his hut.

Hunulf appeared at the entrance of his dwelling a short time later. He was about to speak when he caught a glimpse of Valerius's bow and quiver of arrows hanging from a wooden peg. He stood frozen in place before finally pointing at the weapon. "What are you doing with that?"

Valerius knew what he was pointing at, but decided to act innocent about his possession of the bow. "Doing with what?"

"Your bow and arrows. You are a prisoner here and should not have them."

"Hunulf, I attempted to instruct some of your warriors at your behest to use this weapon. Your men are short on patience. It takes a lot of practice, and I mean a lot, to master this weapon. They all were frustrated in attempting to use the bow and departed. None of them took the bow with them, so I returned it here."

"You cannot have that bow."

"And why not, Hunulf? Do you believe I am going to take it in the middle of the village and shoot everyone? Listen to me. I give you my word as a Roman officer that I will not use it against anyone. Furthermore, no one in your village appears to have any desire to use it, so why not leave it here? I would pledge to use it in defense of your village or if you wanted me to use it on a hunt."

Finished with his remarks, Valerius looked to Hunulf for an answer.

"I will need to think about this for a bit. In the interim, you may keep it here. I came by because I heard from Hereca that there was a disagreement you had today."

"I did, and thanks to the intervention of your daughter, the confrontation did not escalate."

"You need to be careful of Uthrix. He has a quick temper and. like many of the others, he hates Romans."

"I tried to avoid the situation this afternoon, but he would not hear of it—"

"You need to be very careful, Roman. I can protect you only so much." With that he turned and walked away.

That evening, Valerius wandered away from the tribal fires in the center of the village and out into the open field. A cold wind gusted in from the north. He shivered at the penetrating chill. It was autumn, and winter would be here soon. He stared to the east, where a full moon rose, bright orange in color. Silhouettes of migrating birds flew across the moon, their distinctive honks echoing in the distance. He looked down at the ground, his mood despondent. He was a prisoner here and the people hated him, but he had little in the way of options. If he attempted to flee, he would be hunted down by the men of the village and executed. His odds of surviving any escape attempt were nil. He was fortunate that the confrontation with Uthrix did not escalate this afternoon. The outcome would have been bad no matter how he fared against the German. If they had fought, he might have been killed. If he was victorious, the Germans would have slain him. Of that he had no doubt.

His ruminations were interrupted as Hereca appeared next to him. She had a heavy shawl wrapped around her. "Are you trying to escape, Roman?"

Valerius had not seen her approach and was somewhat taken aback. "I did not see you, but to answer your question, yes, I was fleeing. Can you not see the speed at which I am moving?"

She offered a hearty laugh. "More of your Roman humor?" After a brief silence, she asked, "What were you thinking about? Were your thoughts of your home?"

Valerius stared at her in the darkness. Why was she asking him these questions? He replied, "Actually, I was not thinking of my home. That place is forever gone for me now after the death of my wife. There are always the legions, but I have had my fill of military life as well. After the confrontation today with Uthrix, I was thinking about my confinement here. It is a prison. By the way, thank you for your intervention. That would have ended badly for me, no matter what I did."

"You are welcome." She looked back at him. "So, getting back to my original question, were you thinking of escaping?"

"I must confess. Yes, I was pondering fleeing, but only briefly for I believe my chance of success would be extremely slim. It seems just a matter of time before one of your warriors, like Uthrix or Guntar, skewers me for looking cross-eyed at his woman or some other minor transgression."

She replied, "Uthrix is a braggart and a fool. I would be mindful of him. He will seek to provoke you in any way he can." She stopped speaking for a moment and then lowered her voice. "You are a strange one, Roman. You have no wish to return home. You do not like the legions, and you do not like it here, which I understand. What is it you seek, assuming you were free?"

Valerius was silent. He was conscious of Hereca staring at him in the dark, awaiting a response. Finally he spoke, his tone bitter. "I seek nothing. I am sick of the killing with the legions. I have done more than my duty. Rome holds nothing but sorrow for me now. I have no desire to return there. So what option do I have? I am a prisoner here. I guess it is as good as anywhere else. Perhaps death is the answer. Maybe I should goad one of your warriors into a fight and let myself be killed. Once life had promise for me. Not so anymore."

Now it was Hereca's turn to be silent. After a time she spoke. "Roman, you are a troubled man. You need to find a purpose in life, whatever that might be." She turned and kissed him lightly on the cheek, then hurried back toward the village dwellings.

Valerius was stunned. He stared after her retreating figure, conscious of the swaying of her hips. She had never shown any kindness to him, yet her light kiss had a touch of tenderness. The hostility and contempt she had previously exhibited toward him now seemed to be in the past. He was baffled by the turn of events, yet pleased. *These Germans are outlandish people,* he thought. He replayed the scene over and over in his mind, wondering if it had really happened at all.

XVII

Dolgubni Territory
Five Months Later
Early Spring

Valerius stared despondently out the entrance of his hut at the cold, cascading rain. It had been pouring incessantly for three days now, turning the village into a quagmire. He sat on some wood planking to keep his butt dry and had a heavy woolen blanket draped around his shoulders. A drop of cold water landed on his neck. He looked up at the thatched roof in frustration. The past winter had featured heavy snowfall and gusty winds that had wreaked havoc on his dwelling. He was not alone. Others in the settlement were experiencing the same thing.

A figure filled the entrance. Hereca stepped in, shivering with cold. Her face was pale and etched with lines of grief. It had been a tough winter for the Dolgubni clan. While the bountiful harvest had ensured a sufficient food supply to see them through, a fever had spread through the village, taking many lives, including Hereca's mother, Clonid. The loss had struck Hereca particularly hard. The two had a wonderful mother-daughter relationship that was now lost forever. Valerius had sought her out and offered his condolences for her loss. This was the Roman way, and he guessed the Germans did the same type of thing. Hereca in turn appeared to further soften her feelings relative to him.

Valerius's relationship with Hereca appeared to have morphed on to a new plateau, almost that of friendship.

She and the tribune had spoken at length over the winter months. She even called him Valerius now instead of Roman. At first their exchanges had been brief, but as the winter dragged on, their conversations had deepened and expanded to many topics. Hereca almost seemed to enjoy his company. Upon invitation, he would go to Hunulf's lodge to speak with her. He would never go on his own accord, for this might be viewed as too forward. She had many questions for him about the Roman way of life. He tried to explain in simple terms the customs and mores of the Roman people. It was not an easy thing to describe, given the vast gulf that separated the two cultures.

They talked of many things, including the village life, religion, food, wine, and many things Roman. Her curiosity had flowered about the people and lands beyond her village. He had enthralled Hereca with his recounting of his voyage on the great sea from Rome to Germania last year and about the feisty Captain Sabinus. She had heard of the great ocean but had no idea of its vast proportions or of the ships that sailed upon it.

There was little else to do during the fierce cold. For the most part, the villagers huddled in their huts, seeking the warmth of their fires. Heavy snows were common, so little else could be done. Occasionally, the men organized a hunt, but Valerius was never invited, which was too bad, for his bow and its long-range accuracy could have brought more game to the tribal dinner table. Valerius had breached the subject of going on a hunting excursion with the men. Hunulf contemplated the question briefly and then slowly shook his head. He gave no explanation as to why. Valerius assumed he had pushed too far and that he was still viewed with contempt by most.

Valerius gestured for Hereca to sit next to him. She sat down, and Valerius pulled the woolen blanket over both of their shoulders. They sat that way saying little for some time, looking glumly out at the hard rain.

Hunulf entered the dwelling, shaking the rain off his cloak. He frowned in disapproval at the intimate huddling of the couple, and noted tears streaking down his daughter's face.

"What is wrong, daughter of mine?"

"Need you ask, Father? I miss my mother and cannot get over my grief. She was such a guiding force for me."

"And I am not?

"Of course you are, Father. But I long for my mother so much. I am so lonely without her cheerful banter and kind ways."

"I miss her too, child. Clonid and I were very happy together. It was a terrible blow to me when she passed."

Valerius spoke. "Hunulf, if I may speak freely. Your wife was a wonderful woman. If you are the father of this settlement, then she was the mother. All of the wives and children looked up to her for guidance."

Hunulf, his face pinched with sorrow, nodded. "Now listen to me, both of you. Hereca, you cannot be in this man's hut by yourself. People in the tribe will start talking. It is not right."

Hereca's eyes blazed with anger. "Do you think I care what they think? Besides, Valerius has been a good person to talk to and help me console my grief."

Hunulf responded, "I know, my child, but the ways of our tribe forbid this familiarity."

Hereca's anger bloomed. "The ways of the tribe be damned. Do you think I could have a similar discussion with the married or unmarried males of our tribe? They are only interested in getting under my tunic."

"Hereca, enough!"

Valerius interjected, "Hunulf, I apologize if I have broken any of the rules or disturbed the social order of things. I have acted honorably toward your daughter. No offense was intended. I wish I could do or say something that would make her feel better. While I welcome her presence, I have purposely not sought her out for being perceived as too presumptuous in my relationship with her. She has come to me to speak about the nature of things, good and bad."

Hunulf sighed. "I hold no anger against you, Tribune, and Hereca has told me much of what you speak, but I am concerned about the perception of others in this village, especially since I am the chieftain. We will speak of this later. Hereca, come. I need you to help with the evening meal."

Unknown to the Dolgubni, warmer spring weather would be arriving shortly, but so would death and destruction. The band of Cherusci, under the leadership of Safrax, was advancing toward the Dolgubni settlement. He had been waiting all winter for the weather to break. Now the time was near when he would lay waste to the Dolgubni village. He was unconcerned about repercussions. He had Inguiomerus's permission, and he would concoct a story that his raid was in retribution for a Dolgubni attack on the Cherusci people. Besides, Arminius would probably never even learn of the raid, and even if he did, he would most likely do nothing. From what Safrax had gleaned, Arminius was angry about Hunulf's ill-timed remarks in front of the coalition of tribes.

The timing was perfect. The German tribes under Arminius had disbanded many months ago for the winter. The coalition of tribes had been defeated in battle on several occasions last summer, but the Romans had withdrawn back across the Rhine to their winter quarters. If they reappeared later in the spring, then the tribes would unite again. As for now, it was time to punish the Dolgubni, settle his blood feud with them, and take the chieftain's daughter for his own. Her name was Hereca.

The Cherusci band moved en masse, with no advance scouts. Why should they not? No one was expecting them. The group numbered several hundred men, all looking forward to plunder and satisfying their lust with the women of the Dolgubni. It would be another day's march, but they would get there soon enough. The warriors all carried small shields and multiple spears, along with personal satchels of food and water.

The next day was much brighter, with the arrival of temperate weather and a warming sun. Hunulf and Guntar stood outside the dwelling of the chieftain. They were good friends, and each had an important role in the village—one as the chieftain and the other as the village champion. Hunulf leaned closer to Guntar to confer with him. "Guntar, I have not told anyone else yet, but it is my decision that the Dolgubni of this village will not answer the call of Arminius to join the coalition to fight against the Romans in the event that they venture across the Rhine again later this spring. We have suffered great losses from our village in the quest against the Romans, and the plague that hit us this past winter reduced our numbers even more. I will recommend to the other Dolgubni villages near us not to send their warriors against the Romans."

Guntar was silent as he pondered the words of his chieftain. He knew they were not spoken lightly and that Hunulf must have deliberated for some time before making his judgment. That was the kind of man he was, and that is why he was the chieftain. Guntar knew that Hunulf's decision was final, but the chieftain was also seeking confirmation from him that his decision was the correct one.

"Hunulf, you are right about our losses. We have many widows among our tribe, including your daughter, Hereca. The deaths we suffered this winter, including your wife, make it that much worse. I concur with your judgment. I am worried that the decline of the number of warriors has made us weak, which leads me to my main concern. Will the powerful Cherusci tribes to our south seek retribution against us if we refuse the demands of Arminius, and perhaps doubly so since we are now in such a fragile state?"

"Guntar, I share your concern, but do you believe the Cherusci know of how debilitated our tribe has become? I think not. They have problems of their own. If I send a contingent of warriors against Rome once more, I fear we will have more losses. In my mind, we only have one choice, and that is to bow out of this war with the Roman beasts. When I speak with the other chieftains of the Dolgubni over the next several weeks, I will seek to form an alliance with those tribes for mutual protection in the event the Cherusci decide to take vengeance upon us for not joining their coalition."

Guntar was about to reply, but he never got the words out. He looked up in alarm as a dozen Cherusci warriors surrounded the two unarmed men. Before he could raise a warning, numerous spears slammed into his torso. Most men would have fallen to the earth, succumbing to the terrible wounds. Despite his grievous injuries, he managed to swing one of his powerful arms into the face of one of his assailants, shattering the man's jaw. With that, several more spears were thrust into his neck and torso. Guntar emitted a loud grunt, followed by a gurgling sound as he toppled to the earth. Hunulf joined him several heartbeats later.

Valerius was refreshed after his walk around the village. The air had warmed considerably, and he noted buds bursting forth on the trees. If only the thick, ubiquitous mud would dry up. He was in his dwelling and about to eat his morning meal of barley cakes and dried venison when he heard screams and the clash of arms outside. He was startled by the appearance at his doorway of a German warrior with a spear leveled at his midsection. The German screamed a battle oath and charged. Valerius stood abruptly. With no weapon in hand, he grabbed the closest object, a wooden camp stool, and hurled it at the man's feet. The warrior stumbled and sought to regain his balance. Valerius was quick to react. He pounced on the man, picked up the heavy wooden stool, and bashed the man in the head repeatedly until he stopped moving.

Valerius hastily retrieved his bow and quiver of arrows from their hanging place on the wall. He approached the entrance to his hut and cautiously peered outside. What he observed was a horror scene. There were German warriors slaying the men of the village, most of whom were unarmed. Surrender was not an option. Bodies of women and children littered the ground, with pools of blood everywhere. Valerius quickly strung his bow and slipped out of his dwelling, which fortunately for him was at the edge of the settlement. He ran to a clump of thick bushes and hid. There were no shouts of discovery. Concealed amid the foliage, he gazed about, noting the alarming number of enemy warriors. This was no hit-and-run raid. Their purpose was to eradicate this settlement.

He crouched and dashed from his hidden position, and then halted. To his front were two of the German invaders guarding against anyone fleeing the settlement. They stood with spears poised, ready to gut any unfortunate villager who chose to approach in their direction. At their feet lay the still form of an unfortunate Dolgubni man in a pool of blood.

Valerius notched an arrow and took aim. It was not an easy shot as the targets were at an oblique angle, presenting less of a profile. They were about thirty paces away. He let out about half a breath and then held what was left, aiming at the center mass of the closest man. The warrior turned slightly toward him, making him that much better of a target, just as he released the arrow. The man went down hard. Seeing his fallen comrade, the second warrior was gripped with indecision. His hesitation was a costly mistake. A moment later he was down.

Valerius rushed toward the mortally wounded warriors. He ripped the satchel containing food and water from the shoulder of one of the men. He then picked up two spears and an iron knife from his slain foes. He continued circling the settlement, leapfrogging from one position to the next. He heard more screams as he warily skirted the village perimeter. He gazed from his obscured position in a copse of bushes and observed two men holding Hereca. Her father lay unmoving nearby in a pool of blood. Next to him on the ground was Guntar. A large warrior was directing the two men holding Hereca. Was he their leader?

What was Valerius going to do? He could not flee and leave Hereca like this, but how could he rescue her? It would be difficult to hit both of the men holding her. They were not far away, but the slightest miscalculation of his shot might strike her. Temporarily gripped with indecision, he remembered his military instruction when training as a tribune. Above all else, do something, and so he did. He drew his bow back. There was no hesitation, for this only increased the odds for a bad shot. The arrow flew from his bow, narrowly missing Hereca by a hand's breadth and striking one of her captors. The man let go of her and collapsed. Now partially free, Hereca turned and kicked her remaining captor in the groin. He went down with a scream of anguish. Seeing her free, another warrior rushed forward to grab her. He never made it. He was struck by an arrow.

The large German who Valerius presumed to be the leader began shouting at several of his warriors closest to him, pointing at Hereca and in the direction of Valerius. His gesticulations were cut short as an arrow streamed from the perimeter of the village, deeply gouging his arm. He gasped in pain and doubled over, holding his ruined appendage. Valerius charged forward with the bow and spear in his hands.

"Hereca," he shouted, and tossed the spear sideways for her to catch. She grasped it in midair, pivoted, and threw it at an advancing marauder. He was struck in the midsection and collapsed with a grunt. Valerius grabbed her hand and shouted, "This way." Together they rushed out of the settlement. They ran hard through the fields and forest, not looking back.

Safrax was livid with rage. The whole purpose of his raid was gone. The chieftain's daughter had escaped. As one man meekly bound the bloody arrow wound on his arm, Safrax cursed his men. He looked about and turned to his second-in-command. "Brixus, start organizing a search party. I want that woman back and the head of that man who wounded me."

Brixus looked back at him. "Now, Safrax?"

"No, you bloody idiot. Let us wait until tomorrow when they have a day's march lead on us." He struck the man in the mouth with his good arm to make his point. "Now get your ass moving."

Valerius and Hereca ran side by side away from the carnage. There was no sound of pursuit, but he dare not look back, for this would only slow them down. They arrived at a fork in the trail; both hesitated as to which direction to go. Valerius gestured to the left, and the two were off again. The pair continued their flight, running hard for their lives. Finally Valerius slowed down and motioned toward a nearby thicket. They slipped into the foliage so that they would be unobserved by anyone coming down the trail. Panting, both hunched over with their hands on their knees.

Hereca looked up at Valerius, and her eyes filled with tears. "They killed my father. The leader whom you wounded in the arm with your arrow knew my name. He wanted me alive for who knows what purpose." She shuddered at the thought of it.

Valerius looked at her. "Hereca, I do not believe this was a random raid. They were out for blood. It appears that they wanted you as well. If this is true, then this is not good news. That means they will be in pursuit. Who were those killers?"

She spat out a response. "They were Cherusci."

Valerius was stunned at her reply. It never occurred to him that the feuding between the tribes had reached this level of wanton slaughter.

They had tarried long enough. "Come on, Hereca. They are most likely chasing you and want to kill me many times over for the death I have spread among them. We need to make haste."

They sprinted side by side down the dirt trail. Valerius decided to slow the pace so Hereca could keep up. She noticed it immediately. "Do not reduce our step on my account. I can keep up." And she did. They ran all day through wooded terrain and across streams, putting the distance behind them. Valerius looked back occasionally and saw no signs of pursuit, but that did not mean that there were not Cherusci close behind them. Hereca leaned close to him and spoke in a low tone. "You realize that we have been traveling south all of this time?"

Valerius nodded. "Not by design. I ran down the first trail we came to outside of your settlement. After a time, I noted the position of the sun and figured we were going south. Hereca, this suits my purpose. I have no sanctuary here in Germania. The instant anyone identifies me as a Roman, my ass is cooked—no mercy. I intend to journey to the Rhine."

Hereca looked at him deeply. "And what about me?"

"What about you?"

Anger flamed in her face. "So you would ignore my safety and go on your way? Maybe we should part here."

"Hereca, stop this. You think I had this planned with no thoughts of your life? We were headed south through no deliberate action on my part. It was spontaneous. Please tell me what options you think you have available to you. You know better than me. We should decide these things here and now."

Hereca was silent in thought. Tears came to her eyes. She spoke haltingly. "I have no future back at my village. My family is gone from me, my father murdered. The village no longer exists."

"What about other Dolgubni settlements?"

Hereca shook her head. "I would always be an outsider, even among them. Furthermore, the Cherusci are after me. No village would take me in once that is known. I have no safe haven."

Valerius spoke. "Yes, you do. Come with me to the far side of the Rhine. You will be safe there."

"But I am a Dolgubni, not a Roman."

"Yes, you are a Dolgubni woman, and you will fit in nicely. The peoples living on the western bank of the Rhine are from all over, including many Germanic tribes friendly to Rome. You can be among your own, sort of, and will be safe from any marauding Cherusci. Please come with me."

Hereca bit her lip. More tears ran down her face. "You would take me with you and see that I am safe?"

"Yes. Now can we agree you are accompanying me? We need to get moving and out of this area."

"Yes, we need to leave this place, especially since that is a Cherusci village up ahead. This is the northern edge of their territory. Their lands extend well south of here."

Valerius's face blanched. He had no idea that he had led them straight to the heart of danger. Thinking about it, he recalled hearing that the Cherusci were to the south of the Dolgubni. He should have known better, but his flight from the Dolgubni settlement had been so precipitous that he had no chance to think things through. No matter; it was done. Now what? Cautiously viewing the area to his front, he observed a substantial Cherusci settlement. He looked toward the rear from their concealed position. He saw and heard nothing suspicious that would indicate the presence of their pursuers.

He turned to Hereca. "I suggest we back out of here under the concealment of these woods, and we move fast. Assuming the raiders of your settlement track us here, they might enlist the support of this village. If they find out that you are in the company of a Roman officer, no doubt the entire tribe will join in."

The two turned about and silently crept among the trees, steering clear of any open areas. Valerius moved a short distance and then stopped. He turned his head fully in both directions before proceeding, caution forgoing speed for the moment. In this manner, they stealthily padded through the forest and away from the Cherusci settlement. After some distance, Valerius heaved a sigh of relief. He was about to tell Hereca that they could relax now when voices off to his left startled him. Valerius sank to his knees, pushing Hereca down with him. He then dropped to a prone position.

Nudging aside the leaves from a large bush, he peered in the direction of the voices. He spied a small party of women and older men gathering up deadwood. They were headed in their direction. He must choose flight or fight. It was an easy decision. He could not possibly kill all of them, and the survivors would alert the village. Besides, he had not become so callous that he would slaughter women and old men. The only option was to remain hidden and hope they were not discovered, then flee. Valerius pantomimed to Hereca to keep her face down to the earth. This way they would blend in more with the surroundings. Valerius did the same.

The voices grew louder. They were almost on top of them. One of the women complained that her husband was a good-for-nothing and never wiped the mud from his shoes or clothes before entering their dwelling. Another laughed at her complaint and told her not to give him any mating until he learned his lesson. The others chuckled and agreed that this was a good idea. Valerius heard the breaking of dried wood as it was thrust into the sacks they were carrying. There was more laughter, and then the voices faded. Valerius and Hereca looked up from the ground at the same time. He motioned for her to rise. The two scurried forth, putting distance between them and the wood gatherers.

The pair ventured south the remainder of the day. It was now nearing dusk. "Hereca, are you ready to stop and find a place to sleep. I do not wish to stumble about in these woods in the dark."

"I was thinking the same thing. What about shelter?"

Valerius studied the sky for a moment. "I do not think it will rain tonight. I suggest we find some dry ground and make camp there."

Valerius looked into the satchel that he had taken from one of the Cherusci warriors back at the Dolgubni village. "There is some food in here, as well as flints to make a fire. I think we will forgo the fire tonight as there may be Cherusci nearby."

Hereca nodded wearily. "Let us find a place to make camp before it gets much darker."

Valerius pointed. "In that direction is a pine forest. I can see it from here. Let us go there. The pine needles will make a fine bed."

It was almost black when they reached the large stand of pines. The chill was creeping into their bones. Valerius used the spear shaft to scrape up a pile of pine needles for a bed. The two sat down and shared the stale barley cakes and skin of water. He motioned for Hereca to lie down. He placed his bow, quiver of arrows, and spear beside him and settled next to her. He shrugged off his heavy cloak and draped it over both of them. She shivered slightly, and then cuddled next to Valerius, placing her arm around his waist. She fell asleep instantly.

Valerius listened to the night sounds of the forest. A slight wind whispered through the swaying pine branches; insects twittered. He glanced up through the gaps in the pine branches at the star-filled sky, the moon shining brightly above them through the trees. He took a deep breath and exhaled. He felt the physical presence of the woman next to him. Like him, she had endured considerable sadness that would have crushed a lesser spirit. He smiled inwardly. He might, the Goddess Fortuna permitting, reach Roman-held territory. More importantly, he had something to live for.

XVIII

Upon awakening, it took Valerius a moment to realize where he was and how he got there. Dazed, he looked about. It was gray, and the trees were ghostly silhouettes, but he knew that dawn would arrive shortly. He sensed Hereca stirring next to him. Putting his face next to hers, he placed his finger to his lips, indicating silence. Chances were that they were alone, but why take unneeded risks? He rose and prowled around the perimeter of their camp. Hereca watched him from her bed, her eyes wide in fear. She had rolled out of their bed and held a spear in her hand. All was silent, with the exception of the morning birds, which was a good sign for surely they would not be chirping if other men were present. Valerius nodded his head, indicating they were safe.

Seeing they were alone, Hereca rose and stood, brushing the pine needles from her woolen garments. "I do not suppose you have anything remaining to eat in that satchel. I am starving."

"I do not. We will have to scavenge off the land for our food. Do you know of any plants that we can eat?"

Hereca shrugged. "There is not much this time of spring. If we come upon any streams, there are some greens that grow along the edges that are edible."

Valerius nodded. "We need to get moving."

The two advanced south along the dirt path at a fast walk. They made good time, for the going was easy and the trail clear of obstructions. They arrived at a swift-flowing stream, narrow in width. Valerius stopped to refill the waterskin. They both drank deeply of the cold crystal water. Hereca knelt along the edge of the stream, peering along the bank. With a triumphant cry, she pulled up some rich green plants.

"These are good to eat. They are sweet to the taste." She proceeded to put a small fistful of the plants in her mouth and chewed vigorously.

She handed some to Valerius, who proceeded to stuff some of the greens in his mouth. He chewed for several moments and was tempted to spit them out. They did not taste sweet at all. In fact, they had no flavor. Not wanting to hurt Hereca's feelings, he chewed some more. "These are rather good."

The two ate some more of the greens. Hereca looked at him curiously. "Do you really like these?"

Valerius tried not to laugh, but could not help it. "Actually, no."

Hereca frowned, but then she too laughed. She was about to speak when they heard voices off in the distance. The two scurried forward into a thick stand of bushes, where they had a good view of the trail that they had traveled down. A group of five Cherusci warriors advanced toward them, totally unconcerned about any danger to their front. The men were grouped together, talking loudly. Each carried a wooden spear and a dagger. The distance was closing; they were now about one hundred paces away.

Valerius quickly strung his bow. He handed the spear to Hereca and retrieved an arrow from his quiver. It was time to fight. He would surprise them with a flurry of arrows. Hopefully they would panic and retreat from whence they came. He drew the bow back and let the arrow fly. The first man went down hard from the force of the feathered shaft. One of the men started screaming orders at the others. He was the next target. Valerius's arrow took him in the neck, killing him instantly. At the loss of their leader, the other survivors were hesitant as to what to do, but then they began moving toward Valerius. He unleashed an arrow, but missed. The trio ran at him. He hastily withdrew another arrow and unleashed it at his attackers. The arrow struck home, knocking one of the men down. The other two were almost upon them, their spears leveled at waist height.

With a shriek, Hereca leaped from the bushes and hurled her spear, striking one of the men in the chest. He struggled to remove the shaft, falling to his knees. The remaining Cherusci saw the two adversaries to his lone self. He pivoted and bolted back down the trail. With the exception of the moans from the man wounded by Hereca's spear, all was silent.

Valerius quickly scavenged whatever food and supplies the dead men possessed plus two spears. Valerius knelt over the man with the javelin lodged in his chest. Blood pulsed from the wound. He drew his knife and waved it in the man's face. "Who were you after?"

The warrior was sullen, his face a mask of desperation.

"Help me."

Valerius put the knife against the man's cheek. "Who were you after?"

The Cherusci looked at Hereca and pointed with his finger. He whimpered as more blood pulsed on the ground.

Valerius withdrew the knife. "Are there any others after us?"

The warrior said nothing. His fingers twitched feebly, and then he was still.

They gathered up their booty and hurried away from the scene. Valerius spoke. "I believe that was the posse that was after us, well, you more than me. There may be more Cherusci chasing us. That may have been only the tracking group and not the main body. We should put as much distance as possible between us and these bodies. Let's go."

Theudis, the sole surviving member of the Cherusci band that had pursued Valerius and Hereca, stopped on the trail, panting for breath. He had been tracking the pair from the Dolgubni village for two days. He was feeling the effects of the march from the extreme southern portion of Cheruscan territory to the Dolgubni settlement, and then this pursuit. He was relieved to see a group of ten Cherusci materialize on the trail. He smiled. This was the main party.

Theudis hailed Brixus, leader of the Cherusci band. "I am glad you are here. We found the two escapees, but they killed four of our tracking group. I am the only survivor."

Brixus snarled. "You could not wait for us? We were not that far behind you. Now they are alerted to our presence. Safrax will punish all of us if we do not return with the two Dolgubni, especially the woman."

Theudis gestured with his hands. "We thought we could overcome them. Besides, they saw us first and attacked. Three of us were dispatched with the bow, and one succumbed to the spear."

"Enough of your pathetic excuses. How far ahead are they?"

Theudis pointed. "They are not too distant. We should be able to catch them before sundown."

Brixus yelled, "Then get off your ass and show us the way."

The cluster followed at a trot down the dirt trail.

Valerius and Hereca advanced briskly south down the beaten trail. Their pace was quick, close to a running stride. Hereca looked to Valerius. "Do you think that was the extent of the Cherusci hunting us? That last warrior you questioned never did give a response."

"No, he did not, but there may be more of them. My experience in the Teutoburg was that the Germans send an advance tracking party followed by the main group. So if I had to guess, there is another bunch following us, only larger."

Hereca stopped abruptly. "So what do we do?"

Valerius was silent. He looked back up the trail in the direction they had just come from. "I have been thinking about this and what our next course of action should be. We will need to get off this path, but I was hoping to wait until dusk so they could not identify our movements. These men are skilled trackers. Once we leave this trail, our movement will be slowed considerably. So for now, let us proceed on the trail at a brisk pace."

The pair advanced in a southerly direction down the path as the late afternoon gave way to evening. Valerius would stop at various intervals and look back, listening for any sounds, but so far there were no signs of others on their trail. They ventured onward. Valerius viewed both sides of the track, looking for a suitable place to break off the path. He stopped and pointed. There was a small game trail that split off to the right.

"This is what we are going to do. We will leave signs of where we exited the trail. Our pursuers will discover it right away. Make sure you make a visible footprint in that mud there so they cannot miss it."

Hereca looked at him quizzically. "Why are we doing that?"

"Because it will be a false trail. We are going to loop back on the main path about one hundred paces ahead, and then we will stay on the trail for a while before venturing off again into the brush. By that time it will be dusk, and they will not be able to find us."

Hereca replied, "You mimic the ways of the fox. You Romans are clever."

"Sometimes not clever enough. Let us hope this works. I do not relish going head-to-head with a large band of Cherusci."

The pair completed their ruse, leaving the path, venturing into thick foliage, and then returning to the trail one hundred paces ahead. They were off again, venturing farther down the main trail.

A short while later, the tracker, Theudis, followed the signs of disturbance off the main path and into the foliage. Brixus, impatient to capture his prey, urged the men forward. "Move now. Speed is of the essence. They cannot be much farther."

The progress of the Cherusci slowed as they entered the foliage. After a short distance, Theudis held up his hand for them to halt.

Brixus was furious. "You are trying my patience. Now what? Why do you delay us?"

Theudis remained calm, not intimidated. After all, they needed him. "We must be sure of the direction they are heading. Something tells me our adversary is attempting to mislead us. If we lose them in this dense cover, we will never find them. Is that what you want?"

Brixus snarled. "Stop asking me stupid questions and find them."

Theudis slowly walked along the forest floor, his eyes never leaving the ground. He stopped and studied the ground before him. He knelt down on the damp earth, pointing to a break in a vine growing along the forest floor. He knelt down and examined a piece of greenery. "Look at this, Brixus. The stem of this vine is broken as if someone tripped on it. If I am reading the signs correctly, they have changed direction and are heading back toward the main path."

He crawled to his left, his eyes inches from the ground. "Yes, just as I thought. Look at this imprint on the ground."

Brixus squinted in the fading light. "I cannot tell, but I will take your word for it. You had better be right, Theudis, or Safrax is going to skin you alive. Let's make haste back to the trail. I do not want to lose them in the approaching darkness."

They came to a minor curve in the path. Valerius raised his hand up for Hereca to stop. She looked at him expectantly, waiting to hear what was next. He looked up at the evening sky. Darkness was descending upon them. He was not sure if his ploy had fooled the trailing Cherusci, but now was the right moment to exit the trail again and enter the forest. It would be difficult for his pursuers to detect their evasive action in the dwindling light. He motioned Hereca to move to the right into the forest. Valerius looked down the trail for any sign of their chasers, and then followed after her.

Valerius motioned Hereca to come closer. "Tread lightly and only speak in a hushed tone. The Cherusci may not be far behind us. I hope to lose them in the approaching gloom."

Moments later, the band of Cherusci warriors rounded the slight bend in the trail, Theudis in the lead. He walked hunched over, his eyes glued to the trail. He moved past the point where Valerius had exited the track when entering the dense forest, and then halted. Brixus almost crashed into him.

He spoke in a menacing tone. "Now what are you doing?"

Theudis said nothing. He slowly retraced his steps, and then halted. He looked up at Brixus. "They have gone off the trail again and have entered the forest here." He pointed to a spot between two thornbushes. "They are not far ahead of us."

Brixus scowled. He turned to his followers. "Don't just stand there. Go after them." The band of Cherusci hurried back off the beaten path into the brush.

Valerius walked softly next to Hereca, the woods silent as dusk approached. He faintly heard voices back in the direction from which they had come. "Hereca, they are close behind us. Run."

The pair dashed forward. Valerius heard shouts of discovery behind them. They moved as fast as possible. The brush was clearing, not thickening as he'd hoped. He was not sure he could lose his pursuers in time before darkness closed in on them. He made a quick decision. "Hereca, keep running in that direction and do not stop. I will give them some discouragement."

She hesitated.

Valerius shouted at her, "Go. I will catch up with you."

She darted away, not looking back.

He quickly strung his bow and nocked an arrow. In one fluid motion, he drew the bow back and let an arrow fly in the direction of the Cherusci, some of whom were now visible. He sent a stream of arrows in their direction and was rewarded with terrible shrieks as the missiles found their marks. He spotted a figure off to his left, perhaps fifty paces away. He fired quickly, striking the man fully in the chest, knocking him off his feet. Valerius turned and sprinted in the direction where Hereca had gone.

The leader of the Cherusci, Brixus, was down. The arrow had penetrated his chest cavity. He breathed a few shallow breaths and was still. The band of warriors gathered around him, unsure of what to do. Also among the dead was Theudis, the last of the skilled trackers. Several others had also been wounded, some severely. The unexpected carnage halted their chase. The survivors looked at one another, wondering what to do next.

Valerius scampered through the forest, looking for Hereca. He saw no sign of her as nightfall blanketed the wooded landscape. He slowed his pace slightly, so he would not stumble. He smiled smugly. The Cherusci would not be able to track him in the blackness. He had won for now, but he needed to find Hereca. She had to be somewhere up ahead. Valerius continued moving in the direction he thought she was headed. He stopped every so often to listen for sounds of pursuit or of Hereca to his front, but all that greeted him was silence.

He moved through the forest for some time before stopping. It was useless to continue to search in the darkness. He sat at the base of a tree to collect his thoughts. What now? He would never find Hereca stumbling about in the night. Was he wrong to send Hereca ahead? He had made the decision hastily. Was it the right one? He pondered this for a moment. Yes, it made sense. His purpose in confronting the pursuers was only to delay them. If he was killed or captured, it would have served no useful purpose for her to be with him. At least she had a chance on her own. Exhausted, Valerius, sitting with his back to the large tree, closed his eyes and slept.

It was not a dreamless sleep. He had haunting visions that pushed and pulled at his consciousness. In one sequence, an eagle soared high above him in a cloudless sky, and then the face of Clonid, Hereca's mother, materialized. She smiled at him and pointed toward the eagle. She silently mouthed the word, "Go." Out of the darkness strode Arminius. He shouted at Valerius, "You were fortunate once, Roman, but you will not escape me again." In the next sequence, Valerius gazed at the night sky and found the star that always pointed north. With that, scores of shooting stars blazed across the heavens, all heading south. This image was replaced by Germanicus's legions, with eagle standards held high, marching down a long Roman-constructed road. He ran to them, hailing the legionnaires, but they did not acknowledge his presence. Wothar appeared to him, his chest covered in blood, pointing across a wide flowing river.

Valerius gasped, his body bathed in sweat. It was still dark, though the dawn was approaching. He was grateful to be awake and away from those vivid imaginings. What in Hades did it all mean? He heard the first chirps of the birds greeting the new day. He sat and listened, but heard nothing to indicate the presence of other men. Slowly he got to his feet and surveyed his surroundings. Picking up his bow and quiver of arrows, he ventured forth in the direction he believed Hereca had traveled. He moved several miles before he came to a stream. If Hereca had traveled in this direction, she would have had to cross it. He would search both upstream and downstream for signs of her. The Cherusci might be on his trail, but he would ignore that threat for now. Leaping into the creek bed, he began combing the area downstream for signs.

Valerius moved slowly, sometimes crossing to the other side, seeking signs of her presence, halting his exploration after every hundred paces or so, listening for the Cherusci or Hereca. All he heard were the songbirds and the gurgling of the creek. After some time, he stopped and sighed. Nothing downstream. He hurried back to the spot where his path originally intersected the brook. He paused and drank greedily of the cool water. Again he listened, but all he heard were the sounds of the creek and the forest.

He searched painstakingly upstream, but there was still no sign of Hereca. By now it was midmorning. He looked up ahead and observed where a large tree had fallen across the brook. He would go as far as that spot before stopping, and then he would continue across the stream. A strong breeze blew through the treetops. There were tracks of deer and wild boar, plus other small game, in the soft sand at the creek's edge, but no sign of a person. He halted and rubbed his neck, now stiff from constantly staring at the ground. He moved onward to a bed of gravel at the streamside, but saw nothing on his side of the stream. Peering across the small stream, he spotted what looked to be some trampled grass shoots. He waded in the chilled waters and closely examined the break in the foliage. He leaped up out of the creek bed and on to the opposite bank and peered at the earth. There in the mud was a partial imprint of a sandal. It had to be Hereca. There was no one else in this wilderness.

Tracking her was frustratingly slow, for he was not adept at reading the signs of someone passing through the woods. He was tempted to call out her name, but he was unsure if the Cherusci were still following his trace and in the vicinity. Odds were they were not on his trail, for surely they would have found him by now. He bent down and examined the ground. He saw nothing that would indicate the hint of another person. He cursed silently. Had he lost her again? Which direction and how far had she journeyed? Now that she was gone, he realized how badly he missed her. He wanted her next to him and would not continue his flight toward the safety of the Roman garrisons on the Rhine without her. He felt responsible for her safety. They had gone through much together, forming a bond he never would have thought possible. There was no doubt she was a tough woman capable of surviving in this environment, but what would be her ultimate destiny, alone and wandering about?

As if by some divine intervention, he glanced to the side and saw some bruised and trampled grass, but how long ago? A more skilled tracker would know, but he did not. Regardless, that had to be her. His spirit soared. He took off running in the direction suggested by the signs of her passing. He plowed through bushes, avoiding the thornier versions. The vegetation thinned out and then became thick again. He crossed a small brook, jumping from stone to stone to cross it. He approached a wooded glade with a small clearing. He spied her sitting with her knees drawn up, a solitary shaft of sunlight penetrating the tree branches illuminating her. "You are a hard person to find in these woods."

She looked up, startled at the voice. They rushed and embraced. No words were spoken.

It was a long day. Using the sun's position in the sky, they wandered south, or close to that direction as their reckoning was imprecise. Eventually the pair stumbled upon a beaten path, more like a game trail, that headed roughly south. They advanced out of the wilderness and into cleared lands and pastures. The area was populated by many Cherusci settlements and farms. They spent much of the day circumventing these places. Caution was the key. They halted in view of another Cherusci village and skirted around the edge of the settlement, always keeping in concealment.

Valerius asked Hereca a question that had been nagging at him most of the day. "Just for argument's sake, if we were discovered, could we be brazen and bluff our way through? We both speak the language, you much better than me, but if we concocted some story about the purpose of our travel, could we not convince them to let us pass?

Hereca snorted. "Not likely. We could get by from a distance, but upon closer scrutiny, our story would unravel like a cheap piece of cloth."

Valerius was perplexed. "How so?"

"The Cherusci have a distinct dialect, so even I would be identified as someone not of Cherusci blood, and they are a close-knit group. To them, there are the Cherusci, and then there are all other people. Perhaps even more damning is your appearance. You may wear German clothing, and your hair and beard are longer than those of a Roman, but you do not look German. It is your coloring and complexion. Throw in that bow of yours, and you would be branded as a threat. We need to keep out of sight."

Valerius grunted in disappointment. "Nevertheless, just in case, we should concoct some story of why we are traveling out of the lands of the Dolgubni. Think of something, for you will need to be the one who speaks on our behalf."

It was getting late in the afternoon. Valerius regarded the sky and sniffed the wind. "Is it just me, or do you think it will rain sometime tonight? Look at those heavy clouds."

Hereca replied, "I was thinking the same thing."

"I suggest we leave this path and see what shelter might be available. I do not relish the thought of sleeping in the rain."

They cut diagonally through the forest away from the village and soon came upon some rocky crags bordering a clear rushing stream.

Valerius pointed. "If the gods are with us, there should be an overhang somewhere in there. Let's go look. You go to the left, and I will move to the right. We will meet back here at this location. Do not stray too far. I do not want to lose you again."

The pair split up, seeking to find shelter. Valerius wandered up and down the rock faces, but saw nothing that would satisfy their purposes. He ventured back toward the dirt trail, hoping they might have missed something. He noted a narrow winding path that had been used by people before. He decided to follow it, with the expectation that there had to be a reason for this trail. It had to lead somewhere. His logic was rewarded. The small manmade avenue led to a sleeping shelter, complete with a rocky overhang that would shield them in case of rain. It was a hunters' camp that had witnessed occasional use.

Valerius bolted from his position to find Hereca before she wandered too far. He softly called her name several times before she answered.

"Over here, Hereca. I have found us shelter."

She materialized out of a thicket with one of the captured satchels slung over her shoulder and a spear in the other hand. "Good, because I am about at the end of my limits."

The pair walked back toward the shelter. It would do nicely. There was a space of about five feet between the overhang and the ground. It extended back about eight feet, which was more than adequate to protect them from any storms. The previous users of this location had built a stone fire pit to reflect the heat back toward the small cavern. Stout wooden branches formed a rectangular bed, stuffed with dried moss and pine needles.

"Hereca, caution be damned, I am building a fire. In this wooded terrain, no one will be able to see the light from afar. The temperature is dropping, and we need some warmth. It is my sense there is no one around."

Hereca nodded wearily. Valerius, using a flint and his knife, built a small fire, which provided some degree of warmth. The two sat on the bedding munching on the barley cakes and dried venison from the captured satchels. Valerius threw his woolen cloak around both of their shoulders. They sat staring at the fire.

Hereca spoke. "What is it like on the other side of the Rhine? I fear I will not be viewed favorably, being from one of Rome's enemies. What kind of life will I find there?"

Valerius responded, "First, you need to understand that there are peoples from many different tribes that have settled there. You are under the impression that there is a dominant language and culture. There is not. Almost all the people settling there are outsiders. Also, there is not just one town, but many settlements are along the Rhine. Commerce is flowing up the river from the sea. Above all, it will be safe. You will not have Cherusci raiding the settlements. The Rhine is a border the Germans have not crossed in many years. You will be under the protection of Rome and her legions."

"It is hard for me to understand these things. I have lived all my life in our little settlement."

"I know, Hereca. You will have to trust me on this. Anyone who disrespects you will have to answer to me."

"But are you not going back to Rome?"

Valerius shook his head. "I do not think so. That is a place that is now lost to me. I think I will stay in the provinces."

Hereca was silent. She snuggled closer to Valerius.

"I would like that."

A rumble of thunder interrupted their conversation. Rain began falling, and windblown drops of water made the fire sputter. With that the pair bedded down. Valerius smiled as Hereca hugged him close. They fell into an exhausted sleep. If he could have seen Hereca's face, he would have noted that she was smiling also.

They awoke at dawn to a cold pounding rain. Hereca groaned. "Tell me we do not have to venture forth into that mess."

Valerius glanced at the torrent and spoke. "I suppose not. We would be drenched in a matter of moments, and then the chill would set in. I think we should wait it out."

Hereca rolled over facing Valerius. She spoke coyly. "Tell me more of what I might expect of life on the other side of the Rhine."

Valerius was flustered. He could feel the pressure of Hereca's breasts on him. "I do not mean to make light of your lifestyle among the Dolgubni, but you will experience many new things that were not available to you in your settlement. There are many varied foods for sale in the towns along the Rhine. You will find some of these to your liking, I am sure. There are many options of women's clothing accessible to you. Then there are the dwellings. Many have real floors, with roofs made of tile that do not leak rain. So in terms of comfort, you may find this to your liking. I forgot to mention the baths. They have large buildings that house pools of warm and cold water where one can bathe even in the dead of winter."

Hereca opened her eyes wide in amazement. “And this is available to all?”

“If you have enough coin, yes, it is open to everyone.”

“And they have warm water even in the depth of winter?”

“They do.”

“You are not joking with me?”

“I am not. It is all true.”

Hereca looked into his eyes. “And when the women bathe, do they take all of their clothes off?”

Valerius stared back at her. “Of course.”

She reached over and tugged at his tunic. From there, things went totally out of control. Clothes flew everywhere. They were still in bed at the end of the morning.

The weather cleared, and by early afternoon the pair were trekking south once more. The air held a chill, and the wind blew from the north. Onward they went, skirting villages and cautiously advancing down the trail.

The pair stopped walking. Hereca spoke. “I have something good to say and something not so good.”

“Let me hear it.”

“The good is that I believe we have exited the land of the Cherusci and are now in the land of the Chatti people.”

“Great. So what’s the not so good?”

“The Chatti are almost as bad as the Cherusci.”

Valerius frowned. “Thank you for that revelation. So, not to overstate the obvious, we are still in extreme danger?”

“Yes, we are.”

Valerius cursed in Latin. “*Stercus*.”

Hereca, puzzled, asked, “What does *stercus* mean?”

Valerius translated in the Germanic tongue: “Shit.”

Hereca spluttered with laughter. “Well put, Roman.”

Later in the afternoon farther down the worn path, they stopped at a clear bubbling spring and drank deeply. The pair was too preoccupied with their thirst to notice that this was a place often visited. The signs were all there if they had bothered to look. The path to the cool clear waters was heavily traveled. Even more conspicuous were the imprints of many feet around the perimeter. The two were startled as a group of four women materialized out of the bushes carrying a variety of empty containers to fill. The women were alarmed at the presence of strangers at their spring. Their expressions of shock deepened when they saw the variety of weapons they carried.

Hereca was quick to act. She stood and looked directly at the group, now frozen in place. Putting forth her most disarming smile, she spoke. "Hello. Isn't this a glorious day?" Not waiting for a reply, she continued, "Correct me if I am wrong, but you must be of the Chatti tribe. My husband and I are of the Dolgubni and are traveling to the land of the Bructeri to attend a wedding. There was a larger contingent of us, but we departed two days later on account of my mother, who was ill. We have yet to catch up to them. Have you seen any Dolgubni in this vicinity?"

The women were silent, eyeing the couple with suspicion. Finally one of the women, clearly the oldest of the bunch, spoke. "You have come a long way. Are not the Dolgubni lands north of the Cherusci?"

"Yes, they are. It has been a wearisome journey."

The Chatti woman continued, "Why do you have so many weapons?" She directed her gaze to Valerius's bow and spear.

"You have not heard? We were warned that the cursed Romans have crossed the Rhine already and are killing our people." Hereca slipped in the "our" word to get the Chatti women to empathize with them. The Romans were hated by all in this region of Germania.

The women's faces turned to fear. The older woman continued, "We have not heard this. Our village lost many of our warriors to the Roman invaders last summer."

Hereca jumped right in. "So did the Dolgubni. We are united with our Chatti brethren in the loathing of the Romans." She hoped this would elicit some sympathy among the Chatti. It worked.

The woman spat upon the ground. "We detest the Romans and wish to see them destroyed. What is your name, Dolgubni woman, and that of your husband?"

"I am called Hereca. This is my husband, Otho."

"I am Adena." She then introduced the others as Brinditha, Calaris, and Lorinda.

Valerius smiled and offered a grunt in return.

"Does not your husband speak?"

Hereca turned to Valerius.

Valerius nimbly answered, "Forgive me, ladies. I did not mean to be rude. I hope you can understand me. My accent is of the Frisi tribe. We speak a little differently and use some strange weapons." He lifted his bow to show them. He hoped they bought into his ruse. The Frisi were a tribe a long way from the Chatti lands. Valerius hoped that the women had never encountered a Frisi before.

Adena spoke. "A strange combination, a Dolgubni and a Frisi."

Hereca sighed. "It is a long story, which I will not bore you with. But I can tell you that the Frisi men are as lazy as the Dolgubni."

The Chatti women all laughed. Adena spoke. "And just as lazy as the Chatti men."

Hereca grinned back knowingly. "Can you direct us toward the lands of the Bructeri? All we know is that we are supposed to head south along the trail that passes through the Cherusci and Chatti lands."

Adena pointed at the trail. "You are on the right path. The Bructeri lands are two days march from here."

Hereca turned to Valerius. "Two days. We still have a long way to go. Are you ready, husband of mine? We must not tarry, or we will miss the wedding festivities."

After they were some distance away from the spring and the Chatti women, Valerius slowed the pace down. "My name is Otho? You could not do better than that?"

She smiled. "That was the first name that came to me."

In a more serious tone, he continued, "I think we are safe thanks to your glib tongue back there. You certainly put those women at ease. You practically had them eating out of your hand with your comments about our common foe, the Romans, and the fact that the Dolgubni lost many warriors as well. And then that comment about the lazy menfolk that really had them in sympathy with you."

Hereca smiled. "I may seem like a simple German woman to you, but I do possess some guile when needed."

"You would do well in the Roman Senate."

"What is the Senate?"

Valerius sighed. "I will explain it to you someday. Let's get moving."

Hereca grabbed his hand. "Let's go."

XIX

Valerius returned to their small encampment in a copse of evergreens. He held a rabbit transfixed with an arrow. Hereca looked up from her seat around the small fire. "Thank Wodan you Romans know how to hunt. I am starving. Are you going to prepare it so we can roast it over the fire?"

Valerius looked perplexed. "Ah, I do not know how to do that."

Hereca was astounded. "Is this another of your jokes?"

Valerius grinned back sheepishly. "It is not. We always had people prepare our food in Rome, and the same goes for the legions."

Hereca gestured toward the rabbit. "I see. Hand me your knife, and I will show you how."

She proceeded to skin and gut the creature and had it roasting on a spit in no time. She looked back at him. "That is how you prepare game for a meal. Next time you do it."

In a short time the pair were enjoying the roasted rabbit with the last of their stale barley cakes. Valerius licked the grease off his thumb. "I never tasted anything so good."

Hereca replied, "It must be my cooking."

Valerius added a few more sticks to the fire to ward off the night chill and ventured toward their bed of pine needles. He lay down in the bed of pine needles and beckoned Hereca to join him. She gave a throaty laugh and jumped in after him.

The next day proved to be more of the same. They journeyed through dense forests interrupted intermittently by cleared farmlands adjacent to Chatti villages. Valerius stopped and motioned for Hereca to remain where she was while he scouted ahead. They were near the edge of a small plateau that would offer a wide view once they cleared the current stand of timber. He cautiously advanced ahead, reaching the edge of the tree line. He parted some offending branches blocking his sight and peered ahead. He was shocked at what he observed. The view of the valley below reflected great swaths of blackened scorched earth. Off in the distance, he could see the remains of several villages, the wrecked dwellings testimony to the death and destruction reaped by the legions last summer. They must now be in the land of the Bructeri.

Valerius paused and pondered his next steps. Over the last several days, he had perceived their lack of vigilance. As fatigue set in from their arduous journey, the less caution they had exhibited. The meeting of the Chatti women at the spring was clear proof. They should have scouted the area before approaching the watering spot. Their next encounter might not end as well. Now what? The road ahead offered less concealment as the land gave way from forest to wide plain. It would be more difficult to rely on stealth, but then again, how many people would they encounter? The land ahead offered little evidence of habitation, only charred landscape.

The real possibility that he might see Romans again, something for which he had long ago given up hope, weighed on him. How should he proceed? What would Marcellus do in these circumstances? If they became overanxious, they might pay with their lives. With the open ground stretching before him in the lands of the Bructeri and Marsi, it would be impossible to travel unobserved. He assumed that there would be bands of Germans ahead. The Romans had not killed them all. He thought back to his Teutoburg flight to the Rhine. They had sacrificed speed for caution and traveled at night, so that is what he would do.

He returned to Hereca. She looked at him quizzically. "What took you so long?"

"There is a wide plain ahead of us. I believe we are entering into the lands of the Bructeri. Settlements have been razed to the ground, and there is little in the way of cover for us to travel unnoticed."

"How bad is it?"

"It is an ugly scene. I believe we need to restrict our movements to the nighttime. I am almost certain we will encounter Bructeri and Marsi groups if we travel in the daylight. It will be much slower going, but safer."

"How much farther to the Rhine?"

"I did not pay much attention to the distance when the legions advanced through this territory. I would guess maybe four days."

She replied, "And we will need to be careful even in the night?"

"Yes, but I cannot imagine too many people out in the blackness. Why don't we wait here until dusk and then proceed?"

As darkness neared, the pair carefully descended the escarpment to the plain below. They slowly made their way south. Every so often, Valerius would check the heavens for the star that always pointed north, and adjusted their direction as needed. Aided by the light of a full moon, they made their way for some time through the devastated landscape. At one point they trudged through burned stubble. On occasion they passed by the ruined silhouettes of once prosperous settlements. As they trekked over a small rise in the land, off in the distance, they could see watch fires.

Valerius leaned close to Hereca and spoke softly. "If you need to converse with me, do so in a hushed tone. Sound carries much farther at night."

She looked at him quizzically. "Why is that?"

Valerius shrugged. "I have no idea. It just does."

Hereca shivered in the night chill. Valerius moved closer to her and wrapped his cloak around her. They ventured farther south as the night wore on. The landscape was more of the same: devastated villages and fields, with occasional watch fires. They gave the beacons a wide berth, at times going through heavy brush and timber. Finally the pink traces of dawn glowed on the eastern horizon.

Valerius looked about and saw a copse of woods not too far ahead. He pointed with his arm, and the pair moved at a much faster pace toward the refuge. Upon entering the wooded area, Valerius heard the gurgling of a small stream. They needed water and a place to hole up for the day. He found a secluded spot, with dry ground, close to the brook that was sheltered from the wind. The pair slumped down exhausted and hungry and fell asleep.

Later that day, Valerius awoke and decided to go hunting. He looked over at Hereca, noting she was in a sound sleep. There was no sense in waking her. She was exhausted and would need all of her strength to complete the journey. Their bellies were empty, and their strength was waning. In his mind, it was worth the risk to hunt. Food would sharpen their senses, giving them a better chance of reaching the Rhine. He wandered off not far from their day hideaway, hoping to find some game. He soon came to a mixture of field and scrub pine, a promising spot to hunt.

The Goddess Fortuna was with him that day. He spied two rabbits and brought them both down with perfect shots from his bow. But he was not finished. He flushed two more rabbits from the tall grass of the field. He rapidly sighted his bow, but missed the first one. Not to be deterred, he notched a second missile and shot from extreme range, nailing the other one. Grinning from ear to ear, he gathered the third rabbit. *Wait until Hereca sees this*, he thought.

He searched in vain for his arrow that had missed the target, for his supply in his quiver was running low. He was so engaged in finding the arrow that he stumbled into a family who he assumed to be Bructeri: a mother, father, and two young children. Valerius was startled, and put his hand next to his iron knife. Upon closer observation, he realized that this family posed little threat to him. They were a pathetic-looking bunch, scrawny, obviously malnourished, and their faces were encrusted with grime. No doubt life had been hard for them.

The mother and father eyed the rabbits that Valerius possessed, but said nothing. Without a second thought, he stepped forward toward them. The family retreated in fright. He held two of the rabbits out for them. The mother's eyes brimmed with tears. The father stepped forward hesitantly and accepted the offering. "Thank you," he said.

Valerius nodded, not willing to speak with his accented German. No sense in giving these folks any suspicious thoughts, although he doubted they were concerned about a stranger who had just provided them a meal. He turned and ventured back toward Hereca.

Entering their camp area, he noted that Hereca was now awake. Valerius held up the rabbit for her to see. "Dinner," he exclaimed.

"That should do nicely," she replied.

"I had two others, but I stumbled upon a starving Bructeri family, a mother and father plus two young children. I gave them two of the rabbits."

Hereca rushed over to him and hugged him. "You are a good man, Valerius."

He grinned. "So I am told. I am also told that I have extremely poor taste in women."

In mock anger, she picked up a stone and threw it at him.

The travel that night was easy, the weather favorable. They found themselves on a wide dirt road illuminated by a bright moon and clear skies. Better yet, there was no one about. It was deep into the night, about three hours until dawn. The pair strolled hand in hand. Valerius had his bow strapped to his back and a German spear in his hand. Valerius whispered to Hereca, "I am pleased with the progress—"

He never finished. They were suddenly surrounded by dark shadows. The pair halted. Valerius silently cursed his lack of vigilance, wondering what would be the shadows' first move.

One of the figures spoke. "What have we here? Two wayward stragglers moving about in the dark."

Hereca spoke. "We are of the Dolgubni tribe. We are traveling south to attend a wedding."

The same figure spoke again. "I do not care who you are and why you are traveling. We own this road."

Valerius dropped his hand from Hereca's and surreptitiously shifted his grip on his spear. He nudged Hereca with the side of his foot, hoping she got his warning. There looked to be five of them, and the speaker was obviously the leader. Words would not get them out of this confrontation. He decided he would kill the leader first. The group appeared relaxed and not expecting any trouble from the couple.

"What do you want? We have no money," said Hereca.

The leader snorted. "I think we will have you first." The other men snickered. He moved closer. "Let me get a better look at you."

Valerius erupted out of his stance and drove his spear deep into the leader's neck. He quickly yanked it out in a spray of blood and then transfixed the next closest individual. Out of the corner of his eye, he saw Hereca stab the man closest to her in the face with her knife. The two remaining men fled in terror down the road.

Valerius reached for Hereca. "Are you all right?"

"I am. What should we do with these vermin?" She gestured with her knife to two of the men writhing on the ground. The other man, the leader, lay motionless.

"Leave them be. We need to put some distance between us and these bandits. Let's get out of here." The pair broke into a trot down the dirt avenue, leaving the wounded men behind.

Valerius stood at the river crossing at Vetera, not believing that he had defied the odds and made it back to safety, cheating death once more. The travel over the past several days had proved to be uneventful; they encountered no one during their evening sojourns. Hereca gaped at the pontoon bridge spanning the Rhine. There was sparse traffic crossing the bridge this particular morning. "I had no idea you Romans could build such a thing."

Valerius chuckled. "Indeed they do. Now can we get moving? I am starved, cold, and in desperate need of a bath."

The pair walked over the bridge and then on to the Roman paved road on the other side. The first thing he noticed was the lack of bustle. There were few legionnaires about, and the wharf along the river was devoid of any activity. Looking about, he noted the temporary camps adjacent to the permanent fortress of Vetera were no longer occupied. Scanning the road ahead, he wondered where everyone was. Surely the troops should be out of their winter camps by now and getting ready for the campaign. Had they crossed the Rhine already? No, he thought. It was much too early in the spring, and even if they had, he would have observed the activity of the legions from whence he had just come.

The pair approached the main gate of the fortress, with its intimidating wooden towers guarding the entrance. As they neared the access point, their path was blocked by two legionnaires holding javelins. The one to the left spoke gruffly. "No Germans allowed into the fortress without a pass."

Valerius knew that his appearance was hardly that of a Roman officer. The only vestige of Roman apparel he wore was his marching sandals, and they were in tatters. He calmly spoke Latin for the first time in about eight months. "I am a tribune on General Germanicus's staff. He would want to be notified at once upon my return."

The sentries were flustered, not expecting a figure dressed in German garb but speaking perfect Latin. The two looked at each other questioningly. Noting the strangers' blood-spattered clothing, they gripped their spears tightly. When neither spoke, Valerius continued, "Listen, I know my appearance does not fit that of a military officer, but I have been away for a while. General Germanicus knows me."

One of the sentries turned about. "I will get our centurion. He will know what to do. Wait here with my fellow sentry, Calvus."

Valerius, speaking German, turned to Hereca. "We will need to wait here for a bit." The sentry gawked as the guttural words issued forth, no doubt confounding him further as to the identity of this mysterious man.

Hereca said nothing. She stared wide-eyed at the massive Roman fortification.

Several minutes later, the centurion of the guard approached, giving him a curious look. "What's your story, Tribune, if that's who you are?"

"I would like to see General Germanicus. My name is Tribune Valerius Maximus. He knows me. I was attached to his staff. Look,

I have been missing for almost eight months. I was captured by the Germans last summer in the battle in the meadow. I have escaped my captors. Would you please let me pass?"

The centurion gestured to Hereca. "And her?"

"She is with me."

The pair followed the centurion of the guard up the main thoroughfare past the bakeries, watering points, storage areas, and blacksmiths. They reached the Praetorium.

The centurion gestured. "This way."

Valerius and Hereca were ushered into a small alcove. "Wait here," said the officer brusquely. "What did you say your name was?"

Valerius replied, "What did you say your name was, *sir*?"

The centurion eyed him for a moment, then asked the question again. "What did you say your name was, sir?"

"Tribune Valerius Maximus."

The centurion continued down a hallway. They could hear some indistinct chatter as he reported the information about the mysterious Roman officer in German clothing. They did not have to wait long. A tribune whom Valerius did not recognize burst into the room. "Come with me. The general will see you now."

The pair were escorted into the inner sanctum. Germanicus, who was seated at his desk, broke into a wide grin. "By the gods it is really you. Tribune, you are a tough man to kill." He rose and clasped firmly Valerius's hand. He motioned to Hereca. "And who is this lovely creature?"

"Sir, this is Hereca of the Dolgubni tribe. We saved each other on several occasions. She does not speak any Latin."

Valerius turned toward her and spoke in German. "Hereca, this is my commanding officer, General Germanicus."

She looked at Valerius in puzzlement.

He realized his error. "Germanicus is our chieftain."

She turned toward Germanicus and slightly bowed. "Hereca," she said.

A servant brought in a tray of goblets with chilled wine.

Germanicus raised a goblet. "To your safe return, Tribune."

Valerius and Hereca drank greedily from their goblets. Valerius wiped his mouth on his tattered sleeve. "I have not had wine in over eight months. That was the best-tasting grape I ever had."

With that, Marcellus, who had been summoned with the news of Valerius's return, burst into the room.

"Well, I'll be dyed seven shades of shit."

Valerius replied, "Thanks for that warm greeting. I certainly hope that was a metaphor."

The centurion lumbered over and hugged him, lifting him off his feet. "Ha! I cannot believe you returned to us."

"I have." He looked back to Germanicus. "Sir, of course I will provide you a full report later, but I think you should know that there is internal strife among the Germans. I was captured by the Dolgubni, a small tribe with lands north of the Cherusci. About two weeks ago, the Cherusci raided the Dolgubni village, killing most of the inhabitants. This proved fortunate for me, for it afforded me the opportunity to escape."

The general scowled. "Ordinarily that would be valuable intelligence, but sadly not anymore. Tiberius has recalled the legions back to their home bases. The German campaign is finished. Apparently he believes the war has become too costly, as we did not kill Arminius and destroy the Cherusci. I have tried to persuade him otherwise, but he is steadfast in his beliefs. I have been summoned to Rome to receive a triumph for my victories over the Germans. After that I will be posted to the eastern part of the empire."

"So all of our efforts were for naught?"

"Not so, Tribune. We did recover two of the eagles, and we put a licking on the Germans. I do not believe they will be too anxious to cross the Rhine and raid Roman territory." Germanicus beamed at Valerius. "So, enough about the German campaign. What are your plans, Tribune?"

Valerius gazed directly into Germanicus's eyes. "I was hoping that I could be discharged of my military obligation. I have plans to stay here in Germania on the Rhine and start a new life."

The general rubbed his jaw in thought. "What about your parents? They are probably anxious to see you."

"I know, but Rome holds nothing but bad memories. I have no desire to return there."

"I see. Well, Tribune, as to the first part of your request, you will be discharged from your military obligation. I will see to that. You have served me and the legions with distinction. But like it or not, you are traveling back to Rome with me. You are a hero of Rome and will be part of the triumph." He looked over toward Marcellus. "That applies to you also, Centurion."

"Yes, sir," he replied.

Germanicus turned his gaze back to Valerius. "We will be leaving in a few days from now. You will need to get outfitted with new armor and a sword as befitting your rank."

"But, sir, I was hoping..."

"Do not argue with me, Tribune. My pronouncement was an edict, not a request. Besides, you are obligated to see your parents after what they have been through. I can appreciate your feelings about Rome concerning your late wife, but you will need to put them aside. You can return here to the Rhine afterward. Understood?"

Valerius glanced over at Hereca. How would he explain this to her? She would be upset about it, but he was sure he could convince her to go with him, especially since it was only a temporary stay in the capital city. He directed his gaze back to Germanicus. "Understood, sir."

XX

Rome

Many weeks later the flotilla carrying Germanicus and his Praetorian cohort plus the entire Twentieth Legion entered the harbor at Ostia, the seaport that served as Rome's gateway to the seas. The massive transport glided smoothly against the wooden pier, gently nudging the wooden structure with a slight thump.

Hereca stood at the rail next to Valerius and Marcellus, gazing at the massive quay and the town beyond. "This is Rome?" she asked.

Valerius chuckled. "No, Hereca. That is Ostia. Rome lays less than a day's walk from here."

"Oh," she said, disappointment ringing in her reply. "I am anxious to see this city of yours after all you have told me about it."

"Soon. You will be astounded at what you see. Ask Marcellus. He never saw Rome until last year."

Valerius turned toward the centurion and spoke in Latin, repeating his previous statement.

Marcellus proffered a wide grin. "Yes, it was beyond what I had imagined. You will be amazed."

Valerius translated in German to Hereca. He reached down and squeezed her hand for assurance.

The trio boarded a water barge and journeyed up the Tiber toward the city. As the silhouette of the city came into view when the barge rounded a bend in the river, Hereca just stood there, stunned and unable to speak. The marble buildings gleamed in the late afternoon sunshine. Valerius pointed out several, but stopped when he realized that Hereca had no idea of the significance of any of them. They disembarked at a wooden pier and, along with several porters, made their way to Aventine Hill.

The trio arrived unannounced at his home. While his parents knew he would be arriving, they had no idea when. Valerius bounded up the stone steps of his parents' home, pounding on the massive front entry. Horace, the servant who manned the front entry, shrieked and embraced the previous young master of the house. His parents hurried from the atrium where they had been sitting and rushed toward their lost son. His mother and father openly wept at seeing him again.

Hereca and Marcellus stood by watching the poignant moment. Finally Sentius and Vispania broke off their embraces with their son and hugged Marcellus. They released Marcellus and turned to Hereca, eyeing her curiously, wondering who this strange, beautiful woman was, for she was obviously not a Roman, and what her relationship was with their son. The silence was broken as the enigmatic woman put her foot forward and announced her name. "Hereca," she said.

Vispania and Sentius announced their names to her, and then turned and looked quizzically at Valerius. "Mother, Father, this is Hereca. She is of the Dolgubni tribe and saved my life during my captivity and escape from Germania. She is with me."

His parents nodded numbly, not knowing what to do or say. An awkward silence followed. Finally Vispania gave Hereca a light embrace and said, "Welcome to our home."

Hereca understood the Latin word "welcome" and offered a wide smile to Vispania. She spoke in her guttural Latin, saying the word, thank you.

A week later to celebrate his coming back, a huge party was hosted by Valerius's parents in his honor. Germanicus and his wife, Agrippina, attended. His commander spoke glowingly about Valerius's contributions to the successful campaign in Germania, including his role and that of Marcellus in the recapture of the Seventeenth eagle standard from the Chatti village where Segestes and Thusnelda were located. General Apronius, legate of the Twentieth Legion, also paid tribute to Valerius, calling him one of the finest junior officers with whom he had ever served. General Tubero did not attend.

Valerius appreciated the accolades and valued the fact that two of Rome's finest and senior military commanders found the time to attend his return home.

The tribune spent much of the time showing the sights of Rome to his German woman. She had not been thrilled about venturing to Rome, but Valerius had gently persuaded her, stating that they would only be there a short time. It had been a difficult discussion, but in the end she had agreed to come with him on the condition that they both return to the Rhine. She had overcome her initial fears, and it did not take her long to enjoy the many and diverse sights of the imperial city. She gawked at the enormity of the buildings and numbers of people. In the end, she absorbed the Roman culture and took to the many comforts it had to offer.

Valerius appeared restless and never fully at ease back in his home setting. It was clear to Sentius and Vispania that their son, while glad to see them, had ambivalent feelings about returning to Rome. And then there was Hereca. His parents had been taken aback with Valerius's relationship with Hereca, a German woman from the wilds of the north who barely spoke any Latin. This was certainly not the match that they had envisioned, but as time went on during their visit, they came to appreciate all the vitality and zeal the young woman offered. Valerius had relayed to his parents their perilous flight from the Dolgubni village and their battles with the Cherusci. The German princess lacked the refined manners and culture of Roman women, but underneath it all, she was a formidable person who had survived perils that most could not imagine.

Valerius had informed his parents that he was not going to remain in Rome and would be going back to the territory on the Rhine. His parents were disappointed that he did not want to stay in Rome but understood his reluctance to linger, given the bad memories. They also knew Valerius had never desired a career in the imperial city, a statement that he made to them more than once, even before the death of Calpurnia. His father had always had ambitions for him to serve in the Senate, especially now with his favorable relationship with the young prince Germanicus, but Valerius wanted no part of it.

Marcellus and Valerius were gathered with thousands of other troops in the assembly area on the Field of Mars. Armor was polished to a high sheen; the colorful shields of red and gold had been repainted to repair the damage over the past months. The men were groomed to perfection. Today was the day of one of Rome's finest spectacles—Germanicus's triumph. The noise of the crowd was deafening as Valerius and Marcellus marched near the front of the Praetorian cohort in the triumphant processional. Leading the pageant was Germanicus, who rode in a gilded chariot pulled by a team of four magnificent white horses. The general wore a wreath of bay leaves on his head and a golden vest adorned with a palm of the hand, a symbol of victory. A purple cloak trailed from his shoulders, and in his right hand, he carried an ivory scepter topped with a golden eagle. Trailing the lone chariot were two standard-bearers holding aloft the two recaptured eagles of the Seventeenth and Nineteenth Legions. Next came the Praetorian cohort, followed by General Apronius and the Twentieth Legion, trailed by a line of fettered captives.

Valerius glanced about at the cheering throngs. The colonnades were bedecked with garlands, and showers of flower petals descended upon the marching legionnaires. All business in the city had been suspended for the day. The procession circled past the Circus Maximus on to the Sacra Via and then across the forum area to the temple of Jupiter, where the general's arrival was greeted by all of Rome's senators, the emperor, and the family of Germanicus.

As the Praetorian cohort had wound its way on to the Sacra Via and past the temple of the Vestal Virgins, Marcellus bellowed to Valerius above the din, "I have never seen anything like this in my life. All of these people shouting and cheering for us."

Valerius turned toward Marcellus so as to be heard above the din. "A grand spectacle, is it not? I wonder if it was really worth all of the killing and misery the legions inflicted upon the German people, not to mention the loss of so many legionnaires."

Marcellus pondered the question for a moment and then shrugged his shoulders. "Probably not."

Epilogue

Town of Oppidum Ubiorum (Modern-Day Cologne) One Year Later

Upon their return to Germania, Marcellus and Valerius created a trading company that brought iron farm implements, textiles, jewelry, and wine from the many ports of the empire to the flourishing town of Oppidum Ubiorum. Valerius had discussed the possible business venture with Marcellus back in Rome. He needed little convincing. After all, he had spent most of his life in Germania and preferred the colder climate. The centurion, now former centurion, recognized that it was the right time for him to leave the legions. It was an easy decision after the last campaign.

They had two transport ships under the direction of Captain Sabinus, recently retired from the imperial navy. The trading company brought the highly desired goods to the towns of the Rhine. Although it was strictly forbidden, they had a thriving business with the hostile tribes on the other side of the Rhine. Hereca proved to be invaluable in dealing with the German people. The German natives trusted her as one of their own, much more than an ex-Roman officer who spoke the language. Above it all, she had a head for business and was a shrewd judge of character.

Valerius sat at a table in the dining area of his home. It was a Roman-style dwelling, with a red tiled roof, heated floor, fresh water piped in, a bath, a small atrium to let the sunshine in, and several servants to help run the household. Marcellus had a home just like it not too far away. The centurion had always saved his money, and his share of the booty from the last German campaign had made him a rich man. Marcellus had never wasted his money, and his only vice was gambling on the horses, at which he usually won.

Seated at the table with Valerius were Hereca, Marcellus, and the tavern maiden from the Braying Mule, Brida, who was now Marcellus's wife and very pregnant. A pitcher of wine was in the middle of the table, and four goblets were filled to the brim. Valerius sipped the wine and smiled. "I will say this. We bring in good wine from the Italian ports and Gaul. This stuff is excellent. I would like to propose a toast. I have just finished reviewing our financial statements for the last six months. I cannot believe how much money we have made. I know Sabinus will be pleased. So raise your cups and drink to our future success."

They all clinked their cups together, smiling at the success of the business. Hereca stood up and gave Valerius a hug. Valerius grinned in return. He lived every day like it might be his last. He had been so fortunate to have survived the Teutoburg and then his capture by the Dolgubni. They were long odds, but he had endured. Now he was happy. He had a beautiful wife and a successful business with his former centurion and best friend. He glanced over his shoulder at a small closet off the kitchen area. His armor, sword, dagger, and bow were all kept in that enclosed space ready for use, just in case.

END

Author Note

Return of the Eagles is a work of fiction. However, similar to my previous work, *Legions of the Forest,* the book is based upon historical events in Roman antiquity. First and foremost, two of the sacred eagle standards lost in the Teutoburg Forest were recaptured over the course of the campaign against the Germans. The eagle of the Eighteenth legion was never recovered. The battles described in *Return of the Eagles,* including the entrapment of the legions in the forest on the plank road, the Battle of Idistaviso, and the snatch and grab raid to rescue Segestes and capture Thusnelda, actually occurred. Many of the Roman commanders mentioned, including Germanicus Caesar, Aulus Severus, Seius Tubero, Gaius Silus, Publius Vitellius, Cassius Apronius, and Licinius Stertinius, were actual historical figures, leaders of the Roman Imperial Army. Also the German characters of Ariminius, Thusnelda, and Segestes were real persons. Historical sources include the writings of Tacitus, Suetonius, Villus Paterculus, and Cassius Dio.

I have taken certain liberties with respect to the actual timeline. The novel reflects the German campaign lasting over the course of a year beginning in AD 10, while in fact it did not begin until several years later. I did this to have the story flow from the aftermath of the terrible defeat of the Roman legions in the Teutoburg Forest in AD 9, as described in *Legions of the Forest.*

The massive force of eight legions plus numerous auxiliary cohorts described in this work is consistent with historical sources. Germanicus initiated his campaign with an invasion of the Marsi, devastating their lands. His incursion was prompted by the mutinies of the legions in Germania Inferior triggered by the longer enlistment period dictated by the emperor. Germanicus Caesar dispatched the ringleaders and then directed the legions against the Marsi to force their attention to their common foe and away from the injustices within the legions.

With respect to the Praetorian guard, some say they were nothing but brutal self-serving thugs whose sole purpose was to support the legitimacy of the current emperor, while others suggest their role was largely ceremonial and to act as an armed escort for the imperial family. There is some historical evidence that the Praetorians were an elite force and used as a spearhead in tactical situations. I have chosen to depict them as a combination of the three noted above.

Germanicus and Arminius were well-matched opponents. Arminius learned quickly that his new Roman adversary was no Varus. Germanicus, despite his confidence and massive army, could not kill or capture Arminius. Both men were exceptional commanders, who led from the front, but in the end, they both failed. Arminius was unable to exploit his victory in the Teutoburg Forest, resulting in the subsequent devastation of the German tribal lands and the loss of many German lives. Germanicus failed to decisively defeat Arminius and his forces. Ironically, it is highly possible the two men served together in the Roman campaign in the Balkans some years earlier before the Teutoburg battle.

As noted in this book, Germanicus was recalled to Rome and awarded a triumph. The Roman Army he commanded was pulled back to the border of the Rhine. Some say Emperor Tiberius removed Germanicus because he was jealous of his success and was afraid he had become too popular and thus a threat. Perhaps, but the more logical explanation was that Tiberius, a strong military tactician, realized the folly of defeating the Germans. The Romans had been on campaign against the Germans for over two decades, beginning with military intervention by Tiberius's brother, Germanicus's father, Nero Claudius Drusus. Germanicus's campaign had devastated German territory and killed many Germans, but they were no closer to pacifying the lands and absorbing the German peoples into the empire. The cost had been enormous with respect to the imperial treasury, plus the loss of many highly trained legionnaires. Intuitively, Tiberius made the decision to withdraw the Roman forces to the safety of the Rhine, which became the de facto border of the German territory.

After his triumphal spectacle, Germanicus Caesar was posted to Syria to govern the eastern empire. He fell ill and died in AD 19, some say poisoned by his uncle, Tiberius. Germanicus was only thirty-five years old. He was a popular figure among the masses. His birthday was celebrated by the Roman people into the third century. Many historians believed Germanicus was the best and brightest of the Julio-Claudian line. Who knows how the history of the Roman Empire and western civilization might have changed had Germanicus ascended to the position of emperor? The successors to the imperial throne of this dynasty were, in a word, awful. Although Germanicus never became emperor of Rome, his son, Gaius Julius Caesar Augustus Germanicus, did succeed Tiberius. He was also known as Caligula.

In the name of the Senate and People of Rome,

Mark Richards 2016 (legions9ad@aol.com)

About the Author

Mark L. Richards, a graduate of Pennsylvania Military College (now Widener University), served in the US Army as an infantry officer before entering the health-care industry. He worked as a chief financial officer at a large academic health center. Now retired, Richards resides in West Chester, Pennsylvania. He is married, with two daughters and five grandchildren.

A lifelong historian of Roman antiquity, Richards was inspired by his favorite subject to write his debut novel, *Legions of the Forest*, and the sequel, *Return of the Eagles*. He may be contacted at legions9ad@aol.com.

CPSIA information can be obtained
at www.ICGtesting.com
Printed in the USA
FSHW012258010119
54771FS